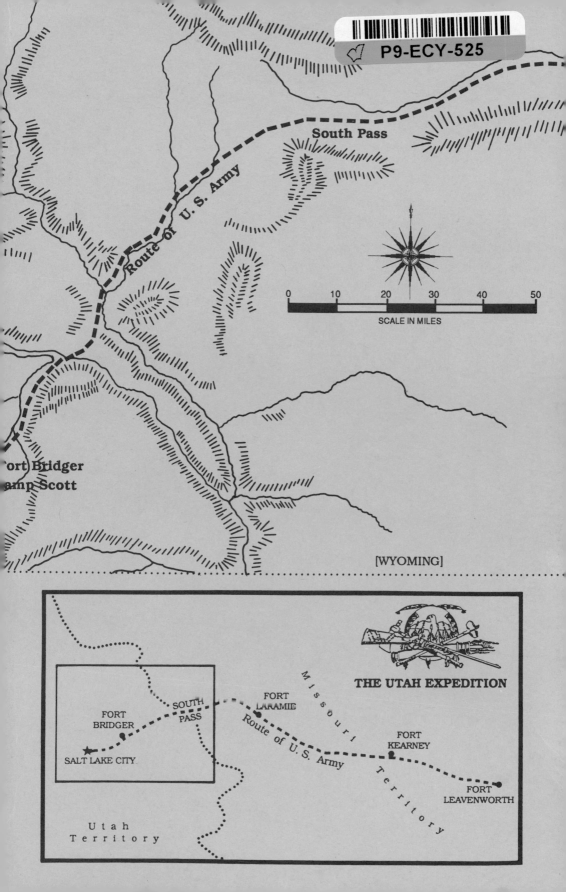

South Pass

Route of U. S. Army

SCALE IN MILES

0   10   20   30   40   50

ort Bridger
amp Scott

[WYOMING]

THE UTAH EXPEDITION

FORT
BRIDGER

SOUTH
PASS

FORT
LARAMIE

Missouri Territory

Route of U. S. Army

FORT
KEARNEY

SALT LAKE CITY

FORT
LEAVENWORTH

Utah
Territory

POWDERKEG

POWDERKEG

Leo V. Gordon
and
Richard Vetterli

LYFORD
B O O K S

Powderkeg blends truth and fiction. Many of the important events portrayed and statements made are a matter of historical record. Nevertheless, the authors remind the reader that *Powderkeg* is a novel.

LYFORD Books
Published by Presidio Press
31 Pamaron Way, Novato CA 94949

Library of Congress Cataloging-in-Publication Data

Gordon, Leo.
    Powderkeg / Leo Gordon and Richard Vetterli.
        p. cm.
    ISBN 0-89141-435-5
    1. Utah Expedition, 1857–1858—Fiction. 2. Mormon—Utah—
History—19th century—Fiction.   I. Vetterli, Richard. II. Title.
PS3557.06688P69   1991
813' .54—dc20   91-19515
                                          CIP

Jacket and interior illustrations by Michelle D. Nosco
Typography by ProImage

Printed in the United States of America

Acknowledgments

From the birth of *Powderkeg* talented and skilled friends have been willing to read the manuscript, offering suggestions and encouragement. To the following we express our sincere gratitude: Cindy Ingersoll, Sherlaine Ure, Wilford Brimley, Howard A. Christy, Robert Totten, Douglas Benton, Sydney Reynolds, Professor John B. Harris, Glenna Shapiro, Wilburta Locke, and especially Fran Howell.

Chapter One

A Potomac night mist, thick, almost impenetrable, blanketed the District of Columbia as the driver of the closed carriage guided his animal up the sweeping driveway to halt under the porte cochere's flickering gas lamps. A tall, gaunt-featured man, swathed in a greatcoat, emerged from the carriage. The honorable senator from the state of Mississippi—Jefferson Davis—mounted the wide steps and tugged sharply at the bellpull. The summons from John Floyd, President Buchanan's secretary of war, had been deliberately vague—a matter of great importance and mutual interest, the note had stated. It had damned well better be, thought Davis. This was no night to go gallivanting about—a man could catch his death—still, a message from the secretary of war was not to be ignored, not even by Jefferson Davis.

The senator from Mississippi was in bad humor, and what seemed an interminable wait for a response to the bellpull served only to heighten his discomfort. Davis had little genuine affection for the war secretary, and some considerable suspicion that Floyd was not the kind of man you'd want at your side when your back was against the wall.

At last the door's view port opened to reveal a pair of searching eyes set deep in a coal black face. "Good evening, Jonathan," said Jefferson Davis. "I believe I'm expected."

The view port closed and there came the sound of a heavy bolt being drawn, then the door swung wide. The senator from Mississippi entered. Jonathan assisted Davis out of his greatcoat, indicating the double doors to the right, "The secretary is in the drawing room, Senator. He said to send you right in."

"Thank you, Jonathan."

John Floyd, a large, florid-faced man sporting a flamboyant brace of muttonchops, turned from Howell Cobb, secretary of the treasury, Jacob Thompson, secretary of the interior, and Georgia Senator William Toombs, and moved to meet the late arrival with extended hands. "At last!" he beamed. "We were about ready to give up on you, Jefferson."

"The fog," shrugged Davis, his eyes taking in the elegant room with a hint of envy as they came to rest on the three men sharing the warmth of a cheery fire in the grate of an Adams fireplace. Their presence brought a quizzical lift to Davis's brow. "Your message indicated a matter of some urgency, John, but I didn't anticipate a cabinet meeting. Do I take it our esteemed president, Mister Buchanan, is going to join us?"

"Perish the thought," Floyd snorted through a laugh. "At this hour, I'm sure he's hiding under his bed, afraid to close his eyes lest the hobgoblins of secession turn his dreams into nightmares."

"And well they should," chortled Cobb, angling to the wine decanter and glasses centered on the long deal table. "Sherry, Senator?"

"If the poker's red, I'll have it mulled," nodded Davis. "There's an unseasonable chill in the air."

"And in the cabinet," smiled Thompson, bending to pluck the cherry-tipped poker from the fireplace flames and dip it into the glass Cobb poured for Jefferson Davis.

"What *is* this 'matter of urgency,' John?" asked Davis, his tone none too congenial.

"Patience, Jefferson," Floyd answered, sharing a knowing smile with Cobb and Thompson. "Permit me to relish the moment—it has been a long time coming."

"Too long," agreed Cobb.

"Before we go into detail, allow me to propose a toast," said Floyd, lifting his glass.

A trace of annoyance flickered in Davis's eyes as he took in the three cabinet members savoring their as-yet-unshared secret.

"To the South, gentlemen," said Floyd, "and the Utah Territory!"

The glass was halfway to Davis's lips when he paused, a puzzled frown knitting his brow. His obvious bewilderment broadened Floyd's smile. "A worthy toast, is it not, Senator?"

Floyd's smile was duplicated on the faces of Cobb and Thompson. A touch of red came to Davis's cheeks as he focused on the secretary of war. "The *first* part, Mister Secretary. As a Mississippian I consider it an honor to raise my glass to the South, but I'll be damned if I'll drink to something I know nothing about. What connection can Utah Territory have with the South?"

"More than you can possibly imagine, Senator," said Floyd. "As of early this morning, the territory of Utah has become a powder keg, whose explosion may well initiate the breakup of the Union—and the fuse is burning even as we speak."

"A delegation of territorial officials met secretly with the president Monday last," said Cobb. "As senior cabinet members, Thompson, Floyd, and I were privy to that meeting, Senator, and I—"

"Get to the point, Howell," interrupted Thompson. "The fact is, Senator, Utah Territory is in a state of rebellion—open revolt against the government of the United States."

Disbelief flooded Davis's face. "Rebellion? You can't be serious!"

"If denial of federal authority by a territorial governor isn't rebellion, I don't know what is," grunted Cobb.

"Our Mormon friends have burned down the United States courthouse in Salt Lake City, destroyed government records, and forced federal officials to flee for their very lives," added Thompson, with a look of satisfaction.

"And that isn't all of it," continued Floyd. "According to the territorial Indian commissioner, a Mister Twist, Governor Young has ordered his people to incite the Utes into attacking non-Mormon settlers. . . . Don't look so startled, Jefferson, do you think we Southerners are unique in wanting independence for ourselves? Is it so difficult to believe that the people of Utah might want it as well?"

"Has any of this been substantiated?" asked Davis. "Have these officials you mention offered any proof of what they say? From what I've heard of Brigham Young, he's not the kind of man to incite an Indian war on innocent settlers, no matter what the provocation."

"We have a sworn statement from the Indian commissioner."

"A political appointee, no doubt," stated Davis with a slight curl to his lip.

"Aren't they all?" sighed Thompson. "At least that's one pork barrel that doesn't pick the pockets of taxpayers."

"No," Davis grimaced, "they just pick the bones of the tribes we entrust to their care. Scavengers, all of them."

"It was not just the Indian commissioner, Jefferson. The entirety of the official territorial entourage has fled Utah, under the direction of Territorial Judge William Drummond."

"Drummond!" spit Davis with invective. "A whoremonger and a blackguard! What have we to do with him?"

His obvious disgust quickly dampened Floyd's flippancy. The secretary of war raised his hands in a calming gesture. "Please, Jefferson, I don't mean to parry with you. If you will but allow me, sir, I believe that Providence has placed an extraordinary, indeed, unparalleled opportunity at our very fingertips. If we can exploit this boon to its full potential, it may be a critical, nay, an irreplaceable factor in the creation and continuance of the Confederacy."

Davis was still agitated, and gave every indication that his toleration of Floyd was becoming strained. He fixed a searing look on him. "I do not see what benefit men who are void of moral conscience can be to the Confederacy. I say there is no truth to their statements."

Floyd's eyes narrowed to slits as he moved overbearingly close to the senator from Mississippi. "I tell you, Jefferson, it makes little difference to us if there's but one grain of truth to the bushel, one drop to the barrel; it still serves our purposes. The one fact that is important is that early this morning, Buchanan informed us he would meet this challenge of rebellion with force. As secretary of war, I have fully agreed with the president that he mount an immediate, punitive expedition against that rebellious territory. And, I might add, our good friends on the cabinet"—he nodded to Cobb—"seconded the motion. What is more, our naive chief executive readily accepted the recommendation that I select the commanding officer of this force, a task I performed this afternoon."

"And?" Davis remained irritated.

"General Albert Sidney Johnston," Floyd responded in near arrogance, "a soldier of unsurpassed reputation and one of us to the core."

"Fool that he is, Buchanan wouldn't dare proceed with this without congressional approval, certainly not without an investigation of the facts."

"But Congress isn't in session, as you are well aware, Senator, and Buchanan *is* commander in chief. As for an investigation, let me remind you that Utah lies twelve hundred miles beyond the western terminus of the railroad. You are talking about months."

"Granted . . . still, the situation can't be considered that critical."

Floyd's smile was confident. "No, Senator? A territory that's defying federal authority, virtually declaring itself sovereign? What if the contagion should spread to the other territories—Oregon, Washington, Kansas, New Mexico, Nebraska, Minnesota? If they go, California goes, and the United States will end at the Mississippi." Floyd paused for a moment, looking from one to the other, then said softly, "The hobgoblins of secession, gentlemen, Buchanan's nightmare. Remember, the president has pledged to hold this nation together. By force, if necessary. Well, here is his first challenge! If he ignores it, waits for a committee to investigate, it will be interpreted as a sign of weakness, an open invitation elsewhere."

Floyd's momentary bravado left the room silent but for the crackling of the fireplace. Then, taking a deep, noticeably wheezing breath, Floyd guided attention to the far wall of books, which framed a formidable and somewhat exaggerated painting of the United States and its territories. He moved quickly to the map, then turned to face the others. "Gentlemen," he began firmly, his lips stretched tightly across his teeth, "my concerns with regard to our great adventure are known to you. For the sake of making clear to you how this event may be of inestimable service to us, let me summarize.

"As Senator Davis knows, I do not share the enthusiasm of some of our brethren for an easy break with the Union. That our secession will be met with armed resistance from the North I have not the slightest doubt." One or two of Floyd's guests shuffled nervously with that declaration, but he did not miss a beat. "When that war comes, unless we gain a quick and decisive victory, time will shift to the advantage of the North. Then our advantage in leadership, generalship, and enthusiasm will fall to other factors."

"How so, sir?" interrupted the perplexed senator from Georgia. "How so?"

"Ah, my friend," Floyd responded compassionately, "the wealth of America is in the North. We are an agricultural people; they have industry. They can make their own weapons in a short period of time and in large quantities. Furthermore, from the great cities of the North our adversaries can conscript massive armies to outnumber us beyond our capacity to survive a prolonged conflict."

The senator from Georgia lowered his eyes and said no more. Floyd, on the other hand, was relentless. "Transportation, shipping, food supplies, logistics all favor the North. I could go on at length pointing out our disadvantage. The claim by our firebrands that secession will be achieved without so much as firing a shot, or that in the event of war Northern forces will be easily dispatched, expresses more arrogance than common sense.

"We have embarked on this venture with historical intent. A short or aborted independence is not our goal. Our mission is secession followed by true freedom and independence. It is not our intention to occupy the North, nor is it within our capabilities. If we win independence on the field of battle, what is to prevent the North from reinvigorating its great potential in preparation for the reestablishment of the Union at some future time? And has anyone given thought to the insecurity we face with our narrow economy during a war and its aftermath? We must not only think of the present. The Confederacy must persevere or its creation is not worth the candle."

Floyd stopped for a moment, allowing his points to take effect on his audience, his slitted eyes striking from one to another. He noticed Jefferson Davis, his brow furrowed, deep in thought. No one volunteered a statement. It was a sobered group of men before him waiting for the next shoe to drop. The secretary of war would not keep them waiting. Refreshing his tobacco-scarred lungs with a great sucking sound, he renewed his lecture. "Gentlemen, we need help, and we must go beyond the confines of the South. Diplomatic recognition and a vast quantity of arms from England are absolutely essential. This will help provide the balance we need against the industrial strength and the military potential of the North. I, among others, am in discreet contact with powerful representatives of the British government. But I must tell you, they are *not* overly enthusiastic about our chances of secession. They must be assured of our ability to succeed."

Jefferson Davis now spoke slowly and deliberately. "If then we accept your analysis, from where do you suppose we'll find a means to provide that assurance?"

Floyd spun about to face the map that had been behind him, slapping the outstretched palm of his left hand solidly on California and the western territories. Then, without moving his hand, he pivoted his left to face his audience once again. The lighting in the room manufactured a grotesque, elongated shadow that towered above and silhouetted his portly body.

"Here, Senator! It is here where the fate of the South may well be decided. Gold from New Mexico and California to buy arms from England,

and open seaports should a Northern blockade of the Southern coast be successful. The Confederacy spreading to the western territories and California—the trails west in our hands, confining the North to east of the Mississippi. With this accomplished we gain the respect of Europe and support for a sustained Confederacy stretching from the East to the West coasts. Power, wealth, territory, resources of every kind, and colonization welcomed from the vast population centers of Europe. In but a generation *we* will be the great nation upon this continent.

Thompson was about to interject a thought, but Floyd stayed him. "Bear with me a moment longer, gentlemen, as I reveal to you the great importance of the territory of Utah." With this he planted his clenched fist momentarily on the map's outline of Utah. "Here is an outcast people, mobbed, murdered, driven into the wilderness . . ."

"And a good riddance say I," mumbled Senator Toombs.

". . . only to be preyed upon by corrupt territorial appointees," continued the war secretary. "It's no wonder they are fed up with a government that has repeatedly denied them equal protection under the law. Brigham Young has publicly vowed that his people will never again be driven from their homes, while Washington turns a blind eye to injustice.

"And now, our esteemed president has ordered a federal army to march on the territory of Utah, to put down a rebellion that may not exist. But I assure you, if that is the case—that there is no rebellion at this time—the situation will change swiftly, once federal troops enter the territory."

"I can almost read Buchanan's mind," ventured Cobb. "He thinks to make Utah a not-too-costly example to the South."

"Exactly," responded Floyd enthusiastically. "But instead, he will succeed not only in driving Utah into *our* camp, but will substantially deplete the treasury, and isolate a federal expeditionary force two thousand miles from where we stand, surrounded by a people who will fight with desperation for their very survival. Utah could become the proverbial bottomless pit, swallowing up the military and financial resources of the nation, until Buchanan, or any other president, would be helpless to force his will on the South."

"They would be fighting on their home ground," interjected Davis, "against an army with twelve hundred miles of wilderness between it and the nearest base of supply. Remember Hannibal, gentlemen? Distance destroyed his army. The Romans just swept up the pieces."

"Either way," added Cobb, "we come out ahead."

"The possibilities are legion," continued Floyd, delighted that Davis was beginning to show some interest. "We have strong disunion movements in Colorado, New Mexico, and California. And now this with Utah. The strategic nature of that territory is obvious. It is the centerpiece of the West.

"With Salt Lake City in *our* hands, the trails to both Oregon and California can be controlled. We would then be in a position to exert a powerful influence over the western half of the continent. *Our* general will be commanding the expedition, a man sworn to our cause. Every disunion movement in the West will be benefited, especially in California, where the balance of power between secessionists and unionists is so very close.

"California. I tell you, without California and the West, we fail to achieve a lasting confederacy. And with Johnston in control of Utah, he would be able to exert substantial pressure on California and the direction it takes. In the event of hostilities between North and South, he will be instructed to move on with those troops loyal to him and seize that prize and hold it for the Confederacy.

"This is our goal, gentlemen, a solid South stretching from California to the Carolinas; the wealth of the Golden State pouring into the coffers of the new Confederacy. Our manifest destiny, Jefferson!

Howell Cobb came to his feet. "A dream about to come true, Senator; and strike me if I can see anything this side of heaven or hell that can prevent it from coming to pass."

The secretary of war lifted his glass. "A toast, to Brigham Young and the territory of Utah—unwitting midwives in the birth of a new nation."

A troubled Jefferson Davis was the last to consummate the toast.

Glasses were tilted and drained, the crystal facets refracting dancing light as a sudden draft brightened the fireplace flames.

Chapter Two

Platte River Station, a motley collection of about a dozen structures—some adobe, some false-fronted frame—owed its very existence to two things: immigrant wagon trains plodding West, and the complement of United States Army troopers stationed at nearby Fort Laramie, with the emphasis strongly leaning on the troopers. The two-hundred-man complement was under the command of Col. Philip St. George Cooke, a highly regarded West Pointer, who, a decade earlier, had commanded the Mormon Battalion in the war with Mexico.

At one end of the short, deeply rutted street that bisected Platte River Station was the Overland Stage Office, with its adjacent barn and corral. At the other end was Sadie's Birdcage, the one and only brothel within a five-hundred-mile radius, understaffed the first five days of each month, overstaffed the remainder. Then, as now, "the Eagle crapped" on the first of the month. Payday. Then, as now, the military couldn't wait to blow a month's wages as quick as they possibly could, and Platte River Station was the only place where that could be reasonably accomplished. This being the third day after payday, there were a considerable number of McClellan-saddled cavalry mounts tied up at the various hitch rails, though not as many as the day before, or the day before that. The hitch rails were a clear indicator of the troopers' preferences: Sadie's and the saloon. Other establishments, such as the local blacksmiths, the Emigrant Supply Store, livery stable, and the apothecary shop, profited from the "dribble effect."

Porter Rockwell clenched the stogie between his teeth, dead center in his mouth, tipping it up past his nose as he stared across the table at Phil Cooke. The colonel wasn't wearing a vest, but he might just as well be, the way he was holding the five pasteboards close to his chest after a one-card draw, his face expressionless, a classic poker face if ever there was one.

Jim Bridger, bearded, muscular, and buckskinned, was no slouch himself when it came to concealing what was going on in the brain behind his weathered brow. The mountain man riffled his cards slowly. "Opener bets. Up to you, Port," he said, fixing an eye on the slab-lean, rock-hard, and not unhandsome man to his left.

Porter Rockwell appeared to be about forty, give or take a year or two, a soft-spoken man with a deceptively casual manner that seemingly belied his reputation as one of the deadliest gunfighters on the frontier. Known as the "Wayward Saint" or "Mormon Gun," depending on whom you talked to, Rockwell was an admitted backslider, a sort of church outcast, a man who knew his weaknesses as well as his strengths, and accepted them. The brace of navy Colts, buckled high on Rockwell's waist, were in a manner of speaking symbolic of both.

Rockwell eyed the other players—the Platte River Station barber and a hulking teamster. Both men, he sensed, were hoping he would check to Cooke's one-card draw. A halfway sizable bet would make them toss in their cards. Rockwell leaned back in the rickety chair, carefully thumbing the greasy pasteboards into a squeezed fan. "They aren't going to change, Porter," said Cooke, reaching for the bottle next to the small pile of coins that was the pot. "Check or bet. Make your play."

"You don't want to be bettin' into a one-card draw, Mister Rockwell," frowned the barber.

"My thoughts exactly, Mister Peavy," nodded Rockwell, bringing his chair back down on all four legs. "Don't want to, but I guess I'll have to. Opener bets four bits."

Disappointment registered on the barber's face as Rockwell added a coin to the pot. "That lets me out."

"By me," grunted the teamster, tossing in his cards.

"Up to you, Phil," shrugged Rockwell.

"Four bits!" frowned Cooke. "I thought this was supposed to be a friendly game, Port."

"Now I know you pulled a good one, Colonel," grinned Rockwell, "and I know you're going to bump me."

Cooke nodded approval. "You called that right. Your four bits, *and* four bits. Cost you a dollar, Jim."

Bridger shuttled a frown between Cooke and Rockwell, tapping a horny finger on his cards. Then he issued an unemotional, "I'm in."

"That makes it four bits to me," said Rockwell, throwing another half dollar into the pot. "You're called, Colonel."

A clatter from the batwing doors arrested Cooke's movement as he was about to lay down his hand. The young lieutenant quickly zeroed in on the colonel, snapping to a stiff salute as he reached the table. "Sorry to interrupt, sir."

"State your business, Lieutenant," growled Cooke, not bothering to conceal his annoyance.

The lieutenant plucked a sealed document from his tunic. "Dispatch, sir, from Fort Leavenworth. Came by special courier."

Cooke sighed, put his cards facedown on the grimy felt, and ripped open the sealed envelope, his face stiffening as his eyes traveled the single page. Folding the document he turned to the young officer. "Round up every trooper in town, Lieutenant. All passes are canceled. Have the men assemble out front."

"Yes, sir!" snapped the young officer, saluting. Wheeling on his heel he addressed the scattering of troopers at the bar and seated at nearby tables: "Attention! All ranks from Fort Laramie, finish your drinks and report to me outside."

A medley of protest came from the troopers, but it was quickly muted as Colonel Cooke came to his feet. He drained the remainder of his drink, then, slipping on his gauntlets, gave the men at the table a small, apologetic smile. "Sorry. Duty calls."

"Sioux out again, Phil?" asked Rockwell dryly, wondering why he had said nothing about the contents of the message.

The colonel did not answer.

"We gonna finish this hand?" interrupted Bridger, turning over his cards and fanning them out, revealing three kings.

Rockwell peered at Bridger with one eye closed, his teeth clamped tightly on his stogie. Then he draped his cards on the table. "Straight, six to ten. You, Phil?"

Cooke flipped over his hand to reveal a spade flush. "Read 'em and weep—all black." Indicating the pile of coins centered on the table, he added, "Hang onto that for me, will you—for next time?"

Rockwell shrugged, raking the pot. "Sure. And you, hang onto what hair you've got left."

With a look of disbelief, Bridger was still digesting the hand that had just been dealt—three kings, a straight, and a flush! He managed a disinterested, "Take care, Phil."

Cooke nodded a smile that took in both Rockwell and the mountain man. "You do the same."

"Your deal," Rockwell said to the teamster, pulling in the cards as Cooke followed the last of the lingering troopers out of the saloon.

Gathering in the deck, the teamster declared the next hand would be five-card stud. He shuffled, the deck almost lost in his huge, paddlelike hands.

The street was a scene of confusion as half-drunk troopers from the saloon and half-dressed customers of the Birdcage, routed out of the nest by an officious corporal, cursed their chosen careers. Cinches were yanked tight, bridles tugged, and unsteady legs thrown over saddles. A big, jugheaded roan, half broken, bucked his rider out of his stirrups, sending him crashing into two of his fellow troopers and knocking one from his saddle.

"Al'right, mount up! Form a column of twos, on the double!" bawled the young lieutenant, achingly aware of Colonel Cooke's eyes boring into his back.

The last refugee from Sadie's hobbled to his mount, boots in hand, outraged indignation puddling his face. As he threw a look back to the laughing girls clustered on the Birdcage's balcony, he wailed, "What the hell's going on?"

His lament was ignored by his fellows; they had their own disappointments to contend with. The townspeople, a few trappers and teamsters scattered among them, found the whole situation highly entertaining, throwing unwanted words of advice to the troopers.

"Move them out, Lieutenant," said Cooke, swinging his mount to the head of the haphazard column, setting the pace at a brisk canter.

"Forward, ho!" bellowed the lieutenant, his voice changing register. Discipline and training took over, and the column moved out with a clatter of accoutrements.

Two riders, their homespun clothing covered thickly with dust, mounts lathered, reined their horses aside as the column passed the Overland Stage Office. The older of the two riders, a solidly built man in his late twenties, eyed the passing troopers stonily, one hand resting near the butt of the antiquated single-shot cap and ball belted to his waist. His name was Lot Smith. His companion, Jud Stoddard, a wiry, smaller man, appeared to be about the same age and, like Lot, had no love for the United States military. Stoddard wore no belt gun; his weapon was a saddle carbine, army model 1841, slung across his back, Indian fashion. Reining back onto the rutted road, the pair headed for the center of Platte River Station. "You reckon he's here?" questioned Stoddard.

"That's his buckskin," nodded Smith, pointing off to an unsaddled horse gnawing the hitch rail in front of the livery stable. "Know'n' Port, he'll be in the nearest saloon, and, seein' how there's only one," he jerked a thumb at the building directly across the street from the livery stable, "it won't take much lookin'. You get his horse saddled and see if the stable boss'll rent us some fresh mounts. Pay what you have to."

Lot Smith stepped down, handing over the reins to Jud, then headed for the batwing doors of the saloon. Stoddard rode up to the livery stable, dismounted, and tied both animals to the hitch rail, next to the sleek buckskin.

It took a moment for Lot Smith's eyes to adapt to the comparative gloom of the saloon. The object of his search—Porter Rockwell—sat with his back to the door, facing Jim Bridger across the table in a game of heads up. The barber and teamster were now huddled at the bar, bemoaning losses they could ill afford. Bridger ceased shuffling, his brow lifted at the sight of Lot. "Hullo, Lot. You're back early."

"Something's come up," answered Smith, sliding into the chair recently vacated by Phil Cooke and centering his attention on Rockwell. "Got to talk to you, Port. If it wasn't important I wouldn't be taking the time."

"What's the problem, Lot?"

"We can talk about it on the way. Jud's gettin' your horse saddled now."

Rockwell's brows lifted. "Am I going somewhere?"

"Five hundred miles, to Salt Lake. And I mean to do it in five days," said Lot with a sudden intensity.

Rockwell exchanged a puzzled look with Bridger, then shrugged. "That's fine, Lot, if you're craving a sore hind end, but include me out. I've still got some serious drinking and poker playing to do. Right, Jim?"

Bridger nodded lamely at Rockwell. "Uh-huh."

Lot's face stiffened as he looked from Bridger to Rockwell. "I said this was important and I meant it. I haven't got time to waste with you two funnin' me!"

"I'm not funnin' you, Lot," Rockwell said softly. "I don't fun a man I respect. Now, what's troubling you?"

Lot looked around quickly, then leaned closer, dropping his voice. "The army—it's gettin' ready to march into Utah!"

Rockwell recognized his own reaction in Bridger's face. "What do you mean—army?"

"Just that! President Buchanan has ordered troops from Fort Leavenworth to march on Utah, to put down a rebellion."

"Rebellion? What rebellion?" frowned Rockwell.

"There isn't any, never was!" said Lot. "It's just another lying excuse to take over what we built up, what we worked for—just like they did back in Missouri and Illinois."

"That's the truth, Brother Rockwell," Jud's voice came over Rockwell's shoulder. The small man slipped into the chair next to Lot's. "When me and Lot got into Independence to pick up the mail, they wouldn't give it to us. Said we wuz traitors. We barely got out of town with our skins whole, and that's the truth."

Rockwell looked to Bridger. "What do you think, Jim?"

"Reckon we should'a let Phil Cooke answer your question—about the Sioux bein' out again."

"Maybe," said Rockwell, turning back to Lot and Jud. "This army, has anybody seen it?"

"The drummer, Caldwell. He was at Fort Leavenworth six weeks back—saw it gettin' ready to move out. It's a real army—all regulars, Brother Rockwell. Even got artillery with 'em," said Jud.

"Artillery?"

"All this talk is wasting time. We should be riding." Lot turned an eye to Jud. "You get the horses?"

"Yeah. All saddled up and ready to go, includin' Brother Rockwell's buckskin."

Rockwell studied the anxious-eyed pair for a long moment, then his own eyes seemed to cloud. "I'd be obliged if you'd tell Mister Blocker to unsaddle my horse. I won't be needing him just yet. And you, Jud— don't call me 'brother'!"

Jim Bridger's surprise was no match for Lot's and Jud's, and Jud's face dropped as if he'd been hit. Rockwell's remark had crushed him. Anyone who knew the small man was well aware that he looked upon Rockwell with something akin to hero worship.

A note of anger in his voice, Lot protested. "Damn it, Port! This is no time for joshin'; this is a war! And President Young is going to need every fightin' man we can bring him!"

Rockwell's eyes hooded as he toyed with the cards. "My fighting days are over. It's your war, you fight it," he said, flat voiced. "Mister Bridger and I have our own problems—right, Jim?"

"Can't argue that," shrugged Bridger, searching the faces of Lot and Jud.

Lot forced back his anger. "I'm not about to beg any man, Port Rockwell, but I'm reminding you, you're still one of us."

"One of you!" snorted Rockwell. "Where the hell have you been, boy?"

"The door is always open, Port."

Rockwell leaned back in his chair, clamping the stogie between strong teeth. "That's what it comes down to, doesn't it? Well, listen close; I don't want to come back. I've found my place, and I'm staying in it. That clear enough?"

"It's our hour of need, Brother Rockwell," pleaded Jud Stoddard, trying to hide the hurt he felt. "You can't turn your back on us."

"I just did," said Rockwell, his voice chilled.

There was dead silence, then Lot rose to his feet, his face suffused with anger. "Let's go, Jud. We're wastin' our time here."

Turning on his heel, Lot Smith strode out angrily. Jud Stoddard hesitated a confused moment, the plea in his eyes ignored by Rockwell. "Ain't right—just ain't right," he muttered as he followed Lot through the batwing doors.

Bridger's searching stare made Rockwell uncomfortable. "Shuffle the damned cards!"

Bridger broke his gaze and scooped up the deck. Rockwell reached for the whiskey bottle; his pour topped the glass, sloshing over to spread a wet stain on the greasy felt. The cold look in his eyes softened, replaced by a strange melancholy, which in turn became self-anger. He lifted the glass and drained it in one gut-wrenching gulp.

"Five-card showdown, two-bit ante," bit out Bridger.

Then Rockwell tossed a coin to the center of the table as Bridger dealt him his first card, faceup—the ace of hearts.

Rockwell was well on his way to disproving the theory of cause and effect, action and reaction, considering the time and the volume and alcoholic content of the sipping whiskey. Jim Bridger watched in wonderment as Rockwell drained the last of the second bottle and called for a third in as many hours. Still, Rockwell showed no visible effects as yet, except for a slight glazing of his normally clear blue eyes. The card table had been abandoned hours ago. The pair now draped themselves at a corner of the bar, away from the town's regulars and the transients drifting through Platte River Station.

Muldoon plunked the fresh bottle down on the bar and flicked a questioning look to Bridger. The mountain man responded with an expressive lift of his shoulders. "Dollar and a half," said Muldoon as Porter pulled the cork and poured.

Rockwell dropped a pair of silver dollars to the bar top. "Four bits for the cup, Muldoon."

"Obliged," nodded Muldoon, scooping up the coins as he moved back down the bar.

Bridger grimaced as Rockwell tossed off a good four-finger jolt of the red-eye and immediately refilled the glass. "No business of mine," snorted Bridger, "but I'd say you was gonna be one miserable sonovabitch when you ride outta here."

"What the hell are you talking about? I'm not riding anywhere."

"Uh-huh," agreed Bridger sarcastically. He knew that Rockwell was hating himself.

There was a peculiar sense of obligation—like a sack of stones—that Rockwell carried toward the people of the Utah Territory. When it got too heavy, he'd try, always unsuccessfully, to lose it in a bottle.

"Keep your nose out of my business, Jim," Rockwell bristled. Then, slowly, the hardness went out of his voice; he sent an apologetic half grin at the mountain man. "They don't need me, Jim—they don't need anybody."

" 'They' meaning Jud and Lot—or the Mormons?"

"One and the same, cut out of the same cloth—all of 'em, from Brigham Young on down," said Rockwell, with a hard edge to his voice.

"Uh-huh."

"There isn't going to be any war. It's all some kind of show to make Brigham knuckle under. That business of kicking out a federal judge was a damn fool stunt to start with. The arrogant fool forced the government's hand."

"You think he will—knuckle under, I mean?"

"No, damn his stubborn hide! He'll fight, if they force it on him."

"From what those boys said, seems that's what they got in mind—artillery and all."

Rockwell directed a scowl at the big man, then resumed drinking.

Case Carney, hard-faced, a big man, reined the four-up, Dougherty-type army conveyance to a halt in front of the saloon. Carney was no ordinary teamster, a fact attested to by the pair of Remington .44s holstered on his belt, along with a mean-bladed Siberian skinner. He turned to the man sharing the bench with him, Henry Magruder, decked out in a white linen duster. "Should get some pretty good pickin's here, Mister Magruder; always a few drifters and hard cases around, lookin' t' pick up a loose dollar."

Magruder nodded. "The hard cases I can use; the drifters I can do without."

"You just let me do the pickin', Mister Magruder. You'll get what you want."

The pair swung down from the seat and headed for the batwing doors just as a townsman, four sheets to the wind, pushed his way through. He paused on the plank walk as if trying to recall where he'd intended to go. Carney brushed the man aside to hold the doors open for Magruder, then followed him in.

"Can I have your attention for a moment, gents?" said Magruder, striding to the center of the room. Carney remained near the door, his narrowed eyes scanning the room's occupants. "My name's Magruder," he continued as the room grew silent and every eye made him the center of focus. "Tell you why I'm here; I'm going to need a lot of good men, and I'm gonna pay top wages, three dollars a day, and an extra dollar a day for each horse or mule a man can provide."

A buzz went up from the listeners. One man called out the question all wanted an answer to: "What kind o' good men you talkin' about, mister?"

"Drovers, jack skinners, bullwhackers, all-around hands. I'll take all I can get."

"Jest what in hell you got in mind, mister?" another voice called from the crowd.

"Hank Magruder," Bridger said to Rockwell. "One of the bloodsuckers your people run outta the territory."

"I know who he is," said Rockwell, his eyes fixed on the man standing at the door. There was something unpleasantly familiar about the face. Rockwell tried to pull recall past the whiskey fog hazing his memory, without success.

Case Carney's memory had no such impediment. He recognized Porter

Rockwell instantly, but he kept the recognition out of his eyes as his right hand shifted position to rest just above the butt of one of the Remingtons.

"What I have in mind, gents," said Magruder, "is supplying rolling stock, provisions, and replacement mounts for the United States Army."

"Army—whut damned army?" a voice bellowed from a corner of the room. "Only damned army we got here is out t' Fort Laramie. Ain't much more'n a handful."

"Half a handful," someone laughed. "Iffen y' only count the sober uns!"

A laugh erupted from the other men. "That's fer sure," shouted someone. "And the best of 'em couldn't whup a pup in a fair fight."

"I'm talking about an army of three thousand men. The army that's going to march into Utah Territory and kick livin' hell out of Brigham Young, chase him and his heathens clear out of the territory and leave it wide open for decent folks to settle in."

A stunned silence greeted Magruder's announcement. He filled it in: "I don't know about you good people, but I, for one, am proud to be part of this. That land should belong to us, not some heathen so-called saints who make a mockery out of the Good Book, and spit on the Constitution of the United States of America!"

A roar of agreement went up from the crowd. The prospect of free land—land already fully developed, productive land—was a heady thought.

"What in hell would he know about the Good Book?" Bridger snorted to Rockwell, who was still trying to fathom where he'd seen Carney before.

"Jud was right, Jim," he said resignedly. "This is going to be Missouri and Illinois all over again. It won't be the army; it'll be what comes with it, and after it."

"Any of you gents want to sign up, now's the time," said Magruder. "Mister Carney, my associate, will take your names."

Carney! The name registered hard in Rockwell's brain, and with it a kaleidoscope of long-dormant images. It was the same face, a decade older, no longer clean shaven, but still the same brutish face. Case Carney, who, with a mob of his own ilk, had led the attack on the Carthage, Missouri, jail that ended with the murder of the man Porter Rockwell had sworn to protect, the man he had failed—Joseph Smith.

Pushing away from the bar, Rockwell crossed to the crowd that was building around Carney, men eager to add their names to Magruder's payroll, and the opportunities that were sure to go with it. The puzzled Bridger on his heels, Rockwell jostled through the crowd to come face-to-face with Case Carney. The big man's eyes showed no fear as they met Rockwell's. "Remember me, Carney?" Rockwell asked in an ominously pitched voice.

"Sure, Rockwell, I remember you. You're the fella who climbed in a jug, back in '44. From the looks of you, I'd say you're still in it."

Bridger growled, clinching his hamlike fists as he tried to move past his friend.

Rockwell arrested Bridger's move, his eyes still locked on Carney's. "Do me a kindness, Jim; go across the street and ask Mister Blocker to saddle up the buckskin for me, will you?"

Bridger passed an uncertain look between Rockwell and the bigger man. "Please, Jim," said Rockwell after a moment.

Bridger sighed his reluctance, then pushed through the ring of silent spectators and exited.

"Trouble, Carney?" asked Magruder, frowning.

"Nothin' I can't handle, Mister Magruder. Just another whiskey-bottle hard case." Carney leaned closer, his jaw jutting aggressively at Rockwell. "Do yourself a favor, Rockwell; go someplace and sleep it off."

"Consider this a down payment, Carney—the rest will come later," Rockwell said through a thin, humorless smile.

"What the hell is that supposed t' mean?" growled Carney.

Suddenly, Rockwell slammed an iron-hard first deep into Carney's solar plexus. The big man's jaw dropped, and his eyes bulged as he buckled, right into the path of the follow-up punch—a right cross that dropped him in his tracks. He was out before his head hit the floor with a resounding thud.

A loud murmer rose from what had now become an audience. "Gol dang!" someone said in an awed voice. "Dropped him like a shot hawg!" "Damn," another murmured. "Never seen a man that drunk move so fast."

Rockwell carelessly flipped a silver dollar to Muldoon, at the edge of the crowd. "When he comes to, buy him a drink, Muldoon. After he gets it down, you tell him it's Mormon-paid-for whiskey he's got in his gut."

Rockwell pushed through the ring of spectators and was almost to the batwings when Magruder called out. "Hold on there, mister! Just who in hell are you?"

"That depends on who you ask."

"I'm askin' you!"

The batwing doors flapped and Rockwell was gone, leaving Magruder's question hanging in the air.

Magruder's brow knitted briefly, then cleared as he dismissed the incident from his mind. He glowered at Carney as consciousness returned to the big man. "Somebody get him on his feet."

A dozen eager hands helped the woozy Carney erect. He seemed to have difficulty trying to focus his eyes.

False dawn lighted the eastern horizon, ending tentative probes toward the distant peaks of the Great Divide as Bridger and Rockwell rode at a ground-consuming canter. Bridger's big black was a good match for Rockwell's buckskin. Rockwell's face was stiff as he fought to keep it expressionless, even though every beat of the buckskin's hoofs clanged like a hammered anvil in his brain. Bridger was right—there wasn't anything worse than a hard ride with a hangover.

"What made you decide to come along?" he managed to holler at Bridger.

"I'm not along," he replied. "Got to get back to my fort."

"Don't know why," Rockwell chortled through a stab of pain, "you're hardly ever there anyway."

The next quarter mile they rode in silence, each with his own thoughts; then the mountain man gave voice to his. "No business of mine, but that Carney fella . . ."

"Killed a man," said Rockwell, after a long moment.

"That all?"

"Joseph Smith."

"The prophet? Yeah, I heard me some talk about that. You was supposed to have run off and let that lynch mob take him. I never did believe a word of it."

Rockwell returned a thin smile.

"Carney, he one of the mob?"

"The top hand," gritted Rockwell. "The court found him not guilty. One day I'll hold court on Carney myself—don't know why I didn't do it last night."

"Uh-huh," snorted Bridger, "and they'd have swung your ass this morning."

"No great loss," shrugged Rockwell.

Some time later, Rockwell turned to the mountain man. "What made you so damned sure I was going to change my mind?"

"The way you was puttin' away that sipping whiskey," grinned Bridger. "Tryin' to make it convince you that you was doin' the right thing, when you knew different. Like the boy said, you're still one of 'em."

Rockwell grunted. "Maybe so, maybe not—but this time I'll be there—"

"Port!" said Bridger, reining in the black to stab a finger toward a brush-covered outcropping off to the right.

Rockwell pulled back the buckskin, his eyes narrowing to pierce the muted light. A thin, almost invisible column of whitish smoke rose wispily from a fold in the outcropping. Bridger scanned the trail dirt, indicating what he saw to Rockwell. "Shod horses, two of 'em."

Rockwell eyed the tracks, then frowned at the column of smoke. "Green-wood fire. . . . Damn fools! That smoke is a plain invite to any bushwhacker or hostile ten miles around!"

Swinging out of the saddle, Rockwell slipped his Merrill breech-loader from the scabbard. Bridger's Sharps carbine was already in his hand as he stepped down. Drop reining the buckskin and the black, both men started for the smoke column, moving soundlessly on moccasined feet.

The click of a hammer being ratcheted back froze both men in instant tableau. Bird dogs on point couldn't have been more still. "You can let down the hammer, Lot—easylike," said Rockwell in a calm voice.

Lot Smith stepped out of the concealing brush, behind Bridger and Rockwell, his big .50-caliber single-shot pistol down muzzled. "How'd you know it was me and not Jud?" he frowned at Rockwell.

"No mystery," said Porter as he and Bridger turned to face the younger man. "Action of a carbine or rifle has a heavier sound to it," he continued. "Jud wasn't wearing a palm gun."

At the sound of his name, Jud Stoddard stepped out of his place of concealment, opposite Lot Smith's, his carbine crooked loosely in his arm.

"Damn!" chuckled the mountain man. "The pups had us flanked, Port."

"Speak for yourself, Bridger," said Rockwell, his look holding on

Lot Smith. There was no welcome on the younger man's face. "We going to stand here all morning," offered Bridger, "or are you going to offer us a cup of that brew you're cookin' up?"

"What do you want, Porter?" said Smith, coldly. "What are you doin' here?"

"This is open country, boy."

Jud took a tentative step toward Lot, eyes wide in anticipation, his tone placating. "Maybe he changed his mind, Lot. Maybe—"

"Then let him tell it," snapped Lot, with a challenging look to Rockwell.

Aware of Bridger's grin at his discomfort, Rockwell grimaced a shrug at the young Mormons. "Thought I'd just ride along for a spell."

A long moment passed, then a grin of welcome was birthed on Lot Smith's face. He stepped forward, hand out thrust. "Glad you did, Port."

Rockwell accepted the hand, his grin a bit wry, as if there were still some lingering doubts that he had made the right move.

"That goes for me, too, Brother Rockwell," beamed Jud Stoddard. "Welcome."

"You boys gonna' butcher the fatted calf?" Bridger mumbled irreverently.

Rockwell looked in disbelief at the mountain man, then to Stoddard. "And you, Jud, you and I are going to have a problem if you keep calling me 'brother.'"

"Time we was movin'," said Stoddard quietly, first looking at the ground in humiliation, then nodding at the fast-lightening sky.

Chapter Three

The sun was directly overhead, beating down with merciless intensity on the small column of immigrants pushing their way west over the airless, rolling plain, broken in spots by jagged outcroppings thrusting up through the dust-dry earth. There were no wagons in the column. The wheeled vehicles were heavily laden handcarts; men and women strained shoulder-to-shoulder against the crossbars, like yoked oxen, while other family members helped push or turn the massive wheels. Younger children straggle-herded a few head of scrawny cows, bringing up the rear. A half-dozen outriders, some walking their horses, flanked the column. These were men of a different stripe, accustomed to the vicissitudes this hard land had to offer—the escort, sent to guide and protect them on their twelve-hundred-mile journey from Independence to Salt Lake City. This group had already traveled four times that distance before reaching their escort in Missouri, a journey that had begun in the rugged highlands of Scotland.

A half mile ahead, riding point, Cephus James, a gaunt, leathery-faced man in buckskin and homespun, reined to a halt at the summit of a low hill, his narrowed gaze fixed on the heat-shimmering plain ahead. His eyes told him a cool, inviting lake lay in the distance, but Cephus knew from long experience that the invitation was an illusion, a mirage that would retreat a step with each step forward, always just out of reach. Cephus squinted harder; there was something else out there, something that was not a mirage. Shifting his Colt revolving carbine to his left hand, he plucked a small, brass-tubed telescope from the pouch whang-leathered to his saddle horn, and brought it to his eye. What he saw was not totally unexpected; nothing ever was in this country, as Cephus had good reason to know. The ten-power glass confirmed what his senses had already told him: Trouble was approaching, in the form of a band of mounted Sioux, some twenty in number, on a course that would bring them head-on with the small immigrant train. The distance, even with the glass, was too great to determine if the braves were wearing paint. But, war paint or no, the small, lightly defended column of immigrants would be a temptation the Sioux would find hard to resist. Returning the glass to the pouch, Cephus wheeled his mount back down the reverse slope, silently cursing himself for having agreed to guide in one more handcart train. All those foreign men, women, and children, utterly defenseless, and his responsibility. Damn!

Luther James, Cephus's eldest son, signaled the column to a halt when he spied his father racing toward them. His haste could mean only one thing—danger. The young man jabbed a finger toward a cluster of boulders cresting a low rise off to his left. "Up there! Leave the carts! Move!"

Angus McCutcheon, a medical doctor from Edinburgh, shucked off the cart harness he shared with his daughter, Anne. "What is it? What's wrong?"

His question was answered indirectly as Cephus thundered up to Luther, now joined by the others of the escort. "Sioux! About twenty of 'em."

"War party, paw?" questioned Luther.

"If it isn't, it will be, if they catch us out here in the open! Get these people movin', son!"

"We can't leave the carts," Anne protested in dismay. "Everything we own—"

"Isn't worth your life, missy," Cephus snapped to the tall, clear-eyed, flaxen-haired girl, trying to ignore her regal beauty. "Now do as yer told!"

Fire flashed in Anne's eyes as Cephus wheeled his mount, shouting instructions to the other immigrants, urging them to haste.

"Easy, lass," said her father, squaring the tam-o'-shanter to match the set of his jaw and plucking a smoothbore musket from the cart. "The man must know what he's about, or they wouldn't'a gi'e 'im the responsibility."

Other men snatched up weapons as their wives did the same with the smaller children, and headed for the rocks. Luther and others of the escort lent assistance to the youngsters hazing the scrawny herd. Livestock was a premium, second in value only to human life in this hard land.

They were almost to the shelter of the rocks when Dan Petrie, a heavily built immigrant nearing sixty, clutched at his chest and fell to his knees, gasping at the pain searing through his breast. "Daniel!" shrieked the thin, washed-out woman behind him as he toppled over on his face.

"Help that man!" roared Cephus.

McCutcheon broke stride to angle toward the fallen man as Luther and one of the other escort riders rode up and leapt from their mounts.

"My bag, child. Fetch it here!" commanded McCutcheon, turning the stricken man over as Anne ran to her father's side.

"No time for that," snapped Luther. "Take care of his woman. Lend me a hand here, Brother Cole," he added, throwing a quick look to the other escort rider.

Together, they dragged Petrie's deadweight partially erect. "Our horses, miss," said Luther, jerking his head toward Anne. "Fetch 'em along, will you?"

Numbly, Anne obeyed, gathering the reins of the two mounts to follow Luther and his companions as they struggled to gain the security of the rocks with their unconscious charge. The injured man's wife twittered concern every step of the way.

Angus retrieved his dropped musket, and gazed off to the distant hill from which Cephus had ridden moments earlier. The gold-brown crest was now dotted with dark, moving figures. A series of high-pitched, ululating yelps pierced the distance as the tiny figures raced down the slope, kicking up a column of dust that grew nearer with every beat of McCutcheon's heart. The thunder of unshod hooves beat a contra- puntal base to the shrill, penetrating cries as Angus continued his climb, the last to reach the sheltering rocks.

Cephus James guided a practiced eye over his charges, now hunkering down among the scattering of boulders. He spotted Luther and other members of the escort party among them. Not one in three of the immigrants had a firearm. Those who did not had armed themselves with a variety of farm implements. Cephus knew that his own men could put up a fight, even against the three-to-one odds, estimating the In- dians to be about twenty in number, but men would die, men sorely needed. There were two schools of thought on how to deal with roving bands of Indians: Put up a solid resistance, no matter the odds; or try to avoid conflict, even if it meant the sacrifice of material things. Cephus James was inclined toward the latter. Things could be replaced; lives could not.

He looked back, past the protective line, to the women and children huddled among the rocks. Beyond them, he could see a gaggle of the half-grown youngsters struggling to keep the spooked cattle in herd.

His eye shifted to McCutcheon and the woman hovering over the prostrate form of Dan Petrie. The Petries were of an age that ill suited them to the brutal twelve-hundred-mile trek from Independence to Salt Lake, a journey to tax the body and spirit of the most hardy. Yet, they came, even older, more infirm. Some made it; many did not. Cephus had a strong feeling that Daniel Petrie would be one of those who would not. He had seen this scene before, and worse. Again he cursed that it had happened on his watch.

Andrew McKee, a British army veteran who had served on India's northwest frontier back in '36, ratcheted back the hammer of his Harper's Ferry .60-caliber musket. He was grim lipped.

"No man fires 'less I give the word," said the frustrated Cephus, raising his voice so that all could hear.

Below, the whooping band of Sioux fell on the abandoned cart train in what seemed like an orgy of vandalism. Leaping from their ponies, the Indians tore into the carts, spilling out the contents of trunks, barrels, and boxes, knife blades ripping open bags, bundles, and sacks with total abandon. Garments, bolts of cloth, tools, china, bags of precious seed, and treasured family heirlooms were scattered in the dust.

Cephus James could see what the newcomers could not—the hunting party, he was sure that's what it was, since the young braves did not carry war shields and wore no paint, seemed no real threat to anything more than property. Unless, of course, they were provoked. His eyes fixed on one of the Indians, the only one still mounted. Cephus could see that he was substantially older than the others—about thirty, he estimated, and, from the feathers decorating his lance, was probably a subchief. If there was to be a fight, he would be the first to die, determined Cephus.

The Indian was well aware of the aimed musket barrels and equally aware that the action was purely defensive. The white faces would not fire unless attacked, and he had no intention of doing that. The risks far outweighed the possible rewards. He would have liked the small herd of cattle the immigrants were protecting, but he knew that the attempt would be unwise. His braves already had whatever was worth having from the abandoned cart train, which, from the looks of it, wasn't much.

A blue and white Wedgwood china dinner plate skittered past the Indian's head and shattered on the baked earth behind him. He slanted a frown at the young buck digging into a chest of china, ripping away the protective batting to skim another plate high into the air, shrilling delight as it sailed high and far before crashing to earth. In a moment he was surrounded by his companions, and the air was filled with sailing china, each brave trying to outdistance the throw of the others.

"Oh, no!" wailed Anne McCutcheon, watching the destruction of her treasures. "My china!"

A craggy-faced, fierce-eyed Scot growled his indignation at Cephus. "Are ye no gonna do somethin'? Are ye gonna wait 'til they destroy everything before ye give the order t' fire?"

"Aye," another immigrant snorted his disgust. "When do we shoot the scurvy heathens?"

Cephus James fixed both men with a steely look. "Nothin' down there worth riskin' lives over—ours or theirs. Keep your fingers away from those triggers."

"We could get half of 'em with the first volley," protested the first man, an immigrant named Ross.

"And the other half would be on us before you could reload," snapped Cephus. "There isn't a buck down there who couldn't get a fistful of arrows off before you tore paper on your next cartridge."

"Arrers!" snorted Ross.

"I've seen an Injun drop a full-growed bull buffalo with one of them 'arrers,' " snapped Cephus.

The words created a vivid picture in Ross's mind. The Scot peered down the slope, as if seeing the Indians in a new light, a discomforting light. Cephus shook his head. Indians he could handle, but these damned fools. . . !

Angus McCutcheon looked on helplessly as death stole into Daniel Petrie's eyes. His overtaxed heart had given up the struggle. Gently,

Angus palmed the dead lids into their final closing. "I told he we shouldn't'a come," Margaret Petrie said in a numbed voice. "I told he we was too old—but he wouldn'a listen, he wouldn'a listen. Why, Daniel? Why did y' have to be stubborn? Why have y' left me alone?"

A sob came from deep within her as she caressed the still brow of the man who had shared most of her life, and would share no more. Angus beckoned to one of the other women, his meaning clear. The woman nodded, came to her feet, and crossed to put a comforting arm about the shoulders of Sister Margaret. "I'll see to her, Doctor," she said softly.

Sadly, Angus McCutcheon pushed himself to his feet. At that moment a shrill, discordant series of sounds drowned out the chatter of Indian voices. McCutcheon blanched, instantly recognizing the sound for what it was—the sound of his pipes. Next to his daughter, Anne, the bagpipes were the most prized thing in his life. Anguish flooded his face as he ran for the line of defenders and peered down at the cart train. A circle of braves stared at his precious pipes, lying in the dust. One of the more bold eased forward to prod the plaid air sack with the butt of a lance, bringing another squeal from the pipes. The bucks jumped back, several unsheathing knives or raising lances in alarm. A guttural command came from their leader. Whatever he said, it instantly eased the tension. Laughs and sheepish looks were exchanged among the young braves. Another command was barked. The braves abandoned their looting and raced for the drop-reined ponies, vaulting onto their blanketed backs.

Their leader surveyed the row of musket barrels aimed down at him from the sheltering rocks, his finely cut lips twisted with disdain. With a suddenly swift movement he reversed his lance so that the butt end was toward the white faces cowering behind the boulders. With a touch of his heel he urged his pony toward the slope and the row of muskets tracking his advance.

"What's he about?" puzzled McKee aloud.

"Gonna touch coup," said Cephus. "Gonna ride up here with his lance reversed—a sign of contempt, proof he's a warrior of great courage."

"Foolishness, if you ask me," snorted Ross.

"Mebbe so," said Cephus James, "but to an Injun it's as much a victory as takin' a scalp; some say more."

Angus McCutcheon's whispered prayer was answered. None of the young braves showed any more interest in his beloved bagpipes, lying in the dust only a few yards away from the mounted Indians. Angus had another prayer—that none of the milling horsemen would trample the precious pipes.

Anne watched with frank curiosity as the tall Indian guided his pony up the slope, his chiseled, hawklike features seeming to possess a certain primitive nobility as well as arrogance.

Cephus James shrugged angrily at his plight and stepped out from behind the rock that had sheltered him, the Colt revolving carbine left behind. The weapon could tempt the Indian and he could very well demand its surrender as tribute.

Luther had a solid bead on the Indian's chest as the brave reined to a halt, his pony's head a mere two hand spans from Cephus. He ran his eyes down the row of musket and shotgun barrels that had him as their center of focus. His lips curled faintly as he turned back to Cephus. "You chief?"

Cephus nodded casually, showing no emotion, no fear. "I'm in charge."

"No gun? Why chief have no gun?"

"We are not here to make war on our Sioux brothers. We welcome you to take what you will, and leave us in peace."

Below, at some unspoken command, the young braves eased their mounts closer to the base of the low hill. In silence they started upward, alert, ready to knock arrows into their powerful hunting bows at the first hint of hostility from the white faces.

Again the Indian surveyed the men behind the leveled muskets. The barest hint of a smile touched his lips as he turned back to Cephus. "You do not want to make war, but you are ready to make war—is true?"

"Only to protect ourselves."

Cephus and the Indian locked eyes, a mutual search for a sign of weakness, of fear. They found none. The warrior uttered a strange clucking sound, which Cephus knew meant he had gained the Indian's respect.

With a ceremonial flourish he touched the butt end of his lance to Cephus's breast, one, twice, three times.

A yelping cry of approval went up from the young bucks gathered below. The Indian thrust his lance over his head, a shrill victory cry ripping from his throat as he wheeled his pony to present his back to the guns of the white men, a gesture of contempt. He hadn't ridden ten yards when the 270-grain slug from McKee's Harper's Ferry musket smashed into his thigh, hurtling him from the back of his pony.

There was a double heartbeat of stunned silence as the echoes rolled away, the puff of white smoke lingering in the still air, immigrant and Indian alike frozen into a momentary tableau of disbelief.

Anne McCutcheon's brain refused to believe the evidence of her wide gray eyes. No! her mind screamed silently. Her hands, till now steady, began to tremble. Smothering an unsaintly curse, Cephus James dove for the shelter of a boulder as outraged cries ripped from Indian throats followed by a volley of hunting arrows and the thundering of hooves. The young braves charged the slope as the subchief dragged himself to a protecting rock, still clutching his lance.

"It was an accident! I didn't mean t' shoot!" wailed McKee, feverishly tearing open a fresh powder and ball charge. But no one was listening.

Cephus James unceremoniously snatched the Colt revolving carbine from his son, bellowing an order: "Over their heads! Fire over their heads!" A ragged volley roared from fowling pieces and muskets, filling the air with white, acrid gun smoke. The thunder of the muzzle blasts spooked the Indian ponies, spilling a number of the young braves. Cephus James's revolving Colt thundered again and again, giving the others time to rod home fresh loads into their single shots and loose another volley.

Heeding the commands of their leader, the young Indians dismounted to seek shelter among the rocks while keeping up a steady stream of arrows flying in search of a target behind the wall of powder smoke. Furious as he was, Cephus James took a moment to silently thank his maker that he and his charges were not facing a battle-tested war party. It would be hand-to-hand fighting, seasoned warriors braving the musket fire to come to close quarters where their knives and fighting axes would make the immigrants' weapons no more lethal than clubs. "Save your powder! Hold fire!" he bellowed again.

A guttural scream sounded a few feet from Cephus. He turned in time to see Ross stagger back, clutching at the shaft of an arrow that had punched through the fleshy part of his upper arm, its bloody head protruding a good six inches. In spite of himself, Cephus felt a momentary satisfaction; perhaps the man would have a little more respect for "arrers" in the future. Cephus chided himself for the thought; a wounded man on a trek wasn't a burden to be taken lightly. Luther and Cole moved quickly to tend Ross, snapping the arrow's shaft and drawing it from the wound. To Ross's credit he suffered the rough treatment without complaint.

Cephus noted the sun, already on its downward turn to the west.

Two things could happen with nightfall: The Indians could launch an attack under cover of darkness; or they could slip away into the night, nursing the injury to their pride, and wait for another day to avenge their loss of honor.

A movement below caught Cephus's eye: A hand, palm facing toward the upper reaches of the slope, appeared from behind a large rock. A shot rang out somewhere down the line, the ball spanging into the shale well beyond the upthrust hand. "Dammit!" roared Cephus. "I said t' hold fire!"

Every eye, immigrant and escort, was locked on that bronze palm as it rose higher, bringing head and torso into full view. The chiseled features of the subchief showed no sign of the pain his wound must have given as he took up his lance and thrust its head into the ground, then once more lifted his palm. "What's he up to?" said a voice to Cephus's left.

"Telling us it's over," he answered, a note of thankfulness in his voice.

From the shelter of the rocks, immigrants and escort watched in silence as the young Indians rounded up their ponies and assisted their wounded mentor to his mount, a crude bandage having been fixed to his wound. Slowly the band re-formed and moved away. The only sound was the scrape of unshod hoofs on shale and hardscrabble. As Cephus had said, it was over. Still, it had cost one life. Not to an Indian arrow, but that was little consolation to the widow of Daniel Petrie.

McKee, veteran of the Afghan wars and India's northwest frontier, tried to explain he had not fired intentionally. The ancient Harper's Ferry musket had a touchy trigger, probably a worn sear; he'd hardly touched it. No one seemed interested in his explanations, least of all Cephus James.

History had seen the bagpipe progress from the pre-Roman Mediterranean through Spain, France, Germany, the Lowlands, England, and Ireland before reaching the Scots in the early 1400s. It was there the bagpipe reached its final state of the art, never to be improved upon—unfortunately, some might say.

The blowtube between his lips, stubby fingers playing over the eight holes in the chanter pipe, Angus McCutcheon paced the ritual steps of the death dirge, each foot pausing a halt beat before touching earth. The melancholy pibroch that had accompanied the souls of countless Highlanders to the hereafter now drifted across this new land, this new Zion.

The last words had been spoken and the last shovel of earth had fallen to cover Daniel Petrie's grave when Angus drew the final somber note from his reeds. The time for the dead was over. Now it was time for the living. There was work to be done.

The sun was well to the west by the time the immigrants salvaged what they could, with particular attention to tools and the precious, scattered seed. The sturdy carts were reloaded, lighter now. Two of the Lowery boys, strapping teenagers, took charge of the Petrie cart while their parents did what they could to take the widow's mind off her sorrows, letting her tend to the needs of a new life—the Lowery's youngest—an eighteen-month-old girl named Rebecca.

Cephus James, trying to hide his ill temper, ordered the evening meal to be prepared. There would be no further travel this day. Darkness would be upon them before the reassembled cart train could travel a mile.

The communal pots had just begun to boil when Luther, from his picket post atop a nearby boulder, spotted the riders approaching on the back trail. He came to his feet, pointed off, and shouted, "Riders, paw! Comin' fast!"

Cephus, with a look of "what's next?" on his face, stood in his stirrups to peer off where his son indicated as a moan of despair welled up from the immigrants, the men hastily reaching for their weapons.

Even at this distance Cephus could see that the approaching riders, four in number, were not Indians, but that was no guarantee that their presence didn't spell danger. More than one immigrant train had been attacked by well-armed bands of roaming ruffians. Mormons, Cephus had good cause to know, were fair game to both red and white, if caught out in the open, few in number, and poorly armed. "Can you make 'em out, boy?" he called to the youth.

Luther James brought his father's telescope to his eye and quickly centered the focus. His jaw dropped at what he saw. Slamming the scope shut he leapt down from the boulder and ran toward his father. "Paw! You ain't gonna believe this . . ."

Irritation flooded Cephus's face. "Believe what? Speak up, son!"

"It's Lot Smith and Jud Stoddard, paw, and—"

Relief eased the tension in Cephus. Raising back in his stirrups, he called to the concerned immigrants. "It's al'right, folks, no cause for alarm. They're our people."

"Thank the Good Lord for that!" said Angus McCutcheon, placing his musket back in his cart.

"But, paw," protested Luther, "they got Jim Bridger with 'em and, and—"

"And who? What's wrong with you?"

"Port Rockwell!" gulped Luther. His words carried back to Anne McCutcheon, sparking instant interest.

"You sure?" frowned Cephus, looking off at the approaching riders. "Gimme that scope!"

Cephus focused on the riders, his jaw tightening. "Well, I'll be hanged, it is him!"

Cole reined up alongside Cephus and Luther, his carbine laid across the bow of his saddle, his hands shaking nervously.

Cephus looked sternly at the younger man. "You be careful with that gun, boy; just let it set! We had one buryin'; I figger that's enough for one day. . . . If Rockwell's ridin' with Jud and Lot, there has t' be good reason," he added as an afterthought.

Anne McCutcheon stepped forward for a better look at the approaching horsemen, trying to single out the man who seemed to have such an unsettling effect on the escort riders.

It had to be the tall one in the bleached buckskins; there was something about the way he carried himself in the saddle. A proud man, and dangerous. She could sense it. And, like women of every time and age, she was intrigued.

Bridger's eye scanned the solemn group before coming to rest on the freshly covered grave on the slope. He sniffed the still air. "Powder smoke and a fresh grave—you folks been havin' a to-do?"

Rockwell observed the several hoofprints still visible among the boot and shoe impressions in the powdery dust. "War party, Cephus?"

Cephus James shrugged. "Naw. Jest some young bucks tryin' t' play growed up."

McKee pushed forward, apology on his craggy face as he indicated the faulty action of his Harper's Ferry musket. "Was my doin'; bloody thing went off all by itself."

"What's done's done, McKee; sorryin' won't change it," growled Cephus, in no mood to be charitable.

Lot Smith nodded at the new grave. "That the only one?"

"Dang shame. Didn't have t' be," Cephus responded grimly.

Anne McCutcheon shuttled a look from Lot Smith back to the man in pale buckskins as he reflected, "You said it yourself, Cephus, sorrying won't change it. What were they, Pawnee? Cheyenne?"

Luther James moved in beside his father, obviously awed by the tall man in the bleached buckskins, and wanting to show his aggressiveness. "No sir, Bro—Mister Rockwell—they was Sioux. 'Bout twenty of 'em. Like pa said, young uns."

Cephus gave his son a look of disapproval, a look that wasn't lost on Rockwell or Anne McCutcheon. Rockwell forced a thin smile at the younger James. "Then I'd say you folks have something to be thankful for. If they'd been full grown there'd be more than one grave up there."

Lot Smith masked his annoyance at the all-too-obvious deference to Port Rockwell, the assumption that he was the spokesman for the group. "Nearest Sioux camp is about two days south, Brother Cephus. Be a good thing if you folks got an early start in the mornin'."

"They'll come a-lookin', that's fer sure," growled Jim Bridger.

Anne McCutcheon read the frustration in Lot Smith's face, and could understand it. They were much alike, these two, and very much unlike. For some reason the word *domesticated* sprang into her thoughts as she eyed Lot Smith—spirited, but restrained. Rockwell, on the other hand, seemed to have an easy freedom about him, exuding independence, defiance of any authority not his own. Be sensible, Anne McCutcheon, she told herself; for all his magnetism this frontier man was not the sort any proper girl should be thinking about.

Jim Bridger's growl broke in on her thoughts, his glowering eyes on Cephus James. "Anyone goin' to ask us to step down?"

Cephus shuttled a tight look from Bridger to the faintly smiling Rockwell. Trail courtesy was an obligation not to be dismissed lightly, to stranger as well as friend. Rockwell was no stranger, but to Cephus James, he sure couldn't be called a friend, not since Carthage, Missouri.

At last Cephus nodded. "Step down. Grub'll be ready when it's ready."

Swinging around to Luther, Cole, and the other escort riders, Cephus bawled, "Aw'right! Get back t' yer posts."

Anne McCutcheon glanced up from her plate to dart a quick, covert look at Porter Rockwell. For a flustering moment his eyes locked on hers. A touch of red came to her cheeks. Rockwell smiled, deepening the flush in her face. She had a difficult time breaking contact. Simultaneously, contrasting feelings of fear and desire surged through her, causing a chill to go up her spine. Never had a man caused such an effect on her. Finally she lowered her eyes, suffering the embarrassment of knowing this mysterious man was aware of her reaction.

"Seems that Rockwell fella's taken a fancy to ye, girl," frowned Angus, breaking the silence. "Not too sure that sets well with me, from what I've been hearin'."

"What have you been hearing, Da?" she asked, breathing deeply, closing her eyes for a moment.

"A renegade, through and through. A deserter."

"Now is that a fact?" Anne responded, her eyes complementing the teasing tone of her voice. She surveyed the small, cart-surrounded enclosure centered by the cooking fires. The light from the flames seemed to dance in Porter Rockwell's eyes as once again they met her own. It was she who broke contact again, as the strange sensations returned. "Maybe, Da—maybe not," she replied to her father, who responded with a shake of his head.

Porter Rockwell had not the slightest doubt he was the topic of conversation between the handsome blond girl and the man he'd learned was her father, Angus McCutcheon. And he had not the slightest doubt of what the gist of that conversation might be.

A shadow fell across Rockwell as Lot Smith, his plate in his hand, stepped between Porter and the cook-fire flames. Rockwell forced a brow up at the thin-lipped, younger man. "Something on your mind, Lot?"

"I been watchin' the way you been starin' at that girl, Port—"

"Don't say it," Rockwell cut him off with a cold look.

Bridger offered a sarcastic smile.

Lot, suddenly feeling inconsequential, still warned in a low, determined voice, "Keep your place, Port."

Turning on his heel, Lot crossed to one of the hang kettles to angrily slop a ladle of fresh stew into his plate. In spite of himself, he looked for Anne. She was in deep, animated conversation with her father. With a mental shrug of resignation, Lot returned to take his place beside Jud Stoddard.

"What'd y' say to him?" asked Jud.

"Nothin', nothin' at all," said Lot, an edge to his voice.

"Maybe we shouldn't'a asked him t' come back with us, Lot. Maybe it wasn't such a good idea."

"We've got to keep our personals out of it, Jud. Look at it practical. Isn't a better man on either side of the divide when it comes to a fight, and it looks like that's what it's comin' to—us against the United States Army."

Bridger, his back against a cart wheel, grunted something Rockwell didn't catch, and wasn't particularly interested in anyway. Something far more important occupied his thoughts—Anne McCutcheon.

This evening there was none of the satisfaction that usually accompanied the completion of another ten miles of progress toward the immigrants' still-distant goal. Daniel Petrie's death had hung like a cloud, dampening the spirits of the newcomers. To come so far, to die so close—it wasn't fair.

Escort and immigrants had gone about their chores with muted voices. Children were bedded down, the milk cows were penned in a makeshift corral fashioned out of roped cart stakes. Weapons, primed and loaded, were placed within easy reach. The picket guards were sent out, and Porter Rockwell and Jud Stoddard were assigned to relieve two of the regular escort riders.

Anne McCutcheon sand-cleaned the five-gallon, cast-iron utility pot that had held the evening meal. Refilled with clear water, the pot would be placed on the sand-banked coals, which would emit just enough heat to have the kettle ready for the morning's porridge.

The combined weight of water and kettle was something over fifty pounds, and it took a girl of Anne's strength to lift it to nest on the bed of coals. "Let me give you a hand with that, miss," Lot's voice came from behind her. He had found his opening.

Anne looked over her shoulder as she straightened up. "Thank you kindly," she said through a cool smile, "but it's no great bother. I've been doing it since we left Independence."

There was a long moment of awkward silence as Lot fidgeted, desperately seeking some way to keep the conversation going. Anne, secretly pleased, took pity on the earnest-eyed young man, so obviously at a loss for words. "You're Lot Smith, aren't you?"

The look of surprise in Lot's face almost brought a laugh to Anne's lips; she compromised with a smile. "Well, it's no great secret, is it now?"

"No," mumbled Lot. "Guess I'm just kind'a glad you took the trouble to remember it."

"No trouble," said Anne, thrusting a firm, sun-bronzed hand to the young mail rider, a twinkle in her eye. "I'm Anne McCutcheon, and it's pleased I am to be making your acquaintance, Mister Lot Smith."

"I'm the one that's pleasured, Miss McCutcheon," gulped Lot through an uncertain grin, taking her hand. He stood for a moment, searching for something additional to say. Nothing came.

Anne's brow lifted over a bemused smile. "May I be having my hand back, Mister Smith?"

"Huh? Oh—your pardon, miss," he flushed. "No offense meant. . . ."

"And none taken," said Anne with a small smile, massaging her released fingers. "It's a fine, strong grip you be having."

The flush in Lot's cheeks deepened as he stammered, "Uh—sorry, Miss McCutcheon, I didn't mean to—"

"Would it be terrible improper if we stopped being so formal, Mister Smith?" said Anne, overriding his apology. "I'd be more comfortable if you'd call me Anne."

Lot was euphoric. "Ah, yes, . . . well *Anne* . . . maybe a short walk later on?" His voice cracked like that of a boy verging on puberty. Her smile exhibited the most perfect set of teeth he was sure he had ever seen.

"Perhaps," she responded in a way that meant yes, and Lot's heart began to thump against his chest wall. He was thunderstruck. He liked everything about this girl—her beauty, the way she handled herself, never giving up an ounce of poise and sophistication even when she carried a heavy pot of water. Her charm enthralled him. He loved the way she tried, with relative success, to mute her Scottish accent when she talked.

Rockwell had just started to return to his blanket after four hours of picket duty when voices carried to him out of the darkness, beyond the camp perimeter. Reversing himself, he eased around the bulk of the cart to peer off into the shadows of a wagon-sized boulder some fifty feet distant. There were darker shadows within the shadows, shadows that moved and spoke. Rockwell recognized Lot's voice. Then, ". . . Scotland isn't the end of the world, you know," said one of the shadows in a sweet, burr-kissed voice that Rockwell knew instantly to be Anne McCutcheon's. The lilt of her phrasing struck a responsive chord in Rockwell's memory—another voice, another time.

He made a conscious effort to stifle the memory of that other voice. He rolled back behind the cart and, with his hands clasped behind his head as a makeshift pillow, gazed at the millions of diamonds that graced the darkened sky. In a moment the voices trailed off into the distance and were overwhelmed by familiar night sounds, bringing with them the peace of sleep to Rockwell's troubled mind. Before his eyes closed he thought he heard Anne speak his name. His name on her lips; it was pleasing to him.

A newborn sun silhouetted the distant peaks of the Continental Divide as the cart train prepared for another day's journey west. It would be nine days on the trails, at ten miles a day, before reaching Bridger's Fort, there to rest up for the final 150-mile push that would take them to their final haven—Salt Lake City. At the fort they would have an opportunity to rest a spell, make repairs, and purchase what trade goods they could afford.

Bridger had decided to stay on with the train; there was no great urgency for him to get to the fort, he had said. But Rockwell knew the real reason: He had decided to remain to help protect this little band of immigrants. That was the kind of man he was. Cephus James was glad to have another good rifle to back up the small contingent of escort riders. But he was more than just a good rifle, Cephus told Angus McCutcheon, Ross, and McKee. The mere presence of Jim Bridger would have a salutary effect should another band of Indians suddenly appear. Bridger was a legend to the red man as well as the white; big medicine, blood brother to half the tribes traversing the great plains; Sioux, Ute, Blackfoot, Nez Percé, and the Crow all knew Jim Bridger, king of the mountain men.

Jud Stoddard was already in the saddle when Porter Rockwell threw a leg over his big buckskin and a tight look at Lot Smith, some ten yards away, next to the McCutcheon cart.

Anne handed the young man a small, cloth-wrapped bundle, which Lot stuffed inside his rough, homespun shirt. As she smiled a good-bye to Lot, she could feel Rockwell's eyes watching her, although her back was to him. She caught her breath and returned her attention to Lot. A few feet away, Angus McCutcheon kept a protective, fatherly eye on his daughter as he tightened the cart harness, drawing out the task, timing it, he hoped, to coincide with Lot's departure. The young pup was struck, no doubt about that, thought Angus. The fact that Lot Smith was a full-grown man, well past the age that most men of the time had wives and families, was lost on McCutcheon. To him, Lot Smith was a pup, and would be until he proved more. At the same time this traditional father was cautiously pleased. It had been a long time since his daughter had shown the slightest interest in any man.

What was it about this woman that turned him all thick tongued and fumbly, Lot groaned inwardly. There were girls as pretty in Salt Lake, some a mite prettier, but never had he seen a pair of eyes like Anne McCutcheon's. It wasn't the color, a pale blue-gray, or the fact that they were pleasingly wide set; it was the way she used them, or rather, the way she did not; there was no coyness here, no fluttering feminine glances. Anne's look was open, direct, and honest, without a suggestion of the wiles some girls believed so necessary.

As if to buttress his thoughts, Anne said, "When we get to Salt Lake, perhaps we can talk again."

Lot looked deep into the cool, gray-blue eyes, and smiled. "Sure thing. I was worryin' you might not want to."

"Only thing I'm worryin' about is the two of ye' taking root," snorted Angus McCutcheon.

"Da!" said Anne, feigning anger. "It isn't proper to listen in on people's conversations."

"Didn't notice much conversation," grumbled Angus, "just a lot o' taffy-eyed lookin'. Say your good-byes and get done with it."

"Bye, Anne. See you in Salt Lake," said Lot, taking both her hands in his. Aware of her father's eyes, Anne flushed, nodding a smile.

Lot pulled himself away and strode for the mount beside Rockwell's. Anne's look held on both men, as if weighing the balance.

"Sorry," Lot said to Rockwell as he swung up into the saddle.

"You're the one who's so anxious to get moving," he responded dryly.

Bridger moved in to hook a hand on Rockwell's bridle. "Reckon you'll have time t' stop at the fort?"

"I'll make time."

"Good," said Bridger. "Tell Little Fawn I'll be comin' in with a party, fifty and some."

"Got it," grinned Rockwell.

Rockwell kneed the buckskin around and touched spur to the animal's flank. The big horse leapt into motion, forcing his rider to shorten rein.

Lot Smith responded to a wave from Anne McCutcheon as he urged his own mount into movement. He and Jud Stoddard raced after the big buckskin, then slowed to a gallop, keeping pace with Rockwell.

"Al'right, we're movin'!" Cephus James called to the immigrants in his characteristically irritated manner. "Cole, you take point. Luther, Jennings, flank riders. Dennison, back trail." The riders rode to take their appointed stations as the small column of carts groaned into movement.

Anne's strong, young body lunged hard against the wide pull straps of the harness she shared with her father, spurring him to greater effort. A side glance at her face told Angus that things were never going to be the same. Something had changed with the arrival of Lot Smith and Porter Rockwell. She was radiant this morning, full of energy, as if she were just beginning a great adventure. Angus wasn't at all sure how to take this. What father from the Old Country would?

Jim Bridger, atop his big black, riding the lead along with Cephus James, looked back at the cart train. Pushed and pulled, it would average a hair better than one mile an hour, every step bringing it that much closer to their destination. A dark thought knitted the mountain man's craggy brow. If that Magruder fella was talking true, these good folks stood a fair chance of winding up with more promise than land. Somehow, it didn't seem right.

Some ten hours and ninety miles later, Port Rockwell and the two mail riders came within sight of Bridger's Fort, a rough rectangle of log and adobe with rifle towers at each corner, situated on a rise that gave it a commanding view of the surrounding terrain.

By military standards, the term *fort* was a misnomer. What it was, in actuality, was a glorified trading post, capable of withstanding a not-too-determined attack by lightly armed Indians, but not much more. The real protection provided by the fort was in the reputation of the man whose name it bore—Jim Bridger.

Bridger was supported by a half-dozen or so tough mountain men who were sort of junior partners. Their presence combined with their ominous reputations contributed to the firepower and the legend of Bridger's Fort. As did Bridger, they moved freely among the Indian nations. Not only their universally feared mystical reputations, but their fairness in dealing with the Indians assured them this privilege. They were led by a giant half-breed, known only as Simon. A brawny seven-footer, Simon was uncommonly handsome, with long, wavy jet black hair and black eyes set off by his light skin and ivory teeth. He had been left with Franciscan monks in Santa Fe by Apache Indians, who claimed that his mother, a captured white woman, had died birthing him. Apparently no other squaw would raise the half-breed. Thanks to the monks, who became surrogate fathers to him, Simon spoke English impeccably, and, for the time and place, was well educated.

There was the inevitable cluster of worse-for-wear tepees and stick shelters, found outside the walls of every fort and trading post in the territories, housing an assortment of bare-bottomed children, aging squaws, old men, dogs, and more dogs. They clung to such establishments as the remora clung to the shark, depending on it for survival and offering much the same service in return. They were scavengers, making use of every cast-off or throwaway that came from within the walls.

"We've got another good two hours of ridin' light, Port. You go give Bridger's woman his message; we'll wait for you here," said Lot Smith as they reined up a few hundred yards from the fort.

Rockwell's voice was stern. "I've done all the riding I'm going to do for one day. If you and Jud want to keep going, don't let me stop you."

Lot Smith searched Rockwell's face and frowned. "Somethin' botherin' you?"

Rockwell ignored the question.

"What's it going to be? You riding or staying?"

"We might as well call it a day, Lot," ventured Stoddard. "Like Brother Rockwell says, a few hours won't make no nevermind."

Rockwell jerked his head angrily toward Jud Stoddard. "I'll say it one more time, Jud. Don't call me brother; I stopped being a brother to fools a long time ago."

Then, urging his buckskin forward, Rockwell galloped down the slope, heading for the wagon road that led to the entrance of Bridger's Fort. Indian dogs, yelping with excitement, raced to intercept the new arrival, a game that was ritual with the mangy creatures.

"Come on," Lot snapped to Jud Stoddard, grim lipped and frustrated. "We're stayin' over." They started down, following Rockwell's path.

From the northeastern tower of the fort, the imposing figure of Simon, who had been apprised of the approaching riders, sang out a hearty welcome to his friends.

That evening, after having washed the trail dust from their bodies and having spent an hour or so talking with Simon, the three riders sat quietly at a plank table in the huge general-purpose room, eating beans and strips of venison. The room served as kitchen, bar, bunk room, and dining room for travelers. Several other structures, nestled within the walls of the fort, served as storage space for a vast quantity of necessities often needed by those same travelers. There was a large assortment of firearms; powder and lead; bags, barrels, and canisters of staples; harness leather; bolt cloth; blankets; camphine oil; sugans; boots; a variety of headgear; and most important, a never-ending supply of tobacco and whiskey. While Bridger was away, Little Fawn was the keeper of the keys. Her assistants, Tiny Elk and Shy Flower, blood kin, were cut from the same mold; short, round, and fully packed.

Porter Rockwell bit into one of the chewy, muffin-sized cookies that Lot Smith brought out of the cloth-wrapped bundle Anne had given him that morning. "Not bad," he grunted.

"Oatmeal and honey. It's kind of a treat in Scotland," said Lot, wearily taking a chunk out of one of the cookies.

"I've tasted worse," munched Jud Stoddard as Little Fawn cleared away the last of their scraped-clean plates.

A few such statements of small talk is all that passed between Rockwell and Lot Smith. Jud sensed a new feeling of strain between them: no doubt, he reasoned, because they were both thinking about the same thing—that beauty of a Scottish lass. Jud felt uneasy. This, he said to himself as he eyed them both, could be a dangerous situation, what with Rockwell's naturally ornery disposition and Lot's quick temper. He would have preferred to hear them arguing over one thing or another, rather than to suffer through this ominous quiet.

Rockwell and Smith, he knew, had a tenuous relationship. There was no doubt they admired each other, but Lot could not accept Rockwell's backsliding, his desertion of the Mormon community. And Rockwell could not stomach the rigid orthodoxy and at the same time the self-assuredness, bordering on arrogance, from such a pup. He hadn't realized that Lot was attempting, as best he could without sacrificing his faith, to imitate the gunman, that imitation was the strongest form of respect. And now, in a matter of just a few hours, another cause for irritation had stepped between them—a Scotswoman, whose striking beauty and unprovoked sensuousness would have turned any man's head.

"Whiskey now?" Little Fawn broke the silence, waddling back to the rough plank table in the center of the general-purpose room.

"No, thank you," Lot responded to her query.

"Speak for yourself, boy," said Rockwell. "Bring me a bottle and a couple of those three-cent stogies, Little Fawn. Better make that a half dozen." Little Fawn nodded and waddled away.

Slowly, Lot put down his oatmeal cookie and climbed to his feet, his eyes fixed hard on Rockwell.

"Something on your mind, boy?" said Rockwell, with a lift of his brow.

Jud looked apprehensively from one to the other and took another bite of his cookie, chewing nervously.

Rockwell kept his seat as Lot stood towering across the table separating the two, supported by leaning on his two fists, his arms straight and rigid, his eyes focusing directly on Rockwell's. "You don't cotton to being called brother," he bit out. "Well, that's fine with me. Now, I'll say this just once: Don't call me boy, or we're going to have a problem, you and me."

With that he spun around and walked briskly to the far side of the room, where he began unceremoniously to arrange his bunk. His body was tense. He expected to feel Rockwell's powerful hands on his shoulders spinning him around at any second. No one talked to Porter Rockwell the way he had.

But Rockwell sat unmoved, saying nothing, and Jud started to choke on his Scottish cookie. Little Fawn, returning with the bottle and stogies, freed one hand and brought it down between Jud's shoulder blades with a resounding thump, almost driving his nose into the plank table. The blow had the desired effect. Through tearing eyes he managed a nod of thanks to the moon-faced Indian woman.

A short time later Lot Smith and a truly relieved Jud Stoddard watched as Rockwell casually crossed to one of the tiered bunks to stash stogies and bottle in the gutta-percha sheet wrapped around his blanket. The tall man then swung himself onto the bunk, shucked out of his moccasins, and lay back on the rough canvas mattress stuffed with dried plains grass. Hay was a luxury not to be found at Bridger's Fort.

Tonight, he was sure, there'd be no whispered conversations to disturb his sleep. Still, a vision of Anne McCutcheon flooded his consciousness. Actually she had never been far from his thoughts since the moment he had first seen her—majesty in crumpled, faded, Scottish woolen. Her image, her aristocratic presence, even her voice, brought back memories of a love that once uplifted and fulfilled—memories Rockwell had thought were lost in time. And now this Scottish lassie had returned to him a sense of warmth and desire he thought to be long dead. If this were another time, another place—but it wasn't; it was now. . . . It was some time before his eyes closed.

At dawn the following morning, Jud caught Rockwell alone, saddling the buckskin. "Porter."

"Yes." Rockwell looked down at the diminutive mail rider, whose faith and courage had made a giant.

Jud was looking down at his feet, his fingers nervously pulling against each other on the rim of the hat he held in his hands. "Well, ah, last night."

"What about last night?"

"When Lot was bracing you the way he did. I was plenty worried. I thought you sure would . . . but you held your temper, and well . . . I thank you for that."

A specter of a smile played about Rockwell's lips. "I couldn't fault a man for being right, could I?"

The kind words and the half smile from Rockwell made Jud Stoddard's day.

Simon watched from the gunwalk over the gate as the three riders headed west, mounts trying to catch up with early morning shadows keeping pace ahead of them.

Chapter Four

E migration Canyon, July 24, 1857, Pioneer Day. Except for a few of the very aged, or infirm, and those who had to care for them, the entire population of Salt Lake City and its environs had gathered in this sylvan spot to celebrate the tenth anniversary of their arrival in the valley. This was a day of rejoicing, a day when ordinary cares were set aside, a day to give thanks.

Ten years before, when the weary wanderers had first set foot in this canyon, they'd found a barren nothingness, a land that seemed hostile to all living things. Now, there was sweet water, rich grassy glades, an abundance of trees, and beyond, fertile fields and lush meadows.

Trestle tables set on the mossy bank of a clear running stream were heavily laden with glazed hams, huge roasts, and pork and chicken cooked in a variety of ways. There were cakes, cookies, and hearth-baked loaves, along with a wide-ranging assortment of vegetables, fruits and melons, and innumerable jars of preserves.

And there were games, for young and old—horseshoes, quoits, sack and egg races, and the inevitable games of tag and blindman's bluff. Amid all this, several of the oldsters managed to concentrate on games of chess or checkers. The women seemed content to exchange gossip or recipes, while keeping a watchful eye on the younger children.

So different were these faces now, compared to what they had been just ten short years before. Gone was the haggard, haunted look of desperation; gone were the doubts and fears, the worn, gaunt bodies, the dispirited eyes. Now, everyone stood strong and erect, bodies full-fleshed, eyes glowing with confidence, secure in the knowledge that they had overcome odds to try the souls of lesser men and women.

For the boys and girls soon to become men and women, the center of focus was the Nauvoo Brass Band, sharing the bunting-clad speakers' platform. Above the platform, on a spliced pole, wafted the Stars and Stripes.

The band ended a medley of lively tunes to segue into Stephen Foster's latest melody, "Come Where My Love Lies Dreaming." Strong, young hands slipped about slender waists; shy glances were exchanged. Indeed, this land would continue to be fruitful.

At the periphery of the festivities, overlooking the valley, a solitary figure stood surveying the panorama of the city, the Great Salt Lake, and the mountains beyond, occasionally turning his head to watch the excitement taking place.

One leg was raised, his foot planted on a small boulder, his right arm resting on his knee, and his hands clasped. He was bareheaded, and the cuffs of his tan shirt were rolled up near his elbows, revealing muscular arms that complemented large, rough hands—a carpenter's hands, one might have guessed. He was clean shaven, which allowed the full expression of his classic features, framed by a tight, muscular jaw and embellished with piercing blue eyes. An observant person would see in him a healthy combination of raw strength and intelligence, an air of sophistication combined with an almost overpowering masculinity. His clothing was no different from that of other men in the large group, for Mormon Church leaders did not wear distinctive clothing, nor did the Mormon people dress as Quakers, or any other religious order for that matter.

Few men have been more revered by their followers than Brigham Young, who was looked to by these festive people for spiritual guidance and, as governor of the territory of Utah, for secular leadership as well. Yet for the moment he was left in solitude. Something in his bearing indicated to his followers that he did not wish to be disturbed, and his privacy was respected by all—although now and then furtive glances were cast his way.

On this anniversary of the arrival of the first wagon trains to the once-sterile valley of the Great Salt Lake, the leader of that body of outcasts had mixed feelings. To be sure, as he took in the faces of the merrymakers, he experienced great satisfaction. Somehow, although they had become tough, durable, and self-sufficient, most of them had escaped the crudeness and meanness of manner often associated with the extremes of frontier life. Colonel Thomas L. Kane, United States Army, had become acquainted with the Mormons when they were on their way west. Having spent some time on duty with the frontier inhabitants of Missouri and Ohio, he later wrote about the Mormons thus: "I can scarcely describe the gratification I felt in associating again with persons of Eastern American origin—persons of refined habits and decent language."

In the summer of 1846, Colonel Kane had been special presidential emissary to Brigham Young, who was then leading his flock to the Rockies. The message from James K. Polk: Would the Mormons, who were in the midst of being driven from the confines of the United States, submit five hundred able-bodied men to serve in the war against Mexico? Brigham Young had agreed, and, under the direction of Kane, who by now had become a close friend of Young's, the Mormon Battalion had been created. The battalion left Fort Leavenworth in August, commanded by a non-Mormon—Lt. Col. Philip St. George Cooke.

As Young's contemplation took him back over the years, he remembered these men well. He was not yet aware that soon both of these officers would again play conspicuous roles in Mormon—and American—history.

So it was not without some satisfaction that Brigham Young surveyed his surroundings. Still, the governor was uneasy. He wondered to himself how long the peace would last. On this brilliant July day, as far as the eye could see, the sky was a flawless, cerulean blue. Yet he knew that dark clouds were forming afar to the east. Since Utah businessmen had assumed the federal mail and cargo contracts, having undercut their corrupt and slovenly competitors, communication with the East had been remarkably efficient for the times. Young was fully aware that the relationship between North and South was deteriorating. Political and economic problems were festering. The question over slavery divided states, communities, even families. Mobocracy was rampant. The deliberations of men seemed to abandon reason. He was reminded of the statement by a United States senator: "Of all things I hate most, it is slavery—except abolitionism."

Now, with each day's passage, Young's concern grew. Would those dark, roiling clouds of disunion reach the western Rockies and beyond? He knew the answer even as he contemplated the question. Disunion was coming; only its form and duration were a matter of conjecture.

With a sense of foreboding, the governor acknowledged to himself that the dark clouds of persecution that his people knew so well were undoubtedly on their way to the territory of Utah. The fat was already in the fire—he repeated the cliche to himself. He estimated that the motley group of federal appointees who had taken French leave of the territory—including Judge William Drummond and his garish whore—must have arrived in the nation's capital some months past. That they would follow through with their threat to declare Utah in a state of rebellion was a foregone conclusion.

The problem had begun simultaneously with territorial designation. Fully aware of the corruption inherent in territorial governments, Young had sued for statehood. Congress would have none of it, but did acquiesce in appointing him governor of the newly formed Utah Territory. From the beginning his tightfisted control of territorial funds caused anger and frustration among the other federal appointees. Their inability to line their pockets had removed all conceivable benefits of having come clear to hell-and-gone to Utah. It was only a matter of time before a reactive explosion would take place. Even Percival Twist, the Indian agent whom Brigham Young called a bloodsucker, was suffering, since the Indians under his charge preferred to trade with the settlers. More than once he had complained that he was the only Indian agent in all the territories who was worse off than his clients.

The final blow had come to their aspirations when they lost their only source of pillage beyond a few judicial fines and their paltry salaries—the cross-country mail and freight services. A frown cut across Young's face as he recalled that blustery day when, nudged by a brisk wind out of the west, he strode across Main Street, entered the Territorial Court, and slapped the new mail and freight contract on the judicial bench directly in front of the startled Judge Drummond, demanding that it be legally recorded and acknowledged. He then followed this with two hundred dollars gold—enough to pay the fine and contempt citation against one Levi Abrams, a respected freighter, who had just suffered the indignation of Drummond's kangaroo court.

Young once again pictured vividly Drummond's face—rage written in every line of his debauched countenance. His puffed, bloodshot eyes had spewed hatred, promising revenge. There was no doubt; this man would never let the affront go unchallenged. Therefore, it was no great surprise to anyone when, a short time later, the entire territorial complement returned to Washington with little more than they had originally brought with them.

As the months passed, Young waited for the repercussions that would surely come. With each new day he watched for some evidence of reaction from the federal government—at best an official inquiry, at worst. . . . But today. . . . He brought his thoughts back to the matters at hand; nothing was going to spoil *this* great celebration.

From the valley floor, up through the pass came a rider, mounted on a lathered Indian pony exploding dust under racing hoofs. He galloped to the fringe of the crowd facing the platform, did a quick dismount, and forced his way to the platform steps. A tin star fixed to his homespun shirt identified him as one of the city constables, Will Moss. He made his way up the steps, ignoring the questions that came from those he excused out of his way, there to confront the two counselors to Brigham Young—Gaskel Romney and John Benson. A brief but animated conversation with excited gestures ensued, most of it coming from Moss.

Then the three turned to look for Brigham Young, who had already begun to make his way toward the bandstand. Few words passed between them before Young motioned them toward his carriage, which was tethered some fifty yards distant in a clump of aspen by the road. Raised eyebrows, curious looks, and inquisitive murmurs came from those who had witnessed the strange happenings. As he left, Brigham Young turned to the bandmaster. "Play, Mr. O'Brian, play!"

"Yes, sir," responded the man, lifting his baton and tapping the music stand.

The joyous melody swelled to fill the canyon as every voice joined in, drowning out the sound of churning hoofbeats and the spinning wheels of the carriage that bore the governor and his ecclesiastical counselors into the city.

"Magruder and Drummond! Greedy little men with no thought but their own pockets. How can the government survive such men!" snorted Gaskel Romney.

"A good question," responded Young, "but the problem we have to concern ourselves with is how are we to survive the government?"

From his position, leaning against the wall near the door of the governor's office, Porter Rockwell, shifting his weight from one leg to the other, was obviously uncomfortable. Lot was standing a few feet away with Jud. Although Young had greeted these two warmly, only a nod had passed between him and Rockwell. From all appearances no love was lost between them. Young had been understandably shocked when he walked into the room and saw Rockwell, but, characteristically, he hid his reaction behind a stern countenance.

As always, with harbingers of bad news, the trio had been relegated to positions of nonimportance once their message had been delivered. For the moment they were little more than spectators, looking on as the powers-that-be evaluated, assessed, and considered the importance of that message. The expression on Lot's face was obvious; he did not like that position one bit. Rockwell, for his part, sighed and shifted his weight again.

John Benson, a lean, angular man in his late thirties, said angrily, "I was afraid that with our territorial status something like this would happen."

Brigham Young nodded. "Perhaps it was inevitable, but I'm afraid that our problems go much deeper than federal appointees. We're all aware of the fragile state of the Union. When secession comes, and I believe it will, the horsemen of the apocalypse will be unleashed, and I don't see how we can fully escape its ravages."

"I had hoped we wouldn't become involved," Benson reasoned aloud.

"It would appear," Young responded slowly, his eyes moving to each person in the room, "we are already involved."

His words struck his listeners like a blow. Even Rockwell raised his head from contemplating the toes of his boots, and placed his weight squarely on both feet.

After a palpable moment of silence, the governor continued: "At this moment an army moves toward us, and it is an army; according to Lot, probably brigade strength, maybe more. Could it be that we have become the entering wedge to disunion, that the first shots of a great war between the states will be fired in the territory of Utah?"

"What are you driving at?" asked the perplexed Gaskel Romney.

"Let's look at the situation facing us. The reality of an army driving toward us is not open to argument. The question is why, and what are we to do about it?

"Our former territorial appointees have undoubtedly convinced the president that Utah is in a state of rebellion, that we had driven them out, burned down the Territorial Court, and abrogated the authority of federal law. What would be the reaction of a president of the United States, facing the specter of secession and civil war?" The question was asked in such a way that he who asked it was expected to give the answer.

"Would he have thought, here is an opportunity for me to give the nation—particularly the South—an object lesson? The conditions would be perfect: an errant territory, inhabited by an outcast, rebellious people, with none to speak in their defense or take up their cause. A man who is as frightened of disunion as Buchanan might well not consider the long-range consequences of his action, and send out an army without an investigation into the charges. It seems inconceivable that Buchanan can't see the dangers of tying up an army two thousand miles or more to the west when those troops may be needed to protect the integrity of the Union, but perhaps the opportunity of showing the strength of his presidency has outweighed caution."

"He also might be sending a message to the copperheads on his own cabinet," offered Benson. "The secretary of war, John Floyd, is known for his secessionist sympathies."

"Good point," responded Young. "Is it possible *both* Buchanan and Floyd may have agreed to dispatch this army for *conflicting* reasons— Buchanan, to put down what he's been made to believe is an insurrection by a territorial government; Floyd, to position a sympathetic general to move his troops on to California and seize it for the Southern bloc when the time is right, using the territory of Utah as a stepping-stone."

"California?" responded Romney, trying to coordinate the enormity of what had just been said.

"California," repeated Young. "The wealth of California, and a solid South, stretching from ocean to ocean."

To Rockwell, who had become an expert on the duplicity of men, what Young had said was all very logical. In spite of himself he spoke out, filling a void following Young's last statement: "Makes sense. Five hundred million has come out of California in the past seven years, and there'll be a lot more. The South could use that gold."

An almost-dazed Romney looked from Young to Rockwell. "The use of the army as part of a plot to destroy the Union?"

Rockwell shrugged.

Brigham Young turned, his steps carrying him to the window overlooking the large walled enclosure, the site of what would one day be an imposing temple. At length, he turned to face the others, the muscles in his jaw taut, his steely eyes penetrating, overpowering. "As God is my witness, I tell you that we'll not be used as pawns in this game! But our actions, whatever they may be, must be thought out with great care. An error in judgment now could undo all we've strived for. Remember this: Our future lies with becoming a state; our obligation is to stand with the Union. But we'll not kneel before it!"

Then Romney opened the question that was on everyone's mind: "Are we facing another Missouri, another Illinois?"

Brigham Young shot a stern look back at him. "We've run for the last time! We'll not submit to pillage and mob rule again!"

"And if the army's coming to do just that?" posited Rockwell.

The governor of Utah Territory did not hesitate a second. *"Then we fight!* But on our terms, not theirs, in ways of our choice, not theirs! This military expedition faces more than a few problems; we'll turn these problems into crises!"

Rockwell felt like cheering but instead appeared disinterested and immune from the tension that was mounting in the governor's office. He was not about to give Brigham Young the satisfaction.

No one suggested the apparent contradiction between Young's pledge of allegiance to the Union and his determination to take a stand against what gave every indication of being an invading federal army.

Benson was the next to speak. "Should we activate the battalion?"

"Slowly," responded Young. "There is time. I want as little disruption as possible now. However, I want the senior officers placed on alert. General Wells will provide us with information on the length of time needed for a full mobilization of the territory's military force, its numerical strength—especially the number and physical readiness of the battalion's veterans—and the condition of our weapons, wagons, horses. Brother Romney. . . ."

"Yes, sir."

"A difficult task, my friend. . . . I want an assessment of our ability to withstand a prolonged siege. Also, I want a plan to bring in and accommodate families and communities that may be in the path of the army." Then, as an afterthought, "I suppose our people in the southern part of the territory will be safe for the moment."

Without waiting for a response, the governor, now commander in chief, looked intently at his three messengers, granting them half a smile. "Gentlemen, for you I have reserved the most difficult task of all. I want to know the size, the makeup, the leadership, and the condition of the expedition. I want to know everything about them—the extent of their current supplies and their means of replenishment, their attitudes and intentions. I want the supply columns infiltrated by our people. I must know the exact route the army will take, and whether or not the intention is to occupy Salt Lake Valley. They must be kept under surveillance at all times.

"For the moment," he continued, "we'll give Buchanan the benefit of a doubt. We must assume that a presidential commission of inquiry is on its way, and that the military will await its conclusions before contemplating occupation under force of arms.

"If, at the end of two weeks, we find no indication of such a commission, we'll send our own emissaries to Washington. We must try to deal with this problem by negotiation rather than confrontation, if possible."

Then Young looked directly at Rockwell, to the utter dismay of Lot Smith. "Porter, how long will it take this army to reach the territory?"

"Depends," he shrugged. "Forced march . . . they might make it in two months. But I doubt if they'll push that hard. They'd outrun their commissary, have to live off the land. I'd figure on twelve weeks, maybe a bit more."

Young pursed his lips thoughtfully. "Late October, early November. . . . We have time!" After a lengthy pause, he took in Lot and Jud. "Now then, Johnston's army must be held at bay until we're able to present our case to the president, or, failing that, until we're better prepared to deal with it. *I want that army kept out of these valleys until at least spring!*"

Jud's eyes opened wide at the enormity of the task before them. Brigham Young was unable to restrain a smile. "We must do what must be done," he said softly, "and of course we shall ask for an early winter."

Porter Rockwell had decided to splurge; a three-dollar-a-week room at Brandon's boardinghouse. He tried to recall the last time he'd slept on a real mattress, within four walls he could call his own, however temporarily—and couldn't.

The pleasantness of his situation temporarily soothed his troubled thoughts, and momentarily arrested the question he'd been asking himself from the moment he entered the Salt Lake Valley: What in the hell am I doing here? He had known only guilt and pain since the day he'd become one of them. He was alone then, questioning, searching. Joseph Smith seemed to have answers, but it all ended in tragedy.

Stripping off his gun belt, he checked the loads of the navy Colts, making sure that each cylinder hole was well greased, that the percussion caps were secure on the nipples.

For some reason he remembered that Case Carney had worn a brace of Remington army .44 calibers. A good gun, but not in the same class as Mister Colt's products.

Case Carney—the mere thought of the man brought a tightening to Rockwell's jaw. Someday, someday he'd give Carney a chance to use those .44s, or that strange-looking knife he had strapped to his belt. Remingtons against Colts, Siberian skinner against the short-bladed Bowie that Rockwell favored. On second thought, he opted for the blades. For a man like Carney, a bullet was too damned quick, too easy.

Carney! That was it. He had a debt of long standing to settle with Carney, and an obligation to the Mormon people—one he must repay before he could free his soul from them.

Before he slept, Rockwell's thoughts returned to the meeting with Brigham Young. He was certain that when the two-week limit was up, Benson and Romney would be dispatched to Washington, to personally lay their case before Buchanan himself. Besides Col. Thomas L. Kane, there was one man in Washington who had proved himself a friend to the people of Utah—the senator from Texas, Sam Houston. If Houston couldn't get them into Buchanan's office, or raise a little hell in Congress, no one could.

By fast coach, reasoned Rockwell, Benson and Romney would reach the railhead at Independence in a shade over three weeks, assuming they ran into no difficulties. From Independence it was four days by rail to the nation's capital, and Buchanan. A recall order from the president could halt the slow-moving army before it got within 500 miles of the Salt Lake Basin.

It was 1,168 miles from Fort Leavenworth to the Salt Lake Valley, logistically a brutal task for an army of probably three thousand men crossing open, unsettled wilderness. They'd be spread out for miles, parallel columns, if possible, Rockwell knew. The problem was forage, for horses, mules, and draught animals. At least four thousand, he estimated, perhaps more. An army wasn't much different from a large wagon train, and Rockwell had seen some huge ones, especially in the early days of the rush for California gold. And he'd seen what happened when those trains tried to pass over ground already stripped of forage by previous trains, or came upon bad water. The animals sickened and died, leaving the immigrants with no means to move their huge Conestogas. They'd had to abandon their wagons, and most of what they held.

Yes, thought Rockwell, the officer in command of Buchanan's army, whoever he was, had his work cut out for him. Not only did he have to worry about his troops, he had to concern himself with a large contingent of camp followers—camp leaders, to be more accurate—the civilian drovers, bullwhackers, muleteers, provisioners, hunters, and scouts, as well as the inevitable collection of gamblers, sharpies, and painted women who have attached themselves to every army since the beginning of organized troop movements.

Rockwell put his Colts on a small table and rolled onto the bed with a sigh of contentment. It had been an interesting afternoon. He smiled as he thought of Brigham Young. He was half fox, half wolf. If there were a fight it would be "on our terms, not theirs, in ways of our choice, not theirs," he had said.

Rockwell knew that Young had no intention of having the battalion meet the army head-on, not when a determined harassing effort could slow the army to a virtual crawl in open country, a ponderous giant swatting at mosquitoes bleeding its extremities. The Mexican army took full advantage of these techniques; *guerrilla tactica,* they called it—hit and run—and it was effective, Rockwell remembered.

Delaying tactics were what was needed; gaining time, time to let the cruel grip of winter get its hold on the land, immobilizing the army or forcing it to turn back. This would give Brigham Young breathing space, a chance to put the facts before the president or Congress, rally the support of men like Sam Houston. A chance; that's all it was, Rockwell knew.

Brigham Young. As much as he disliked the man, Rockwell had to admit he had guts.

Chapter Five

Anne McCutcheon sank to her chin in the hot, soapy water that filled the huge oaken tub, half a five-hundred-gallon wine-aging cask that some enterprising immigrant from Italy, dreaming of a broad new vineyard on the slopes of central California, had been forced to abandon. Anne didn't know about the Italian, or his dreams. At the moment she was fulfilling one of her own—a steaming-hot bath, the lather of good, hard-milled English soap. Heaven. After months on the trail, bathing, when possible at all, in icy streams, she felt like a sybarite, and darned if she'd be guilty about it. There was nothing, absolutely nothing she wanted more than what she was enjoying now.

The heat of the steaming water lulled her. Ten more days to Salt Lake City, a new land, a new home—a new life. What would it be like? she wondered. In a way she would miss Edinburgh; old cities had a way of making you feel that you belonged, were part of them; there was a continuity. On Sundays, as a little girl, her father would take her to the heights of Edinburgh Castle. From the battlements she could see Edinburgh spread out before her, and know that a hundred generations of her people had looked down from these same heights, watching a village gradually transform itself into a great city. The heights, her father had told her, had originally been a stronghold to the ancient Picts, long before the legions of Julius Caesar had set foot in Britain. Four hundred years the Romans had stayed in Britain, and for four hundred years the Picts held them at bay, never allowing them to set foot in Scotland.

Mary, the tragic queen of the Scots, had trod these same battlements. Her hand had probably rested on the cold iron barrel of Mons Meg, the giant cannon that dwarfed all others, a symbol of Scotland's determination that no foreign power would impose its will on Scottish hearts.

Stop it! Anne told herself; you're becoming maudlin. These were events long buried in time—and so, too, had her life in Scotland slipped into the past. With a twinge of conscience she recalled how she had encouraged her father, bereaved at the death of her mother, to come to America and make a new beginning. But she had to admit to herself that her own desire to seek a new life was at least as important a motivation.

She had tried, she rationalized, to find someone to love among the young men in her community, someone she could imagine fathering her children, but to no avail. Her expectations were too high, her choices too uninviting. She was fully aware of her beauty, and was not about to sacrifice it. Suitors stood in line, each one in his turn summarily rebuffed. And to make matters worse, with each passing year she had grown more desirable. The pleadings of her parents grew more incessant—people were talking. A beautiful woman approaching thirty was a threat to the community. In effect, she had become a spinster by choice, but a very unusual one, indeed.

She had continued to stand aloof, spending time alone, becoming more and more introspective. Each afternoon, chores and weather permitting, she would hike to the top of a hill near her home and, sitting on the soft blanket of green grass, her back propped against a two-hundred-year-old oak, devour books of great adventure and magnificent love, simultaneously becoming more and more determined not to offer herself to the plight of so many of her friends—loveless marriages in drab, colorless, and depressingly predictable relationships.

Through her voracious reading she had become infatuated with the American West. The glamorized stories of the frontier and the men and women who were conquering it piqued her interest. She came to associate Scotland with the past, America with the future.

Then the missionaries came from across the Atlantic. She was quick to follow her father's lead into the new religion, which one Scottish writer described as "a truly American religion, born of the adventure and promise of the frontier."

Now, reclining in a heavenly tub of near-scalding water, safely inside

Bridger's Fort, her vivid imagination filled her mind with images of a bright and beautiful virgin land and a determined, resolute people. And although in the past months frequent periods of nostalgia had returned her in spirit to the mist, the streams, the crags, and the heather of the Highlands, the memories grew dim, overpowered by exhilaration and expectation.

As she envisioned her western Camelot, she was filled with an excitement she had never before known. She longed unabashedly to express the passionate womanly charms she had held within her for so long. A man, a real man, to whom she could give herself completely, body and soul; a home of her own, children. . . . In glorious sequence she thought of Porter Rockwell, Lot Smith . . . and, yes, Simon!—men spawned from the wild beauty of the wilderness they had made their own.

Simon had been the first to welcome her to Bridger's Fort. She was struck instantly by his incredibly handsome face, his jet black hair intensifying the lightness of his skin, his firm, muscular jaw, and the darkest, most piercing eyes she had ever seen. This vast land seemed to abound with a new breed of man.

But Rockwell! What was it about him, she asked herself, that had energized every feminine impulse in her? She imagined his arms embracing her, and her body tingled; she knew that doors had been opened in her deepest feelings that would be difficult to close. She was no longer a child. She knew this couldn't, shouldn't, be happening—but it was.

Rockwell! How did *he* feel? She was aware he had taken an interest in her—certainly not to the degree of Lot Smith—but how deeply she could not tell. His hypnotic eyes revealed just so much. This was a man whose thoughts were going to be hard to penetrate. Yet, she knew she had to try.

A bucket of ice-cold water jolted Anne back to the present with a gasp. Shy Flower gave her a gap-toothed grin as she lowered the bucket. "Time up. You finish now."

Anne glared at the Indian woman, then suddenly broke into a good-humored laugh and reached for the coarse towel draped over Shy Flower's pudgy arm.

The nineteen-year-old dispatch rider from Fort Laramie handed a sealed letter to Jim Bridger, requesting him to see that it reached the hands of Porter Rockwell as soon as possible. Bridger's fishing expedition didn't bear any fruit: The rider had no idea of the letter's contents; he knew only that Colonel Cooke had told him to get it to Bridger's Fort. "But something's up," the young trooper had added. "The colonel rode out a week back, just him and a small escort, heading east. Major Hemming's taken over command at Laramie."

Twenty minutes later the young rider was enjoying a hot meal, and the letter was in the hands of Cephus James. Whatever the letter contained, it had to be important, Bridger had told him. Colonels don't send dispatch riders all over hell-and-gone without good reason.

"You think it's got something to do with that army they're sending to the territory?" frowned Cephus.

"Wouldn't surprise me none," shrugged Bridger. "Port and Phil are close friends ever since they served together down in Mexico."

Cephus frowned, eyeing the envelope. "Maybe this is something President Young should see."

"That's for Port Rockwell to decide. I wouldn't take it kindly, him getting that envelope and finding he isn't the first to see what's in it—if you get my meanin'."

A nervous smile formed on the scout's lips. "It'd be hard not to, Mister Bridger. You have my word."

"Good enough," nodded Bridger, easing the hint of hardness that had come into his eyes. "Your boy Luther tells me you and him're plannin' to ride on ahead in the mornin'."

Cephus nodded. "The train won't have any trouble from here on. A four-man escort can do as well as six, and besides," he shrugged, indicating the envelope, "it'll be that much sooner this gets to where it's goin'. Just one thing I have to take care of before I leave these folks. . . ."

"But why?" asked Angus McCutcheon when Cephus James told the assembled immigrants an army was marching that very moment toward the Salt Lake Basin—a real army, not one or two companies of lightly armed troops. Angus's question and his bewilderment were echoed in the faces of the others.

"Can't tell you the why's of it. Guess we won't know that 'til they get to the territory. All we know for sure is, they're comin'."

"It has something to do with the courthouse, and some man who had a government freight contract," said Anne.

Every eye swung to her, bringing a tinge to her cheeks. "Lot Smith told me about it," she ended weakly.

"And you kept it to yerself?" glared Angus.

"What's wrong with you, girl!" another voice called out.

"You should'a told us!" growled McKee.

Anne's back stiffened as she took in the ring of accusing faces. "And what good would it have done?" she demanded. "What good did it do for Brother James to be tellin' you now? Changes nothing. Would you feel better if you had another ten days of worrying over something we can do nothing about?"

Silence blanketed the common room. Faces, which just moments before had been filled with the joy of knowing that their long journey would soon come to an end, their goal within reach, were now filled with troubled, sober thoughts. Was it all in vain?

"There is something you can do, if you've a mind to," said Cephus James, breaking the silence. "There are two trails leading out of here, one to Salt Lake, the other heads north, to the Sublet Cutoff. From there you can take your choice—the Oregon Trail, or the Humbolt, to California." Cephus scanned the silent faces, then added, "Whatever you decide, nobody's goin' to fault you."

"There's nothing to decide." said Angus McCutcheon, tight jawed, coming to his feet. "We dinna' cross an ocean and two thirds of a continent just to give up almost within sight of our goal. On we go, and that's that!"

"Ye have a fine way with a word, Angus," said Ross, nodding grim agreement. "I could nae' have said it better meself."

"If there's going to be trouble, we'll stand with our brothers, come what may!" said McKee, slamming a hard fist on the tabletop, glaring a look that challenged dissent.

There was none.

Colonel Fitz-John Porter shifted in his saddle with a silent moan. Damn George McClellan, he growled inwardly, damn his new-fangled saddle, and double damn the War Department for accepting it! McClellan, he knew, had been one of a number of officers sent to observe military operations during the late Crimean conflict. Observe and recommend. The best George could do was this damned saddle! A monstrosity. Thank the Lord we didn't have it ten years ago, he said to himself, or California and the new southwest territories would still belong to Mexico.

Napoleon Bonaparte was wrong, he mused wryly: An army didn't march on its stomach; it marched on its rear end—excepting the infantry, of course.

Shifting again, Porter fanned a panoramic look at the route—stepped columns of troops plodding across the open Kansas prairie. It was a hodgepodge—infantry both foot and mule mounted mixed in with artillery caissons, squadrons of dragoons mingling with ambulance and supply wagons—all marching to their own beat, and, at the head, Brevet Brig. Gen. Albert Sidney Johnston.

Colonel Porter couldn't resist a twinge of jealousy as he thought of Johnston. A few short months back the new brigadier had been a colonel. Now, he was in command of the largest single body of troops in the army, thanks to the secretary of war, John Floyd.

Perhaps Porter was being unfair; Johnston was a good soldier and a courageous officer. He'd proved both at the battle of Monterey— three horses shot out from under him in the thick of things. An amazing career, Johnston's. One of the top men to graduate in his class at the Point, he'd resigned his commission in '36 to enlist under Sam Houston, fighting for the Republic of Texas. Two years later he was commander of the Texas army; a year after that, secretary of war for the new Republic—a position he surrendered to take a commission as colonel of the 1st Texas Rifle Volunteers when the war with Mexico broke out. Reinstated in the United States Army after the war, he soon became paymaster, with the rank of major, thanks to General Butler.

For seven years, that had seemed to be the end of the line for Johnston; but it wasn't, thanks to Jeff Davis, the then-secretary of war and now senator from Mississippi. Davis transferred Johnston from his desk job to an active command with the 2d Cavalry, jumping him in rank from major to full colonel. No question about it, the man went up and down like a bob on a fishing pole, but each time he came up, he went a little higher. How high would he bob this time, Fitz-John wondered. That would no doubt depend on how well he carried out what could be a very ticklish enterprise. There was already a lot of opposition to this march into the Utah Territory.

Fitz-John turned in his saddle to watch the straggling columns, paying particular attention to the artillery units, equipped with the latest howitzers and long guns, carrying enough grape and round shot to lay siege to a heavily fortified garrison. Was it all show, designed to intimidate, or would the troops actually be called upon to shell their fellow citizens? He shrugged, dismissing the thought.

The subject of these speculations rode at the head of the column. Albert Sidney Johnston was an imposing figure of a man for his fifty-four years, with a heavy ledge bone over dark, piercing eyes, full mustache, and a square, unyielding jaw. It was a face that truly reflected the man's dominant characteristic—a bulldog tenacity.

His aide, Capt. Randolph Barnes Marcy, was an acknowledged authority on overland crossings of unsettled territory, and was currently negotiating with *Harper's* for the publication of his book, *The Prairie Traveler,* a recounting of his own travels dating back to the 1840s. The book also contained a number of proven itineraries, and a selection of helpful hints to adventurous argonauts.

Marcy had strongly recommended the southern route, along the Arkansas to Bent's Fort, then a swing north on the Cherokee Trail, which would take them to Bridger's Fort, bypassing the troublesome Platte River crossings.

Johnston had listened politely, and then, equally politely, rejected the advice. The route would be from Fort Leavenworth, northwest to Fort Kearny, then due west to Fort Laramie, Bridger's Fort, and the Salt Lake Basin. The fact that an average of three hundred miles separated each of the forts didn't seem to concern Johnston; nor did the fact that it was late in the season for the northerly route.

What troubled Marcy most was the unusually high proportion of civilian employees contracted to service the troops, and not including the personal servants accompanying many of the officers, or the gamblers, prostitutes, and miscellaneous opportunists who had attached themselves to the army. All would have to be fed, sheltered, and protected. Past experience had taught Marcy that any number of things could go wrong on a thousand-mile march, and probably would. There was only one certainty, he thought acidly: The only ones who would really profit from this little excursion would be the civilian contractors and the politicians. Wisely, Captain Marcy kept such thoughts to himself.

Ten days out of Fort Leavenworth the army had traveled less than a third of the way to Fort Kearny—ninety miles. Already a number of the baggage wagons and several artillery caissons had lost wheel rims, collapsing the spokes. There were spare wheels, but at this rate they'd be used up before the column was a quarter of the way to the Great Salt Lake Basin. Marcy would prevail on Johnston to strip Fort Kearny of every farrier and wheelwright on the post—commandeer them, if necessary.

Marcy had no way of knowing that his thoughts were not too dissimilar to those of the man riding beside him, Gen. Albert Sidney Johnston.

The general had told Secretary Floyd that he could accomplish his mission with a third of the forces he now led: March into Salt Lake City, arrest the seditionists, install an interim military government, and establish order. A small force would move faster, be more efficient, and get the job done quicker.

Floyd's response had been enigmatic. "There's a larger game afoot, Sidney."

The general hadn't inquired as to what that larger game might be.

Brigham Young's personal courier caught up with Porter Rockwell and Lot Smith a few miles out of Logan five days after Cephus James and his son had reached Salt Lake City.

Rockwell, Smith, and Stoddard, along with some fifty other riders, had been covering the territory, alerting every farm, hamlet, village, and town that trouble may be on the way and to prepare. Grim-faced settlers didn't ask the why's or wherefore's; they simply set about doing what had to be done. Stores of food and weapons were cached in preselected hiding places; caves in the surrounding hills were made habitable as places of security for women and children; and men with military experience and veterans of the battalion made ready to bid farewell to their families and start the long trek to Salt Lake City. The rest of the able-bodied males, from fifteen to sixty, prepared themselves to defend what the Lord and hard work had made their own.

The weary courier handed over Phil Cooke's letter to Porter Rockwell, still sealed. "President Young told me to keep riding 'til I found you, Mister Rockwell—and that's what I've been doin' for most of a week now."

Rockwell eyed the now-grimy envelope, instantly recognizing Phil Cooke's scrawl. Frowning, he ripped open the envelope and quickly scanned the single page it contained, his frown deepening.

"Something wrong, Port?" asked Lot Smith.

Rockwell ignored the question to throw one of his own to the dispatch rider. "How'd this get to Salt Lake?"

"Army dispatch rider brought it to Bridger's Fort. Cephus James brought it the rest of the way. President Young thought it might be important, said to get it to you quick as I could."

"Appreciate it," Rockwell nodded.

At the mention of Cephus James, Lot Smith's face lit up. "Did Cephus bring in that immigrant train already?" he asked the courier.

"Not likely." interjected Rockwell. "Figure the time. He must've ridden on ahead."

"That's right," agreed the courier. "Him and his boy, Luther."

Lot's face fell.

"Anything you want me to tell President Young, Mister Rockwell?" added the courier.

"No," said Rockwell, folding the letter and stuffing it into a pocket. "Tell him myself." Turning to his drop-reined horse, Rockwell called over his shoulder, "Climb into your saddle, 'Brother' Lot, we've got some riding to do."

"Just like that?" flared Lot as Rockwell mounted the buckskin. "No reason why, no explanations?"

"Didn't feel you'd need any—considering that Cephus left Bridger's Fort a good ten days ago, and that immigrant train should be reaching Salt Lake City any time now. Was I wrong?"

Lot flushed angrily. He strode to his mount and swung into the saddle, his jaw clamped tight. A touch of the spurs and he was off, leaving Rockwell standing.

A grin broke out on Rockwell's face as he turned to the puzzled courier. "See you back in Salt Lake."

Rockwell spurred out after Lot. The big buckskin would overtake Lot's bay with ease.

The young courier silently thanked the Good Lord that Rockwell had decided to personally deliver any messages he might have for Brigham Young. Hunkering down on a rock, he pulled off his boots for the first time in five days. It felt grand.

The immigrant train had been in Salt Lake two days when Rockwell, Lot, and Jud rode in. The train had been met by members of the Immigration Committee, who would look to the needs of every newcomer, assuring each one a place and whatever assistance they might require in adapting to their new home. Those with special needs, such as the widowed Mrs. Petrie, would be provided for.

Angus McCutcheon and his daughter were warmly welcomed by Doctor Milford Ames, a septuagenarian who had made the trek to Utah at the age of sixty, among the very first to set eyes on the Great Salt Lake Basin. Now, like Angus, a widower, he was eager to share his large house with a colleague from across the sea, and share his patient load as well. Doctors were always in short supply and if this business about the army marching on Utah proved to be more than rumor, the need would become critical. "I guess I've got a little of the Scot in me myself," he said, a twinkle in his eye as he looked at Anne. "Not only get myself a colleague, but a goddess for a housekeeper t' boot!"

Anne liked the old man from that moment on. And discounting the five or six arguments per day, Doctors Ames and McCutcheon were to hit it off famously. Debating every issue imaginable, working together with patients, and relaxing with a chessboard in the evening by a crackling fire—what more could one ask. . . .

A squadron of the battalion cavalry went through their paces within the walled temple site—lean, whipcord-tough–looking men who sat their horses as if the animals were an extension of themselves. A few of the older wore remnants of the uniform they had distinguished in the late Mexican war, under the command of Phil Cooke.

Porter Rockwell and Lot Smith, dust caked and red eyed, reined their travel-worn mounts to a halt a few yards from the temple-site wall. Perched on the wall, observing the squadron's maneuvers with a critical eye, was Gen. Daniel Wells, commander of the battalion. "How're they coming along, General?" called Rockwell.

Wells swung a look to the two riders, his frown erasing itself as he recognized the pair. "I don't think the Spanish Riding School has to worry about competition, if that's what you mean; but all in all, not too bad. How'd you boys make out?"

"We spread the word, General," said Lot. "Folks are doing what they have to do. Reserves and volunteers ought to be pouring in here pretty soon now."

"They've *been* pouring in," said Wells. "I have most of them bivouacked outside the city. Brigham doesn't want Salt Lake to look like an armed camp when that delegation from Washington gets here."

A bellow from the grizzled three-striper putting the squadron through its paces shattered the air as a pivot maneuver ended up in a shambles.

"They never were much good at that column left, column right business," grumbled Wells, shaking his head.

"May be," answered Rockwell, "but I'd take them over a squad of parade-ground troopers any day of the week. Pretty doesn't count for much when the shooting starts."

"Doesn't look like there's going to be any," grunted Wells. "Brigham is dead set against calling for a full mobilization, making it official."

"President Young knows what he's doing, General," said Lot, expectedly.

"I hope so, Lot—I sincerely hope so," responded Wells. "But being ready for trouble is a good way to avoid surprises, to my way of thinking."

Rockwell nodded, frowning at Lot. "I'd have to go along with *you* on that, General."

"Then I suggest you tell that to Brigham. Lord knows I've tried."

"Just what I had in mind. Let's be moving, 'Brother' Lot," said Rockwell sarcastically, reining his buckskin into motion.

Wells looked after the pair for a moment, then turned his attention back to the squadron.

A half hour later Porter Rockwell, Jud Stoddard, and Lot Smith were in Brigham Young's study. With some difficulty Rockwell had persuaded Young's housekeeper to awaken him from his nap—something she viewed with only slightly less trepidation than arousing a disgruntled grizzly from hibernation.

Brigham Young nodded a welcome to the dust-stained trio facing him across the study table. Slipping the single page from the envelope Rockwell had handed him, he read, his expression growing more grim by the moment as his eyes traveled down the page.

With something like a sigh, he placed the letter on the tabletop. Driving the fingers of his right hand through his disheveled hair, Young crossed to the study window to peer out at the orchard beyond.

Lot shot a quizzical frown at his companion, but the man in buckskins kept his eyes focused on the broad back of Brigham Young, waiting.

"Now we know," said the governor after a long moment, his back still to Rockwell and Smith.

"Now we're *sure,* Brigham," answered Rockwell. "I think we knew all along."

"Would someone mind telling *me* what it is we're supposed to be sure of?" blurted Lot. "Sorry, sir, but for three days I've been trying to find out what's so important about that letter."

"Read it," said Young.

Lot didn't need a second invitation.

Dear Port,

I heard about your run-in with Magruder's man, and the fact you and Jim Bridger rode out of Platte Station right after it happened. I didn't need a crystal ball to tell me you'd be heading hell-bent for Salt Lake City and Brigham Young. Too bad you didn't stay around for a few days longer, I wouldn't have had to write this letter.

I don't think it would be a breach of military security to tell you what everyone in Platte Station, Fort Laramie, and points east knows by now, thanks to Mister Greeley's newspaper and Henry Magruder's mouth—President Buchanan has ordered a punitive expedition to march on Salt Lake, with instructions to invest the city, suspend civil government, disarm, arrest, and detain all seditious elements, and establish martial law. He means it! The expedition will be escorting a new territorial governor, a Southerner, Alfred Cumming, and Judge Lamar Dawson.

From what I could gather from Magruder, Young will be the first to be taken into custody. "The head of the snake," as he put it.

I have been instructed to report, forthwith, to the commanding officer of the expedition, Brig. Gen. Albert Sidney Johnston, currently enroute via Fort Kearny. I assume the War Department must feel that my experience, as former commander of the Mormon Battalion, will serve some purpose in the event of armed resistance. I sincerely hope this will not be the case; but, as you know, I am a soldier, and must carry out my orders, whatever they may be. My deepest respects to Governor Young.

Yours in friendship,

Phil

"Martial law! Arrest President Young! They can't do that!" blurted Lot, disbelief and anger in his face.

"They can, and will, if we let them," said Rockwell, more to Young than Lot. "Johnston's just about the best field commander the army has. The only choice he'll give us is to surrender or fight. And, if I know Johnston, he'll be hoping it's to fight."

Young turned from the window, seeming to have aged. "It all fits in," he said, a tone of resignation in his voice. "Johnston's an outspoken Copperhead, tied coat and tail to the secessionists."

"You can believe one thing, Brigham," said Rockwell. "There isn't going to be a commission coming from Washington to investigate."

Young nodded, a line forming on his jaw. "Your point is well taken, Porter. Brother Benson and Brother Romney will leave immediately for Washington. Buchanan won't have to seek out the truth—we'll deliver it to him."

"*Try* to deliver it, you mean. You know what it's like in Washington, Brigham; the bureaucrats will have Romney and Benson cooling their heels for weeks, maybe months, before they get in to see the president. And if Davis and Floyd have anything to say about it, they'll never get in."

"We are not entirely without friends in Washington. A way will be found—in time."

"Seems to me that's the one thing we're short of," said Rockwell.

Young leaned forward, resting his large hands on the tabletop, his square jaw thrust forward. "Then we shall have to find a way to buy us more." He repeated the charge he had made the last time he had met with Rockwell in the governor's office. "Johnston's army must not reach Salt Lake City before we get a response from President Buchanan!"

Rockwell returned Young's sternness—his eyes on the governor, questioning. . . . "Is that an order—stop the army? I want it clear, no mistakes."

"You'll stop the army, delay the army, do whatever you have to do to give us time," responded Young.

"Can't ask for anything clearer than that." Rockwell smiled with satisfaction. "We'll give you your time, Brigham—I just hope Romney and Benson can make good use of—"

"There is one condition that goes with that order," Young cut in. Then, after a beat, *"You will shed no blood!"*

For a moment, dead silence reigned. *"What did you say?"* blinked Rockwell.

"I said, you will shed no blood!"

Anger suffused Porter Rockwell's face. "And just how do you propose we avoid it! They sure as hell will be trying to shed *ours!"*

Young shrugged. "That's a risk we must take."

Rockwell's frustration exploded. He slammed a heavy fist on the tabletop, his eyes boring into Young's. "Damn it, Brigham! You're hamstringing us! We can't do it that way!"

Young's own fist crashed down like a thunderbolt, splintering the delicate inlay. "Damn it, Rockwell—you *will* do it that way! *You will shed no blood!"*

A heavy silence fell as the two men continued to lock eyes, jaws knotted, a clash of frustration and determination.

Lot broke the stillness. "We'll do our best, President," he said in a firm voice.

"I'm sure you will, Lot," Young responded authoritatively, his look still directed at Rockwell. "The death of one boy, one American soldier, by our direct hand, and we lose what friends and supporters we have, and any chance for a fair and just hearing. What's worse, we'd be playing right into the hands of the men behind Johnston."

Jud Stoddard was flabbergasted. He could not believe what he had seen and heard. He just stood there, as if his feet were planted, his mouth wide open, his arms hanging loosely at his sides. He did not even notice when his hat slipped from his fingers and fell to the floor. It was Lot who took him by the arm and led him out of the office.

"There they were," he said later that evening to his intended, Mary-Beth Anderson, "a yellin' and a cussin' at each other and slammin' the table. Why, President Young fair splintered the gol dang thing! And I'll tell you something else. I can't figure Porter Rockwell. Why, he's left a dozen or more graves along his way, and yet I saw him braced by both Lot and Brigham Young, and he took it both times. I don't know why he don't just ride off. . . ."

Brigham Young was having the same thoughts, alone in the governor's office. When the three had left, he examined the damage his powerful fist had done to the tabletop. It could be repaired, and it would give his hands something to do while his mind engaged itself with problems of greater scope. He had never lost his love of working with wood. It gave a man an honest satisfaction to build something useful with his hands. He had to admit that life had been a great deal less complex when he'd been a simple carpenter.

What to make of Rockwell. . . . That was indeed a complex question. A tragic man—blaming himself for something that he could not have prevented.

Why had he come back during this crisis? Was it to pay a debt to a man long dead? Was he now determined not to fail Smith's followers, Brigham Young included? Or was he seeking revenge? If it was the latter, Young reasoned, then Rockwell could bring disaster on all of them.

There was no question—Young needed Rockwell, but. . . .

His thoughts drifted briefly to the group of new immigrants who had arrived from Scotland just two days before. How long ago it seemed, the two years he'd spent in the British Isles.

Then Gaskel Romney and John Benson came to his thoughts. They'd have to succeed, make Buchanan realize he was being used as a foil to further the ambitions of unscrupulous men. If they could accomplish that, they'd have served both Utah and the Union.

Chapter Six

It was shortly before sundown when Col. Philip St. George Cooke and his escort of six mounted troopers from Fort Laramie passed through the picket lines and were directed to the command tent of Brevet Brig. Albert Sidney Johnston. Cooke sensed anticipation; he and Johnston went back a long way.

Six weeks on the march had toughened the men under Johnston's command, honed away the softness of garrison life, brought them down to lean muscle and sinew. From an average of nine miles a day at the beginning of the march, they now were easily capable of tripling that distance, but, like all armies, they were limited to the pace of their support elements—the baggage and supply wagons, the remount herd, the walking commissary of beef cattle, draught oxen, and reserve mules—and the ever-present problem of forage and water. Still, they were now averaging eighteen to twenty miles a day, a respectable distance in any man's terms.

Cooke took note of the neatly aligned, precisely spaced campfires, each with its complement of officer's tents and the new shelter halves recently adopted by the army for enlisted personnel. Off to his left was the wagon and artillery park. He could hear the ring of hammers on anvils as repair teams labored to make damaged wagons ready for the morrow's travel. From beyond the wagon park came other sounds—a concertina, raised male and female voices, a banjo strumming a lively tune. This, he knew, was coming from the camp follower's tents, positioned just beyond the camp perimeter.

A rank-conscious young adjutant escorted Phil Cooke to the big Sibley command tent with a brigadier's pennant at the entrance, and assured Cooke that his escort riders would be fed and bedded down for the night before starting the long ride back to Fort Laramie.

Cooke snapped a stiff, regulation salute to the tall man behind the map-covered camp table. The light, from a brace of camphine lanterns, told him that the intervening years had been good to Albert Sidney Johnston; the man hadn't seemed to age a day. "Colonel Philip St. George Cooke reporting as ordered, General," he said crisply.

Cooke held the salute, forcing the brevet brigadier to return it. "Al'right, Phil, that's enough formality," Johnston smiled, extending a hand.

Cooke accepted it, returning the smile. "The formality is for that star you're wearing, Sidney—congratulations."

"You'll have one yourself one of these days," said Johnston, moving to lift a cut-glass decanter and brandy snifters from the top of his camp chest. "Drink?"

"Is that brandy?" asked Cooke as he slipped into a camp chair, eyeing the decanter and glasses.

"Imported," nodded Johnston, pouring. "It goes with the star. Rank does have its privileges, as well as prerogatives. What shall we drink to?"

Cooke passed the snifter under his nose, savoring the aroma. "How about to what we're drinking? I can't think of anything better at the moment."

Johnston expressed agreement, lifting his glass. "To French brandy, the only good thing to come out of France since Bonaparte."

"Who happened to be a Corsican." Cooke sipped the brandy, rolling it over his palate appreciatively. "Almost makes the ride from Laramie worth the effort. Talking about prerogatives, was getting me relieved of my command one of them? Not that I'm objecting, mind you—just curious."

Johnston's eyes hooded momentarily. "That wasn't my doing, Phil. It came from higher up, though I can't say I'm displeased. Your knowledge will be an asset."

"Knowledge?" Cooke lifted his brow.

"Don't play coy with me, Phil. You know damned well what I'm talking about—the Mormon Battalion. You commanded them during the Mexican war. I want to know what I may be up against."

"That depends on what you have in mind."

"What I have in *mind*, Phil," said Johnston firmly, "is carrying out a presidential order to put down a rebellion against the authority of the United States government. I'd like to carry out that order with as little bloodshed as possible."

A small smile played across Cooke's lips. "You won't object if I take that statement with a large grain of salt, will you?"

Johnston's features stiffened. "I suggest you clarify that, Colonel."

"Informality over?" questioned Cooke, draining the snifter and placing it on a corner of the camp table. "Al'right, General, I'll give it to you straight—there is no rebellion, there never has been one. Man for man I don't think there's a more patriotic group of people in this country."

"There seems to be a difference of opinion."

"The question, Sidney—pardon me, General—is whose opinion are we talking about? Whose interest is being served? It certainly isn't the government's."

Johnston forced a thin smile. "Don't get into politics with me, Phil. I'm a soldier, the same as you. Our responsibility is to carry out our orders—not question them."

"Being a soldier doesn't mean we have to abrogate moral responsibilities, Sidney. Believe me, if I knew for a fact that the people of Utah were in rebellion, I wouldn't have the slightest hesitation in marching against them. The same applies to Baptists, Episcopalians, Catholics, Jews, or any other group you can hang a label on. And—just for the record—that applies to copperheads as well."

"Are you questioning my loyalty?" asked Johnston, an ominous tone in his voice.

"I don't know, General—you tell me."

Johnston held Cooke's eyes for a long moment, then let go his pent-up breath, his thin smile returning. "You never were one for dissembling, were you, Phil? Well, also just for the record, the day loyalty comes into conflict with my convictions is the day I'll resign my commission. Does that satisfy you?"

"Guess it'll have to. You'll forgive me for repeating myself, General, but you're on a rabbit hunt where there are no rabbits. There is no rebellion in Utah."

"Then we have nothing to worry about, do we?" said Johnston over an icy smile. "Care for another brandy?"

"Don't mind if I do," responded Cooke, reaching for his snifter, thinking that whatever Johnston is or is not, he is a man of his word. If he said he would resign his commission if his loyalty came into conflict with his convictions, he more than likely meant it. Still, thought Cooke, these were perilous times, times when men's loyalties and allegiances were being challenged by unbridled idealism.

The midday meals had been a revelation to Phil Cooke. There was no general mess for the officers; each seemed to have his own dining arrangements, complete with personal attendants to prepare and serve.

He'd seen linen coverings and sterling flatware on camp tables. Hampers filled with tins of imported viands and fine wines. Many of the officers, he noticed, had brought along personal weapons, mostly of foreign manufacture. One infantry officer had a magnificent Whitworth target rifle, complete with telescope for long-range shooting. The excess baggage carried along must have filled a dozen transport wagons.

There were exceptions, however: Captain Marcy, who had cordially invited Cooke to share his table, and Col. Fitz-John Porter. Marcy was a gregarious young man, open and friendly. The colonel was quiet, withdrawn. Cooke didn't need Marcy to tell him that Fitz-John Porter was rankled at being placed under the command of the brevet brigadier; it was evident in every fiber of the man. Be that as it may, both Marcy and Fitz-John Porter eschewed the fripperies affected by their fellow officers, dining instead on simple fare served them by a man from the enlisted ranks.

Albert Sidney Johnston invariably had his meals with the two government officials accompanying the army—Alfred Cumming, the man Buchanan had appointed to replace Brigham Young as governor of Utah Territory, and Lamar Dawson, Buchanan's selection to fill the seat vacated by Judge Drummond. Cooke was surprised to find that both were highly competent men. And both were Southerners, which was no great surprise to him at all.

In the ten days since Cooke had joined the column, except for his initial meeting with Johnston, the men had not exchanged one word, except for an occasional "good morning" or "good evening." Cooke hoped that their discussion that first night had not built a wall between them. But if it had, so be it.

Cooke rode stirrup to stirrup with Captain Marcy. The young captain was a fund of wilderness lore, and liked nothing better than pouring his knowledge into a receptive ear. Cooke, after the first few days, developed a knack of looking attentive without listening, while he gave weight to thoughts of his own. This army, he told himself, would be in for a rude awakening if Brigham Young refused to submit to martial law and the installation of new political hacks in positions of authority over his flock. The Mormon leader, he knew, had three loyalties: to God, his people, and his country—and in precisely that order. Cooke's loyalties were but two: God and country—and he wasn't sure which took precedence. The question had never been put to the test.

Three more days would see them at Fort Laramie. Johnston didn't intend to rest his troops at the fort. That would come at Platte River Station, which, as Cooke was aware, was already preparing a warm welcome for the army, and making a substantial profit in the doing.

En route to join Johnston, Cooke and his escort had encountered several large groups of heavily armed Missouri Wildcatters heading for the Platte, and what lay beyond. The stink of pillage was in the air, luring would-be scavengers from every part of the territories.

Cooke shuddered at the thought of such men loosed on the peaceful valleys of Utah, backed up by the might of Johnston's guns. Damn! he growled to himself, if I was Brigham Young, I'd fight.

A one-legged man in a butt-kicking contest! Porter Rockwell grumbled to himself as he stepped down from the buckskin to tie off on the rail fronting Kimball's Emporium. Stop the army, but shed no blood! Just how in hell was he supposed to do that?

A gust of chill wind whipped across Temple Square, penetrating the laced openings of Rockwell's deerskin shirt. A grin split his face; maybe Brigham's prayers for an early winter had been heard. If so, it would make things a damn sight easier. At the first heavy snow, Johnston's army would grind down to a crawl, his forage problem increased tenfold as his animals had to root beneath the snow for the last of the fall grass. Time to pick up a sugan or a poncho while I'm at it, he told himself. His purpose in coming to Kimball's was a fresh supply of Kynoch's fine grain—the best pistol powder on the market, imported from England, and expensive. Well, no problem, he'd charge the bill to Brigham, now that he was considered on active service with the battalion once again.

Rockwell wondered if he should have accepted Lot's invitation to a family meal at the Smith home. No, he affirmed his earlier decision; he just wasn't comfortable in a family setting, except for possibly Jim Bridger's, and that couldn't really be called a family—or could it?

"Interesting conversation, Mister Rockwell?"

Rockwell turned to see Anne McCutcheon smiling broadly at him, her arms filled with an assortment of packages from Kimball's. Rockwell flushed a grin and stepped up on the walkway.

"Talking to myself is one way to get answers I agree with, missy."

Anne's smile faded. "I'd appreciate being called by my name, Mister Rockwell. Somehow, I don't think 'missy' goes along with a woman my size."

"Nothing wrong with your size, Miss McCutcheon."

"You don't have to be so formal. 'Anne' will be fine."

"Fair enough—if you'll call me Porter, or just Port, if you like. Agreed?"

"Agreed," she said, trying to free a hand to extend to him. The attempt was unfortunate; several of the packages slipped from her grasp.

In the scramble to recover them, they momentarily came face-to-face. Her irises had tiny gold flecks in their pale gray, Porter noticed. He'd never seen eyes quite like hers before. Anne reddened, breaking contact, silently cursing herself for being so clumsy. "A 'missy' wouldn't be so awkward, now would she?"

"How far are you going with all these?" asked Porter as both came to their feet.

"That far," she responded, nodding to a canopied spring buggy tied to the Kimball hitching rail.

Responding to the question in Rockwell's eyes, she added, "It's not ours; it belongs to Doctor Ames. We're staying with him until Da can make some other arrangements."

They deposited the packages in the buggy boot. "It's not charity, mind you—Da is helping Doctor Ames with his patients," Anne continued.

"I haven't come across anybody yet who hasn't needed a helping hand at one time or another."

Anne's eyes widened. "You surprise me, Mister Rockwell."

"Port. Remember?"

"If you'll pardon me for saying so, Porter, you don't sound very 'Wayward' to me."

A soft laugh escaped Rockwell. "I'm glad to hear that, 'Sister' McCutcheon."

"Anne. Remember?" she laughed.

The sound of her laughter did something to Rockwell; it made him want to hear it again, to keep on hearing it.

"Have you seen Lot Smith?"

"What?" he asked, trying to retrack his thoughts.

"Lot Smith. Have you seen him?" she repeated, a contrived glow of anticipation in her face.

Rockwell's confidence plummeted. "Haven't seen much else these past weeks," he mumbled.

"When you see him again, would you please tell him I'm—we'd be staying with Doctor Ames?"

"I'll do that. Nice seeing you again—Anne."

Touching his hand to the brim of his hat, Rockwell moved around the woman and entered Kimball's Emporium.

After Anne had climbed onto the buggy's seat, she put her hand on her chest and breathed deeply, smiling. Now she knew. Rockwell *had* been taken by her. There was a strong—perhaps too strong—attraction between them! And, he was jealous of Lot Smith.

But why then hadn't he attempted to find her, as Lot had? Perhaps it had to do with this business of the great army that was on its way. Then she wondered if he had a woman—somewhere. . . .

That evening Anne and Lot Smith walked together through the much-frequented wooded park, with its bright fall attire of orange and gold, near Doc Ames's home. Doctor McCutcheon had allowed the stroll to take place, given the brightness of the moon and the number of other couples doing the same thing. After all, he explained to Doc Ames, she was no longer just a girl.

This was not the last time that Lot came courting, and he deported himself with all the propriety expected of him. Each time Anne was with him, she came to like him more. She enjoyed his company, the conversations they had, the laughter they shared. And it didn't hurt at all that he was tall, and ruggedly handsome. Yet when she was not with him, she thought of Porter Rockwell.

John Benson and Gaskel Romney set forth on the long journey to Washington at daybreak, with an armed escort. The big Concord coach would head east to Bridger's Fort, then south along the Cherokee Trail to the Arkansas River, where it would again turn east, thereby avoiding any possible encounter with the army approaching on the Fort Kearny–Fort Laramie trail.

As Brigham Young watched the coach disappear in the distance, his thoughts went back to the persecutions endured in Missouri and Illinois, and anger welled in his heart. This anger, he knew, was not in his heart alone. There were many tormented by the same bitter memories, and there were many who would look forward to exacting an avenging pound of flesh for past cruelties inflicted upon them, such as the old man from Provo he'd spoken to the previous day, still carrying an ounce of lead in his body from the Haun's Mill massacre— a frenzy of murder, rape, and pillage against a Mormon community by an Illinois mob. The old man would like nothing better than to pay that ounce back, with usurious interest.

Everywhere men were arming themselves, and at the same time preparing their families to once more strike out for a distant land, another search for safety. Young contrasted the joy he had seen at the Pioneer Day celebrations with what he saw in his people's faces now. The young ones, those with memories unsullied by the tragic events of the past, went their way without great concern; but the faces of those who did remember reflected an ominous gloom, and with it a determination never to submit to the indignities of the past. Never again!

On September 15, 1857, Brigham Young, governor of the Utah Territory, would give the order for full mobilization of the battalion and declare martial law. Porter Rockwell would have his opportunity, but if he failed, if Johnston's army attempted to march into Salt Lake City. . . .

General Wells tracked a finger across the large, easel-mounted topographical map, set up in Brigham Young's office, of the Utah Territory and portions of the adjoining areas. "The commander of the expedition will probably rest and refit his troops at the Platte before pushing across the divide to Bridger's Fort. From there, if he takes the Echo Canyon trail, he can be within striking distance of the city within ten days. You can double that if he swings south and comes at us through Bear Lake Valley. My guess is he'll take the shortest route, Echo Canyon."

"And why is that, General?" asked Brigham Young.

"For one thing, he'll be short of supplies. Every day costs him, and every pound has to be carried with him."

"He'd be a damn fool to try Echo Canyon," said Rockwell.

"Be the best thing that could happen, if he did. We'd have him boxed in tight," added Lot Smith.

"You're forgetting something—he's got Phil Cooke with him. Phil knows this country as well as we do. He won't let Johnston put himself in that kind of a bind."

"I understand that Colonel Cooke has always been a friend to our people," frowned John Kimball, a close confidant and aide to Brigham Young.

"He is," answered Rockwell, "but he's also a soldier. He won't put friendship before duty."

"What are our options should Johnston come by way of the valley, General?" asked Young.

Wells shook his head slowly, a look of concern written on his handsome face. "Not many, President. If he is able to break through our ranks and gain sight of the city, we are in desperate trouble." Wells paused. "If only he didn't have artillery. . . ."

"But he has, General," said Rockwell. "A frontal attack and your boys will be running head-on into grape and canister. He'll cut them to pieces before they can get close enough to fire a shot. And once he gets that artillery within range of the city, it's all over. He'll pound away as long as he has to."

"If that happens—if he does get within artillery range of this city—he will find nothing to aim his cannon at," said Young ominously.

A palpable silence fell in the room as each man interpreted Brigham Young's words in his own way. Wells broke the silence, murmuring, "Kutuzov. . . ."

"Did you say something, General?" asked Young.

"Sorry, President. I was thinking aloud."

"Perhaps you'd care to share those thoughts, Daniel," Young pressed.

"I was thinking of the Russian commander who gave the order to burn Moscow—General Kutuzov. It must have been a terrible decision for him."

"It was the *only* decision, Daniel," came the solemn reply.

"Seems to me we're getting the cart ahead of the horse, Brigham," said Rockwell. "Johnston's army isn't here yet; he's still on the far side of the Platte. A lot can happen in the five hundred miles between here and there."

Young fixed his attention on Rockwell and Smith, nodding. "That's the purpose of this meeting, Porter. Have you and Lot formed some plan of action?"

Rockwell half laughed, half sneered. He was not about to play games with Brigham Young. "You know we have, Brigham," he responded caustically, "the only option open to us—hit and run, *guerrilla tactica*—'on our terms, not theirs, in ways of our choice, not theirs.' "

"Alright, alright," responded the governor, without the slightest hint of a smile. "Can you do it—stop them until spring?"

"I don't know, Brigham, we'll try. And about that early winter?"

Now Young really did smile. "I don't know, Porter, we'll try."

For some time, the Mormon leader fixed his gaze on Rockwell, as if he were pondering his next move. "As of this moment both you and Lot are recommissioned as officers of the Territorial Militia. You will share authority and responsibilities equally."

Both men erupted simultaneously, and only General Wells's military training kept him from voicing the strongest protest. Lot's free spirit rebelled against the discipline of military life, and he was damned if he was going to be on an equal footing with Rockwell; but all that escaped from his mouth was a plea to be left in his current status—scout and courier.

"Now hold on, Brigham," Rockwell protested. "I'll take no commission!"

"You will each resume your previous rank of major. Only the legally constituted militia of this territory will stand at its defense. We must not be accused of hiring mercenaries. Furthermore, I want a chain of command; if something goes wrong, I want to know who's responsible."

"By wrong, you mean the shedding of blood?"

"Exactly." Young's face grew ever-more stern. "If it happens, I'll know who to hang."

Rockwell and Young locked eyes for a long moment. "Then you'd better set aside a rope, Brigham."

"I've given you an order, and you will obey it," came the searing response.

Young sensed that Rockwell was about to walk out. Without betraying his authoritative bearing, he silently prayed that this would not happen. There was no question—if Rockwell left now, he would not be back. But Young had to know if the gunman would obey orders. Otherwise, he would be a disaster waiting to happen.

A strange, wry smile formed on Rockwell's lips. "I'm good at obeying orders, Brigham, remember?"

Young remembered. So did everyone in the room. When the Mormon prophet Joseph Smith rode out of Nauvoo, Illinois, for Carthage to answer a bogus summons that fateful summer morning in June 1844, he had ordered an angry, pleading, cursing Porter Rockwell to remain behind. That evening a mob, led by Case Carney, shot Joseph Smith and his brother Hyrum to death. Since few knew of the order, a hundred stories concerning Rockwell's absence from Carthage had circulated through the Mormon community and beyond.

For an interminable moment Young and Rockwell pierced each other with their eyes. Young saw the searing agony that had been consuming the gunman's soul.

"Pardon me for saying so, President, but that's water long under the bridge," said General Wells, breaking the oppressive silence. "We have to concern ourselves with now."

Young nodded. "No pardon necessary, Daniel. You're right." He turned to Lot Smith, his brow lifted.

"Well, sir," said Lot nervously, clearing his throat, "Port and I thought the best approach would be hit-and-run raids, the kind the Mexican irregulars used back in '47. We figure to worry him the way a hound dog worries a bear. Every which way he turns, we'll be there, snapping at his heels and flanks. We'll make Johnston wish he'd never heard of Utah."

General Wells, a traditional military officer, was unconvinced. "Guerrilla tactics won't stop a determined commander, Lot," he broke in.

"No," responded Rockwell, "but they sure as hell can slow him down. If we can keep him at a distance 'til the weather changes, we've got him. You were talking about Moscow, General. If Kutuzov could have held up Bonaparte's advance another few weeks, he wouldn't have had to burn Moscow. The Russian winter would have stopped Napoleon in his tracks, forced him to retreat."

"That's Russia. This is Utah."

"Snow and cold are the same everywhere, General. And from the looks of things, we're going to be in for a lot of both this winter."

Brigham Young breathed an unnoticed sigh of relief. For some reason, he was not certain why, Rockwell had again swallowed his fierce pride. Young had gotten his way once more with the gunman. He wondered how many times he could go to that well. Rockwell had been uncharacteristically tractable . . . perhaps too tractable, he mused.

"How many men will you need?" asked Young, casting a silencing look at Wells as the general was about to voice another objection.

"Fifty should do it, for now," said Lot, looking to Rockwell for agreement.

Rockwell nodded. "And two remounts for each man. We'll be covering a lot of ground."

"See to it, Daniel," Brigham nodded to Wells.

"One more thing, General," added Rockwell, his voice losing none of its bitter tone. "Tell them we want volunteers. Some of those boys might not like the idea of getting shot at and not being able to shoot back." This last statement was directed more at Young than Wells. Neither responded.

As the group turned to leave, Young's hand detained Rockwell. "Just a moment, I want to talk to you." The governor hesitated, searching for what he hoped would be the right words. "Porter, I know you revered Joseph Smith, as did we all, but there were too many in that mob. Your presence there could not have changed what happened. Would you have forfeited your life knowing there was no hope to succeed?"

Rockwell jerked his arm from Young's grasp. A suspicion of wetness laced his eyes. "Yes, damn it, yes!" he hissed between clenched teeth.

Young remained stoic. "Porter, your death would have served no purpose!"

"Then," responded Rockwell bitterly, "I'd have had a drink in hell that night with at least twenty of those Missouri bastards!"

Young was unmoved. He shot back firmly, "Fool's talk! When Joseph Smith ordered you to stay in Nauvoo, he knew what he was doing. He knew he was going like a lamb to the slaughter. He wanted you to live. He had his reasons. Don't make a mockery of that decision!"

Rockwell started to answer, then abruptly turned and left the room.

Lot Smith and Porter Rockwell had found no shortage of volunteers, even when the men were told of the restrictions imposed by Brigham Young. They would carry arms, but only for purposes of intimidation, if and when required. Those selected, with one exception, were quite young, averaging twenty years of age. All were men who'd spent much of their lives in the saddle—drovers and ranch hands for the most part, and all with military experience. The exception was Cephus James. He and his boy, Luther, had been among the first to volunteer.

Rockwell had initially rejected Cephus, telling the leathery escort rider that this was a job for younger men, but Cephus had insisted. If this was the only way he could escape escorting in another one of those damned handcart companies, then so be it.

"You're all too clean," said Rockwell, surveying the double-ranked line of scrubbed faces. "Get some dirt on you!"

"Don't have to be dirty to fight!" a voice called out.

"We're not fighting. Get that through your heads right now," said Lot Smith. "What Major Rockwell is trying to tell you is that you, that *some* of you, are going to infiltrate the enemy camp, get at them from the inside. For now, we want men who can get hired on to work for the army, men who look like they haven't done an honest day's work since they were pups."

"What you want is a passle of them Missouri Wildcatters!" grinned a rawboned, towheaded youth, Andrew Moss.

"You've got that right, Andy," said Lot Smith. "Wildcatters, border ruffians, drifters, drunks, and the like—that's the only kind Henry Magruder hires. If you can't pass for one, there's no point in sending you to Platte Station."

"Magruder—that rules me out," grumbled a distraught Cephus James. "He knows my face good as his own."

"There anybody else here Magruder might recognize?" asked Rockwell.

Several raised their hands, and were told to step aside. In the next few minutes Rockwell and Smith cut the ranks down to less than half, culling out those with faces too open, too ingenuous to pass for anything but what they were—clean-cut, decent young men. There were disappointed protests until Lot assured them they'd have other tasks to perform, equally important.

Rockwell was pleased with the Cartwright brothers. They wouldn't have to alter their appearance one bit. They were big, steel strong, and as mean looking and ugly as any frontier drifters or Missouri bushwhackers he had seen. "Good men, but naturally ornery," Lot had confirmed. These were two at least Rockwell needn't concern himself with taking care of themselves.

The remaining twenty, Luther James and Andy Moss among them, would be suitably outfitted for the long journey to Platte River Station. They'd enter the town separately, posing as drifters in search of employment.

"Look for a fella named Case Carney," Rockwell told them. "He's Magruder's ramrod, the one who does the hiring." As an afterthought, he warned, "And watch your step around Carney. He's got a thing about Mormons—he likes to see them bleed."

"If you run into any problems," added Lot, "get back across the river. The rest of us will be around, somewhere."

Rockwell and Lot exchanged few words as they headed for Kimball's

Emporium with a shopping list of needed supplies for the new unit. Foremost on the list would be heavy clothing and gutta-percha canvas to provide warmth and shelter for men who would be spending a good part of the coming winter in the open country. As Rockwell had told General Wells, Utah might not be Russia, but Utah's winters were nothing to be glossed over lightly. Many a wagon train captain had good cause to regret a late start across the divide, if he survived to regret.

Rockwell's mind pictured a kaleidoscope of images, most dealing with the five hundred miles of mountain, river, and prairie that separated Platte River Station from Salt Lake City—Johnston's army from the territorial capital. Could they do it, delay Johnston long enough for winter to take hold? He'd sure as hell try. Case Carney's face formed in his mind's eye, and with it the words Carney had thrown in his face in Muldoon's saloon: "You're the fella who crawled into a jug back in '44. From the looks of you, I'd say you were still in it. . . ." Was he, Rockwell wondered, or rather, would he be again, when all this was over?

Lot cast a covert look at his companion, puzzled by the dark, brooding expression on Rockwell's angular face. What was he thinking? Lot wondered. Good question; few folks knew what went on behind the face Rockwell presented to the outside world. Fact is, Lot didn't know anyone who knew a damned thing at all about Port Rockwell.

The day before leaving Salt Lake City, Rockwell was surprised when Lot came to the boardinghouse with an invitation to supper at Doc Ames's place. Rockwell's first inclination was a polite refusal, but Lot reluctantly told him that Anne McCutcheon had insisted.

All in all, it hadn't been a bad evening. The pot roast was the best Rockwell had tasted in years, and the conversation with Angus and Doc Ames was good. But most of all, the Scottish beauty with unforgettable eyes graced the table. Her bright, lilting conversation, her warm yet sophisticated bearing, her graceful and uninhibited femininity filled the room with an essence that resurrected in Rockwell every beautiful and desirable thought associated with the word *woman*. Time and again, from across the table, her eyes seemed to touch his with a tenderness that penetrated his cold exterior. Past the usual amenities, they said nothing to each other. But there was electricity between them; and what is more, everyone in the room sensed it—including the frustrated Lot Smith.

The only sour note was Angus McCutcheon's insistence on topping off the evening with his pipes. To Rockwell's unappreciative ear the instrument was about as melodious as a sack filled with squalling tomcats.

As Rockwell and Lot left, Doc Ames presented them with a kit containing a supply of bandages, sutures, ointments, laudanum, a pint of 190-proof alcohol—"for medicinal purposes mind you"—and other items needed for emergencies.

Rockwell was the last of the guests to pass under the door's portal. Anne stood close to him as he hesitated a moment before leaving. Their hands touched and then slipped together, each holding tightly. "God be with you," she whispered.

The following morning, Brigham Young rode his prized stallion to the mouth of Emigration Canyon to see them off, wishing them Godspeed and protection. Rockwell knew they'd need both.

At the last moment, Young caught Rockwell's eye and, jerking his head, motioned him a short distance from the rest of the group.

"You wanted something, Brigham?"

"Tell me, Porter, if you and the weather are successful in delaying Johnston, would he still be able to find shelter and provisions at Bridger's Fort?"

"Somewhat, yes."

"Alright, burn it!"

Rockwell was nonplussed. "What did you say?"

"Burn it!"

"You listen to me, Brigham! Bridger and I . . ."

But the governor of Utah Territory had already reined his mount away and was spurring the animal toward the valley.

Rockwell watched Young's broad shoulders and straight back, moving in perfect unison with the gait of the horse, grow smaller in the distance. At length the gunman turned to lead his little band of guerrillas into God knew what. His face was fairly purple with rage.

Chapter Seven

With eleven days' growth of beard, slouched, feature-concealing hats, and buffalo-hide trail coats, Porter Rockwell and Lot Smith blended in with the drovers, skinners, bullwhackers, and all-around hands mingling with the troops in Platte River Station.

The single-street town had burgeoned to the size of a small city with the influx of Johnston's army and the civilian employees living off that army. Construction was going on at a frantic pace as tent buildings were thrown up to form side streets off what a week before had been the only street. Permanent structures were being expanded as workmen added a second floor to the Platte River Inn and an annex to Sadie's Birdcage, and tore out the rear wall of Muldoon's saloon to add a large canvas-roofed extension. A number of canvas-covered, plank-topped bars and gambling establishments were already giving Muldoon substantial competition. The games ranged from three-card monte to chuck-a-luck, and all of them were rigged in favor of the house—a fact of life readily accepted by the patrons. Sadie's Birdcage, despite the workmen, was doing a land-office business, if the line of troopers and civilians outside the front door was any indication.

The Overland Stage Office was now the Magruder Freight and Transport Company. A cluster of applicants and a hand-lettered sign at the entrance indicated that Magruder was still hiring.

From somewhere, a hurdy-gurdy and a tinny, out-of-tune piano struggled to compete with the sounds of hammers, saws, and street noises.

Surrounding the town, virtually enclosing it, was a small sea of regulation-spaced Sibley tent, wagon, and artillery parks. Beyond their perimeter, drovers kept alert eyes on the herds of foraging animals fanning well out into the surrounding hills. At the riverfront a company of engineers was beefing up the pull rafts to sustain the weight of the big supply wagons and gun caissons.

"Haven't seen so many troops in one place at one time since Mexico," Lot said with a frown.

"Makes our job a lot easier," responded Porter Rockwell, lifting his shoulders. "Bigger the herd, the bigger the target."

A tight grin creased Lot's face. "Maybe so, but *this* herd is carrying rifles. We'll be the target."

Rockwell eyed the badge on the tapered "tar-bucket" shako of a passing infantryman. The man was from the 2d Cavalry, a mounted infantry unit. Rockwell knew that mounted infantry were a fairly recent development, resulting from the army's experience in dealing with the forays of marauding Indians on the frontier. When a mounted infantry unit caught up with a raiding party, they'd dismount and fight on foot. The Indians, accustomed to the individual combat of pony soldier against cavalryman, were no match for the concentrated firepower of well-disciplined infantry.

An hour in one of the canvas-topped, plank-bar saloons allowed Rockwell to identify other units in Johnston's command: the 5th, 10th, and 2d Infantry, a mounted rifle company, the 2d Dragoons, and the 9th Field Artillery. The troopers, mixed in with an almost equal number of civilians, were crowded five deep at the bar, keeping a dozen bartenders busy pouring red-eye and raking in money.

From a disgruntled mule skinner, three sheets to the wind, Rockwell and Smith learned that Magruder was hiring on replacements for the balance of the trek to Salt Lake, men who'd go along with kicking back part of their pay to Magruder and Company. There had already been a number of clashes between the latecomers and the men from back east, men who wouldn't go along with the kickback. "You ain't thinkin' of signing on with Magruder, are you?" the skinner glowered at Rockwell and Smith, suddenly hostile.

"Not us," Rockwell grinned assurance, and bought the man a drink.

A few minutes later, conversation with a sergeant of the 2d Dragoons proved there were no military secrets in Platte River Station. Johnston, worried about the weather, was planning a forced march on

Salt Lake City. Several of the infantry companies would remain in Platte River Station as reserves, bringing down the troop count with Johnston to twenty-five hundred men, almost all mounted. A large portion of the baggage and supply wagons would also remain on the east bank of the Platte, allowing Johnston's forces to move at a faster pace to Bridger's Fort, where they would resupply for the final leg to Salt Lake City.

"Do you think the Mormons will fight?" Lot asked casually.

"Fight or run, makes no difference," grinned the sergeant. "Either way there won't be a pair of Mormon long britches left in the territory when we get done with 'em."

"I know exactly what you mean, Sergeant," Rockwell smiled tightly. Clapping Lot on the shoulder, he added, "How about you and me trotting over to Magruder's office and signing on, partner? No sense in lettin' the army have all the fun, is there?"

Passing back by the Platte River Inn, Smith and Rockwell observed a color sergeant unfurl General Johnston's command pennant from the building's balcony. Two sentries, with fixed bayonets, were posted at the entrance.

Rockwell pulled up short as a tall, clean-shaven young man stepped out of the Platte River Inn entrance. He might have been a carbon copy of Rockwell twenty years earlier. He wore fringed buckskins, a wide-brimmed, flat-crowned hat, and a brace of long-barreled navy Colts buckled about his waist.

Rockwell turned his back as the man passed and continued across the street to disappear into Muldoon's.

"You know him?" asked Lot Smith.

Rockwell nodded. "Ran into him last year, in Kansas, a little town called Monticello. He was town marshal."

"Him? He looks awful young for a marshal."

"He's old enough, and big enough," said Rockwell. "You didn't see those guns of his dragging on the ground. His name's Hickok."

"Never heard of him," shrugged Lot, unimpressed.

"You will, if he lives long enough."

"Wonder what he's doing here," frowned Lot.

"Same as all the rest of them, I guess—looking to cut himself a slice of the pie."

"He just might be cutting himself a bellyache doing it," said Lot, still fuming over their exchange with the dragoon sergeant.

"We've seen all we came to see," said Rockwell. "Time we were getting back."

They angled across the street and headed down the narrow alley that would bring them to the rear of Blocker's Livery Stable. They untied the bay and buckskin and were mounting up just as a trio of tanglefooted cavalrymen made an appearance from the other side of the building. The largest of the three, a burly corporal whose features revealed an apparent long history of bare-knuckle resolutions to differences of opinion, instantly focused on Rockwell's big buckskin. A wide grin flooded his face as he pulled up short. "Hot damn! Now that's a man-sized horse!"

Moving in, he grabbed the buckskin's bridle just as Rockwell turned the big horse. "Hey, fella," he frowned up at Rockwell, "you wouldn't turn down a good offer for this critter, would you?"

"Depends on what you have in mind," said Rockwell, coolly darting a warning glance at Lot.

A smirk filled the corporal's face. He threw a wink to his grinning companions, then turned back to the man in the saddle. "Give you ten dollars—hard money. How's that for a fair deal?" The offer brought snickers from the two troopers as they eyed Rockwell for his response.

"Does that ten dollars include saddle and bridle?" asked Rockwell calmly.

The corporal blinked a frown, then grinned, shaking his head. "Naw, that would be takin' advantage. Step down, mister. You just sold yourself a horse."

"Mind if I think about it for a while?" said Rockwell in a deceptively mild voice.

This brought a cackle from one of the troopers. "He wants to think about it, Riley!"

"Shut up, Coogan!" snapped the big man, focusing on Rockwell.

"Sure, mister. You got ten seconds to think on it, then I start whippin' your ass to help you make up your mind. Fair enough?"

"I'd take the ten dollars if I was you, boyo," grinned Coogan.

"Hell, no!" the second trooper protested. "I got a better idea—fight him for the horse, Riley."

A mean grin spread over the corporal's battle-scarred face. He nodded, eyes locked on the man in the saddle. "Good idea, Ez. That okay with you, mister?"

Rockwell sighed. "Fine with me, if you're sure that's the way you want it."

"Now hold on, Corporal," Lot Smith broke in. "We're not looking for any trouble—"

"Save your breath, Lot," said Rockwell, cutting him off. "Time for talking is over."

"Right as rain, saddle tramp," the corporal nodded, flexing his shoulders with a grin. "You steppin' down, or do I pull you down?"

Rockwell shrugged, then leaned into his left stirrup as if to dismount. Suddenly, his right foot lashed out with vicious force, catching the big man flush on the point of his chin. Riley went down as if pole-axed, and his companions found themselves looking down the barrels of a brace of navy Colts. They froze, suddenly sober. Belatedly, Lot Smith pulled his own weapon to level it on the pair.

"If I were you boys," Rockwell smiled thinly, "I'd take me a walk somewhere and let Corporal Riley here sleep it off for a while." To add emphasis to the suggestion, Rockwell eased back the hammers of the Colts. The clicks seemed deafening in the sudden silence.

Coogan, wide-eyed, looked at the big man crumpled in the mud. "Hell, mister, it ain't our fight. Come on, Ez."

Ez didn't need any further urging. He scrambled after Coogan, stumbling around the building and out of sight.

"You scared the hell out of me, Port Rockwell!" Lot glared. "First time I've seen you pull on a man and not fire."

"If we don't move, I might have to yet. Those boys'll be coming back, with help," said Rockwell, holstering the Colts.

A perimeter guard shook his head as the two riders raced past him, heading away from Platte River Station. "Crazy drunks!" he muttered to himself, with a trace of dry-throated envy.

It had taken Smith, Rockwell, and the volunteers eleven hard days to reach the Platte and ford it some miles above the River Station. They could have done it in less time if they hadn't had to worry-along the remounts, and didn't lose half a day at Bridger's Fort. Bridger was gone, Lord knows where, as usual. The stop at Bridger's wasn't a total loss, however. Rockwell purchased a wagon, several kegs of triple X black powder, and fifty feet of waterproof fuse line, something that was in short supply at Kimball's Emporium.

The volunteers, now fifty-one in number, with the addition of the indefatigable Jud Stoddard, who had threatened to tag along anyway if he wasn't included in the group, were camped in a hollow some three miles above Johnston's army, waiting for Smith and Rockwell to return from their scouting mission to Platte River Station. It was a far different-looking group now than it had been eleven days previous. Like Rockwell and Smith, all had allowed their beards to grow, and had taken pains to look as scruffy as possible.

The men selected to infiltrate Platte River Station would split up and move into town singly or in pairs, some mounted, some afoot. Rockwell made the decision that no man would carry a sidearm, but all would be allowed to keep their knives. No man traveled the territories without a blade of some kind. He'd sooner be without his britches than his knife.

Jud Stoddard protested the sidearm order, proudly displaying the new Colt pocket model .36 he'd purchased at Kimball's before leaving Salt Lake. Rockwell was firm. He reminded Jud and the others they'd be mingling with the scum of the territories, men to whom drinking and fighting were as natural as breathing, men quick to take offense at any slight, real or imagined. A man with a gun was too often a temptation to other men with guns; if you carried one, you were expected to be ready to use it. If any of them got in a brawl, they were expected to fight their way out of it, or take their lumps. Under no circumstances were they to use a weapon that could draw blood. Rockwell could feel Lot's eyes boring into the back of his neck as he laid down the admonition.

His final words were a warning about Case Carney—see the man, get signed on, and then stay the hell out of his sight as much as possible.

Dobie Lewis, a thin, gangling youth who looked older than his nineteen years, eyed the others of the group that would be infiltrating Platte River Station on the morrow. He wondered if they too felt a little knot of fear like the one gnawing at his own innards, or were they stronger than he? A whole flock of Daniels going into the lion's den, he thought to himself.

A little more than three miles distant, Brevet Brig. Gen. Albert Sidney Johnston signaled the end to the staff meeting by proposing a toast. "To our winter quarters, gentlemen—Salt Lake City. I intend to be there within forty days."

Phil Cooke frowned over the rim of his glass, hesitated a moment, then drank. His hesitation did not go unnoticed.

"Something on your mind, Phil?" asked Johnston, a hint of chill in his voice.

"Five hundred miles in six weeks is a safe enough margin, Sidney—weather and the battalion permitting," shrugged Cooke.

Johnston was aware that Cooke's statement had given some of the others pause.

"Weather could be a problem, Sidney," said Fitz-John Porter, ponderously. "We're already getting hoarfrost in the mornings, and up on the divide it'll be a good forty degrees colder. One heavy storm, and there goes your schedule."

"If there's a storm, we'll force our way through it. It's going to take more than a little snow to stop this expedition. As for the so-called battalion," he continued with a pointed look to Cooke, "I don't intend to concern myself about the military prowess of a gaggle of farmers."

A grin suddenly appeared on Cooke's face, in spite of his attempt to repress it.

"Did I say something amusing, Colonel?" asked Johnston.

"Sorry, General," said Cooke, still unable to fully wipe the smile from his face.

"Don't apologize, Colonel. Share your good humor with the rest of us—what did you find so amusing?" insisted Johnston, a steely edge to his words.

Cooke realized that Johnston wasn't going to let it drop. Well, if that's the way he wants it, fine with me. "I was just thinking of someone who might have said much the same thing, Sidney—the English general who sent his troops against 'a gaggle of farmers' . . . Lexington and Concord."

The smiles that broke out on the faces of the assembled officers were quickly stifled as Johnston's brow darkened. "I would hardly consider that an apt simile. The men of Lexington and Concord were patriots."

"Not to King George."

A thin smile formed on Johnston's lips. "I wish you'd make up your mind, Phil. For weeks you've been telling us these people are loyal; now you're suggesting just the opposite. Which is it? Are they loyal, or in rebellion?"

Cooke met Johnston's smile with one of his own, aware that every eye in the room was on him, awaiting his response. "Does it matter? Either way, you intend to march this army into Salt Lake."

"May I remind you, Colonel, that these are United States troops, marching into United States territory. No loyal citizen could find that cause for objection. Do you agree?"

"I'd say that depends on how those troops conduct themselves, General. From the talk I've heard among the men, I'd think twice about welcoming them with open arms if I were a Mormon."

A dry laugh escaped Johnston. "Sometimes I get the impression you are, Philip."

A sudden silence fell in the room, and Cooke's face stiffened. "If I were," he said in a flat tone, "I'd be on the other side of the Platte, making damn sure this army never did get to Salt Lake City."

"I don't doubt that for a moment, Phil," chuckled Johnston. "Which makes me all the more appreciative of the fact you're on my staff. I need a man who knows how these people think, what they may do under a given circumstance. Yes, I consider you a very valuable asset. We all do."

Obligatory murmurs of agreement came from the other officers. "I'll drink to that!" said Captain Marcy, lifting his glass—as did they all.

There were two ways to post sentries in open country. At night, low ground posts were best. A sentry on low ground could more easily detect an approaching hostile against the relative lightness of the sky. The opposite was true in daylight, when elevation gave a sentry a wide view of the surrounding terrain.

Rockwell, unable to sleep, relieved Luther James and took over his post. A few minutes later Lot Smith moved in to hunker down beside him. "I've been thinking," Lot ventured after a long moment of silence.

"Glad to hear it."

"We're missing a good bet, Port."

"Yes?"

"The ferries! There's still time to slip down before sunup and cut the cables. Got to take 'em a couple of days to restring 'em."

"Already thought about it."

"Well?" Lot frowned impatiently.

Rockwell shook his head. "That would tip off Johnston too early, make him change his plans."

"That's in our favor, if it gets us time."

"Sure, it'll buy us two days, maybe three, but then he'll know we're going to be on his back. He won't risk leaving those reserves and supply wagons behind; everything will go with him. Those wagons are the key—the more of them he leaves at the station, the better for us." A grin split Rockwell's face. "I could've kissed that dragoon sergeant when he told us Johnston was planning to resupply at Bridger's Fort. That means his troops will leave the station with just enough rations to get there. I figure to just lay back, let him get about halfway between here and Bridger's—South Pass—then hit him hard."

"Hit him hard *how?*" said Lot, suddenly concerned.

"By pinning his army's belly to its backbone, that's how. No trooper's going to march twenty miles a day on an empty gut."

Lot's eyes lit up. "Yeah! He'll have to send back for more supplies, or ahead, to Bridger's."

"That's what *I* was thinking about. . . . That, and thinking we ought to cut back on the boys we're sending in to get jobs with Magruder."

"Cut back? Why?"

"I don't figure we'll need them all, even if they can get signed on now that Johnston's moving light."

"How many do you think should go?"

"Maybe half a dozen. Enough to do a little damage, to slip in and out, let us know what's going on."

"The others will be disappointed. Most of them are real het up about tomorrow."

"They'll get over it. Before this is finished, a lot of them will be wishing they hadn't been so quick to volunteer."

Lot Smith thought for a pensive moment, then asked, "Can we do it, Port? Can we stop Johnston's army?"

Rockwell regarded the younger man. "Perhaps."

From somewhere in the distance came the lonesome call of a prairie wolf. It was not answered.

The next morning Jud Stoddard was the first man through the door when the office of the Magruder Freight and Transport Company opened for business. Behind him, spaced among the other applicants, were Dobie Lewis, the Cartwright brothers, Walt Staggs, and Harvey Arnold.

Stoddard signed his name on the employment register and handed the pencil stub back to the man seated behind the chest-high desk, Case Carney.

"There'll be four bits a day commission deducted from your pay, fella. Any objections?" challenged Carney.

"Not from me, mister," grinned Stoddard. "I'll pay four bits to get two and a half dollars anytime."

Soon the would-be spies were signed and had disappeared into the roving crowds who filled the street.

In the morning they were the first six men in line at the company office, thus giving them a better chance of being assigned to the same wagon company.

It was noon when Rockwell, Smith, and the rest of the volunteers rode across a ford eleven miles north of Platte River Station. They'd come down the opposite side of the river and observed Johnston's army cross and begin its march to Bridger's Fort and Salt Lake. From that moment on, Johnston's invaders would never be out of their sight.

At about the same time, Henry Magruder was once again registering a protest to Albert Sidney Johnston—the same protest he had made five days previously, when Johnston informed him of the forced-march plan. "I still say you're cutting it too thin, General. Anything goes wrong and you'll be marching on short rations."

"Nothing is going to go wrong, Magruder. We'll have a twenty percent safety margin—twenty-four days' rations for a twenty-day march. And—," he raised a hand to cut off the protest forming on Magruder's lips, "if, by some remote possibility, we do happen on misadventure, the hunters are well able to keep us in fresh meat until we reach Bridger's Fort and resupply."

"If you're counting on buffalo, General, forget it. The herds started moving south a month ago, meaning we're in for a real bad winter."

"A winter I have every intention of spending in Salt Lake City, Mister Magruder. Now, if you will excuse me, I have work to do."

Magruder sighed defeat. "You're the general, but if you ask me, you're making a mistake."

"Now we get to it, Mister Magruder," Johnston said icily. "I am *not* asking you. Good-day!"

When Magruder left, Johnston's thoughts returned to an earlier meeting with Alfred Cumming and Lamar Dawson. The Buchanan appointees had suggested that Johnston provide them with an escort and send them on ahead to Salt Lake City with the idea of resolving what was basically a political problem without a show of military force.

Johnston would have none of it. "I'll not risk civilian personnel entering the territory before it is secured by the military," he answered curtly. "You must remember that your predecessors had to flee Salt Lake City in fear of their lives."

"It's a risk Judge Dawson and I are willing to take, General," Cumming insisted.

"But not one *I'm* willing to take, Governor Cumming," said Johnston. "Your safety is my personal responsibility. What would happen if Brigham Young wasn't prepared to negotiate a peaceful settlement? What if he decided to take you hostage?"

"I don't consider that a likely possibility, General," said Dawson. "What would they gain by such a foolhardy act?"

"We are dealing with a people who time and again have flouted the laws of this nation, a people who have proven unable or unwilling to live in peace and harmony with their neighbors. I'm sorry, gentlemen, I fully appreciate your good intentions, but prudence forces me to deny your request. If there are to be any negotiations, they will be made from a position of military strength."

Reluctantly, but only for the time being, Cumming and Dawson accepted Johnston's refusal; at this distance from Salt Lake City, they had little choice in the matter.

The ferry crossings had started at the crack of dawn, and by noon the ten wagon companies, each comprised of forty wagons, had crossed the six-hundred-yard expanse without incident. Upstream, drovers swam the mules and remounts across, followed by the dragoons, cavalry, and mounted infantry. The regular infantry made the crossing by ferry. Last of the military units to cross were the artillerymen with their heavy guns and ammunition caissons. These were followed by the carriage carrying Cumming and Dawson, and Henry Magruder's slab-sided Conestoga that served him as both office and living quarters. By seven that evening Johnston's army was camped five miles west of the Platte.

From the crest of a distant bluff, Port Rockwell, Lot, and the volunteers had watched the crossing with interest, noting that there were no camp followers' wagons following Johnston's column. This must have taken a bit of doing, Rockwell mused. Focusing a telescope, which he'd borrowed from Luther James, on the far side of the river, he soon found the reason—a company of the reserve infantry had been posted at the ferry head to prevent unauthorized crossings and turn back the angry camp followers. It became clear to him that General Johnston intended to get his army to Salt Lake in fighting shape. There'd be no carousing, drunken brawls, and morning hangovers on this march, not without the free-flowing, overpriced whiskey offered by the camp followers.

For the next ten days Rockwell planned to march a parallel course to Johnston's army, on his northern flank and well out of sight of the advancing troops. The important thing, he stressed, was to let Johnston proceed, unopposed and unsuspecting, until they had him where they wanted him. There would, however, always be someone on the alert, with a clear view of the wagon columns in the event that Jud or any of the others had some need to contact the main body of volunteers.

As Stoddard had anticipated, when they got to the Magruder office the morning after he and the others had signed on, assignments were on a first-come, first-served basis.

Case Carney assigned four of them to 1st Company, under the command of a civilian captain, Jubal Hathaway, a grizzled, bad-tempered giant who Jud was sure hadn't drawn a fully sober breath since Andy Jackson was a pup. Fortunately, most of the other teamsters had already picked out wagon mates, so it was no trick at all for Jud and three of his charges to do the same, isolating them, to some degree, from too close contact with the other members of the company. However, they got separated from Walt Staggs and Harve Arnold.

The wagons of 1st Company carried a mixture of supplies, ranging from sides of bacon to hundred-weight sacks of grain for the livestock. The grain would be necessary to supplement what the animals could get on the trail in the way of forage. Jubal's wagon was of particular interest to Jud. In addition to bales of army greatcoats, it carried a supply of gunpowder—a dozen fifty-pound kegs.

It was the fifth day into the march to Bridger's Fort when the trouble started. In an eight-hour period there were almost as many breakdowns and accidents among the wagon companies. Three of the transports were damaged beyond repair, forcing a redistribution of their cargoes among the other wagons. No time was lost, however; the wagons that could be repaired limped into night camp several hours behind the rest.

Later that evening, after taps, Jud had noticed Jubal Hathaway in quiet conversation with the other company captains. It wasn't a matter of any great import to Stoddard—not until the following day, when three more wagons suffered unexplained accidents, severely damaging two. So far, Jud was aware, none of the breakdowns or accidents affected 1st Company, their own.

Now Jud began putting things together, and his conclusion brought a quiet grin to his lips. If he was right, he told Dobie and the others, they wouldn't have to do a thing to sabotage the wagons—the other teamsters were doing a good job of that themselves. Tomorrow, Jud guessed, there would be more "accidents." No doubt rankled by Magruder's "commission" scheme that was taking four bits a day out of the teamsters' pockets, the company captains had gotten together and decided to make up that loss by throwing Johnston's schedule out of whack. The longer it took them to get to Salt Lake, the longer they'd be on the payroll. Jud smiled. Magruder's greed would cost him, in the long run. But most important, it would cost Johnston time. For the first night in almost a week, Jud Stoddard and the young volunteers slept an untroubled sleep.

The following morning, however, Jud waited uneasily for the expected sabotage from Carney's cutthroats. The thought had occurred to him, with a start, that if these "accidents" were recognized for what they were—deliberate attempts to slow down the expedition's progress—then he and his companions might somehow be exposed as spies. He knew that under intense scrutiny, they would be vulnerable.

Then at five minutes past ten, Jubal Hathaway's lead wagon careened down the slope of a narrow defile, as the result of a snapped linchpin, and crashed into a projecting boulder. The wreckage effectively blocked passage of the other wagons.

Up ahead, Johnston called a halt. Grateful troopers eased their weary rumps out of the saddles while infantrymen sat down to relieve their aching feet.

Henry Magruder sat his horse in smoldering anger as Case Carney shouted orders at the men struggling to right the heavily laden wagon and replace the two smashed wheels. Most of the men, Jud and his little band among them, had stripped off their jackets to give them freedom of movement. Using stout poles, with rocks as fulcrums, they brought the wagon to even keel and began removing the shattered wheels.

As Carney passed on the leeward side of the wagon, he was hidden from those who labored to replace the two wheels on the opposite side. Amid the grunts and shouts and the strained wrenching of the wagon joints, he heard hushed voices that made him stop, his jaw tightening into a hard ridge.

The two speaking were alone, up front, holding secure the tongue of the wagon. A split second before he saw Carney, Dobie Lewis spoke too loud to Jud Stoddard: "By the look of things, President Young's been given another day."

"Shut your mouth!" yelled Jud in near panic, "and hold that damned bar!"

Too late! Carney had caught every word as if they had been shouted. Jud, his heart racing, shuddered. Dobie felt his heart sink to his boots.

Carney glared at them but for a brief moment, then stepped across the wagon tongue and singled out Jubal Hathaway, who was directing the repairs. "The linchpin, lemme see it."

"Ain't no good," responded Jubal. "Threw what was left of it away."

"Where?" snapped Carney. "Find it!"

Jubal's eyes betrayed the location of the snapped linchpin half. One look was all Carney needed to tell him that the pin had been sawed two thirds of the way through. "Look at it," he growled, shoving it under Jubal's nose.

"How in hell did it get like that?" Jubal asked innocently.

"That's what we're going to find out," snapped Carney, glaring at the men laboring to repair the wagon.

"What's wrong, Carney?" asked Magruder, easing his horse forward.

Carney triumphantly held up the pin to Magruder's view. "I knew all these breakdowns wasn't natural. We got spies with us, Magruder! And I know what kind."

In a trice Carney had the men of 1st Company lined up in front of him. Hands on hips, he glared at them, jaw outthrust. "Al'right, I want the man who sawed that linchpin!"

The line of teamsters made a show of exchanging puzzled looks. Jud and the volunteers gave an equally good impression of bewildered innocence.

"Had to be more than one man involved, Carney," Magruder said from behind him.

"I know that, and I'm gonna root 'em out. In this company, and all the rest."

Carney walked past each of the men as if he were an officer on parade. They stiffened as the big man peered into their eyes. The fear of Carney was recognizable in every face.

"Was it you, Ben?" he grilled one of the terrified drovers. "You Tennessee slop bucket! You, Jess? You Missouri pig thief! Or was it you, Dobie? You spyin' Mormon sonovabitch!"

With that, Carney pulled Dobie out of the ranks by the throat; then, snarling a curse, he drove his fist into the small man's face.

Vainly, Dobie tried to defend himself, but it was no contest. Carney's fists drove him backward, stumbling over his own feet. Instantly, the rank of teamsters broke to form a loose circle, cheering Carney on. Jubal Hathaway's cheers were the loudest. Jud's warning look kept his two young companions back, but when Dobie went down and Carney began to launch kicks into the defenseless boy's curled body, it was too much. With a cry of outrage, Jud hurled himself at Carney. The sudden attack drove the big man back. Jubal, glad to have found a scapegoat for the wagon sabotage, jumped forward to make a grab at Jud, seizing his arms in a powerful grip. Carney promptly went to work on Jud, smashing rights and lefts into his unprotected face and body. This was more than the two Cartwright brothers could take, and they threw themselves into the fray. A howl went up from the rest of the teamsters and a number of them plunged into the battle.

That day the young Utahns gave a good accounting of themselves. As Dobie was to tell it later, Carney had damned near killed Jud before he went down. Even though Hathaway had pinned his arms behind him, he got a kick squarely into Carney's groin. Bent over and bellowing like a wounded bull, Carney tore into him with uncontrolled rage.

The young Cartwright brothers, with whom Rockwell had been so impressed, seemed to be in their element. They were everywhere at once. One after another of the teamsters went down in front of their relentless fists, knees, feet, and teeth. Years later, Dobie recalled how good it felt, in spite of his own bruises and spilled blood, to see Will Cartwright demolish Jubal's nose with one sledgehammer-like blow from his right fist, while another drover lost two teeth from Will's left fist in less time than it took to tell about it. "There was three of 'em on the ground bleedin' before they got Willie down," Dobie recalled excitedly. "And they never did get Luke Cartwright down. The first drover to get near him was dropped like he'd been shot. After it was all over, he was still on his hands and knees, a'wonderin' where he was."

Another came at Luke from the side with a skinner. Luke caught the movement out of the corner of his eye a split second before the blade would have plunged into his unprotected body below his right elbow. As he pulled back, it ripped through the front of his shirt, slicing a nasty but not deadly horizontal wound in his stomach, just above the navel.

With the precision of a striking rattlesnake, Luke's left hand closed around his attacker's wrist, pulling him forward, his right hand securing a vicelike grip on the man's upper arm. Following through with what seemed to be a single motion, Luke brought his attacker's extended arm—palm up—down hard on his simultaneously upward-driving knee. There came a resounding, sickening crack, like the rending of a piece of kindling, as the assailant's elbow gave way in the opposite direction that nature had intended.

The agonizing, bloodcurdling scream that followed had the effect of stopping the melee for a brief moment. Then it began again. A maddened Case Carney, having left Dobie writhing on the ground, and Jud's face a bloody pulp, reached for one of his Remington 44s, as other teamsters began to close in on Luke.

The crack of an army revolver brought things to a sudden halt. "What the hell's going on here!" roared Col. Philip St. George Cooke.

"This is civilian business, Colonel," snapped Henry Magruder, turning his horse toward the mounted officer. Just then, the teamsters and Carney pulled back, revealing the four battered young Mormons and twice that many bloody and cursing of their own. Jud, his head reeling, his mouth pulverized, and his right eye pounded shut, and Luke Cartwright, his sliced stomach covered with blood, immediately went to the side of Dobie, still crumpled on the ground.

"I asked what was going on, Magruder."

"Stinkin' Mormon spies," snorted Carney, plucking his hat out of the dust. "They're the ones causing all the breakdowns we've been havin'."

Cooke urged his mount closer to them, frowning. "Is this true?" he asked.

"Is what true?" asked Will Cartwright defiantly, wiping the smear of blood from his lips on his torn shirtsleeve.

Carney pushed forward, holding up the sawed linchpin to Cooke's view. "Course it's true, see for yourself!"

"I was asking him," Cooke said coldly. "Well, son?"

Jud came to his feet, his face suffused with anger. "We're Mormons, if that's what you're askin!" he said, only barely audible with his bleeding and swollen lips.

"Satisfied, Colonel?" smirked Magruder. "Now if you—"

"But we didn't have nothin' to do with the wagons breakin' down," Jud overrode him. "There might not have been any breakdowns if Carney and Mister Magruder wasn't forcing the men to kick back part of their pay every day. Ain't that right, Jubal?" he ended, spitting a mouthful of blood and half a tooth onto the ground, eyes accusingly on the company captain.

"Don't know what the hell you're talkin' about," Jubal Hathaway glared. "Don't blame us for your doin's, ya stinkin' whelp!"

Cooke turned to the smug-faced Magruder. "Al'right, get them out of here," he said, indicating Jud and the others.

"You mean you're goin' to let these spies just walk outta here!"

"Unless you want a full investigation on kickbacks!" snapped Cooke.

Magruder and Carney became suddenly silent.

Cooke confronted Jud again. "Let me tell you this—if there are any more of you, get them out. Take them with you and don't come back, or I can't answer for your safety." Then the colonel swung his mount around and galloped off, his back stiff with anger.

Dobie Lewis moaned deeply as two of the boys tried to get him to his feet. "Think I got a busted rib—or something."

As Jud and his little band of would-be spies and saboteurs moved off, Magruder shook his head angrily at the sight of half a dozen of his own men still in the process of pulling themselves together.

Jud waited until the tail end of the wagon column was barely visible in the distance before using the small pocket mirror to flash a signal off at the hills north of the trail.

He was worried; Dobie was in a bad way. A broken rib would be a blessing, if that's all it was.

Three minutes after his first signal, a flash of light appeared in the distant hills. They were not alone.

A stiff dose of Doc Ames's laudanum had dulled Dobie Lewis's pain enough to allow Porter Rockwell's probing fingers to determine that no ribs had been broken, but Dobie would be one sore young man for the next few days.

Case Carney, Rockwell had thought to himself as he made the examination; one more score to be settled—and settled it would be, he promised himself—Brigham Young's "no blood" order be damned!

Dobie Lewis forced a hazy, painful, apologetic look up at Lot Smith and Port Rockwell. "Guess I ruined everything."

"Don't worry about it, Dobie," said Lot gently. "We've still got two men in the camp they don't know about. We'll get all the information we need from Walt and Harve. Stop talking now, and let that laudanum put you to sleep. You'll feel a sight better in the morning."

Dobie nodded, closed his eyes, and stopped fighting the numbing effects of the opiate.

Rockwell had to smile at Jud's barely recognizable, bruised, swollen, and bloody face. Typical—the tough little cowboy had been right in the middle of it, doing more than his share, taking his lumps without complaint. Good man! Someday, Rockwell promised himself, he would tell him so.

When all the wounds had been treated, Rockwell and Smith eased to their feet and walked over to the fire in the center of the floor of the small box canyon that served as rendezvous camp for the volunteers. The canyon was an ideal shelter for the men and horses, well protected from casual discovery if Johnston sent out flank riders or scouts.

Johnston's arrogant confidence would be his undoing, Rockwell thought grimly. He hoped this business with Dobie and the others didn't alert the general to take more precautions. Of one thing Rockwell was sure, Johnston wasn't taking any advice from Phil Cooke. Phil would have had scouts combing the advance area and picked up their sign ten days ago.

Another three days would take Johnston's army through South Pass, to the far side of the divide—just where Porter Rockwell wanted them, midway between the Platte and Bridger's Fort.

Chapter Eight

Foreign ministers appointed to Washington quickly learned the desirability of consulting a map of the United States when compiling guest lists. Party affiliations were no assurance of harmony in a gathering of Washington politicians; there were proslavery Republicans as well as antislavery Democrats. Lord Lyons, the British minister representing her majesty's government, had long ago come to the conclusion that in America, North was North, and South was South, and never the twain would meet—not at one of his gatherings.

To Lyons, Washington was an appalling place—dismal, devoid of culture, poorly situated. Leave it to the ruddy Americans to select a swampy marsh to be the site of a nation's capital, he snorted to himself, and leave it to a ruddy Frenchman to plan for its construction there! Lyons tried to recall a city, in all his travels on government service, with so little charm, so few things that made life civilized, and he could not. Even those brutes the Russians had their St. Petersburg.

The guests at Lord Lyon's H Street mansion that evening were, but for one exception, from below the Mason-Dixon Line. The exception was the senator from California, William Gwinn, a staunch supporter of Southern views. The others included Supreme Court Chief Justice Roger B. Taney, a native of Maryland, who had only that past March written the majority decision on the Dred Scott case, ruling that free Negroes were not to be accorded the right of citizenship in the United States; John Floyd, Buchanan's secretary of war; Jefferson Davis, the senator from Mississippi; Senators Benjamin and Slidell, from Louisiana; and Wigfall, the scar-faced senator from Texas.

Over cigars and Madeira, the question Lord Lyons had been anticipating was voiced by Jefferson Davis: Would her majesty's government recognize a confederation of Southern states as a sovereign nation in the event of secession from the Union?

Lord Lyons shrugged softly and smiled, exposing a row of decaying teeth, an aberration in his otherwise meticulous appearance of black offset by white lace bursting from beneath the sleeves and lapels of his coat. "Her majesty's government, Senator, makes it a policy not to become involved in the internal affairs of foreign governments. If, however, this confederation did in fact become a reality—something more than merely a persistent rumor—it would be given prompt consideration."

"And would you venture to say if that consideration would be favorably inclined, Sir Edmund?" asked War Secretary Floyd.

Lord Lyons peered over his delicate tented fingers. "Let me put it this way, Mister Secretary. The mill owners of Birmingham and Manchester would welcome your confederation with open arms. I'm sure her majesty's government realizes that what is good for Birmingham and Manchester is good for England."

"You have the mills, we have the cotton," Senator Slidell shrugged matter-of-factly.

"You also have slavery, gentlemen. An institution my country abandoned half a century ago. We have our abolitionists, too—some of them in positions of great power."

"General manumission is just a question of time, Minister," interjected Chief Justice Taney. "In a few years there won't be a slave in the South."

"In the meantime, my government is faced with a choice—moralist or pragmatist," said Lord Lyons.

"No contest, Minister," grinned the senator from California. "Hit a moralist in the pocketbook and you find a pragmatist."

Moralist indeed! thought Judah Benjamin, painfully aware that his English coreligionists were forbidden by law to run for public office in England until but a handful of years ago. Disraeli, a brilliant statesman, had to foreswear his faith in order to run for Parliament. So much for British moralism! Masking his feelings, he smiled. "I'd have phrased it differently, sir. But in essence my colleague from California is right, Lord Lyons. England's economy is based on industrial production. In order to produce, she needs raw material, *our* raw materials."

The British ambassador eyed the smiling senator from Louisiana and thought to himself, another damned Levantine. Pursing his lips, he nodded. "How true, Mister Benjamin, how true . . . at the present time."

He was well aware that England was still the driving force behind the industrial revolution, but others were doing their best to catch up. The American New England states, he knew, had embarked on a crash program of industrial expansion, and every bale of cotton that went to a New England mill was one less for the British.

Lyons's instructions from Whitehall had been explicit: Do all possible to encourage the schism between the North and South; support the disunionist cause, but not openly. Lyons must tread carefully. After the recent troubles in India and the Crimea, England's exchequer needed time to recoup; a new military adventure would be highly undesirable at this time. None of this showed in Lord Lyons's face as he nodded at the senator from Louisiana.

"However, I must say that *some* of my friends," Lyons forced a somewhat nauseating and insincere smile, "and, of course, *your* friends as well, are rather concerned about the other edge of the sword. Some question whether the South, as an independent nation, can survive with an agricultural economy, you see."

Floyd couldn't let this go by. He and Lord Lyons had discussed the issue more than once before. Floyd wasn't sure whether the ambassador was rubbing their noses in it, or was on a fishing expedition. Floyd knew that whatever was discussed that evening would be annotated, interpreted, and forwarded to Whitehall.

Removing a slim cheroot from his mouth, Floyd said calmly. "I can assure you, Lord Lyons, that when the time comes, your government won't be dealing with a small handful of agricultural states. It will be dealing with a nation that spreads from the Atlantic to the Pacific, a land area greater than all of western Europe!"

"Really!" responded the ambassador, removing a silver snuffbox from the cuff of his laced sleeve, flipping open the top, and with effeminate fingers drawing the powder to his nostrils. Then, with eyebrows raised and head cocked, he addressed Senator Gwinn. "Does that, perchance, include California?"

Gwinn nodded a confident grin. "If Texas goes, California goes, and all the land in between."

"And Texas will! Sam Houston be damned!" growled Wigfall.

Lyons didn't attempt to conceal the fact he was impressed. "Yes, that *could* put a different light on things. But," he continued, eyeing Gwinn searchingly, "I was under the impression that California was leaning heavily toward the abolitionist camp."

Gwinn exchanged glances with Jefferson Davis and John Floyd, and nodded. "Things have a way of changing, Lord Lyons, if you help 'em along."

The Englishman, aware of the play between the three, pressed on. "Then, am I to understand that it is not a fait accompli—as yet?"

"Not quite, Lord Lyons," said Floyd. "But the wheels are turning."

Lord Lyons wrote to his prime minister, Lord Viscount Palmerstone, that evening.

The union of American states draws closer to disunion with each passing day. President Buchanan is a weary old man astride a runaway horse, desperately afraid his presidency will preside over the dissolution of the nation. Surely the words of Louis XIV, "After me, the deluge," must be part of the old gentleman's nightly prayer.

I am as yet not fully aware of the reasons for, or the worth of, the Utah Expedition. Using my imagination I can devise a number of possibilities, if properly exploited, possibilities that might prove to be of immense benefit to Great Britain, both economically and territorially. Furthermore, I would think a continental Confederacy could open doors for European colonization in the West, with England assuming, may I say, "the lion's share". Jefferson Davis, the man seemed destined to the leadership of this new confederation of states, has made it quite clear that, in exchange for British support and recognition, England would be granted exceptionally generous trade agreements with the new nation. He further assured me that the Oregon Territory would not be brought into the confederation, thus effectively isolating Oregon from the Union and giving Britain grounds to abrogate the 1846 agreement ceding Oregon to the United States. The vastly weakened Union would be in no position to enforce a claim of sovereignty.

It is encouraging to note that those who are setting the stage for secession understand the importance of the western territories to the fulfillment of their desires. Still, I repeat, what role Utah will play is not yet clear to me, perhaps not even to them. Whatever their machinations, however, the disposition of California must play an important role. If General Johnston's army successfully invests the territory, perhaps it will then be in a position to swing the balance of power in California to the pro-Southern cause, by force if necessary; who knows?

Of one thing we can rest assured: Some of the Southern border states have made it clear that they would not vote secession without a guarantee of California's participation in the new confederation. I suppose much depends on the California state legislature, which reconvenes in the spring.

Lord Lyons ended his communication to Viscount Palmerstone strongly recommending that Britain, too, wait at the very least until spring before making any overt commitments to the Davis-Floyd faction.

Culturally and geographically, Washington was a southern city, deep in the very bosom of the South, surrounded on three sides by Maryland, and Virginia on the fourth—two of the staunchest proslavery states in the Union.

Southern members of both House and Senate delighted in offending the sensibilities of their Northern compatriots by flaunting their retinues of liveried slaves, who accompanied them to the city when the Houses were in session. The most pocket-poor Southern congressman managed at least one slave, usually his carriage driver.

On any morning you could find a score of cheroot-smoking men in large planter's hats discoursing on matters of the moment in front of Washington's most famous hostelries—Willards on 14th Street, the Kirkwood on 12th, and the National on 6th. As the men talked, slaves hurried in and out of the hotels' bars with fresh juleps to help their masters get the day off to a good start. At the curb was the ever-present array of coupes, landaus, and victorias, many with both driver and footman, all black, and all slaves.

Half of every year, Washington was a somnolent place, the half when the Houses were not in session. The local gentry, referring to themselves as "the chivalry," often departed for cooler, more salubrious climes during the summer and early autumn months, malaria being prevalent in those times.

No one knew who first started wearing the blue cockades, tucked in hatband or pinned to lapel, but everyone in Washington knew what they meant: The wearer was declaring his preference for disunion, his identity with the Southern cause.

The prounionists were quick to follow suit with their own cockades in the national colors—red, white, and blue. The South Carolinians, ever individualists, sported miniature palmetto and rattlesnake flags, their state emblem.

South Carolina had thrown down the gauntlet to the federal government once before, in 1832, rebelling against what they considered an unfair imposition of trade tariffs. Their readiness to fight had caused Andy Jackson to quickly back down and modify the tariff regulations.

Now, conflict was again on the political horizon. With a population of four hundred thousand, half of it slave, the Palmetto State was not about to bend the knee to Yankee abolitionists' demands. South Carolina spelled it out in no uncertain terms: She had voluntarily entered the Union; she could equally as well voluntarily depart from it. Unlike some of the less determined Southern states, South Carolina was prepared to go it alone, if necessary, confident that her well-trained and well-equipped militia would be more than a match for anything "Bumbling" Buchanan could throw against them. The fact that of the six departments of the United States Army only one was commanded by a Northerner may have had something to do with that confidence.

The topic of conversation this particular morning was Sam Houston's tirade on the Senate floor the previous day. To the wearers of the blue cockades, the man was a scoundrel, a disgrace to his heritage and his state, and to the South, a turncoat! Nor was he a favorite of the current administration. Houston's challenge in the Senate to the president and his cabinet over the sending of federal troops to Utah had been scathing. "Where," he thundered, "is the evidence of this so-called Utah rebellion? Where is the proof that these people have taken up arms against the lawful authority of the United States? What blood has been shed, what battles fought? In short, gentlemen, who hath measured the ground of this 'rebellion'? No one! And yet, our president has seen fit to mount a military expedition that will deplete our armed forces and the treasury to a horrendous degree, without a shred of positive evidence that this rebellion does, in fact, exist! I maintain that the president's actions have been out of all proportion to any clear and present danger this alleged rebellion could possibly present to this Republic. I call on this body to demand a full and impartial investigation of the facts, to demand the recall of General Johnston's army pending the conclusion of that investigation, to stop the army before it crosses into the Utah Territory, lest it spark rebellion where none had existed before.

"Any people will resist armed invasion, gentlemen. As a Texan I have good reason to know, and so does General Santa Anna."

"You speak for yourself, sir!" bellowed Wigfall, the scar-faced junior senator from Texas. "The state of Texas speaks with another voice!"

"You would have us coddle treason, sir?" another voice called out. "Wait until the traitors' knives are at the throat of this nation? Shame!"

Houston turned to the author of the charge, Senator Iverson from Georgia, a florid-faced man in his sixties. "You have spoken the word *treason,* sir, not I. But now, since the cat is out of the bag—yes, there is treason afoot in this land, but it is not in Utah, gentlemen!" Houston's gaze swung to hold accusingly on the senator from Mississippi, Jefferson Davis. "It is within the walls of this chamber!"

The gaunt-faced senator from Mississippi came to his feet, white lipped. "Explain yourself, sir!"

"As you wish, Senator," said Houston calmly. "Each and every man in this august body has sworn an oath to uphold the Constitution of the United States, to defend it against all enemies, foreign *or* domestic. I submit to you, Senator, that there are men seated in this chamber today who have consciously violated that oath. It is *they* who are the traitors, *they* who would conspire to treason!"

The floor of the Senate erupted in bedlam—cheers from the majority of Republicans, scathing denunciations from the bulk of the Democrats. A blow was struck, another returned; men of sixty grappled with others half their age. Senator Somner of Massachusetts lashed out at Toombs of Georgia with his walking stick as the president pro tempore of the Senate gaveled furiously for order. In the spectators' gallery, partisan elements engaged in their own battle, with considerably more effect. A shrill voice came from the melee. "That's tellin' 'em, Sam!" Senator Slidell went down under a Republican fist; the senator from Vermont buckled from a blow delivered by his Florida counterpart.

In the gallery, his back against the wall, Col. Thomas L. Kane had a grin of satisfaction on his face as he kept his eyes on the tall figure below. Standing in the center of it all, drawn to his full six feet four on top of two-inch-heeled Texas boots, Sam Houston was a calm island in a sea of fury. Wigfall pushed his way through the struggling bodies to confront Houston with blazing eyes and clenched fists. Kane couldn't hear what Wigfall said to Houston—the hubbub drowned out his words—but he did see Houston's response to his fellow Texan. He threw back his coat, letting it fall to the floor, and brought clenched fists to bear. Wigfall spouted a few more unheard words, then spun away from Houston.

John C. Breckinridge, the vice president and close personal friend of Jefferson Davis, left the dais, his face livid with anger as the president pro tempore continued to gavel in a frenzy, calling for the sergeant at arms to clear the chamber.

The passage through South Pass had been without incident, and Johnston's army moved down the western slopes of the Great Divide in good order.

Before entering the pass, Johnston did pay heed to Phil Cooke's warning—sending out advance parties to scout the terrain. Cooke felt that if the Utahns were planning armed resistance, South Pass would be the ideal place. The fact that there had been no resistance, neither hide nor hair of a military presence seen, troubled Cooke. It was not like Young's people to patiently await the headman's ax, not after Nauvoo. Cooke was certain they were up to something, but what?

"So much for your saintly Spartans, Colonel," General Johnston later chided Phil Cooke through a confident smile. "There were no brave three hundred at the pass."

"If there had been, we'd still be on the other side, General. Count your blessings."

"I'm not so sure, Phil," responded the general, the sarcasm gone from his voice. "No battalion of ignorant frontiersmen and slovenly foreigners, however daring, is going to stop this army. These are good men, the best units in the country."

Cooke nodded his head slowly. "You're right, Sidney—they are good men, and they are commanded by the best field officer in these United States, North or South. But as your junior officer and friend, I ask you to be cautious. Don't assume that what you have come to believe of these people is true. They are necessarily a tough, but nevertheless an intelligent, decent, God-fearing, Bible-reading people.

"And don't be misled by their lack of action so far, or their use of the term *battalion*. This title simply honors those who fought in the war with Mexico. Actually, the battalion includes the Territorial Militia, making an army of probably brigade strength when it's fully mobilized. If they decide to make a stand, we'll sure as hell know we've been in a fight. I wonder if you want that, Sidney. It would be a war neither side could win."

Johnston eyed the dour-faced colonel for a long, puzzled moment. In spite of himself, he had been touched by Cooke's obviously honest praise. "Well, Phil, I've learned more about our enemy in the past two minutes than I have been able to get out of you from the first day of your arrival under my command. Now," a smile escaped the general, "a final question. If the people of Utah Territory are indeed decent, Bible-reading citizens, may we not then expect them to render unto Caesar. . . ?"

"No question about it, Sidney," smiled Cooke, "but *only* that which is Caesar's."

The air was crisp, with a crystal clarity that made distances appear deceptively closer. The peaks flanking South Pass stood out like silent, white-capped sentinels against a flawless sky, and a strong easterly breeze rolled ruffles in the waist-high, golden yellow prairie grass that blanketed the land from the floor of the valley to the saddleback ridge five miles away.

For two hours Porter Rockwell, Lot Smith, and a dozen volunteers had been watching the approach of Johnston's army as it snaked down the wagon trail, the morning sun reflecting off metal accoutrements and the white canvas of the wagon tops. Johnston had moved the artillery and wagon companies to the center of the column, a precautionary measure in the event of attack—something Rockwell had anticipated.

The head of the column was less than a mile distant when the rear guard passed through the saddleback. Rockwell lifted Cephus James's telescope to his eye and focused it on the lead riders, some hundred yards in advance of the main body of troops. One was Hickok; the other two were cavalrymen—a sergeant and a lance corporal carrying a guidon. Rockwell shifted the lens to the column head. Phil Cooke's image came clearly to his eye, riding stirrup to stirrup with the sharp-visaged commander of the army. They were followed by two other officers— one a full colonel, the other, much younger, a captain. Rockwell had no way of knowing that the men he was looking at were Captain Marcy and Colonel Fitz-John Porter. Behind them was a heavy carriage driven by an army teamster. After the carriage came the main body of troops, led by a unit of the 2d Dragoons.

Rockwell slid the glass to the low, boulder-strewn mesa off to the right of the column, now almost abreast of the wagon and artillery companies. There wasn't a sign of movement among the boulders, he noted with satisfaction.

Lowering the glass he grinned at Lot Smith. "Think it's about time we got this little party started."

Lot returned the grin with a nod, then called out to the others, "Light her up!"

A dozen matches were lit and touched to the tinder-dry grass, causing it to catch fire instantly. Rockwell and the others then scrambled down the slope to where their horses waited in a hollow. By the time they reached them, the dozen small fires had spread to unite, exploding into a wall of flame, crowned by dark billows of rolling smoke.

James Butler Hickok reined in and stood high in his stirrups to peer ahead at the dark, low-lying cloud that had suddenly boiled up in the distance, glowing red at the base.

"What the hell's that?" frowned the sergeant.

"Looks like a thunderhead," said the lance corporal.

"Never seen a storm cloud with a red belly. That's fire!" yelled Hickok. Wheeling their horses around, the three raced for the head of the column, shouting the alarm.

A particularly strong gust of wind leapfrogged the flames ahead, and they rapidly fanned out into an ever-widening inferno, its hungry tongues reaching skyward to suck nurturing oxygen from the air.

"Fire!" raced the length of the column, bringing a sense of panic to troopers, infantrymen, and wagoneers alike as they took up the cry.

Johnston could see immediately that there was no way his infantry and wagons could outrun the flames roaring up from the floor of the valley. The mounted troopers could outflank the fire if they moved fast, but not the others.

"The mesa!" Cooke bellowed in his ear, pointing.

Rapidly the order was passed down the line as troopers and wagoneers fought to control animals suddenly walleyed with terror, their sensitive nostrils alerting them to danger before sight of the actual flames.

Infantry units swung into an oblique, double-timing toward the mesa. Artillerymen lashed the gun carriage teams savagely, the limbers fishtailing over the bumpy ground, spilling much of the contents. The crews cut the traces to free the teams before running to the mesa's protection.

Two of the freight wagons, attempting a turn, locked wheels, snapping an axle of one, toppling the other to its side. The drivers, screaming curses at each other, ran for the rocks.

The fire, creating its own wind, advanced at a pace faster than the heavily burdened infantrymen could run, forcing many to abandon weapons and knapsacks. They scrambled madly for safety as the billowing, spark-filled clouds of eye-stinging smoke rolled over them.

Porter Rockwell, Lot Smith, and the dozen volunteers followed the burn, keeping pace with the wall of flame that swept up the valley toward the saddleback. Their faces covered with bandannas, they squinted through the rolling billows of black smoke, ears attuned to the shouts of panicked troopers, and orders bellowed by officers and noncoms. Another hundred yards would bring the army to the base of the mesa.

Rockwell slipped a three-foot length of oil rag–tipped sapling from the whang leather holding it to his saddle horn. Leaning, he touched the oil-soaked end to a patch of still-smoldering prairie grass. Instantly the sapling end burst into flame. Lot and the others followed suit, lighting their torches.

The wall of flame raced toward the mesa with a thunderous roar and swept around it to meet on the far side—the mesa became a rocky island in a sea of fire. The intensity of the heat could not be endured by man or animal—dense smoke and swirling embers choked and blinded, searing throats and lungs, scorching flesh, burning holes in tunics. Many men threw themselves to the rocky ground, covering their faces with neck cloths and tunics saturated with water from their canteens, the moisture cooling the superheated air pulled into starved lungs. Terror-filled draft animals and mounts sought escape, trampling dozens of huddled troopers and civilian drivers. The canvas tops of wagons burst into flame, adding to the intensity of the heat.

A powder wagon blew up, scattering flaming debris over a wide area, causing other wagon tops to ignite. With the flats of their swords officers drove groups of men to their feet to rip smoldering canvas from the bows of wagons before the flames took hold. Others smashed open water barrels to wet down ammunition limbers and powder wagons, some already in flames. A number of wagons, caught in the core of the inferno, literally exploded into balls of fire, much like pine trees in a forest fire.

Through momentary gaps in the wall of smoke Rockwell and the others got glimpses of the desperate struggle atop the mesa. Rockwell estimated a minimum of three dozen transports had already been destroyed. There would be more.

Colonel Cooke, with an iron grip on the halter of Governor Cumming's lead carriage horse, held the frightened team steady, keeping it to the center of the mesa. A deafening explosion rent the air, and Cooke knew that another powder wagon or ammunition limber had gone up. The echoes were still rumbling up the valley when three pistol shots sounded from somewhere, in rapid succession. They were followed instantly by shrill, high-pitched cries as more than a score of mounted men with flaming torches broke cover to charge in among the wagon companies, tossing the firebrands into the open backs of the supply wagons. A break in the smoke momentarily revealed the torch-bearing riders as they raced in from the burn area to add to the confusion. Cooke caught a glimpse of the man in the lead. His face was covered but Cooke instantly recognized the big buckskin mount as Porter Rockwell's.

Jubal Hathaway—what was left of his nose cradled in a soft leather cup that narrowed to strings on either side, resting on his ears and tied at the back of his head—lashed at his team savagely, guiding it toward the center of the mesa. A rider appeared out of the blackness to hurl a flaming firebrand through the opening behind Jubal, the knob end of the flying brand knocking off Jubal's hat as it whipped by to land in the wagon's bed. Then the rider was gone, lost in the smoke. Jubal bailed out, managing to get some fifty feet before the casks of powder blew, sending him sprawling face first onto the rocks with a painful thud.

Several of the more alert troopers managed to get off shots at the fast-moving riders, but no saddles were emptied. Case Carney, standing in the boot of Magruder's wagon, emptied both of his .44 Remingtons into the wall of smoke that closed behind the riders as they rode off, their cries fading in the roar of wind and flame. Zebulah Weems reeled in his saddle; one of Carney's slugs had found a home.

A grim-lipped Albert Sidney Johnston scanned the blackened, burned-out valley through smoke-seared eyes as troopers attempted to salvage what they could from the smoldering hulks of what once were supply and commissary wagons. There wasn't much left. On the mesa, noncoms tried to bring some semblance of order, re-forming platoons and companies.

The medical officer, Major Poole, moved among the burned and injured, thankful that the casualties were less than he'd anticipated. But there were many painful burns, some severe, a number of broken bones, and a large number of men suffering from varying degrees of smoke inhalation. Some had the hair singed from their heads and faces.

The air was strangely stilled, as though the fire had carried the breeze away with it in its passage. Ash fell like ghostly snowflakes, covering man, beast, and rolling stock in gray uniformity. Dragoons, cavalrymen, mounted riflemen, and teamsters saw to their animals. Here and there a shot rang out as some trooper put an end to an animal's suffering.

Johnston stepped down from his vantage point atop a boulder to face the silent group of officers. He singled out Cooke. "So this is the way our gallant foes make war, Colonel," he said with cold anger.

"I never told you they'd go by the book, Sidney," Cooke responded. "It could have been worse."

"Wouldn't have had to be at all," said Henry Magruder, pushing through the circle of officers to level an accusing eye on Cooke, "if you'd'a let us take care of those spies the way we wanted!"

"That's a fact," said Case Carney, moving in to stand beside Magruder, jut jawed.

"And how is that, Mister Magruder?" snapped Cooke. "By beating a handful of boys into the ground?"

"We wouldn't have turned them loose, and let them do this," Magruder said, waving a hand to indicate the devastation about them. "That's for damned sure!"

"Should've hung 'em, that's what we should'a done!" glared Case Carney.

Anger welled up in Cooke's eyes as they fixed on Carney's. "And we'd have been burying a lot of our own dead right now, *Mister* Carney, and you'd be one of them. Port Rockwell would have seen to that!"

"Rockwell?" asked Johnston, eyes narrowing. "Who is this Rockwell?"

"A man I had in my command in Mexico," said Cooke. "He did the same thing to General Delgado's relief column marching on Cerro Gordo. It took the Mexican burial parties two days to clean up the mess."

"I remember that," said an infantry captain. "Chopped hell out of Delgado's lancers—rode out of the smoke and cut them down left and right."

"And you think this was the same man, Rockwell?" asked Johnston in an oddly ominous tone.

"Didn't see his face, but I'd know that buckskin of his anywhere."

Johnston nodded, then turned to the other officers. "We'll bivouac here for the night. I want a double ring of pickets out. Company commanders will report to my tent after mess. Mister Magruder, I'll expect a full inventory of losses your wagon companies have sustained. That's all, gentlemen."

Johnston turned his back on the assembly as it broke up. He stood stiffly, his hands clasped behind him as he eyed the devastation littering the valley floor. A quick count revealed approximately a fifth of the column's wagons destroyed, as well as several gun carriages and caissons. It wasn't the number of wagons destroyed that posed the problem, Johnston knew, but what those particular wagons carried— food, grain, and winter gear—all the things vital to an army crossing relatively barren country in the face of approaching winter.

Why, he wondered, didn't these marauders, and this man Rockwell, take full advantage of their opportunity to strike a real blow? In like circumstances, Johnston knew he'd have ordered his men to seek out and cut down as many of the enemy officers as possible. On reflection, he thought he had the answer: They had no intention of a head-on clash with the army, a clash they must know would end in their being crushed. This was a delaying tactic, nothing more. Well, they would be in for a big surprise; Albert Sidney Johnston's mission would be carried out to the letter, come fire, hell, or high water.

Porter Rockwell took no part in the burial of Zebulah Weems, and no comfort in the words Lot Smith spoke over the nineteen-year-old boy's shallow grave. The bullet that killed Weems had entered his back just below the right kidney, tearing out through his groin to lodge in his saddle bow. Rockwell had dug out the slug; bent and misshapen as it was, he knew it came from an army .44, a Remington.

Somehow, Zeb stayed in his saddle for the full five-mile ride back to the hidden campsite, the others unaware he'd been hit. At the camp he'd dropped his reins, then slowly leaned forward, and died, draped over his saddle horn. The patient animal stood motionless as Lot and Will Cartwright eased the dead boy from the saddle, his face still contorted from the pain he'd hidden from his companions. Gut shot, thought Rockwell angrily, no more miserable way for a man to die. No, not a man, a boy. One way or another, Rockwell intended to even the score with Case Carney before this was all over, Brigham Young be damned.

A shadow fell on Rockwell and he looked up to see the anguish-filled eyes of Lot Smith.

"We'll come back for him," Lot said softly, indicating the fresh grave at the foot of a scrub oak.

"What the hell for?" said Rockwell, easing to his feet. "He won't know."

"His folks will," answered Lot.

"A lot of good that's going to do them," bit out Rockwell. "You'd better plan on digging a lot more graves, *'Brother'* Lot!" he said acidly.

Lot looked at the ground, unsure of himself. He had never seen Rockwell so distraught. "It's time we were moving," Lot said softly.

Rockwell strode to the lariat remuda and tightened the slacked cinch on his big buckskin. Lot looked at the tall man for a long moment, his brow knit in a troubled frown.

Dobie Lewis was the last man to ride out. With a grimace of pain, he twisted in his saddle for a final look at Zebulah Weems's grave, and was guiltily grateful it was not his own.

There was something akin to smug satisfaction in Henry Magruder's face when he handed Gen. Albert Sidney Johnston the list of inventory losses. His satisfaction grew in direct proportion to the anger and dismay reflected in Johnston's face as his eyes traveled down the list.

Fully fifty percent of the army's rations had been lost, a goodly portion of winter gear and grain as well, not to mention three fieldpieces, a caisson, and two ammunition wagons. These last items were not on Magruder's list, but General Johnston was all too aware of them, having already received reports from his company commanders.

"How bad is it, Sidney?" asked Cooke.

"Bad enough. The attackers knew exactly which wagon companies to hit."

"How does this affect your plans, General?" asked Alfred Cumming, with a worried frown.

"It doesn't, Governor. We'll continue on to Bridger's Fort, as scheduled."

"Going to be tough on the men to force march on half rations, General," offered Col. Fitz-John Porter.

Johnston turned a cold eye on the older man. "I'm not in the habit of *asking* subordinates, Fitz-John. In ten days I intend to resupply at

Bridger's, and ten days after that, this army will be quartered in Salt Lake City."

"We could do it," ventured Captain Marcy, "if the weather holds."

"We *will* do it, Captain," snapped Johnston, dropping Magruder's list to the campaign desk. "Now, I suggest you all get a good night's sleep, gentlemen. We move out at first light."

As Governor Cumming and the officers filed out of the Sibley tent, Johnston asked Phil Cooke to remain for a moment. Cooke stood silent as Johnston poured two glasses of brandy, apologizing for the absence of snifters, one of the vicissitudes of life in the field. The light of the camphine lamp made the amber liquid glow in the thick-walled tumblers. Taking his chair, Johnston indicated the seat vacated by Governor Cumming. "Sit down, Phil. Good brandy isn't made to drink on your feet."

Cooke slipped into the camp chair facing Johnston's desk, noting how the overhead lamp accentuated the sharp ledge bone of the general's brow, shadowing his eyes. Both men savored the liquor in silence, then Johnston spoke. "What's next?"

"What's next *what*, Sidney?" responded Cooke, fully aware of Johnston's meaning.

"I think you know," Johnston smiled over his glass. "I want you to tell me what other little tricks your friends might have up their sleeves." A slight edge came to Johnston's voice as he continued. "After all, that's what you're here for—you're the expert, correct?"

"I never claimed to be. That was some nitwit's idea at the War Department, not mine."

"Modesty becomes you. Or is it reluctance?"

"Neither. If you want to know what they'll do, just ask yourself what *you'd* do under the same circumstances. It's as simple as that."

"I'd stand and fight. I doubt very much if your Mormon friends have the stomach to do the same."

Cooke's face tightened. "I'd appreciate it if you didn't say 'Mormon friends' as if it were some kind of insult."

Johnston chuckled easily. "No offense meant, but I think you can understand my feelings at the moment. This man Rockwell, what can you tell me about him?"

"About *him*, or what I think he's *thinking?*"

"Both," said Johnston.

Cooke savored the brandy appreciatively. "Not a great deal I can tell about his personal life. Far as I know, he really hasn't got much of one; he's a drifter, a man with a reputation of being too fond of the bottle, too quick with his guns."

"I hear they call him the 'Mormon gun.' "

"Some do," nodded Cooke. "Who told you that—Magruder?"

"That's right. Magruder's man, Carney, said Rockwell was Joseph Smith's bodyguard at the time Smith was pulled out of jail and murdered."

"So I've heard, but I've never asked Rockwell about it. There are some things you don't ask a man—not that man."

"A drunk and a gunfighter. Hardly your typical Mormon, wouldn't you say?"

"Port Rockwell is hardly your typical *anything*," said Cooke with a wry smile.

"Do I detect a subtle note of admiration in your voice?"

"Not so subtle. Porter Rockwell is one helluva man. I'd feel a lot better if he was two hundred miles back, in Platte Station. Today was just the beginning. We'll be seeing more of him, you can put money on that."

Johnston leaned back in his chair, nodding. "I intend to—a price on Rockwell's head—five hundred dollars, gold, for the man who brings him in."

Cooke straightened in his seat. "A bounty? What in hell for?"

"Destruction of United States property, assault on military personnel, and treason."

"How can you charge treason? We are not in a state of war."

"We weren't, until today. I think a military court would sustain the charge. I'm sure of it. If there's any problem about the legalities, they can be corrected, posthumously."

Cooke settled back in the chair, sipped again, nodding. "Excellent, as always, Sidney—the brandy. As for someone trying to collect that bounty on Rockwell, I doubt you'll find too many willing to take the risk. I sure as hell wouldn't."

"Time will tell," responded Johnston. "Let's get back to the present, Phil. What happens between here and Salt Lake? Where could Rockwell hit us again, and how?"

"I've been giving that some thought," Cooke said soberly. "I don't think he'll attack the column again, not head-on. He doesn't have to—the damage has been done. Men can march on half rations; draft animals won't last a week."

Johnston nodded agreement. "I'm reserving what's left of the grain for the draft animals. The saddle mounts will have to get along on forage."

"If there *is* any forage. I have a feeling we'll be seeing a few more prairie fires before we sight Salt Lake City."

Johnston's jaw tightened. "Then, by God, we'll march in on foot, and on schedule!"

"And what happens when we get there, Sidney? Do you think they'll just lie down, let you walk in over them? If I'm any judge, I'd say Brigham Young will have an army waiting for you, willing and able to fight."

"So much the better. We'll clean out this pestilence once and for all."

"As I've mentioned, that might be easier said than done."

Johnston eyed Cooke for a moment, then smiled without humor. "I'm afraid I still don't share your admiration for their fighting abilities, Philip, not if today was an example. Rockwell could have done some real damage, if he knew what he was about."

"I can't argue with that. Any man wearing shoulder boards could have been a target."

"*Would* have been a target if *I* had conducted the raid."

Cooke nodded, then lifted his glass to feign a puzzled look at it. "Damn thing must have a hole in it, Sidney. It's empty!"

Johnston smiled, reaching for the brandy bottle. "I guess we'll have to do something about that, won't we?"

A troubled frown knitted Cooke's brow as he watched the brevet brigadier pour. What was driving Johnston, he wondered; why this great urgency to push on at reckless speed? Salt Lake City wasn't going anywhere. A week or two change in the schedule was of little importance, now that they were through the divide. This brought another nagging question to mind: Why didn't Rockwell make his stand in the mountains? There were a hundred ways he could have brought the army to a standstill, at least for a time. Or was Johnston right and himself wrong? Had the ten years since he'd commanded the battalion so changed the character of these people that they no longer had the stomach to fight for what they believed in? Somehow, Cooke couldn't accept that.

He did, however, accept the freshly filled glass Johnston poured for him.

That night, the temperature dropped to near freezing, and the wind returned with a vengeance, bringing with it a sleeting rain in the lower reaches of the divide, and thick snow flurries at the higher elevations. Men and animals, soaked and chilled, huddled for body warmth, the troopers cursing the officers in their tents, and Magruder's civilians sheltering themselves in the big baggage and supply wagons, while the toopers had to brave the elements under shelter halves. There were no roaring campfires; there was little left to burn.

Morning dawned through a murky gray haze, residue of the night's storm. Glistening frost blanketed fields, men, animals, and equipment. Troopers, moving stiffly about in soggy uniforms, grumbled oaths as they struck camp, breakfasting on hardtack and water, tormented by the rich smell of coffee coming from the officer's tents. Slowly, the haze burned off as the sun rose over the white-shrouded peaks of the divide, turning the air crisp, crystalline clear.

An hour later, the army was once more on the march, anxious to leave the higher elevations behind them.

Corporal Riley was in a foul mood, but, then again, Corporal Riley was almost always in a foul mood. This morning more so than most, however, brought on by his glimpse of a big buckskin that had appeared out of the smoke the day before. It was the same horse, he was sure. The same horse whose rider had jaw-kicked him back in Platte River Station. The son of a bitch was out there, somewhere, and if there was any kind of justice in this crappy world, Corp. Terrence Riley would encounter that man and that buckskin again, and this time. . . .

Farther to the west Jim Bridger peered over the gun walk of his fort with a grimace. There were a dozen more wickiups, tepees, and buffalo-hide shelters crowding against the fort walls than there had been the night before. Bridger spotted Navajos, Sioux, Utes, Blackfoot, and Crows mingling without any trace of their traditional enmity. These were blanket Indians—old, infirm, the very young, families without young braves to provide for and protect them. They had no time or inclination for hostilities; their concern was with survival.

At a rough count Bridger estimated there were a good three hundred men, women, and children—and dogs, dogs, dogs. It was the same every year with the coming of winter; his fort became a hub, surrounded by a sea of Indians unable to survive on their own in the wilderness. It was the same with every fort on the frontier, a fact of life to be endured.

This year, however, there were more than usual, and earlier than usual. Ordinarily it was mid to late October when the blanket Indians showed up in any great numbers, shortly before the first snows. It was going to be one bitch of a winter, Bridger thought to himself, and it was coming early. The Indians were never wrong when it came to the weather.

Moving to a gun tower, he looked east toward the wagon road. No sign of Port Rockwell and his men, and no sign of the advance guard of Johnston's army. Too early for the army, he knew; another two weeks was his estimate. But Rockwell could show up anytime, and probably would.

Chapter Nine

Gaskel Romney and John Benson fought their way through the crowds at the Baltimore and Ohio Railroad's Washington depot, bone weary after twenty-six days of constant travel by coach and railcar. Four days on the grimy, jam-packed and soot-filled railway coach had taxed their endurance to the breaking point. Ninety-six hours of shrill voices, stumbling feet, sonorous snores, belches, and grunts had left them numbed, red eyed from lack of sleep.

The capital's streets were filled to overflowing, humming with both foot and carriage traffic. Silks and satins interflowed with patched hand-me-downs; grand barouches, drawn by high-stepping teams, mingled with hacks, ornate victorias, and buckboards. Shops ran the gamut, from the ultraelite, with liveried doormen, to dingy, dark-windowed holes-in-the-wall.

Their hack driver, a manumitted Negro, proud owner of his horse and vehicle, obligingly took them from Willards to the Kirkwood, from the National to Browns, knowing full well that each was booked to capacity by the hordes of legislators, lobbyists, delegations, office seekers, performers, claimants, and assorted opportunists who flooded the nation's capital each fall.

Passing the Washington Theater, on C Street, Romney got a glimpse of a billboard that told him Charlotte Cushing and the scandalous Edwin Forrest were currently appearing in a revival of the play *Fashion*. Suitable, Romney thought to himself—a farce about people putting on airs. This

was the place for it. Romney had seen the play some ten years earlier, when it had opened in New York, hailed as the first successful
American comedy. He hadn't thought much of it then, and doubted it
would be much improved with age.

The small rooming house on K Street was modest in price, by
Washington's standards, and reasonably clean and comfortable. Benson
informed the landlady they had just arrived from the New Mexico Territory,
Santa Fe, deeming it prudent at the moment to avoid any mention of
Utah.

As fate would have it, the man they had traveled so far to see had
left Washington on the very day of Benson's and Romney's arrival in
the city. Senator Houston was in New York, an aide had informed them,
a guest of the army's general in chief, Winfield Scott. No, the aide
told them, he had no idea when Senator Houston would return.

Each morning for the next three days, the two travelers picked their
way through a sea of mud, marble facings, segmented columns, cast-
iron frames, lumber, crated statuary, cranes, and workmen's sheds to
enter the scaffolded Capitol building. The original dome of the struc-
ture was being removed in order to replace it with a newly designed,
cast-iron dome, to be topped by Thomas Crawford's colossal statue
"Freedom," commissioned the year before. And each of those three
mornings they were turned away; Houston had not returned.

Fortuitously, on the fourth day they encountered Col. Thomas L.
Kane, who had also come to inquire when the senator would return
to Washington. Kane, like Sam Houston, was a friend of the Mormons—
had been since the late war with Mexico. He and Brigham Young had
corresponded for more than a decade. Romney and Benson quietly
informed the colonel that they were emissaries from Young, urgently
in need of a meeting with the senator from Texas.

As usual, the dining room at the National was filled to bursting. Kane
and his guests had to wait twenty minutes for one of the more undesirable tables, and another twenty minutes for the attention of a disobliging
waiter.

Kane recommended the broiled terrapin, a house specialty, shouting over the din to make himself heard. His guests accepted the recommendation and eyed the occupants of the huge room in open amazement. It was a scene bordering on bedlam as people wandered from
table to table, bellowing conversations over bellowed conversation,
oblivious to all else around them. A cluster of jewel-bedecked women

in watered silks held sway in the center of the room, chattering like bright-eyed magpies as they forced dining room help to find passage around them.

The accents, broad-brimmed plantation hats, and ubiquitous blue cockades told Romney and Benson that the National Hotel catered almost exclusively to Washington's Southern elements. Bits and pieces of overheard conversations fairly dripped with sedition, open and unabashed contempt for anything Yankee, anything Northern. Not once, however, did they hear a reference to Utah, or Johnston's army.

The two men from the West watched in amazement as waiters passed with huge trays laden with gourmet foods: canvasback duck, terrapin, poularde, capon, woodcock, Virginia hams, and every variety of fish, all beautifully garnished works of culinary art. There were clarets, Burgundies, sherries, and Champagnes; every imaginable kind of imported liqueurs; rich pastries of every sort; chocolate, hot and creamy; and, over it all, the rich aroma of blended coffees.

The terrapin was all Kane said it would be—succulent, almost sinfully delicious to palates accustomed to plain, though wholesome, western cooking. Submerging slight twinges of guilt, Romney and Benson cleaned their plates with relish, secretly envying Kane as he enjoyed a brandied coffee at the end of the meal. Its fragrance tantalized their olfactory senses as they sipped chilled water from cut-glass goblets.

Initially, they had been reluctant to discuss their mission in such open surroundings, but Kane assured them they had no need for apprehension. People in Washington, he told them, only heard themselves speak; listening was an unknown art in America's capital city.

The "Utah War," he went on to say, was getting little attention from anyone of late. Even the press seemed to have lost some interest in what was happening in the West. In the beginning, when charges of treason and rebellion had been leveled at the territory of Utah, and Johnston's army had begun its trek across the Great Plains, eastern newspapers headlined the events—and none with greater invective than the Horace Greeley chain. John Fremont, who during the war with Mexico had been thwarted in his attempts to gain personal control over all of California by the timely arrival of the battalion in Los Angeles, offered to raise an army of volunteers to invade Utah and stamp out the "Mormon menace." Politicians joined the cry to "disestablish" the territory of Utah. Stephen A. Douglas, for instance, had charged the Utahns with being "nine-tenths alien born," and with "forming unholy alliances with Indian tribes." It was the duty of Congress, he demanded, "to apply the knife and cut out this loathsome and disgusting ulcer. No temporizing policy, no half-way measures will answer," he had stated. "The first step should be the absolute and unconditional repeal of the Organic Act—blotting the territorial government out of existence, on the ground that they are alien enemies and outlaws, denying their allegiance and defying the authorities of the United States."

Now, according to Kane, with the army well on its way west, other stories challenged it and each other for printed space. Newspapers attached a good deal of importance to Europe, especially the imperial adventures of England. *Harper's New Monthly Magazine* and its upstart competitor, the *Atlantic Monthly,* religiously devoted article after article, column upon column to the siege of Kanpur, the relief of Lucknow, and the retaking of Delhi. Accounts of the Royal Navy's destruction of the Chinese fleet and the subsequent capture of Canton brought a tingle of pride to those Americans who could lay claim to a single drop of Anglo-Saxon blood in their veins. On the other hand, much space was given to the fact that England and France had both speculated heavily in American railroad shares—hundreds of millions of dollars. And now, both were involved in colonial wars, Britain in China and India, France in Algeria. To make matters worse, the Prussians were saber rattling again, threatening war in Europe. If that happened, the English and French could be forced to call in their American investments, and there would be financial panic in the country.

And, of course, the growing schism between North and South captured its share of the information market. Sam Houston, Kane reminded his guests, was conspicuous in that debate and also was doing all in his power to expose what had come to be called the "Mormon rebellion" as an insidious hoax, with dangerous ramifications.

Romney looked about at the nearby patrons. "I don't sense any great mood of apprehension here, Colonel."

"No," agreed Kane with a thin smile. "These people know that cotton is still king, Mister Romney. Peace or war, Europe and the world need Southern cotton. The South will survive. I have my doubts about the North."

It was almost three when Colonel Kane dropped off Benson and Romney at the K Street rooming house, with the promise he'd inform them the moment he got word of Sam Houston's return. Kane suggested it might be wise not to put in another appearance at the senator's office.

Houston had enemies in the Capitol, now more so than ever, in view of his recent challenge to Jeff Davis on the Senate floor. The less people knew, even Houston's own aide, the better.

"Time is important, Colonel," said Benson. "What are the possibilities of our getting directly to President Buchanan?"

"I'm afraid that will be up to the lady with the violet eyes," Kane smiled, "Harriet Lane, Buchanan's niece. No one gets near Old Buck without her express approval."

"A bachelor president, with a spinster niece to advise him." Romney shook his head.

Kane smiled. "I've found few men in Washington who would object to taking advice from Miss Lane, gentlemen, given the opportunity. She's a magnificent creature."

Romney and Benson stood on the sidewalk as Kane's hack drove away, sharing a feeling of helplessness. The fate of their people might well be in the delicate hands of the lady with violet eyes. "Will she believe what we have to tell her?" Benson wondered aloud.

Romney thought about this for a moment. "I doubt if our word, or proof, or evidence much matters, old friend. We're dealing with political animals here; the only truths they understand are expediency and pressure. But if what Colonel Kane told us means anything, we've got the one man in Washington who Buchanan can't afford to ignore. Sam Houston may have his share of enemies, but he has more than his share of powerful friends."

"General Scott?"

Romney nodded. "General in chief of the army."

"Under the command of Secretary of War Floyd, however."

"Cabinet members come and go," said Romney, suddenly feeling in a better mood. "Old 'Fuss and Feathers' goes on forever; he *is* the army." And that's a fact, he added silently. Winfield Scott's career had extended over half a century. A brigadier general in the War of 1812, he had risen to full commander of the army in the late Mexican war. In appreciation of his heroic service, Congress appointed him lifelong general in chief of the army, a rank held previously by only one man, the father of the country, George Washington.

In 1852 the dying Whig party had run a reluctant Scott for the presidency. The public, sensing his reluctance, gave the victory to Franklin Pierce, but only by the narrowest of margins.

Franklin Pierce, the hero of many a well-fought "bottle," as his enemies were wont to sneer, had turned out to be a one-term president, paving the way for "Bumbling" Buchanan. A pity, thought Romney. How different things might have been if Old "Fuss and Feathers" had won the election in '52. There was no doubt in Romney's mind that Scott would have been a two-term president, and be seated in the presidential chair at this very moment—when the nation so sorely needed a leader with a firm hand and a strong heart.

James Buchanan, native Pennsylvanian, fifteenth president of the United States of America, squinted across the massive desk at his trio of visitors, his brow furrowed angrily as he focused on the most imposing of the three, Senator Sam Houston. "You are not the head of a sovereign government now, Senator Houston! This is not the Republic of Texas!"

"Damned if you're not making me wish Texas still were a republic, Mister President! We'd be a damn sight better off running our own affairs!" growled Houston.

"Does General Scott share those sentiments, Senator?" asked the president's niece, Harriet Lane.

Sam Houston's attempt to mask his surprise at the query failed as he looked at the woman in the pale blue taffeta. His reaction brought a small smile to Harriet Lane's lovely lips. "There are no secrets in Washington, Senator, as I'm sure you are well aware."

"What about it, Sam?" said Buchanan. "What did Winnie have to say about our little punitive expedition to the Utah Territory?"

"Politically, a mistake. Militarily, an invitation to disaster," answered Houston.

Buchanan's voice broke in on Houston's thoughts. "I take it you agree with General Scott, Senator?"

"In the military sense, you're damned right I do, Mister President."

"And politically?"

"There we had differences," responded Houston with impatience. "Let's get down to cases, Jim; forget all this senator–mister-president crap and talk plain turkey, man to man."

Harriet Lane's well-formed lips thinned as she moved with a rustle of taffeta to place a hand on the president's shoulder, cutting off his intended response to Houston's plea. "It wasn't my impression man-to-man talk required the usage of profanity, Senator Houston. Am I incorrect?"

"Your pardon, Miss Lane," said Houston with a note of asperity.

Damn! thought Romney, Houston's making a botch of it. It was clear to anyone with half an eye that Harriet Lane was the real power behind the Buchanan throne, as everyone in Washington, with the seeming exception of Sam Houston, was well aware.

It had taken a week to get an appointment with the president, and now Houston was alienating the one person who had any real influence on him, the lady with the violet eyes.

Since their arrival in the nation's capital, Romney and Benson had learned a great deal about Harriet Lane. They knew that she had accompanied the bachelor president throughout his political career, from the Congress to ambassadorial posts at the courts of St. Petersburg and St. James, and from there to the presidential mansion. It was commonly acknowledged that her presence on the campaign stump garnered more votes for Buchanan than his speeches and platform. The woman's popularity was incredible, as evidenced by the latest song currently making the rounds in Washington, from cutpurse saloons to the music rooms of H Street mansions, dedicated to her by the composer of "Listen to the Mocking Bird."

There was much more to Harriet Lane than her undeniable physical beauty; there was a razor-sharp mind behind those magnificent violet eyes. A society columnist had unabashedly compared her favorably to one of the truly great women of history, Eleanor of Aquataine. There were others, however, who likened her to one of the more infamous of her gender, Lucrezia Borgia. What Borgia did with poison, they maintained, Harriet did with a whispered word in the ear of James Buchanan. The effects of such a word might not be physically lethal but were, without question, politically fatal. No one in Washington, Northerner or Southerner, unionist or disunionist, would knowingly offend her—no one except the man Benson and Romney had chosen to lay their case before the president, the senior senator from Texas. Well, too late now.

"You are an incautious man, Senator," said Harriet Lane in her softly rich contralto.

"A bloody fool is more like it!" growled Buchanan. "What would you have me do, Houston? Let this rabble run roughshod over the law of the land?" he added sardonically.

"Nobody is running—"

"Don't interrupt!" snapped the president, silencing Houston. "The day I took office I swore an oath, Senator, to defend this nation against all enemies, foreign *and* domestic! I intend to honor that oath!"

"We are not the enemy, Mister President," blurted Benson. "The loyalty of our people goes without question."

"Our people!" snorted Buchanan. "Your very choice of the word gives you the lie, sir! This is one nation, not yours, not ours! And, by thunder, I intend to keep it that way. There will be no 'Land of Deseret,' no sectional clericism, no nation within a nation! I will not tolerate it!"

"You're talking through a plugged hat, Jim!" thundered Houston. "Sectionalism is as much a part of this country as the rivers and land! Winnie Scott knows it, I know it, and so do you. He called it a goulash, and I agree. But goulash can be a damned tasty dish, if you can keep all the ingredients in one pot."

"Which is exactly what the president's administration is determined to do, Senator," said Harriet Lane. "My uncle was elected on a platform of national unity, sir—his promise to hold this nation together. He must keep that promise!"

Houston fixed a hard eye on the tall blond woman at Buchanan's shoulder. "Then, Miss Lane, I suggest the president review his cabinet appointments. There *are* seeds of rebellion germinating, not in Utah, ma'am, but here in Washington, and in high office. Look about you, Miss Lane; the blue cockade of disunion is everywhere, on the tongue if not the lapel."

"Difference of opinion does not spell disloyalty, Sam," growled Buchanan. "The president's cabinet should be representative of *all* sections of the country. You're no stranger to the Madisonian concept; it's what makes our form of government unique—representation of all points of view, a balanced give-and-take."

"Does that balanced give-and-take include the people of Utah, Jim? Or are they the exception?"

Buchanan slammed a heavy fist to the desk top. "There *are* no exceptions! I would have acted in precisely the same way if the people of my own state had rebelled against federal authority! I'd crush them before the poison of anarchy could spread!"

"And I'd do the same, Jim," said Houston, "if I were sure there *was* anarchy, there *was* rebellion. But I'd make damn sure of the facts before I sent an army marching in to incite rebellion where none existed before.

There are a good many thousands of people in Utah, Jim, and by God, if you're making a mistake, and I think you are, you'll have your rebellion, and an army ten times the size of Johnston's won't be able to put it down. They won't run, not this time. They'll fight!"

There was a heavy silence; Buchanan looked to Benson and Romney and saw the truth of Houston's words reflected in their eyes. A sigh escaped the president. "Why in the hell couldn't you people have gone somewhere else. . . ."

"We did, President, twice before. There won't be a third time."

"Tell me *that* isn't the talk of rebellion, Sam!" challenged Buchanan.

"Not rebellion, sir," said Benson. "Survival. We ask no more than the rights given to other citizens of this country. We will accept no less."

"Those rights do not include burning down a federal courthouse, destroying public records, and running lawfully appointed officials out of the territory, sir!"

"Lies, Mister President. Lies told by petty little men, angry because our people wouldn't sit idly by and let them steal the wealth of the territory," said Romney. "President Young sent us here to—"

"There is only one president in this country, Mister Romney, and you're looking at him," Buchanan broke in.

"I did not mean president in the secular sense, sir."

"Why *were* you sent here, gentlemen?" asked the implacable Harriet Lane, a faint twist to her lips.

"To present the truth, Miss Lane," said Romney. "We are the victims of vicious lies. Presi . . . Governor Young—"

"*Mister* Young," snapped Buchanan. "The governor of Utah Territory is now Alfred Cumming."

"Will you let the man have his say, Jim!" rumbled Houston.

"Do you have proof, Mister Romney," said Harriet, overriding Houston's request, "proof that your protestations of allegiance to the Union are valid?"

Romney and Benson exchanged a look of despair. "At this point we have only our word and our honor to support our petition," replied the latter.

"How inconvenient," smiled Harriet unconvincingly.

"OH DAMN!" blurted the frustrated Houston.

"My apologies, Senator," interjected Harriet with acid sweetness.

"I imagine you're more comfortable dealing with squaws. Would it help if I removed my shoes?"

Houston bristled, his face darkening angrily. Then, although he fought desperately to maintain his demeanor, he suddenly burst into hearty laughter. After a moment, to everyone's surprise, Harriet Lane joined him, her violet eyes dancing with a sudden humor.

"On the contrary, my dear Miss Lane," choked Houston. "It is I who must apologize. Indeed, I am no match for you. I humbly surrender, and place myself at your mercy." His hands were outstretched in resignation.

"Senator Houston," was her composed reply, "I must tell you that I have admired your courage and your integrity since I was a small child, but never more than at this moment."

Bowing, the six-foot-four senator from Texas slowly took her soft, manicured hand in his great paw, and kissed her fingers ever so gently.

The tension that had filled the president's office disappeared.

Then Harriet Lane looked at the two wide-eyed, open-mouthed petitioners. "What would you have the president do, gentlemen?"

"With all due respect, ma'am," offered Romney, quickly regaining his composure, "what should have been done to start with—send someone to Utah to investigate the charges against us."

"That's all we're asking," added Benson, addressing the president. "A fair hearing, nothing more."

"You'll have your hearing, sir, when Governor Cumming and Judge Dawson arrive in Salt Lake City. If what you say is factual, and there *is* no insurrection, you have nothing to fear."

"Haven't you heard a thing we've been telling you, Jim?" snapped Houston. "Dawson and Cumming are with Johnston's troops! Once that army sets foot in the basin, it's all over. The people of the territory will look on it as an army of occupation. There are already rumors that Johnston intends to arrest Brigham Young and place the territory under martial law."

"And so he will, if the need be there."

"It will, Mister President, because Johnston will create that need, force it if necessary!"

"And why would General Johnston do that, Senator?" asked Harriet Lane.

Houston took a deep breath, choosing his words carefully. "Because I don't think Albert Sidney Johnston, or the men behind him, give two hoots in hell about what's happening in Utah. They're using this so-called rebellion as an excuse to get the largest single body of troops in the country within striking distance of California!"

A moment of stark silence fell. Then, James Buchanan broke that silence, an ominous tone to his voice. "Do you realize the implications of what you've said, Sam? You've just accused a career officer and a member of my cabinet of conspiracy to treason."

Houston's jaw jutted firmly. "Not just one cabinet member, Jim. I can think of at least three, not to mention a whole gaggle of congressmen and senators, Jeff Davis being high hog of the litter. Come spring, Jim, I'd say your unity platform is going to come tumbling down around your ears. There's more to this disunion business than just talk. If I'm right, and Winnie Scott seems to think I am, the Southern legislatures are going to vote for secession. Your promise to hold this country together won't mean a thing without troops to back it up."

"You mentioned California, Senator," said Harriet Lane. "California came into the Union as a free state."

"By the skin of its teeth, ma'am. A handful of votes and it could have gone the other way—proslavery. Fremont took California with less than two hundred men. Think what Johnston can do with thousands. Think of what will happen to this Union if California joins in secession. It'll be the end."

Buchanan suddenly looked weary, defeated. "What do you suggest, Sam?" he asked softly.

"Cover yourself, Jim. Send someone you trust to Utah to determine the situation. If there is no insurrection, recall Johnston before he gets to the Salt Lake Basin and creates one."

"And if there *is* rebellion—what then, Senator?" asked Harriet Lane.

"Then we all lose, Miss Lane—the president, the people of Utah, and the country."

"If there's any truth in your speculations, sir," she reasoned, "it's already too late. General Johnston's troops will have crossed the Platte by now."

"It's a long five hundred miles from the Platte to the Salt Lake Basin, ma'am," said Romney. "And I have a feeling that General Johnston is going to run into some delays."

"Delays?" snapped Buchanan suspiciously. "What delays?"

"That's rough country out there, Mister President," said Benson, "and not much forage this late in the year."

"He's right, Jim," said Houston. "If Johnston can average ten to twelve miles a day, he'll be doing good. We can have a man in Salt Lake in five weeks, before Johnston can get within a hundred miles of the city."

"This man you keep referring to, Senator," said Harriet Lane, "I take it you have someone in mind?"

Houston nodded firmly. "I do, ma'am, subject to the president's approval."

"I'm listening," said Buchanan.

"Tom Kane," responded Houston.

"Colonel Kane, of the militia?" questioned Harriet.

"That's the one," nodded Houston. "He can be on a packet boat to the isthmus within forty-eight hours. Three or four days to cross, then take a coastal steamer to California, and by coach and horseback the rest of the way to Salt Lake."

"I know Tom Kane," said Buchanan. "A good man."

"You won't find better, sir," agreed Houston.

"There's one problem you seem to be omitting, Sam," sighed Buchanan. "It'll take another five weeks or more for Kane to return with his report on conditions in Salt Lake. By then Johnston will be in the city."

"That's a problem readily resolved, uncle," said the lady with the violet eyes. "Colonel Kane can carry orders to Governor Cumming, instructing him to tell General Johnston to turn back, should the reports of rebellion prove false."

Buchanan shot her a sharp look. "And if they do not?"

"Then the general will occupy the city," she said without emotion. "The sooner Colonel Kane leaves for the Utah Territory, the sooner we'll have a resolution of those doubts, uncle," her words more directed at Sam Houston than the president of the United States.

Buchanan, his eyes moving from Houston to his niece, sighed again. "I can't argue against the both of you. Al'right, Sam, I'll have my secretary draft the required document for Colonel Kane to deliver to Governor Cumming, giving him the authority to order Johnston out of the territory should he deem such action appropriate."

"Generals have a way of ignoring orders from territorial governors, Mister President," said Houston with a faint smile of recollection. "I was pretty good at it myself. Of course, *that* governor happened to be Mexican."

"If you have a point, Senator, make it!"

"A direct order from the commander in chief, Mister President. There's no way Johnston can ignore that, not before Jefferson Davis and his cronies vote disunion."

"Lord, how I despise that word," mumbled Buchanan. "So be it," he continued with a nod of resignation. "But that order will be given to General Johnston at the discretion of Governor Cumming, not Colonel Kane. Is that clear?"

"Wouldn't have it any other way, Jim," grinned Houston with a satisfied nod. "Your choice of Cumming was a wise one. I know him well. He is a man of unquestioned integrity, and although he is a proud Southerner, he is no Copperhead. He'll do the honorable thing."

A look of incalculable relief flooded the faces of John Benson and Gaskel Romney; they had accomplished what they'd traveled two thousand miles to do, thanks to Sam Houston and, in no small measure, the lady with the violet eyes.

At two o'clock the following afternoon, Col. Thomas L. Kane, wearing mufti, was on a coach headed for Charleston, where he would board the *Masapequa,* a side-wheeler, bound for Colón. From there he'd cross the isthmus by train to take a coastal steamer to the California port of San Pedro, then overland through the San Bernardino Mountains. Finally, he'd connect with the Old Spanish Trail that would take him north along the western flank of the Wasatch Range and into Salt Lake City—a grueling last leg of a nearly eight-hundred-mile ride between the port town and his destination. There was one minor consolation— he wouldn't have to worry about weather . . . he hoped.

Tucked safely in Kane's traveling belt was an envelope bearing the presidential seal, addressed to the newly appointed governor of the Utah Territory, the Honorable Alfred Cumming.

Chapter Ten

The crossing at Black's Fork would be the ideal site, Lot was quick to agree. Here, the Green River averaged five feet in depth, and was a good two hundred yards in width. A mile upstream were a number of feeder branches that cut through low hills. It would be no trick at all to dam up the largest of these streams, and drop the river's level to almost nothing. There was something else that made this spot ideal for their purposes: The soft, saturated sand of the river bottom made it imperative to cross at speed, even in the best of times. Anything slow moving was sure to be bogged down.

A mile up from the crossing they found what they were looking for, a place where the largest stream poured through a narrow gap. Beyond the gap was a shallow basin, which would allow a buildup of water when the stream was dammed. Riders were dispatched to keep an eye on Johnston's progress, and work was started on the dam.

The temperature had dropped to near freezing as Rockwell and the others, stripped to the waist, battling cold and current, struggled to construct a seven-foot-high wall across the thirty-foot-wide gap, cutting off the stream's flow. In two fourteen-hour days the work was done, and the crossing at Black's Fork was no longer five feet deep, no longer fast flowing. Johnston's army was only a day away.

As usual, Jud Stoddard had done twice his share of the work, refusing to take time out at the warm-up fires, kept going to take the chill out of the men's bones. And now, Jud was paying the price. A deep, wrenching cough racked his small body, and his eyes were dull with fever. Rockwell had seen enough of pneumonia to recognize the symptoms. So had the others.

Over feeble protests Jud was placed on a travois and warmly bundled for the trip to Bridger's Fort. Rockwell knew that the "crisis" would come on the third or fourth day, before Lot and the others could get Jud to the fort.

It was in God's hands; Jud would survive the crisis, or he would not. If he did, he'd still be in need of care, and the closest place to get that care was the fort, at the hands of Little Fawn and her cousins.

The Indians, as every frontiersman was aware, could do more for the winter lung sickness than any high-toned doctor from the eastern medical schools. That was a fact.

Some years earlier Rockwell had come down with the lung fever, up in the Nebraska Territory. The last thing he'd remembered was falling out of his saddle in the middle of a frozen plain. He'd awakened stark naked in a Dakota sweat pit. The steam and Indian poultices had drawn the sickness out of his lungs. It was several days before Rockwell had the strength to seat his horse and leave the Dakota village. But he left alive.

Over the past weeks Rockwell had developed a genuine affection for "Little Jud," as he thought of him. Stoddard, like most men of small physical stature, made a conscious effort to make up in deed what he lacked in size, always doing more than was asked of him. The thing about Jud was that he did it quietly.

Lot and the others moved out at daybreak, Jud Stoddard strapped securely in the travois, still protesting he was able to ride. Lot had wanted to remain behind with Rockwell, but, as the tall man told him, it took only one man to light a match. Too, Will Cartwright and Harve Arnold, who had been sent some miles east to keep tabs on the army, would join Rockwell soon. "See you at Bridger's," Rockwell said. "Get there fast!"

The column of volunteers rode out, Lot at the point, and Rockwell knew his first moments of solitude in weeks. It felt good. He moved down to the base of the riprap dam to check the fuses for the tenth time, hoping there was no water seepage that would affect the kegs of black powder buried deep in the dam's base.

The backed-up water was now within a foot of the dam's lip, and still slowly rising. The basin beyond was now a fair-to-middlin'-sized lake. Rockwell tried to mentally calculate the acre-foot volume of the water held back by the dam, but was skeptical of his accuracy. Of one thing he was certain—when that dam blew, there was going to be one helluva lot of water looking for someplace to go.

Rockwell and the volunteers had ridden hard to get to Black's Fork Crossing well ahead of Johnston's relatively slow-moving army, covering a distance in two days that would take the army five.

This was the fifth day.

It was near noon when Will Cartwright and Harve Arnold rode in to inform Rockwell that Johnston's army had broken night camp and was on the march. "They're moving right along, Major Rockwell," said young Will. "Should get to the crossin' by three, the way I calculate."

"Where are the others?" asked Arnold, scanning a look around the abandoned campsite.

"Sent them on to Bridger's; no need for them to be here. You can catch up with them, if you've a mind to."

The boys exchanged a look, then both grinned, shaking their heads in unison. "Shucks no!" said Will Cartwright, surveying the riprap dam. "Wouldn't want to miss seeing *that* go up!"

"The column," asked Rockwell. "Where are the supply wagons placed?"

The young men's faces quickly sobered. "Smack in the middle, Major Rockwell," said Will. "And they got infantry on flank march."

"Got 'em boxed in real good. No way to get near 'em without fightin' your way through," added Harve Arnold.

"Fine," nodded Rockwell. "Long as they're bunched up, I don't care what they have around them."

It wasn't quite two thirty when Johnston's point riders reached the east bank of Black's Fork Crossing. Through Cephus James's telescope Porter Rockwell had a clear view of the distant horsemen. One of the riders was Hickok—again.

Within ten minutes the riverbank was crowded with officers and men. Beyond them, the army had ground to a halt, the rear elements still a good three miles from the river.

Rockwell focused his glass on the group of men surrounding the officer wearing the hussar's dolman. Even at this distance he could make out the single star on the officer's shoulder boards—General

Johnston. Phil Cooke was in animated conversation with the general. Rockwell would have given a quart of good sipping whiskey to be able to hear what Cooke was saying.

What the colonel was saying was, "I don't like it, Sidney. I've crossed here a half-dozen times, and I've never seen the river this low."

"Are you suggesting we look a gift horse in the mouth, Phil?" smiled Johnston.

"That depends on *whose* gift it is, sir."

Johnston swung his look to the captain. "Marcy?"

"I'm afraid I have to agree with Colonel Cooke, General. That bottom looks awful spongy, damn near quicksand. We'd be better off with high water; at least that way we'd have some buoyancy for the supply wagons."

"But not for our artillery. We can't have it both ways, Captain."

"Yessir," nodded Marcy, properly chastened.

"I hate to be insistent," pressed Cooke, "but there's a good crossing about nine miles south of here. We—"

"Would lose time," Johnston finished for him. The general fished his watch from an inner pocket and snapped open the gold case. "We still have ample daylight to get across and set up camp on the other side."

"I think you're making a mistake," Cooke persisted. "At least let me send out patrols to scout those hills. We won't lose that much time if we cross in the morning."

Johnston eyed Cooke, then turned to the other officers. "Follow me, gentlemen!"

Spurring his mount, Johnston galloped down the bank into the shallow water, the big gelding kicking up a spray as it thundered across to the opposite bank, followed by Captain Marcy, Col. Fitz-John Porter, and a number of cavalry and dragoon officers.

Cooke remained where he was until the others were across. He surveyed the wooded hills upstream, and damned Johnston for his obstinacy. Five minutes later Cooke was on the far bank with the command staff.

Rockwell lowered the glass with a relieved smile. "You had me worried there for a bit, Phil," he murmured.

"You say something?" Harve Arnold asked.

"Nothing worth repeating. Might as well settle down for a spell," he added, rolling over on his back and tilting his hat down over his eyes. "Be awhile before those wagons reach the river."

Infantry crossed on the double-quick, cavalry and dragoons at the gallop. The artillerymen lashed their animals into a run as they approached the crossing, depending on speed to keep the heavy gun carriages and caissons from bogging down in the water-logged sand of the river bottom. Within an hour well over half the troopers and all the artillery were across, and ground was being cleared for a campsite.

Cooke stood on the bank as the carriage carrying Governor Cumming and Judge Dawson began the crossing. On the far side he could see Magruder's men fanning out their wagons as they approached the bank, obviously intending to cross on a wide front rather than single column. It was the smart thing to do, Cooke approved; less chance of bogging down in the churned-up river bottom that way. Cooke didn't think much of Henry Magruder as a man, but he did seem to know his business.

If anything was going to happen, it would be in the next few minutes, Cooke told himself as he squinted at the hills a short distance upriver. And, something *was* going to happen, he hadn't a doubt in the world. As a young field officer in Mexico, Cooke had learned to trust his instincts; and now those instincts were sending him warning signals he couldn't ignore. He turned to look at Johnston, some fifty feet away, in conversation with Marcy and Fitz-John. At that moment the general's eyes found his. Johnston's brow lifted slightly; a thin smile came to his lips, patronizing. Cooke looked away, feeling a surge of anger. Damn the man!

A shout from across the river brought Cooke around to see the wagoneers lashing their animals to top speed as they raced toward the river on a front ten wagons wide, quickly followed by another ten, and another.

From a mile away Rockwell saw what Cooke saw, but from another angle. The first line of wagons was approaching center stream when he touched the match to the six-foot length of fuse at the dam's base. "Let's get the hell out of here!" he shouted to Harve and Will, running for his buckskin.

The fast-burning fuse line hissed and sputtered along its length to disappear into the face of the tightly packed earth-and-log dam. For a brief moment there was a sudden stillness, then, almost lazily, the dam began to lift, upward and outward, as though thrust up by some giant, unseen hand. Then it fragmented, hurtling rocks, earth, flame, and logs skyward with an ear-shattering roar. A thirty-foot length of the dam had been dissolved, freeing a near million gallons of pent-up water to the pull of gravity.

Colonel Cooke felt the jolt of the explosion before its sound reached his ears. There was a sinking feeling in his stomach as he pulled his eyes from the strings of wagons making the passage. Fully half had already been committed to the crossing, the first string not more than fifty yards from the west bank and safety, but Cooke knew they'd not reach it. His instincts had been right, and now he knew why the river had been so low—a dam!

The shock waves of the blast rolled over Johnston's army, drawing every eye upstream to the column of smoke and debris that rose above the trees a thousand yards distant. The noise of the explosion was followed by a deeper sound, a rumbling thunder that grew louder with each passing second. Cooke looked quickly at General Johnston and the men clustered around him. Johnston's eyes met Cooke's for a brief fraction of time, and Cooke saw rage in the general's eyes. In spite of himself Cooke felt a momentary satisfaction in Johnston's pain. He'd warned the man.

Several hundred yards upstream, it appeared—a wall of rushing, debris-filled water, taller than the highest wagon bow, racing toward the trapped wagons with express-train speed. Panicky wagoneers lashed at their animals in a frenzy; others deserted driver's benches to splash for dry land and safety. A dozen mounted troopers plunged into the river in a vain attempt to rescue the abandoned teams.

Then it was upon them—a maelstrom of raging power that ripped, tore, and splintered everything in its path, tossing men, wagons, and animals to its crest, or rolling over them to grind them along the river bottom. A handful of wagons managed to avoid immediate destruction, being carried downstream at millrace speed for a distance until they too were torn asunder by the rampaging waters, spilling food supplies, camp gear, tents, spare weapons, and every variety of personal luggage that had been stored for transport.

The surge passed, quickly followed by another as more of the dam face gave way upstream.

The first impact had hurled Gilly Walsh, a Missouri skinner, back into the body of his wagon, the parted reins still in his hands. The wagon went over broadside, snapping the single-tree. The power of the water crushed the bows, wrapping Gilly in the stout canvas as the wagon body was sucked under. It scraped along the bottom until it came to rest with several others, broken and battered on a cutbank outcropping some hundred yards downriver.

James Butler Hickok raced his mount to the cutbank and dived from the saddle, a six-inch blade locked firmly in his right fist. He came up near the cluster of wreckage, sucked in a quick breath, then dived again.

Gilly Walsh knew he was a dead man—the water-pressed canvas would be his tomb—still he scrambled to free himself, fighting desperately to hold what little air was left in his tortured lungs.

Blinded by the detritus churned up by the swift-moving water, Hickok worked by feel, hacking away at the canvas locked around Walsh's body. Then, suddenly, he felt living flesh. A final cut, one that sliced a deep gash in Gilly Walsh's thigh, also freed him.

Both men broke to the surface, and willing hands pulled them from the river's clutches. Gilly Walsh was happy as hell; he could feel the pain in his thigh, feel the thick red blood on his fingers. He was alive! Squinting through sand-filled eyes, he gasped to the man standing over him, "I owe you, Mister. . . ."

The tall man nodded, sheathed his knife, and moved away.

Bill Donner, an Arkansas mule skinner, took the longest ride that day. His teamless wagon had been carried almost a mile downstream, high on the crest of the first surge, the white canvas sparkling like the sails of an ancient galleon soaring on Caribbean waves. The end came with a grinding crunch as the wagon slammed into a boulder thrusting high up from the riverbed. Donner was thrown from his perch by the impact and crashed violently against the boulder. He heard the bone in his arm snap like a dried stick. Strangely, he felt no pain as he locked the fingers of his good hand on a rocky projection, holding tight against the pull of the river sucking at his dangling legs. His galleon was no more, just splintered boards and rent canvas, still voyaging downstream. Donner heard a voice, "Hang on there, bub! We're coming!"

Now the pain came. Donner pressed his face against the rough surface of the boulder that had both injured him and preserved him. "You betcha sweet ass I'll hang on," he groaned.

Mort Coleman, a Georgia teamster, went to the bottom three times before he was caught up by a massive, fast-moving tree stump. Clinging to a cluster of thick roots, he went spinning, bobbing, and swirling downriver, first this way, then that. Half drowned, retching, eyes unable to focus, scared crapless, Mort still could function enough to compare his situation with something he'd read, a story about whaling men, what they called a "Nantucket sleigh ride." Damned if he wasn't on one!

A looping rope snagged a section of root and Coleman found himself and his impromptu whaleboat being pulled to the shore. From that moment on, Mort Coleman was determined he'd read no more stories about the sea.

The crest of the final surge passed, leaving behind it a churning mass of debris dotted with the bobbing heads of men and animals. Troopers, mounted and on foot, plunged into the now-chest-high water to pull dazed, half-drowned teamsters and draft animals to dry land.

A jagged tree limb speared Corporal Breen's mount, tearing a gaping wound in its flank. The mare went down with a scream, carrying Breen with it. The young trooper found himself pinned by the wildly thrashing animal, his mouth filled with bottom mud. Dimly, he heard a muffled shot, then strong hands brought him to the surface.

Jubal Hathaway, his entire head bandaged save slits for his eyes and mouth, tangled in the traces of his team but fought his way clear. His wagon was a goner, its bed stove in, its contents carried away by the rushing waters. Jubal cursed aloud, thinking of the jugs of trade whiskey he'd buried beneath the bundles of army greatcoats—gone! The big man pulled himself to the bank, his face bleeding profusely again, ignoring the outstretched hand of an injured driver seeking assistance.

Case Carney threw a puzzled look at Hank Magruder. The man was actually smiling. "I don't see nothin' to smile about," rumbled Carney.

Magruder's smile widened. "That's the difference in you and me, Carney. You see what's in front of your eyes; I look at what's beyond."

Carney waited for Magruder to elaborate. He didn't.

Alfred Cumming silently thanked his coach driver for not abandoning him and Lamar Dawson to the fury of the watery onslaught. The coach had been twenty yards into the stream when the explosion came. The driver lashed his team clear of the flanking, heavier wagons, first ahead, then around to return to the east bank. The wall of water had missed them by a fraction of a minute. Cumming knew that the comparatively light vehicle would have been crushed, smashed to fragments by the relentless force of the raging waters; and he and Dawson would have fared no better.

Concealed by a stand of trees creating a hillock, Porter Rockwell, Will Cartwright, and Harve Arnold had a clear view of their handiwork, a very satisfying view indeed. Then, mounting up, they rode west.

It was a miracle, thought Phil Cooke as he moved among the injured being treated by the medical officer and his assistants. Broken bones, cuts, scrapes, and bruises, some severe, but not one life had been lost, excluding the animals. A good thing that dam hadn't been built closer to the crossing. If it had been, there'd be burial parties at work now.

Rockwell had missed his chance again, just as he had with the fire. Both instances could have taken a heavy toll of casualties; it was just a matter of timing and location.

Then, a thought struck Cooke—*did* Rockwell miss his chances, or was it by design? Was he making a conscious effort to avoid taking human life? The more he thought about it, the more certain he became— design! The army could tolerate the losses of equipment. The loss of men's lives would not be tolerated. The people of Utah would be made to pay in kind, and with a vengeance.

At that moment Rockwell's plan became clear to the cavalry colonel. Rockwell was playing a delaying game; he had no intention of meeting Johnston's army head-on. He was attempting to cripple the army, bleed it of supplies until Johnston was forced to turn back to the Platte. Yes! Rockwell was buying time—but for what?

Cooke didn't know the answer to that question, but he had a damned good idea of where Porter Rockwell and his men would strike next— Bridger's Fort.

Far into the night, torch-bearing troopers ranged downriver, scouring both banks for salvageable goods from the supply wagons; there wasn't much. Johnston's Sibley tent and his campaign chest were recovered, as well as a fair portion of the heavier camp gear that had lodged on a sandbar. The feed grain sacks were nowhere to be found.

Lieutenant Coy, proud owner of the Whitworth sharpshooting rifle, thanked his stars for having the foresight to keep the expensive weapon with him, lashed behind the cantle of his saddle. A year's pay might have been washed away had he left the rifle in the baggage wagon. Other officers hadn't been so fortunate; prized possessions were irretrievably lost, not to mention spare uniforms, tents, and camp furniture. The lower ranks were, in a way, more fortunate. Anything of value they had, they carried with them.

Immediately after the explosion, a number of dragoons and cavalrymen had charged toward the column of smoke still hanging in the air. Johnston snapped an order to his bugler: sound recall. Pursuit, he knew, was an exercise in futility, chasing will-o'-the-wisps. But the time would come, he vowed to himself.

Private Coogan discovered a tin box half buried in the silt along the east bank of the river. Lettering on the box told him it was the property of Capt. Werner Frietag, A Company, 2d Cavalry. Moving off into some concealing scrub, Coogan pried open the box and was well rewarded for his efforts. Along with some letters and a silver-framed daguerreotype of a horse-faced young woman, he found a chamois sack containing a half-dozen octagon-shaped California gold slugs—fifty-dollar gold pieces—weighing two and a half ounces each.

Coogan couldn't believe his luck—three hundred dollars, gold! A bleedin' bloody fortune! As he pocketed the coins and dropped to his knees to begin scooping out a hole in the sand to hide the tin box, Corp. Terrence Riley stepped out of the shadows. "What 'cha got there, Coogy? Find something good?"

Coogan jumped. "Kee——Riley! You scared the crap outta me!"

Regaining his composure, Coogan indicated the box and its contents, shrugging. "Naw, nothing worth bothering with, just some letters and stuff."

In one smooth movement Riley stepped in to grasp the smaller man by his collar and jerk him to his feet. "You wouldn't hold out on a buddy, would you, Coogy?" he glared, thrusting his lantern jaw within an inch of Coogan's nose.

"Hey! C'mon, Riley! I wouldn't do that. C'mon, let me go, will ya!"

"Sure, just as soon as I see what you put in your pocket," said the big man.

Coogan tried to twist away as Riley's free hand dived for the pocket containing the gold coins. It was a futile effort on Coogan's part. Riley's eyes widened as they registered what he held in his hand, then narrowed viciously. "So you wouldn't hold out, ye little scut!"

"I was gonna tell you, Riley, honest I was. I just—"

Riley's fist closed over the heavy gold coins, then smashed brutally into Coogan's unprotected face. The blow sent the small man reeling. Tripping over a root, he went down. Dazed, he tried to push himself to his feet, but he never made it. Riley's camp knife went deep into Coogan's back, just above his right kidney. The corporal held Coogan's face in the smothering sand until all movement ceased.

"Damn!" Riley growled to himself as his anger subsided. He hadn't meant to kill Coogan. When the rage was on him, he lost all control.

But self-recrimination was not a luxury Riley was prone to indulge in for any length of time. What's done is done he said to himself. Completing the hole Coogan had begun, he dumped in the tin box and covered it over. A quick look around told him that none of the other searching troopers was in view. Effortlessly, he lifted Coogan's body and carried it the few paces to the river, then watched it float downstream.

The greatest and most critical loss was among the slow moving, heavily laden commissary wagons. Broadsided by the powerful surge, they were carried away, rolling and tumbling like so many wooden chips in a millrace. The smashed and battered hulks spewed out cases of tinned food, biscuits, sacks of coffee, countless hundred-weight bags of flour, and sundry other foodstuffs. What didn't sink to the bottom, or disintegrate into the tempestuous foam, ended up miles downstream, dispersed and damaged beyond practical recovery.

As Magruder's men and the troopers salvaged what they could of the damaged wagons, cannibalizing wheels, bows, lumber, and canvas from those wrecked beyond repair, company cooks sliced flank and rump meat from the draft animals that had been slaughtered because of injury. In two or three days the thin strips of meat would airdry, becoming jerky, a welcome supplement to men who would now be marching on less than half rations.

Magruder made a tally of the remaining wagons. They totaled two hundred and nineteen, just over half of the original number that had left Platte River Station. A number of the lost wagons were the property of Magruder and Company, leased to the army. He'd bill the War Department for triple the replacement costs. And they'd pay, just as they'd continue to pay on his contract for the growing number of teamsters who now, through no fault of their own, had no wagons to drive. But all this was secondary to Magruder. The real money would come when the Magruder Mail and Freight Company was reestablished in the Utah Territory. And this time, he'd have an army to back him up.

"Filthy no good murderin' bushwhackers!" snarled Corp. Terrence Riley when a search party brought in Coogan's body the following morning. "They kilt' him, Ez! They kilt' poor Coogy!" Riley's feigned anger was matched by a genuine outrage in the other troopers gathered about the remains of Pvt. Walter B. Coogan, 2d U.S. Cavalry, native of Elmira, New York.

"Killin' fair is one thing," growled an iron-jawed infantry sergeant, "back stabbin' a man is another." The sentiment was shared whole-heartedly by both officers and men.

Phil Cooke voiced the unspoken question in General Johnston's mind: "Why would they do it? What would it get them? It doesn't make sense."

"I can tell you what it will get them, Colonel," Johnston answered icily, "a hangman's rope for every armed rebel we take. And, I assure you, *that* will make sense."

Johnston turned to the infantry sergeant. "Bury him. We move out in thirty minutes." Turning on his heel, he stalked away.

"It *was* a damned fool thing for them to do, Colonel," said Marcy, falling in with Cooke as he strode away from the cluster about Coogan's body. "The general will get his pound of flesh for this, make no mis-take."

Cooke swung around to face the younger officer, anger sparking in his eyes. "And what about you, Marcy? How many Mormon scalps do you plan to hang on your belt?"

Marcy was momentarily taken aback by Cooke's sudden vehemence, then he bristled, "With all due respect, that was uncalled-for, Colonel!"

The anger went out of Cooke's eyes. "You're right, Captain, it *was* uncalled-for. My apologies."

"Forget it, sir," said Marcy, relaxing the stiffness in his face. "We're all a little on edge. But," he continued thoughtfully, "if you're right, if the Mormons weren't responsible, that means—"

"One of our own men," Cooke finished for him.

Marcy frowned, unconvinced. "I can't accept that, Colonel. If Coogan had had *that* kind of enemy, someone would have known and spoken up. There are no secrets in army barracks."

"Except from the officers," Cooke added wryly. "Whoever the man is, whatever his reason, he gave Johnston the excuse he's been look-ing for. There won't be any appeals to reason now, Captain. Our bre-vet general is going to have his war."

"Excuse me, gents," a voice came from behind them. Marcy and Cooke turned to see the tall young man in buckskins.

James Butler Hickcok's smile was one of easy self-confidence. "Hope I'm not interrupting anything."

"Nothing that can't wait," said Cooke with a slight frown. "What can we do for you?"

"Just a little information, if you don't mind, Colonel. I understand you know this man Rockwell. That right?"

Cooke's frown deepened slightly. The man's dress, size, and manner were remarkably similar to the man he was asking about, even to the way he wore his guns, but this man was a younger version. "It is. Why do you ask?"

Hickok spoke slowly. "I ran into a fella with that name down in Kansas last year. I was wondering if it might be the same man."

Marcy shuttled a look between the pair and sensed a sudden tension in Cooke. "If you'll excuse me, gentlemen," he said, including Hickok in his casual salute.

"Of course, Captain," said Cooke, returning the salute.

Hickok watched Marcy move off, then nodded approval. "Fella has real good manners. I like that."

"I'm sure Captain Marcy will be gratified to know," said Cooke with ill-concealed asperity.

If Hickok was aware of Cooke's annoyance, he didn't acknowledge it. "I'd be obliged if you'd give me an idea of what the Rockwell you know looks like, Colonel."

Cooke looked the young man up and down. "Find yourself a mirror, look in it, and add fifteen years. That satisfy you?"

Hickok's smile widened as he nodded. "Sure does, Colonel. He's the one. I'd have felt kind of foolish, bringing in the wrong man. Much obliged."

Cooke arrested Hickok's movement as he turned to go. "I'd think twice about trying, if I were you, Mister Hickok. There are easier ways to make five hundred dollars—and safer."

"Mebbe so, but I can't think of any right now. Thanks again, Colonel."

Cooke followed Hickok with his eyes as the younger man sauntered off with the arrogance of self-confident youth. A long-forgotten image came to his mind's eye—the woods of Wisconsin, a sleek, powerfully muscled young wolf stalking a battle-scarred veteran, challenging him for leadership of the pack. It had been a fight to the death, and the young wolf had won. Cooke thrust the thought from his mind; the comparison of men and wolves was not fair—to the wolves.

Cooke turned his thoughts back to Albert Sidney Johnston. The man was a puzzle, no question about that. One moment he was cordial, as gracious as a man could be; the next, haughtily distant, bordering on the supercilious. But there was one constant under it all—Johnston's determination to forge ahead, despite all obstacles. What was driving the man? An ambition to make that brevet star permanent? Or was there something more? Someone like Johnston did not throw caution to the wind without a damned good reason. The thought could not escape Cooke—was Johnston struggling to keep a certain timetable? Too, Johnston was not one to take defeat amiably. He knew only how to win. The systematic destruction of his supplies had raised the fury in him. It could well be that he had first misjudged his adversaries, and now, embarrassed, was going to have his revenge. Johnston was a soldier's soldier, Cooke knew. He would not allow his command to become discouraged, lose their pride and bravado, not if he could help it.

Thirty minutes later the army moved out, less than two hours behind Johnston's preplanned schedule. A remarkable feat, considering the damage done by the rampaging waters.

It would be five days to Bridger's Fort, and resupply—maybe. Cooke had voiced his concern the night before, urging Johnston to dispatch a strong cavalry unit to secure the fort pending the arrival of the main body of troops. Johnston had dismissed the suggestion out of hand. He would not split the command with a large hostile force in the area. He was obviously not concerned about the safety of the fort.

Cooke was far less sanguine about the prospects. He knew Porter Rockwell. He would not have been surprised at all if Rockwell and his band of guerrillas were racing toward Bridger's Fort at that very moment.

There were three of them; the oldest, not a day over fifteen, had caught a scattergun load square in the chest, blowing his sternum out through his backbone.

The range, Rockwell knew, had to be point-blank; the shot didn't get out far enough to spread more than a hand's span.

The obscenely mutilated corpses lay in a clump of brush some fifty yards off the trail, hidden there by the killers. Blood and drag marks indicated that the two younger boys had tried to make a run for it when their companion had been gunned down; their wounds were in their backs. Apparently, the youngest was still alive when his murderers had reached him. They had cut his throat, a vicious swipe that almost severed his head.

The bodies had been stripped of the silver bracelets and throat ornaments traditionally worn by young Utes approaching manhood, and all had been scalped. The boys' weapons, hunting bows, had been left where they had fallen.

Will Cartwright and Rockwell had no trouble reading sign and reconstructing what must have happened. The Indian youths, riding unshod horses, had encountered a wagon on the trail. The Utes, curious, as the usually quiescent tribe were wont to be, had approached the wagon to see what could be traded. They were gunned down without warning.

After the slaughter the wagon had continued on. The tracks of the Indians' ponies, mingling with the deeper prints of shod oxen, clearly indicated that the killers had rounded them up.

Still, fresh droppings from one of the horses told them that the killers, whoever they were, could not be more than half a day ahead.

Both Will and Harve were in full agreement with Rockwell's determination to go after them. An incident such as this could, and probably would, have far-reaching effects, turning the normally peaceful Utes to the warpath, seeking revenge. It wouldn't be the first time innocent homesteaders bore the brunt of Indian outrage at some senseless slaughter perpetrated by strangers passing through.

A shallow grave was scooped out of the earth beside the trail, a grave large enough for three. It would be clearly visible to those who would come in search when the boys failed to return to their village.

It was three hours later when Rockwell and his young companions reached the spot where the telltale tracks branched off the trail toward a timber-crested hill. The people in the wagon were following a practice common to small groups of travelers crossing the plains—always make camp on high ground, if possible. The flat, open plain offered little protection in the event of attack by wandering hostiles, red or white.

Quietly, the trio dismounted. They fanned out amid the trees and approached the fire at spaced intervals.

The men around the wagon froze when they saw Rockwell walk into their encampment, Will emerging from the left, Harve from the right. There were five of them—a father and four grown sons—big, hard-looking men with suspicious eyes and hands never too far from ready weapons. They had parked their battered Conestoga just inside the tree line, out of sight of anyone passing on the trail below.

"Well," offered the old man, "you fellas sure as hell put a scare into us. Ain't that kinda dangerous, jus' walkin' up on a body?"

Rockwell looked at them and said nothing. His piercing eyes sent a chill up the old man's back. "Ah . . . well, come on over. Set a spell . . . there, have some coffee. We jus' stopped for a rest and a bite; be on our way in a minute."

From the corner of his eye, Rockwell saw what he figured to be the next oldest, slowly, cautiously, moving back the right side of his coat to expose a holster and handgun. When Rockwell's intimidating eyes switched quickly to him, he stopped cold.

The old man nervously picked up what had been his solitary dialogue. "I'm pleased to meet you gentlemen. I'm . . . I'm Anse Wheeler . . . ah, from Missouri. We . . . my boys and me, is on our way to the Oregon Territory to stake out a homestead." He didn't bother to introduce any of his sons.

Finally, Rockwell, whose face had stiffened at the mention of Missouri, hunkered down beside the campfire and nodded at the three Indian ponies, drop reined and grazing nearby. "Indian ponies?"

"Might be, might not," grunted the patriarch, now more nervous than ever. "Found 'em wanderin' loose awhile back. Sure you don't want some coffee?" he added, taking an uneasy look at Will and Harve, who had drifted in to form a loose, silent half circle about the camp.

Another of the sons eased away from his brothers, closer to the big, double-barreled scattergun leaning against the Conestoga's rear wheel. Will casually swung the carbine crooked in his arm so that the muzzle was in the son's direction, and smiled.

"We found some dead Indians awhile back," said Rockwell. "Same number as those ponies you found. Don't reckon there's a connection, do you?"

"Maybe, maybe not," said the old man. "Don't see how it's no concern of your'n, mister."

"Those dead Injuns were just boys," said Will, his voice menacing.

"Well they ain't gonna be men, that's fer damned sure!" snorted another of the sons.

"Shut your face, Micah!" snapped Anse Wheeler. He turned an uneasy grin on Rockwell. "Yeah. We seen 'em, too. Figgered they must've got into a scrap with some other Injuns, and come out short."

"Possible," nodded Rockwell. "Except for one thing—Indians aren't partial to scatterguns."

"Wouldn't know about that," shrugged Wheeler, his left eye twitching.

"But you would know about scalping, wouldn't you?" Rockwell asked softly, a thin, cold smile on his lips.

The old man surveyed the silent strangers, then looked at Rockwell, frowning. "You some kind of law?"

"Close enough. You didn't answer my question."

"What question?"

"I asked if you knew about scalping."

Wheeler came to his feet, his hands shaking, his face flushed with anger. "Listen, mister, this is our camp. Nobody invited you to come here. So why don't you jus' mosey on about your business, and leave honest folks to their'n!"

Rockwell eased to his feet. "We'll do that—just as soon as we find out how honest you honest folks are."

Harve found the still-bloody scalps inside the wagon, tied to one of the bows for drying. He discovered the stolen bracelets and neck ornaments in a box under the wagon's seat. The Missourians' protests went unheeded. They genuinely couldn't understand why Rockwell and the others were making such a fuss about the killing of three no-account Indians. No one bothered to enlighten them.

Suddenly and simultaneously, Micah's right hand raced for his exposed handgun holstered at his side, and his younger brother grabbed the scattergun.

Micah's hand never reached its destination, let alone pull the gun from its holster. Rockwell's draw was so swift it seemed to Anse Wheeler that the Colt had sprung into his hand. Never in his life had he seen anything remotely like it.

Nor did Micah's younger brother even get his finger on the scattergun trigger. Before he could bring it up from its resting place against the Conestoga wheel, Will's carbine directed a bullet through his face, blowing out the back of his head.

The remaining Wheelers were thunderstruck. Any movement on their part was immediately arrested. In unison they threw their hands in the air.

Trembling violently, the old man looked down at Micah, now on his knees, his face staring blankly into death, blood exuding from the corners of his mouth, his two hands clutching his breast where Rockwell had fanned in two shots with such uncanny speed that the repercussions sounded as but one explosion.

At length, Micah, now quite dead, fell forward on his open mouth and glazed, protruding eyes.

"Oh my God, my God," wailed Anse, "my boys . . . you bastards! You killed my boys . . . over some damned Injuns. We done nothin' to you. . . . Oh my God!"

"Shut up, pa," yelled one of the boys, "they ain't listenin'."

Will, now breathing easier, his palpitating heart beating somewhat slower, surveyed the situation. "Got us a problem," he frowned. "Gonna have to send them back to Salt Lake, under guard."

Rockwell shook his head. "A waste of time, and we can't spare the men."

"We gonna hang 'em here?"

"No lynching," responded Rockwell, venomously. "We're going to ride out of here leaving these Missouri pigs just the way we found them— almost. Going to let justice take its natural course."

One by one, Rockwell tied the surrendering Wheelers hand and foot, and then securely whang-leathered them to the wagon's wheels. Finally, he hung the bloody scalps about their necks.

Anse was the first to realize Rockwell's intention. "Oh my God, no!"

"Shut up, pa!" one of the boys retorted.

"Don't 'cha see . . . fool!" yelled Anse. "They's gonna leave us here for the Injuns . . . gonna let the daddies of them boys get us!"

With that the blood drained from the faces of the strapped Wheelers for the second time that afternoon. Now all three screamed for mercy. "Ain't you human bein's?" cried one of the boys at the top of his lungs. "At least kill us; shoot us now, in the name of our sainted mother, kill us, *KILL US!*"

Anse stretched his neck to take in Will and Harve, his face contorted in terror. "You boys, same age as my young'ns here. You're good boys, yes you are, you look it, I can tell. Please, you good Christian boys, you take us to Salt Lake to stand trial. Yes, that's the Christian thing to do. I'll bless you till my dyin' day."

Neither Will nor Harve could stand to look at them; both turned away. Harve leaned against a tree and retched.

A few minutes later, amid the curses and pleas of the Missourians, the stonefaced Rockwell and his distraught companions rode out of the encampment.

No one spoke for several miles.

Chapter Eleven

L ot Smith peered toward the eastern horizon for the hundredth
time since he and his small band had arrived at Bridger's Fort,
ignoring the biting chill in the air that came as the afternoon wore
on. Still, no sign of Port Rockwell or the two lads who had remained
with him at the river.

Lot and his followers had made good time from the river, averaging sixteen hours a day in the saddle. Jud Stoddard had lapsed into a
comalike sleep the first day out and was thankfully unaware of the grueling
journey and the jolting of the travois as it bumped and twisted over
the uneven trail.

Twenty-four hours earlier, Lot had led the group through the squatters
encircling the fort, marveling at their number; there must have been
five hundred or more, an areola, with the fort as its nipple. Within minutes
Little Fawn and her cousins had the comatose Jud stripped to the buff
and bedded down in a blanket-tented bunk, a poultice on his chest,
and acrid-smelling steam from a half-dozen pots and kettles pouring
vapor into the blanket tent.

Jud's fever had broken with the arrival of dawn; the crisis was over,
and already the feisty little man was protesting the ministrations forced
on him by Bridger's women.

A fear gnawed at Lot Smith's vitals. Could something have gone
wrong when Port Rockwell blew the dam? A short-burning fuse that

didn't give him time to make his escape? Could he and the boys have been taken prisoner by Johnston's troopers, or worse?

His speculations came to an end as the report of a rifle shot rolled out of the dusk, followed by the insane yapping of the semiwild Indian dogs racing toward the three riders cresting a knoll. The distance was too far for Lot to recognize the riders with his naked eye, but a feeling of elation filled him. He knew it was Rockwell and the boys; it could be no others.

"What held you up?" said Lot as he wheeled his saddleless mount to flank Rockwell's buckskin a quarter mile away from the fort.

"You barebacked out here just to ask me that?"

"Dammit, Port! You had us worried!"

Rockwell ignored the friendly scolding. "Guess Jud made it al'right. We didn't pass a new grave on the trail."

"Yeah, he made it. Bridger's squaws have him bundled up like a sick papoose, and he's squalling like one. Got him sucking in the vapors."

"Kill him or cure him."

They rode for a moment in silence, ignoring the yapping mongrels making a show of snapping at the horses fetlocks.

"How far are they behind you, Port?" asked Lot, unable to hold back the question any longer.

"Four, maybe five days. Johnston isn't letting any grass grow under him. It's forced march, from first light to last."

"Damn!" said Lot. "What about his supply wagons—how many did we get?"

"One out of two would be a fair guess," said Rockwell. "We didn't stay around to run a tally. He has to be on half rations, maybe less. Got foragers out looking for game."

"He isn't going to find much, not this time of year."

"He won't need much—just enough to get him here to Bridger's," said Rockwell quietly.

"We waited too long, Port. We should've hit him at South Pass, like Jim Bridger said."

"You'll get no disagreement from me on that, but aren't you forgetting something?"

It took a moment for Rockwell's meaning to penetrate Lot's frustration. The anger went out of him, replaced by a wry, humorless smile. "And shed not one drop of blood."

"That was Brigham's order," nodded Rockwell. "You thinking on going against it?"

"I can't, Port. You know I can't. But he was wrong, much as I hate to say it. The only way we're going to stop that army is to make it bleed some; otherwise, they're just going to roll right over us, knowin' we won't fight."

"Maybe," said Rockwell, softly, as if to himself. "We'll see."

All of a sudden, as if he had waited until the last second to begin some repugnant task, Rockwell reined in the buckskin and dismounted, motioning Lot to do the same.

"What's goin' on, Port?"

Rockwell's faced hardened. "Where's Bridger?"

"Out trappin' with half a dozen of his boys. Said he'd be back in a week."

Rockwell's eyes narrowed. "Good," he said, almost inaudibly. "What about Simon and the rest of the clan?"

"There's three of 'em in the fort; Simon's got two with him out hunting. Expect him in tonight."

Rockwell sighed. "Damn!"

Lot gave him a puzzled look. "Something up?"

"You could say that."

Rockwell was hurting; to Lot there was no doubt. He could see it in his eyes behind the stern facade. It was not physical pain. There was reflected a searing, desperate anguish, the kind that twists your guts and burns your soul.

Lot could find nothing to say. He dropped his eyes from Rockwell, and began to fidget nervously.

At length Rockwell spoke, deliberately, as if he had to force each word into expression. His eyes caught Lot's and held them in a hypnotic grasp. "Now you listen, *'Brother'* Lot, I'm giving you an order. Do as I tell you and don't ask questions."

Rockwell, his orders given and having mounted the buckskin, rode away from a stunned Lot Smith and the fort in the direction he knew Simon would be coming.

Once, he stopped and, turning in the saddle, looked back from whence he had come. He saw that Lot had gathered his band of cossacks at the far corner of the fort's corral, and appeared to be giving directions vigorously. Rockwell nodded to himself, then rode on.

An hour later he saw the imposing figure of Simon coming over the rise with two of Bridger's tough frontiersmen. He was riding a buckskin the image of Rockwell's. His long black hair waved freely in the cold breeze that blew in from the north. Pack mules bore eight gutted deer.

The sun was down now, a rapidly dissolving orange hue barely defining the purple mountain peaks to the west. Rockwell was relieved. Lot and the boys back at the fort would have plenty of time.

"Ah, Rockwell," greeted the giant half-breed, with the wave of his powerful arm.

"Simon."

"Where you heading?"

"Didn't want you to get lost in the dark," he responded facetiously.

With that Simon bellowed a hearty laugh. "Well, come along then and guide us home."

The temperature, already unseasonably low, was dropping precipitously. Occasional spits of iced rain, issuing from an overcast sky and propelled as missiles by the wind, stung the riders' faces. Rockwell reached for his fur-lined jacket, cinched behind his saddle. As he snuggled into the soft wolf's fur, he was reminded, with a sinking sensation in his stomach, that Bridger had ordered Little Fawn to make it for him as a gift just a few months previously.

For some time Rockwell could not find words to speak to the big man riding next to him. From time to time Simon glanced at him with a puzzled expression. He could see, as had Lot Smith, that his friend was disturbed about something.

Finally, Simon turned to Rockwell. "We have a problem, Port?"

"Yeah, Simon, we have a problem."

"You want to talk it over?"

"Maybe over some whiskey back at the fort."

"Sounds right."

Cautiously, the young Mormons, now matured beyond their years by the events of the past weeks, sought out Bridger's junior partners, one by one. They moved about the fort with complete freedom, causing not the slightest concern to anyone. After all, these wholesome young men were above suspicion, a fact that made their task of deception all the more distasteful to them.

Lot Smith mumbled a fervent prayer that Rockwell's plan of treachery would be executed without violence. He knew that Rockwell was suffering even as he was. This wasn't Rockwell's idea, Lot knew. Brigham Young had given the original order. Lot could not abide to think about the man. His burning conscience momentarily filled him with hatred.

The plan worked, as Lot had hoped so desperately. Before Simon and his companions, including Rockwell, had reached the fort, the mountain men who had remained behind had been subdued and disarmed. Dazed, humiliated, and furious, they had been bound and shepherded into a storeroom by their equally frustrated and curiously apologetic captors.

The light from sixty or more campfires danced forlornly on the walls of Bridger's Fort, as Rockwell, Simon, and the other two mountain men rode through the mass of outcasts to the corral. The smell of urine and defecation from both animals and humans joined with the pungent smell of smoke. The riders looked neither to the right nor the left as they passed through the pitiful sight.

When they dismounted, Simon did not think it amiss when several young Mormons, including the pale, emaciated Jud Stoddard, surrounded his two companions on the pretense of helping them lug the deer to the smokehouse. Simon and Rockwell headed for the general-purpose room inside the fort, where Lot was waiting for them.

"Run that by me one more time, Port," said Simon as he reached for the stoneware jug on the table between himself and Porter Rockwell.

Lot Smith kept a polite distance from the two, but was attuned to every word and gesture that passed between them.

"I didn't stutter, Simon," said Rockwell as the mountain man sloshed five fingers of sipping whiskey into the tin mugs. "I want the fort and everything in it. I will give Bridger a promissory note for any reasonable figure."

Simon leaned back his hulk of a body, half emptying his mug in one long, gut-wrenching swallow, then pawed the back of a hand across his mouth and indicated Rockwell's mug. "Lost your taste for whiskey, Port?"

In answer, Porter Rockwell lifted his mug and, in three long swallows, emptied it.

Lot Smith felt his stomach churn as the biting aroma of the 140-proof trade whiskey bit into his nostrils. This was the second time the tin mugs had been drained by the pair at the table—better than a pint for each man. But for all the effect it had on Rockwell and Simon, they may as well have been downing sassafras tea.

Port slammed down his mug, nodding at the jug for a refill. Simon obliged him, then topped off his own mug. "If you don't mind my asking, if we *did* give you a figure, just how in hell would you get the money to meet it?"

Rockwell knew that Simon was baiting him. "Don't worry about it," said Rockwell. "It'll be there."

Simon squinted at Lot Smith before turning back to Rockwell, a knowing look in his suddenly crafty eyes. "You serious about this?"

"Dead serious, Simon."

The half-breed screwed up his face and leaned across the table. "Then tell me, Port, why are you talking to me? This is Bridger's decision to make, you know that. You'll have to wait a week or so until he gets back."

"I can't wait, Simon; there's an army on its way here heading for the Salt Lake Valley. I mean to deny it supplies and shelter. I'm sorry Bridger isn't here, but—"

"The *hell* you are!" Simon broke in, his voice rising.

Rockwell smiled dryly. "You're right—"

Simon finished his thought. "Because you don't have the guts to face Bridger," he snarled, "and tell him you're going to burn his fort!"

"Yes," replied Rockwell without emotion, "that and one other reason. If I have to kill someone, I don't want it to be him."

The talking was over. But in thinking about Bridger, Rockwell had carelessly eased his caution. With a bone-chilling growl, Simon sprang to his feet with the agility of a panther and heaved the massive table into Rockwell's lap, all in one motion. Rockwell found himself skidding across the rough planking of the floor, pinned by the weight of the table.

In an instant Lot was driving hard-thrown punches into Simon's face, momentarily distracting him from pulling his handgun, and giving Rockwell a chance to gain his footing.

Unimpressed with blows that would have easily felled an ordinary man, Simon grabbed Lot by the crotch and one shoulder, effortlessly lifted him above his head, and cast all two hundred and ten pounds of him into a pile of stacked chairs.

At that moment, Rockwell, with all the strength he could muster, smacked the barrel of one of his Colts across the back of the big man's head where it joined his neck. Simon's legs buckled momentarily; still he managed a disgusted look at Rockwell before he was brought down by a second blow to the same spot.

Lot managed to get to his feet, his head swirling and body aching, to help Rockwell immobilize the mountain man with stout strands of whang leather, securely binding his hands and feet.

There was little sleep to be had within the walls of Bridger's Fort that night. The conspirators carefully watched their prisoners, trying not to look them in the face. Lot and Rockwell stayed with the revived Simon, whose piercing black eyes revealed the betrayal he felt. But he said nothing.

Little Fawn and her cousins had fled the fort and had been absorbed among the blanket Indians outside.

Rockwell spent the night quietly reassessing the situation. In the end everything turned on the location and condition of Johnston's army. There was no doubt he had been hurt by the prairie fire and then the flood. Now finding Bridger's Fort in ashes in what appeared to be a fast-approaching winter would add to Johnston's frustration and the disarray of his timetable, whatever it was. But, damn his hide, thought Rockwell, he was still pushing on—much slower to be sure, but inexorably.

When all was said and done, timing would be at the helm of a victory for Albert Sidney Johnston, or be the midwife of Brigham Young's determination to keep the expeditionary force out of the territory of Utah. Rockwell and his band of guerrillas had bought Brigham Young time. But was it enough?

Benson and Romney were in Washington by now, and if Rockwell was any judge, winter had arrived—its full expression soon to appear in gale winds, blinding blizzards, icy drifts higher than a man's head, grazing forage covered with a blanket of deep whiteness, wagon wheels clogged with ice when temperatures dropped, with mud mixed with compacted snow during brief periods of thaw. Winter's legacy would be ripped and uprooted tents, a scarcity of food and firewood, uniforms that never dried, coats that intermittently froze stiff and then became soggy, government-issue boots that twisted and shrank, frozen fingers and toes, stock dropping dead in their tracks. If the ravages of a high-plains winter were to hit soon, all Johnston's determination would be for naught. The army would grind to a halt, at least until spring. And if Brigham's neophyte ambassadors could somehow find success in the nation's capital, then—well, as much as Rockwell hated to admit it, the man's strategy might vindicate itself.

As the first light of dawn began stretching upward through intermittent dark clouds, illuminating the eastern horizon with magnificent patterns, Rockwell put the torch to Bridger's Fort. He refused to allow any of the young cossacks to help him, an order that each one secretly appreciated.

Two hours later, the last remaining wall of Bridger's Fort, its base gnawed away by the flames, collapsed inward, sending a cloud of showering sparks skyward.

The last of the squatter Indians had left more than an hour before, taking everything that was movable with them—blankets, tinned goods, hams, sides of bacon, barrels of flour, salt pork, and beef. They took pots, pans, cutlery, bolts of cloth and canvas, sacks of dried lentils, beans, and peas. The only things Port Rockwell prohibited were the stores of weapons and gunpowder and the casks and jugs of trade whiskey. The battalion would find use for the guns and powder; the whiskey was left to add to the inferno.

Rockwell turned in his saddle to eye Simon and his five humiliated mountain men. Somehow, the half-breed seemed older, smaller than he had been just hours before, as if the flames of the fort had in some way diminished him.

Rockwell tossed at his feet a paper tied with a strip of rawhide. On it he had printed with one of those new graphite sticks a promissory note to Jim Bridger for ten thousand dollars, payable on presentation to Brigham Young. Also included was a promise that when hostilities were at an end, the battalion would rebuild the fort.

Then, addressing Simon matter-of-factly: "There are wagons and supplies, including your weapons, at the ten-mile fork. I have two of our people there guarding it all for you. They have been told not to leave until they see you coming over the rise. I trust you will allow them to ride away in peace. This," his hand swept in the direction of the blazing rubble, "is *my* doing. These men followed *my* orders, and as you can see, reluctantly. I suppose you and Jim will be wanting to see me about this. I won't be hard to find."

Simon did not speak, but his black eyes penetrated Rockwell's being, symbolically cutting out his heart. For a long moment Rockwell reined in the nervous, prancing buckskin. He seemed to be searching for something more to say. The search was in vain. Why, he asked himself, momentarily giving vent to self-pity, was he destined to hurt those he loved and admired most?

The guerrilla band, maintaining a steady gait, was well on its way before Lot dared to direct a question at Rockwell. "What do you suppose Bridger will do, Port?"

Staring straight ahead, Rockwell reasoned, "He and Simon will more than likely take their people south to the Wasatch Range and winter with Little Fawn's tribe."

"And then?"

"What do you mean, 'and then'?"

"You know damned well what I mean!"

"In the spring, Bridger and Simon will come looking for me," Rockwell replied without emotion.

Sixty miles to the east, Gen. Albert Sidney Johnston's army had spent the night cursing torrents of wind-lashed rain whipping down from the high reaches of the Rockies, a torment to man and beast. The gusting winds, often approaching gale force, made it impossible to erect shelter halves or the big Sibley tents. Toward midnight the rain became an icy sleet that continued until the gray haze of morning had appeared over the crest of the mountains to the east. Morning brought with it a bone-chilling freeze, solidifying the mushy ground, anchoring the wheels of wagons and gun carriages as solidly as cement.

Two hours after sunrise the army groaned into movement. Colonel Philip St. George Cooke sat his horse and eyed the numbed troopers as they passed, their mounts slipping and sliding on patches of sheet ice. Most of the men had wisely dismounted, lead reining their animals. It was the gun crews who suffered most, particularly those with the huge Parrot guns, twenty-four pounders, weighing well over a ton. The declines were the worst; studded iron-rimmed wheels had no purchase on the icy, downward slopes, forcing the crews to haul on restraining lines in a desperate struggle against gravity and weight.

Cooke hated the cold. A man could march and fight in the worst of subtropical heat, and do it well if he had to—but cold! It immobilized man and beast, turning their movements slothlike, freezing flesh to gun and musket barrels, searing the lungs with every breath, making every step an agony of effort.

The colonel called to mind a poem written by a cast-aside English soldier:

> God and soldier,
>   men alike adore;
> When Danger threatens,
>   not before;
> Danger over,
>   all is righted;
> God forgotten,
>   soldier slighted.

Strange, Cooke thought to himself, all these years and he still remembered, having heard it only once.

His eyes once more focused on the struggling column. How many of these men, he wondered, would sacrifice lives and limbs to no real purpose? At least the British soldier of Wellington's day had the satisfaction, such as it was, of knowing he had contributed to the security of the empire. What would be gleaned here? What would this unwarranted adventure accomplish that was worthy of the cost? "Insanity," he grumbled half aloud.

"Did you say something, Colonel?" asked Captain Marcy, urging his mount a step closer to Cooke's.

"Words on the wind, Captain, words on the wind." Cooke heeled his mount into movement, leaving a puzzled Captain Marcy to fall in behind him.

Corporal Terrence Riley's massive frame shuddered; his army greatcoat felt as if it weighed more than he did. The gutta-percha shelter half had been no protection against the wind-driven sleet and rain of the night before. The garment was soaked through, and so was Riley. The six fifty-dollar gold slugs that had cost Coogan his life were of little comfort to Riley at the moment; six or sixty wouldn't buy a hot meal or a warm shelter this day.

A civilian rider passed Riley, giving him a momentary start and causing him to reach instinctively for the carbine in his saddle boot. A closer look told him that this was not the jaw kicker from Platte Station. This one was younger, the one they said had been a town marshal—Hickok. What the hell was he doing here? Riley wondered briefly.

His eyes followed the tall man as he rode for the head of the column. Civilians, Riley snorted to himself, coming along to sop up the gravy after boys like himself did the real fighting. Well, thought Riley, I have a few ideas of my own about that.

At the head of the column, General Johnston sat erect in his saddle, seemingly impervious to any suggestion of discomfort, as though already warmed by the comforts he would find at Salt Lake City. The men would endure, he had convinced himself. A few weeks billeted in comfortable surroundings, their taut bellies stretched with solid food, and grumblings would be forgotten; they would be once more ready to assume whatever was asked of them. Whether that would be to garrison the territory of Utah, or march to the west or to the east, only time, and orders from the secretary of war, would tell.

Colonel Fitz-John Porter eyed the ramrod-straight back of his commanding officer with a grimace of annoyance. There was no need to push the troops to the breaking point; the people of Utah Territory weren't going anywhere. What the hell was Johnston trying to prove? Fitz-John Porter had asked himself that question a dozen times since leaving Platte Station, and the answer was always the same—a blank. I'm getting too old for this, he told himself, snugging his caped greatcoat tighter around him. This expedition would be the end. He'd put in for his retirement when he returned to Fort Leavenworth. Somehow, he felt better for having made the decision.

Case Carney handled the reins of the wagonmaster's team, envying Henry Magruder's comfort in the warmth of the camphine stove–heated wagon. Magruder was a selfish bastard, make no mistake. There was ample room in the wagon to share, and any one of the wagonless skinners or bullwhackers could handle the reins as well as Carney; but no, Magruder insisted that Carney take the driver's bench, let Carney get his ass froze solid! Bastard!

An hour into the march the rain began to fall again, a steady downpour, unbuffeted by the night winds. With it came a rise in temperature. But the increasing warmth had its price, turning the frozen trail into a clinging, mushy sludge, sucking at hoof, wheel, and boot with equal impartiality, equal tenacity.

Men cursed and animals strained, the rain continued to fall, and the pace slowed.

Alfred Cumming, governor designate of the Utah Territory, threw a wistful, long-suffering eye at the vapor-opaqued windows of the coach he shared with Lamar Dawson, and pulled the tartan-patterned coach robe higher, until no more than his eyes and the bridge of his nose were visible between hat brim and robe.

It was not just the beastly weather that caused Cumming's discomfort; Lamar Dawson, the newly appointed federal judge to the Utah Territory, was a significant contributing factor.

There was no question as to Dawson's ability as a jurist; the man had a brilliant legal mind. But to Alfred Cumming's dismay, Dawson also had a heroic constancy toward flatulence. The man was an unending source of winds, a disburser of effluence that bordered on the Olympian. A thunderer! The most modest release of the thin jurist was sufficient to shrivel olfactory nerve endings and bring tears to the eyes, even when filtered through the thick folds of the tartan coach robe. Dawson's appointment to the Utah Territory, Cumming was grimly convinced, served a dual purpose: the filling of a vacant judicial post, and a distinct improvement in the quality of air in the nation's capital.

Lamar Dawson shifted on the padded seat across from Cumming, easing his weight to one buttock, slightly elevating the other as he threw a small, apologetic smile at his traveling companion. "Sorry," he murmured.

Alfred Cumming sank deeper into the folds of the robe, and braced himself. It occurred to him that he might neutralize the foul gas with cigar smoke, but almost thought the better of striking a match.

The coach shuddered, and the layer of vapor on the windows seemed to grow more opaque.

Chapter Twelve

It had been agreed that Lot Smith would return to Salt Lake City, along with Jud Stoddard and several other members of the troop incapacitated by minor injuries or illness. The young soldiers had been driven hard; time, weather, and conditions had taken their toll—and would take more. There would be other Zeb Wheems's before this was over. Neither Lot nor Rockwell had any doubts about that.

Rockwell would remain to carry on his guerrilla activities, his "little war," delaying Johnston as long as humanly possible. Lot and Rockwell knew that there was opposition to Young's "no blood" order; many of the younger men were eager to tangle with the army, prove their mettle, show the world they were no longer willing to turn the other cheek. This was evident even among their own troop, as witnessed by the parody of "Camptown Races" contrived by young Will Cartwright:

> Old Buck has sent, I understand,
> Du dah, du dah,
> A Missouri ass to rule our land,
> Oh, du dah day!
> But if he comes we'll have some fun,
> Du dah, du dah,
> To see him and his soldiers run,
> Oh, du dah day.

Wiser, older heads were more thoughtful, but, from long experience, Rockwell knew that wisdom and age had a way of taking a hind seat to youthful exuberance. It was those who had yet to experience the bitterness of battle who clamored loudest for it.

But it would take more than a song to make Johnston's army run. Rockwell recalled the battle of Monterey, when the Mexican Lancers had ridden into the fray with a song on their lips. The song had turned to screams as canister and grape shot cut twenty-foot gaps in their ranks, allowing the Yankee cavalry to break through their lines to hack away at close quarters, where the long lances were useless against slashing sabers. It had been sheer butchery; there was no other word for it.

The contingent of returnees—seven in all, including Jud Stoddard, strapped to a horse litter despite his protests that he was well able to ride—set out for Salt Lake City. Lot promised to return with fresh volunteers as soon as possible.

By evening Rockwell and his troop had established a secluded base camp on a hill overlooking the remains of Bridger's Fort, a mile distant.

The following day brought a light snow, whipped by gusts of swirling winds that slashed down from the western slopes of the divide. They fashioned windbreaks and shelters, insulating themselves and the animals from the biting cold.

Rockwell turned his glass to the east, against the dark backdrop of the distant mountains. Somewhere out there was an army; men were marching—no, slogging their way through, cursing the elements and the men who commanded the army, but they'd continue on. They had little choice.

Will Cartwright and Harvey Arnold amused themselves with improvised slingshots, hurling frozen potatoes, which they'd taken from the fort, across the landscape with surprising accuracy and velocity at a distant boulder that had assumed a roughly human form under its blanket of snow.

Rockwell called a halt to the activity. A thought struck him, bringing a thin smile to his lips. The lads would soon find a more suitable target, he was sure.

Brevet Brig. Gen. Albert Sidney Johnston sat stiff in his saddle, dark eyes hooded, as he gazed at what little remained of Bridger's Fort.

His men would find no succor here, no warmth to take the chill out of their bones, no fresh food supply to supplement their reduced rations, now down to eight ounces of flour and four ounces of fat pork per man per day. Equally critical was the loss of winter gear, gone with the burning of the supply wagons.

The general, of course, was furious, all the more so since Cooke had practically pleaded with him to treat the battalion as any other hostile force and to send an advance contingent to the fort to secure it for the later arrival of the body of troops. Johnston would not, however, he promised himself, give anyone the satisfaction of knowing how he felt. He noticed he was grinding his teeth, and stopped. Cooke stared at him with a combination of anger and frustration, but the general refused to acknowledge the junior officer.

The dragoons and mounted infantry had fared relatively well; it was the foot soldiers who had the worst of it, with their sixty-pound packs and nine-pound muskets weighing them down, trudging endless miles in boots falling apart at the seams, held together with strips of whang leather and string. Their bodies were covered with scraps of canvas or half-cured hides, anything that would give some protection against the piercing cold. The foot troops would break camp at first light and be on the march two hours before the dragoons and mounted infantry, who would pass the slogging troopers at midday. Each night saw them stagger into the next campsite hours after their more fortunate comrades had arrived, most too tired to bother mixing their flour ration to make ash cakes or sear the fat pork in the small campfires.

Johnston scanned the distant bluffs. Rockwell and his men were out there, somewhere. He could feel their eyes; he damned their souls. A handful of will-o'-the-wisp marauders, systematically turning his army into a column of shambling, half-starved, half-frozen, dull-eyed individuals, each intent only on his own immediate needs, and to hell with the hindmost.

Junior officers had reported a growing incidence of conduct bordering on the mutinous, rumblings of desertion, vicious fights to stake a claim a few inches closer to the feeble flames of a campfire. Magruder and his teamsters were another thorn in the sides of the weary troopers, with their seemingly endless supply of rotgut whiskey, sides of bacon, and tinned beef, not to mention the three dollars a day paid by the government. Three whole dollars a day for a damned bullwhacker against thirty-six cents a day for a trooper; ninety dollars a month against eleven! What in hell kind of justice was that?

The talk of desertion was the least of Johnston's worries. Desert to where? Even if the snow didn't get them—a highly unlikely possibility—the people of Utah wouldn't have them, and the more warlike tribes would find deserters easy pickings.

One thing Johnston knew was crucial—he had to get his army into Salt Lake City while it still *was* an army. One hundred and fifty miles. Fifteen to eighteen days, at their current rate of march, paced to the average forced on him by the slow-moving foot troops.

When the scouts rode in to report the destruction of Bridger's Fort, Johnston gave thought to Phil Cooke's suggestion—split the forces and push on with the dragoons and mounted infantry. Without the drag of foot troops to hold them back, the mounted men could cut the time to Salt Lake City by half, possibly more. A thousand men would be more than sufficient to take the city, of that he was certain. The Mormons would not be about to stand and fight, not when they could hide and run. Fleeing from conflict was in their bones, built into their very nature—as proved by their relatively short history. And if they did attempt to make a stand, a thousand men were more than enough to crush them, men anxious to bloody sabers and bayonets, and do it with relish. If ever an army had cause to rampage, his was it. Every hungry moment, each footsore step, all the days and nights of misery would be paid for.

These cowardly outcasts, thought Johnston with wry distaste, hadn't the stomach to stand and hold. They'd have to be hunted down, rooted out of hiding, like the vermin they were, but the end result would be the same. He shrugged inwardly; they had no one to blame but themselves.

The nearest fuel supply was a stand of virgin timber some five miles to the south of Bridger's burned-out fort. The ideal place, Johnston decided, to establish a temporary base camp for his worn-down infantry. The foot troops had become a liability, a drag on the faster-moving dragoons and mounted infantry units.

A few weeks' rest, warmth, and hot food, and not a little extra discipline, would bring them up to snuff, ready to follow their more able comrades into Salt Lake City, or what was left of it. Johnston had already entered the name of this temporary camp in his journal—Camp Scott—

an offhand gesture to the general of the army, Old "Fuss and Feathers," Winfield Scott. It paid to be politic, mused Johnston; but more than that, it would instill pride in his men.

Porter Rockwell moved his small troop to a boulder-crested rise some half mile from the site of Johnston's new camp. They observed the transition of organized confusion to military order as Sibley tents and shelter halves were neatly arrayed, fieldpieces were secured in lunettes, livestock was corralled, and a steady stream of woodcutters and foragers made good use of the timber stand. The weaker animals were culled out for slaughter, their meat smoked and dried for provender.

On the third day, a twenty-foot stripped sapling was planted in the camp quadrangle, and the color guard stood by as a bugler sounded the crisp notes of assembly. Cephus James's spyglass gave Rockwell a clear view of the activity as the quadrangle quickly filled with well-ranked troops under the stern eye of General Johnston. On this occasion he wore an elaborately frogged, gold-braided hussar's dolman. Rockwell hadn't seen anything quite like it since the Mexican war. The high-ranking Mexican officers were very partial to glint and glitter, much to the delight of *Yanqui* sharpshooters. Rockwell shifted the lens to focus on the mounted men behind the general, centering on a familiar face, that of Col. Philip St. George Cooke.

Try as Rockwell might, he could read nothing in the strong features of Cooke, no more than he could in all those poker games back at the Platte, or in Fort Laramie. Rockwell knew that Phil Cooke would play out the hand dealt to him, no matter his personal feelings concerning the dealer or the other players in the game.

A dozen drummer boys, not a one over fifteen, rattled out a long roll as the color guard raised the Stars and Stripes, the troops standing smartly to present arms. A brisk gust whipped the flag as it unfurled, the colors well-defined in the crystal-clear mountain air.

"They'll be doin' that in Salt Lake City pretty soon, Major," said an angry voice next to Rockwell.

The voice belonged to Luke Cartwright. The young man's expression bore out the tone in his voice.

"They won't have to. The same flag's already flying over the town hall."

"I know," said Cartwright, "and that's what I can't understand. That army's coming to whip us, whip us good. President Young's got to know that. We should'a stopped 'em back at South Pass, when we had the chance. So why is he makin' us cat and mouse with 'em?"

"Because that's the way Brigham wants it. He believes a lot more in what that flag represents than many in Washington do."

Luke eyed the older man searchingly. "What about you, Major? What do you feel about it?"

"Not a fair question. My feelings are my own, and they don't count any more than yours."

"Fair question or no, I'd still like an answer."

"So would I," shrugged Rockwell. "Time was I fought for that flag. It meant something different to me back then—a belief, a way of doing things, a flag for all the people. Now, I'm not so sure. That's the fairest answer I can give you, or myself."

Luke accepted this with a bleak nod. "Let me ask you just one more question, then I'll shut up. Brigham Young—he's callin' the shots. Is he right?"

Rockwell thought for a moment, then shook his head. "I don't know. In the beginning I didn't believe he was. Now, I'm not sure. I guess we'll just have to play it out."

"This Brigham Young. You know him . . . what kind of man is he, Major?"

Rockwell waited some time before answering. Behind his furrowed brow, images of Young over the years passed in review. Will was about to give up on the question when Rockwell finally spoke, softly, almost reverently. "He's the kind of man who men, when they are young, want to become; the kind of man who men, when they are old, wish they had been."

"This a private jaw, or can anybody join in?" grinned Harve Arnold, pushing in for a look at the camp below.

"Nothing special," grunted Rockwell, turning once more to the spyglass.

"Looks like they're plannin' to settle in for a spell, don't it?" said Arnold.

"Just a spell," answered Rockwell. "They'll be moving soon enough."

"What if they don't wait? What if he just keeps on marching?" asked Cartwright.

"I doubt if Johnston will, for a while, anyway. He needs those supplies he left back at the Platte, and his infantry is just about down to the nub. If he does move, it'll be at a crawl."

"He crawls long enough, he's gonna get there," said Luke. "What then? Do we fight, or let them crawl all over us without doin' a lick to stop it?"

Rockwell could see the same question reflected in Harve Arnold's earnest young face. In truth, it would show in his own, if he let it. "You're asking the wrong man," he shot back.

"Didn't mean to get you riled, Major," Luke said softly.

"Luke ain't said more than all of us have been thinking, Major," offered Arnold.

The tension in Rockwell eased, softening his face as he looked from one to the other. "I know that, lads. You've got minds of your own; it wouldn't be natural if you didn't question things you don't understand. I've no quarrel with that, as long as you do what has to be done."

"Meanin' follow orders," said Luke.

Rockwell nodded. "You called it. Now, is this jaw fest about over, or is there something else you want to discuss?"

Harve Arnold shook his head with a boyish grin. "No sir, you about said it all, I reckon."

The grins sent a pang through Rockwell, bringing a vision of another such grin to his mind's eye—Zebulah Weems's—before a .44-caliber slug wiped it away forever.

General Johnston traced a finger across a large map pinned to the slanting wall of the Sibley tent.

"The line of march will take us through the Bear Mountains to the crossing at Ham's Ford. From there it's less than a day to Echo Canyon. Without infantry to hold us up, we'll reach our objective within a maximum of fourteen days." He paused, dark eyes raking the assemblage crowded into the large tent. "Any comments, gentlemen?"

"Am I correct in assuming you intend to attempt passage through Echo Canyon, sir?" asked Colonel Cooke, anticipating the flash of irritation he knew the question would bring.

"It's the shortest damned distance between two points, Colonel. I should think that would be obvious to the lowest rank in this command."

"It's also the most dangerous, *sir*," Cooke replied calmly. "Echo Canyon is twenty miles through, some of it narrow twisting trail, flanked by sheer cliffs on both sides. You couldn't offer an enemy a more ideal defensive area. Compared to Echo Canyon, South Pass would be a picnic, if it came to a fight."

Johnston studied Cooke a long beat, and nodded. "Your comments are duly noted, Colonel. Anyone else care to voice an opinion?"

Colonel Fitz-John Porter took the plunge. "It would seem to me that prudence might be in order, General. How much time would we lose by taking the Bear Valley route—a week, ten days at most? If what Colonel Cooke tells us about Echo Canyon is . . . is accurate—"

"It is," interjected Cooke. "The battalion could immobilize us without exposing a man, bottle us up and cut off our line of retreat."

"Retreat?" snorted Johnston, color flooding his face. "There isn't going to be any retreat, and there isn't going to be any fight, Colonel; sorry to say, I might add. Your vaunted battalion has shown a remarkable aversion to anything approaching armed resistance, unless you consider the murder of a defenseless, half-drowned trooper a noble use of arms."

James Butler Hickok eased his lean frame a step forward. "Excuse me. Jumpin' the gun on that, aren't you, General? There was murder, al'right—but as to who did it, I haven't seen anything that points a finger to the who of it."

"I'm afraid I have to agree with Mister Hickok, sir," added Captain Marcy.

Johnston slid cold eyes to Capt. Werner Frietag; Major Poole, the medical officer; Lieutenant Coy; and the other junior officers. "Since we seem to have an open forum on the subject, does anyone else care to enlighten me?"

Fitz-John Porter braced himself and broke the long silence following Johnston's acerbic question. "I think we're losing sight of the main issue, General. I believe it would be a tactical error to attempt passage through Echo Canyon, a route that could prove disastrous."

Johnston gave the older man a look that reeked with contempt. "You need not concern yourself, Colonel. If you so desire, you may remain here at Camp Scott."

Porter blanched, then reddened. "I resent your tone, sir! *And* your inference. I am ready to follow you through Echo Canyon, or anywhere else. You asked for an opinion, sir!"

Johnston's cold, penetrating look gradually warmed. "Very well, Mr. Porter," he said, dismissing the subject.

Turning back to the camp table, Johnston pulled a sheet of paper from under the map. "Marching orders," he addressed Cooke. "You will see that the indicated units are ready to move out within the week."

Cooke scanned the list, shooting a lifted brow at Johnston. "I don't see Cumming or Dawson listed, General."

"Governor Cumming and Judge Dawson have no function on this endeavor, Colonel. There'll be ample time for politicians once we've secured Salt Lake City. That will be all, gentlemen."

Cooke and the others, with the exception of Hickok, came to a semblance of attention, hand saluting.

"We can forego the formalities, gentlemen. Dismissed."

Cooke was the last man to reach the tent flap. He paused and turned back to Johnston, a quizzical lift to his brow. "I hope I'm wrong, Sidney, but if I'm not, every man on this list is a potential casualty."

A smile broke on Johnston's face, changing his visage to a remarkable degree. "Then permit me to join in your hope, Phil. I'm sure your Mormon friends will see that it bears fruit."

Cooke stepped through the opening, blinking at the harsh winter light refracted from the light carpeting of snow. The man's a fool, he told himself—foregoing a safe route to avoid an extra few days' march, days that would mean nothing in the overall scheme of things. A worm of doubt gnawed in Cooke's breast; had the Mormons gone soft, as Johnston believed; would he just march in and take the city without a shot fired? Somehow Cooke couldn't accept that. The time would come when they'd resist, with all the force at Brigham Young's command.

In the decade since the signing of the Treaty of Hidalgo, ceding almost half a million square miles of Mexico's territory to the United States, the army had yet to fight a single battle against anything remotely resembling organized resistance under a central command. True, there had been a plethora of actions against the more warlike Indian tribes, but these were rarely more than minor skirmishes. The fact remained that if Brigham Young gave the order to resist, there'd be a well-equipped army of frontiersmen scattered throughout the territory, ready to strike anywhere at anytime, and with devastating effect. The thought brought to Cooke's mind Wellington's Peninsula Campaign of 1809. The French forces were systematically decimated by the attacks of civilian guerrillas, harassed to the point of open rebellion against their commanders. When Wellington did strike, he found his enemy in total disarray.

Henry Magruder's gravelly voice broke in on Cooke's reveries. The colonel turned to see the teamster contractor with his ever-present number-one man, Case Carney. Both were well bundled against the cold. The reek of rotgut whiskey traveled on the vapor of Carney's breath, offending Cooke's nostrils.

"You're just the man I've been looking for, Mister Magruder," said Cooke, masking his distaste for the pair.

"Oh? Why's that, Colonel?"

"I believe the general intends to commandeer some of your wagons, Magruder."

"Hell, Colonel, he don't have to commandeer 'em. My boys are ready to roll 'em right into Salt Lake for you."

"The wagons," said Cooke, *not* your drivers."

A look of sudden belligerence flooded Carney's liquor-flushed face. "What kind o' crap you handin' us, soljer boy!"

"Shut up, Carney," snapped Magruder, his eyes searching Cooke's face. "Where my wagons go, my drivers go. I got me a contract, Colonel."

"Damn right," growled Carney.

"Subject to military expediency, Mister Magruder. You should read the fine print. And there's more. I'll want an inventory of the personal provisions you and your people are transporting. Anything in excess of immediate need will be distributed among the troops."

"In a pig's eye!" snorted Carney, his jaw thrust grimly at Cooke in challenge.

Magruder's eyes narrowed speculatively as he forced a tight grin. "What's gotta be is gotta be, Colonel."

Carney's mouth opened in surprise. "Damn it, Henry, they got no—"

"I told you to shut up." Carney's jaws clamped tight as he turned a glowering look back to Cooke. "No problem, Colonel," smoothed Magruder. "O'course, I'll have to add a little something to the goin' rate, pricewise, for the inconvenience, ye understand."

"The little somethin'—it wouldn't be in the neighborhood of double the going rate, would it?"

A broad grin split Magruder's lips. "Right on the head, Colonel," he said emphatically. "A man's got to live. Right, Colonel?"

"A popular misconception, Mister Magruder, unfortunately."

Magruder's brow knit darkly. "What in hell's that supposed t' mean?"

"Think about it," said Cooke, striding off.

"I don't like that sonovabitch," rasped Carney.

"Like or dislike don't mean a damn, Carney, not as long as we can make a profit. C'mon, let's get back to the wagon; freezin' my ass off out here."

Case Carney didn't need a second invitation.

Chapter Thirteen

Word of roaming bands in war paint had spread quickly, and there wasn't a man in the territory who didn't know it was only a matter of time until some unwary settler or traveler would fall victim. There were holdouts, Mormon and Gentile, who'd refused to come to the basin's protection, sure that the normally peaceful Indians would do them no harm. Brigham Young's long-established policy in dealing with the red men would get its just reward: Better to feed them than fight them.

General Wells sent out detachments to bring in the diehards. This time there wouldn't be any discussion about it. Young's order, as president to his followers and governor to all, carried official weight—it would be obeyed.

Lot Smith's twenty-man detachment would move north, along a tributary of the Green River, already icing over where the flow was slow moving. The men were a dozen miles out of Salt Lake City when Jud Stoddard caught up with them. The feisty little man was determined to go along in spite of Lot's protests, telling Lot that Doc Ames had declared him fit for duty.

Lot couldn't help but smile at the figure Jud made, little more than eyes and a red-tipped nose visible in the folds of his buffalo-hide coat, the brim of his thick felt hat pulled down to his brows. "You in there somewhere, Jud?" grinned young Luther James. "I never saw a papoose bundled up snugger'n you."

"I'm in here, right enough," snuffled Stoddard, pawing a mittened backhand under the watery nub that served as his nose.

"Room in there for two of you," chortled Luther.

Jud's eyes glittered warning. "I can peel out right quick, if I've a mind to, flannel mouth."

"Stop being so touchy, Jud," said Lot. "Fact is, you do look a mite comical. Where'd you get that buffalo coat?"

"Borrowed it from Sven Lindstrom. Ain't my fault Sven's so overgrowed it takes two hides t' make him a pair of mittens," said Jud, his good humor restored. "Reckon I do feel kinda lost in it."

Lot wanted to ask the small man if he'd seen Anne McCutcheon at Doc Ames's, but thought better of it. No sense in giving the boys something to pick at him with. After all, he'd been with her almost every day since he'd been home. The night before he left again, he kissed her for the first time, and she had returned the kiss. He could tell. She was leaning against a willow tree, Lot's arms bracing the tree on either side of her shoulders. He was overwhelmed with her beauty, her bearing. Her full lips touching his thrilled him in a way he had never felt before. He held the kiss for a full half minute, and she had made no move to end it. He wanted to tell her how much he loved her, but when he started to speak, she gently put her fingers over his mouth. "Not now," she whispered softly, her eyes caressing him. Then she ducked under his arms, away from the willow, taking his hand in hers, and without a word, they walked the short distance to Doc Ames's home. On the porch she allowed him to kiss her once again. Then she disappeared into the house.

In the morning, before he left, he'd ridden by the Ames's place. To his disappointment, Anne had been out with her father to tend to folks who needed doctoring. Perhaps it was just as well, he thought. But when he returned to the valley, he promised himself, he was going to ask Anne to marry him. At that point, he could not imagine his life without her. No woman he had ever known had caused him to feel this way. And there were plenty who had wanted him to, he reassured himself.

Salt Lake City was spilling over with the influx of farmers, ranchers, and people from outlying communities. There wasn't a spare room or bed anywhere in the city. Lot had heard talk that President Young was planning to move the women and children somewhere they'd be safe if Johnston's army made it into the basin. Some folks had already left the city, heading south, or west to the Nevada Territory. A smaller number were determined to cross over into Mexican lands and build new colonies there. But for every family that left the basin, there were two or three coming in, some from as far away as the Yellowstone, up in Nebraska Territory.

The small detachment rode on. Six hours later, the pale sun well to the west, they made night camp.

James Butler Hickok lovingly hefted the beautifully balanced Whitworth rifle. There was a lethal beauty in the fine, fiddleback stock, artfully crafted brass work and case-hardened frame. The thirty-inch octagon barrel was a deep, rich blue under the glareproof tube of an eight-power Telsar telescope. Hickok threw the weapon to his shoulder to sight on a distant outcropping well beyond the camp limits. The magnified image was sharp and clear through the excellent German lenses. Hickok's finger caressed the double-set triggers. That whisper of a touch brought the rifle's hammer down on the naked nipple with a crisp, clean stroke. Hickok lowered the weapon to turn an apologetic smile on the weapon's owner, Lieutenant Coy. "Sorry, didn't mean to dry-fire."

Coy shrugged forgiveness. "No harm done, Hickok. With a set trigger, a whisper's all it takes to drop the hammer. You can say one thing about the English, they know how to make a fine weapon—none finer in the world. My father had it ordered in time for my graduation from the academy—a year's pay for a shavetail second lieutenant."

Hickok nodded, then squinted at a cluster of boulders on the crest of a low rise some half mile distant. In past days his sharp eyes had seen movement among the boulders, not animal but human—an observation post keeping tabs on the army.

"What's the maximum range for accuracy?" he asked.

"On a bench rest, a thousand yards. She'll drop about eight feet, with seventy grains of powder, using a minié ball. Don't know what she'll do with a round shot—never tried it."

"Uh-huh," nodded Hickok, his pale, almost colorless eyes narrowing speculatively as he once again looked at the boulder-crested rise. He estimated the distance to be a shade over twelve hundred yards from where he and Coy were now standing.

False dawn was probing its way up the craggy peaks to the east as Hickok snaked past a sleepy picket guard and made his way to a clutch of greasewood and oak brush some 250 yards beyond the camp perimeter. Settling himself for prone fire, he slipped the long barrel of the Whitworth through the dry branches, using a rolled poncho as an improvised bench rest. His position brought him well within the thousand-yard range of the English long gun's effectiveness. The weapon was on half cock, loaded with seventy grains of black powder seated under a double-patched, two-hundred-grain minié ball. Hickok thumbed the big percussion cap, cramping it down firmly on the nipple. He then focused the Telsar scope on the boulders topping the rise. The lenses brought the rocks eight times closer than the naked eye could see. The almost invisible cleft between two of the largest boulders now showed sharp and clear in the objective lens. To his left, the sun had just pushed its way into view over the peaks. Night still clung to the valleys and hollows. Hickok waited.

Luke Cartwright had pulled himself out of his blanket at the first hint of dawn and steel-flinted a small pile of buffalo chips into smokeless flame under a blackened pot. When the water came to a slow boil he added powdered chocolate from a five-pound tin.

The chocolate, imported from the prestigious provenders Fortnum & Mason, London, had been a gift from Abram Levi, one of Salt Lake City's most versatile entrepreneurs. The popular merchant had literally stripped his shelves of anything the battalion might find use for, refusing all offers of payment. This was Abram Levi's fight, too, he reminded them.

Luke savored the aroma of the steaming chocolate. It was a luxury that in other times was rarely enjoyed; hard money had to serve more important needs, not be frittered away lightly on pleasurables. He grimaced to himself; a fella could get in the habit real quick when it came to hot chocolate and hard biscuit—real quick.

Porter Rockwell had come awake at the first scrape of steel on flint. His eye traveled from young Cartwright to the blanket-covered forms of the other lads, still sleeping soundly. Rockwell had told them there was no need to post night watches. The slightest activity from the camp below would give ample warning in the night stillness. A sally by mounted troops would be an exercise in futility. He and the boys would be long gone before the troopers could prod their weary mounts within musket shot of the crest.

Rockwell rolled out of his blanket to reach for his pistol belt, a ritual as long as he could remember.

Nodding a "mornin'" to Cartwright, he accepted a tin mug of the steaming brew, then moved to boot-nudge the others into wakefulness.

As they stirred to life, Rockwell angled to the cleft in the boulders that gave a clear view of the camp below. Perching his mug on a shelf of rock, he lifted Cephus James's scope to his eye.

The camp was still partially in shadows, but there was ample light to reveal its awakening. The brassy notes of reveille had sounded sharp and clear. Groggy, half-awake troopers milled about, gravitating to the numerous cook fires that promised warmth for their bodies and something hot for their innards.

James Butler Hickok eased back the Whitworth's hammer to full cock and settled the butt snugly into his shoulder. The cross ring of the Telsar rifle scope centered squarely on the distant cleft. At a thousand yards the eight-power magnification wasn't powerful enough for Hickok to see any detail of the man who had appeared in the cleft. He was hardly more than a dark spot against the swiftly brightening sky. Not that his identity mattered—he had to be one of them.

An eight-foot drop at a thousand yards, Coy had told him, but that didn't allow for an uphill shot. Hickok estimated he'd need another two feet in elevation. Fortunately, he'd not have to worry about windage; there wasn't a breath of breeze.

Hickok raised the scope's cross hairs until his target appeared at the very bottom of the objective lens, in perfect alignment with the vertical cross hair. Gently, he stroked the set trigger, locking it with an almost inaudible click. He then shifted his finger to the main trigger and exhaled slowly. At a thousand yards the minié ball would strike home a full two and a half seconds before the sound of the shot that sent it. Hickok feather-touched the main trigger. The Whitworth roared, slamming the fiddleback butt hard into his shoulder.

Rockwell was lowering his telescope when something caught his eye, a puffball of powder smoke. His reflexes took over even as his brain told him that the range was far too great for an effective shot. He spun away from the cleft, flattening himself against the boulder. A heartbeat later a slug cracked through the cleft and whined away into the distance.

Surprise flooded Rockwell. Whoever the son of a bitch was, he could shoot! Rockwell flung a look back through the cleft as the delayed report reached his ears. The telltale puffball of powder smoke was wisping away. He brought the telescope to his eye, centering it on the source of the smoke—a patch of greasewood. A figure rose from behind the patch, rifle in one hand, the other shading his eyes as he looked up at the boulders. The twenty-power magnification was enough to tell Rockwell who the figure was—that damned lawman turned scout, Hickok.

Why, wondered Rockwell, was Hickok taking a personal hand in this? A scout's job was just that, to scout the lay of the land, not take it upon himself to do the army's job. Rockwell's anger increased when he thought of what might have happened if it had been Luke or one of the other boys standing where he'd been.

The handcart company, under the command of Orley Stuart, a dour-visaged New Hampshire man, had been trailing Johnston's army all the way from the Platte, taking care to keep a safe distance between themselves and the slow-moving military column. They'd passed broken-down, burned-out, and abandoned army wagons; free-roaming oxen, horses, and mules, most with U.S. Army brands; and the discards of an army on the march, both personal and government issue. They'd also passed the grave of Pvt. Walter B. Coogan, late of the 2d Dragoons. They paused a moment to offer up a short prayer before continuing on.

It was a small company, four families, totaling twenty-two souls. Orley Stuart knew that it was only a matter of time until they'd catch up with the army's rear guard, a situation Stuart felt must be avoided at all costs. Thumbing through his well-worn copy of Colonel Masters's *The Argonaut's Guide to the West,* published in 1853, Stuart decided to branch off the main trail at the Sublet Cutoff, head northwest to the Bear River, then cut south for Salt Lake City. The change in itinerary would add another hundred miles to their journey and play havoc with their carefully calculated food supply, but would keep the company well clear of the military expedition. Stuart wouldn't let himself think of what might happen if he and his small party arrived in Salt Lake City to find it already under occupation; he'd face that problem if and when they came to it.

The previous night the company had made night camp on the east bank of the Bear, a sixty-yard-wide expanse of relatively shallow water, dotted with sandbars. Stuart's oldest boy, Daniel, had crossed without difficulty, although the water, averaging four to five feet in depth, was brutally cold and ice flecked. Fortunately, the current was slow moving. Still, getting the company across would be a time-consuming effort. Carts would have to be unloaded and floated to the other side, their contents hand carried across.

As the evening meal was being prepared, the camp routine was broken by the arrival of Ansel Greene and his family, one of the non-Mormon Utahns ordered into Salt Lake Valley by Brigham Young.

The big farmer ungraciously accepted the hospitality of the immigrants, he and his family sharing in the meager evening meal and ignoring Daniel Stuart's suggestion that he lighten the big farm wagon before attempting a crossing. The bottom was soft, and the sandbars were mushy. Better to make several trips than chance bogging down in midstream with an overload. Ansel assured them that his mules were up to the job, and that he'd be well on his way while they were still foolin' around with their "pushy carts." Daniel and his father exchanged a look that clearly conveyed their doubts; Ansel Greene and his mules had more in common than he knew.

The morning proved Ansel Greene half right; his big wagon sank to the wheel hubs on a sandbar midway between the riverbanks. As Greene, muttering a constant stream of oaths, belatedly followed the advice given him the night before and unloaded the heavy wagon, Orley Stuart ferried his people and their goods to the sandbar. Daniel had already gone to the west bank to prepare a large fire. Bodies would have to be warmed, wet clothing dried.

Greene climbed back into the wagon seat and slap reined the team, bellowing encouragement as the big animals strained against their collars, but the sucking sand held the wheels in a firm grip. A nod from Stuart brought half a dozen willing hands to the wheel spokes and wagon body. Slowly, reluctantly, the big iron-rimmed wheels began to turn.

Before the wheels had completed a full revolution, Greene's lead mule reared up with a scream that was quickly swallowed up in a fusillade of shots mingled with war cries. The Indians, some forty in number, had approached in the concealment of a gully some fifty yards back from the east bank of the river. Now they burst out of cover like a torrent, racing their ponies toward the river, firing trade muskets and arrows at the people on the sandbank. The lead mule crashed to its side, dragging down its mate in a fury of wildly lashing hooves.

Whatever else Ansel Greene might be, he was a frontiersman. Leaping from the wagon seat, he roared a command to take cover, then loosed both barrels of the ten gauge at the charging Indians as the first of them plunged his mount into the chilling stream. The broad pattern of the double-barreled straight bore hit low, scathing into chests and front legs of the Indian ponies, spilling three of their riders. Stuart damned himself for not double-charging the ten gauge with buckshot; the light-weight bird shot could do no real damage to man or beast at thirty yards. Still, it was enough to disrupt the charge, giving Stuart and his men time to reach for their own muskets and scatterguns. They didn't score any hits, but the smoke and muzzle blasts were enough to send the Indians scurrying for the shelter of the gully.

Greene and the others took advantage of the momentary respite to throw up a barricade of carts, using the Greene wagon as the hub. An erratic fire of muskets and arrows came from the gully lip. Daniel Stuart, aided by covering fire, plunged into the river to swim for the sand-bank, musket balls kicking up geysers of water around him.

"Don't waste powder," Greene shouted to the others. "Save it for when they come at us again!"

Musket balls plunked into the barricade; arrows thudded into the slab-sided wagon and side-turned carts. Greene moved low to cut the traces, freeing the uninjured mule. The big animal bucked wildly for a moment, then made for the far shore, bellowing protests at his un-seemly treatment.

Reloading the ten gauge, Ansel Greene squeezed a look at the In-dians' position. A 60-caliber ball chewed a foot-long splinter out of a handcart inches from his head. In a sudden fury, ignoring his own advice, Greene came to his feet and let both barrels go at the gully lip. The return fire was instantaneous, and fairly accurate, considering the low quality of the Indians' trade muskets. They consisted primarily of ancient flintlocks converted haphazardly to percussions.

"What now?" asked Orley Stuart. "You think they might go off 'n leave us be?"

Greene gave the immigrant a scathing look. "If'n t'was t'other way around, would you? All they gotta do is keep us pinned down 'til dark and Injun up on us out of the water. Won't see 'em or hear 'em 'til they're right on top of you."

Lot Smith had reined up, signaling the column to a halt as the roll-ing boom of a big-bore shotgun and rattle of musket fire echoed from somewhere upriver. "How far would you reckon, Luther?"

Cephus James's boy squinted, then shrugged. "Hard to say—sound plays tricks over water. Could be a mile, could be five. No way of tellin'."

"There's one way," countered Lot. "Getting to where it's at." Sig-naling the column to advance, Lot spurred his mount into an easy yet ground-consuming canter. He had no intention of riding into trouble with blown horses.

Luther's first estimate proved the most accurate. A mile and a half upriver Lot dismounted his troop to move them through the trees in skirmish formation. The musket fire was now desultory, random shots punctuated by periods of silence. Lot scouted ahead to the tree line overlooking the west bank of the river, the woodsmoke of Daniel Stuart's fire strong in his nostrils. From the shelter of the trees he had a clear view of the situation, mentally chalking up a mark of approval for the people pinned down behind the wagon and cart barricade. They'd made the most of a bad position, but it wouldn't last.

He couldn't tell how many Indians were in the war party across the river, getting only a now-and-then glimpse of a feather-bedecked head as its owner popped up to loose a shot or arrow at the sandbar.

"I'll take half the troop upriver, cross over, and flank 'em," he told Luther. "You and the rest of the boys be ready to get those people off the sandbank and back into the tree line."

Luther frowned. "Wouldn't it be better if me and the boys crossed over downriver and come at 'em on the other flank?"

Lot shook his head firmly. "We'd have a real fight on our hands. I want to spook 'em, not fight 'em. Don't want 'em followin' us all the way to Salt Lake, trying to avenge their dead. This territory's in enough trouble with whites killin' Indians. Going to end up with all the tribes on the warpath."

A half mile upriver Lot and his men crossed to the east bank. Taking advantage of natural cover, they moved in on the Indians' position, leaving their mounts concealed in a scrub-sheltered cutbank. Bellying to the crest of a sandy knoll, they found themselves with a clear view of the gully. They were in a perfect position for raking fire on the unsuspecting red men. Lot passed an order reminding the men of his intentions—spook 'em, not fight 'em.

The leader of the band of young Snakes was in no hurry; the whites on the sandbank weren't going anywhere, and even if they could, they'd have to leave all their possessions behind. Who knew what treasures he and his braves might find in those many boxes and bundles scattered over the sandbar.

His ruminations came to an abrupt end as a volley of shots whistled over the gully, not from the sandbar but from a small knoll some fifty yards on his right. Gunsmoke clearly marked the source of the fire.

The same smoke was a cue for Luther James. "Let's go!" he shouted to the stripped-down men grouped in the shelter of the tree line. Racing across the narrow bank, they plunged into the frigid water, some swimming, others stroking toward the startled party huddled behind the breastwork of carts. It was all confusion for Orley Stuart and the immigrants. On one side of the river he could see the Indians spilling out of the gully, some on foot, others hanging low over the necks of their mounts. On the other side were white men shouting undecipherable commands as they pushed across the thirty-yard gap between bank and sandbar.

For once in his life, Ansel Greene was glad to see Mormons. More'n likely some of those battalion boys, he thought, from the way they'd snuck up on them Injuns, just like regular soldiers. Ansel punctuated his moment of elation with the ten gauge, sending a double load of buckshot at the tail ends of the fleeing Indians.

Jud Stoddard gritted his teeth as he forged his way across the thirty-yard gap between sandbar and riverbank. The cold penetrated to the bone as though driven by a knife. Hetty Greene passed young James to the small man. Hoisting the three year old to his shoulder, Jud began the return journey, the first of three crossings he'd make within the hour.

Lot and his men kept up a harassing fire at the Indians, who'd come to a halt just out of musket range to scream insults at the white faces. Two of the party had been sent back to bring up the horses, but they'd not cross the river until all the immigrants were safely on the other side.

Ansel Greene was outraged: Leave the wagon and goods, not to mention Hetty's musical box, to them painted savages? Damned if he would! Throttling back a more realistic response to the situation, Lot told Greene that the choice was his; if he wanted to make the Indians a present of his scalp, he was welcome to do so. Greene wasn't the only one losing his property; the immigrants would come away with little more than the soggy clothing on their backs. The Indians had already returned to the shelter of the gully, and could launch a charge at any moment. Lot had no intention of waiting around for them to make up their minds.

The troop moved out, women and children on horseback, bedroll blankets offering some little protection to chilled bodies. Jud's borrowed buffalo coat was shared by a young mother and her ten-month-old infant. The troop had barely disappeared into the tree line when the Indians, shouting victory cries, surged onto the sandbar, ripping and tearing at the abandoned boxes, bundles, and sacks. Their leader swiftly appropriated Hetty's musical box, much to the chagrin of a younger brave. Rank had its privileges.

An hour's march south of the crossing, Lot led the troop off the trail to a defensible clearing, ordering picket guards posted on the back trail. Fires were built, rations broken out. With night approaching, with its attendant drop in temperature, Lot knew that the immigrants and the Greenes, not to mention his own men who had braved the icy waters, would need all the warmth and hot food that could be provided, such as it was.

Ansel Greene's mood hadn't improved. If he'd listened to young Daniel Stuart, had lightened his wagon before attempting the crossing, he'd stood a chance of being well away before the Indians jumped the cart train. This wasn't true, of course, but Ansel had to place blame somewhere, and he placed it squarely on the shoulders of young Stuart—he should have insisted.

Jud Stoddard had volunteered for one of the perimeter guard posts some seventy-five yards from the camp. There was little chance the Indians would follow and attempt a night attack, but it didn't pay to take things for granted. He pulled the big buffalo coat tighter around him and peered up through the canopy of fir branches. The night sky was satiny; the stars gleamed alluringly, abundantly. He snuggled deeper into his coat. A wind had come up, gusting through the overhead branches, bringing with it a sudden drop in temperature. Jud shot a longing look at the gleam from the campfires that filtered between the boles of hundred-year-old trees. Another hour, he estimated, and he'd be relieved, and not a moment too soon, he thought. He'd never felt cold like this before, and he'd weathered a dozen blizzards or more in his short life. This cold didn't just gnaw into a man's flesh, it seemed to come from deep inside, a burning cold that clutched at his chest, bringing with it sharp, sudden stabs of pain.

Got to move, he told himself, get the blood circulating. He pushed a mittened hand into the layer of fir needles to bring himself to his knees. It was then he realized there was no feeling in his legs, no feeling at all. The pain in his chest came again, radiating throughout his upper body with a searing heat that clouded his eyes, sent tingling fingers over his scalp. For the first time in his life, Jud Stoddard admitted to himself that he was afraid. Something was wrong, bad wrong. A sudden sheen of sweat broke out on his face and body; he could feel his heart beating rapidly, each beat bringing with it a quick stab of pain that traveled to someplace behind his eyes and exploded in his brain. Using the musket butt for leverage, he struggled to his knees. Desperately he tried to get a foot under himself, pulling hard on the musket barrel. The pain was now agonizing—bands of hot steel squeezing his thin chest. Still he struggled to gain his feet. "Got to get up," he gritted through clenched teeth, "got to." His fingers fell away from the musket barrel of their own accord, and Jud felt himself topple sideways into the soft bed of fir detritus. He knew his face was toward the sky but he could see nothing. The pounding of his heart slowed, then stopped with a final explosion of pain. Jud Stoddard's body was dead. His brain lived for another eight seconds. A long, silent scream of protest echoed in his skull, then faded to nothingness.

Fighting back tears, Lot Smith lashed out at Luther James, "Why'd you let him go in the damned water! You knew he had no business going in the water!"

"I tried to stop him," Luther answered softly. "But you know how he was—nobody could stop Jud from doing what he wanted t' do. That was jest the way he was. . . ."

Lot studied the still, blue-tinged face nestled in the big buffalo robe, then nodded. "I know . . . he always wanted to do as much as the biggest, and he damned well did."

Gently, almost lovingly, Lot closed Jud Stoddard's eyes, for the last time, feeling that something of himself had died with the little man.

Chapter Fourteen

A mid darkening clouds and freezing temperatures, where frostbite, raspy coughs, and short tempers were increasing with each
day's passing, Albert Sidney Johnston read for the third time
the report handed him by Major Aarons, the quartermaster officer. The
reading did not improve with repetition. Losses since leaving the Platte
included an undetermined amount of ammunition and weapons, 2,720
pounds of ham, 92,700 pounds of bacon, 68,832 rations of dessicated
vegetables, 7,781 pounds of hard bread, and 25,000 pounds of various other food supplies, plus the loss of 200 wagons and the bulk of
the army's winter gear. The army's walking commissary, beef on the
hoof, no longer existed. What hadn't been run off by the marauders
had wandered away in vain search of forage, necessitating the slaughter
of the weaker draft animals and saddle mounts for food.

These losses gave added impetus to Johnston's determination to forge
ahead in his drive for Salt Lake City. Every pound of lost supplies,
every ounce, would be compensated for, twice over. He'd strip the city
down to its foundations, if need be. If that meant that its inhabitants
would have to weather the winter months on starvation rations, so much
the better. Hunger had a way of making the most resolute more tractable; that had been proved time and time again during the campaigns
to drive the so-called civilized tribes from their ancestral lands. Like
the Cherokees, the Mormons would have their own trail of tears. Where

it would end was of no consequence to Johnston. As far as he was concerned, the attacks against the Utah Expedition were unprovoked.

Captain Randolph Barnes Marcy's voice broke in on Johnston's thought. "You wanted to see me, General?"

"Ah, yes. Come in, Marcy."

The captain advanced several steps, uncovered, and snapped briskly to attention.

"Stand easy," said Johnston. "I've a question for you, Marcy: How long would it take a small group—extra mounts and packhorses—to reach Fort Union, forced march?"

Marcy frowned. "Traveling light—eighteen to twenty days, sir; that is, weather permitting."

"Cutting it short, aren't you? They'd have to go all the way back to Fort Laramie to pick up the Cherokee Trail."

Marcy indicated the map on Johnston's camp table. "I wasn't thinking of the Cherokee, sir. May I?"

At Johnston's nod, Marcy bent over the map, studied it for a moment, and traced a line. "Save a lot of miles by heading due south to the Green, then east across the Sierra San Juans, through Chochetope Pass."

Johnston eyed the track of Marcy's finger. "I don't see any trail indicated between here and the San Juans."

"There isn't; we'd have to cut one. Shouldn't be any problem, General. I've been over most of that country back on the '48 survey. We'd pick up the Cherokee where it crosses the Arkansas at Bent's Fort. From there it's a straight shot to Fort Union, clear trail all the way."

Johnston stabbed a finger at a point on the map. "This pass, Chochetope, suitable for cattle and wagons?"

"Couldn't be much better, General. No water to cross, more level ground than most, and much of the way should be clear of snow, for a while at least."

"And hostiles?"

Marcy closed his eyes for a moment, then shrugged his shoulders resignedly. Johnston need not have asked the question. "May I ask what you had in mind?"

"Supplies, Marcy. Don't want to have all our eggs coming through the South Pass basket, do we?" Johnston smiled thinly.

"I'll write up a requisition order to the commander at Fort Union. Take a small detachment, no more than five men. Hire what drovers you need in Santa Fe. Take Hickok with you. He is to be in charge of selecting the cattle and bossing the drovers. Good man—tough. But don't tell the arrogant bastard I said so. You'll have your orders in the morning, Captain. Be ready to move out."

When the tent flap closed, Johnston settled himself into his folding camp chair. It felt good to get off his feet.

Reaching for pen and paper, he began to write the requisition order that Captain Marcy would carry to Fort Union, an order that would have behind it all the weight of Secretary of War Floyd's office. Johnston had no doubt the battalion would try to interdict the supply wagons from Fort Laramie. But perhaps a small force could slip away to Fort Union unnoticed. To be sure, Johnston assured himself, he would be in command of Salt Lake City long before Marcy and Hickok returned from Fort Union.

He knew that the task he had handed Marcy and Hickok was a long shot, to say the least. The greater probability was that bad weather would stifle any attempt to bring cattle into the area. More than likely he would not see Marcy till spring, if then.

A near-impossible task, Johnston said to himself, and Marcy had taken the order without a wink. That was Johnston's kind of man, the kind of man he was himself. He'd see to it that the captain was rewarded. Then his mind went back to his predicament. "Godforsaken hellhole," he mumbled. For the life of him, he could not understand why anyone would want to move west—California excepted, of course—and actually settle in this frozen desolation.

Johnston was troubled. Events had not turned out at all the way he had planned. He had been a fool and he knew it. Whatever the cause, he should not have separated his troops from their supplies. It was a textbook mistake by which more than one commanding officer had met disaster. Yet he refused to acknowledge, even to himself, that some damned good officers in his command had warned him, and properly so. Still, he cursed himself for having to resort to such an untenable means to secure even minimum rations for his command.

Again his thoughts were interrupted. This time the intruder was a thoroughly irritated Alfred Cumming. Johnston had anticipated the governor designate's displeasure at not being included in the final push to Salt Lake City, another minor irritant among the many. "Damn it, General," Cumming protested, "my instructions are to proceed to Salt Lake with all possible dispatch, and I intend to do so."

"And you shall, Governor, the moment I'm assured the rebels are pacified. I have a responsibility for your personal safety, sir. The field of battle is no place for civilians, Governor."

"Field of battle!" snorted Cumming. "I'm not a military man, Johnston, but from what I've seen, the people of Utah seem to be bending over backward to avoid armed conflict. If they wanted to make a fight of it, Lord knows they've had ample opportunity to do so in these past few hundred miles."

Johnston shrugged. "We're still in Nebraska Territory on the wrong side of the line, sir. Things could be very different once we cross over into the Utah Territory. I can assure you they won't limit themselves to harassing tactics on their home ground: They'll resist with every means at their disposal."

"That remains to be seen, General. In any event, I relieve you of all responsibility in regard to my personal security. I speak for Judge Dawson as well."

"Sorry, Governor. I can't accept that."

"You *will* accept it, General Johnston. Judge Dawson and I may not be soldiers, but we are no less obligated to carry out our orders than you, sir. Must I remind you, General, the armed forces of this nation are subject to civilian authority?"

A flash of anger flared briefly in Johnston's dark eyes, but he masked it quickly. "Allow me to point out an unpleasant fact of life, Governor. Without the means to enforce compliance, there can be no authority, civil or otherwise. If the civil authorities had the foresight to establish a strong military presence in Utah, as it has in other frontier territories, we wouldn't be faced with what we are today. The insurrection would have been nipped in the bud."

"A strong word—*insurrection*."

"Calling for strong measures."

"True, if in fact it does exist, and that's what I intend to find out. It's possible we're confusing legitimate protest with something far more sinister, General. President Buchanan has sent Judge Dawson and me to make that determination, firsthand. If there *is* rebellion in Utah, we'll be the first to call for measures to put an end to it, by whatever means necessary."

Johnston shrugged acceptance. "May I suggest you rest early, Governor, we move out at first light."

"Damned politicians!" Johnston uttered to himself after the governor designate left the tent. It was always the same—make a mess of things, then call on the army to clear it up. Well, this time it would be different. It would be martial law, not civil, that would rule Utah.

If no more than a handful of hotheads opened fire on United States troops, Johnston would have all the legal grounds needed to place the Utah Territory under martial law and declare himself military governor. So much for Alfred Cumming and his civil authority.

The sky was still dark when the notes of reveille pulled Porter Rockwell from his blanket. Muffled shouts and commands came from the army encampment, blending with brays and neighs from irritable equines, and the rattle and clink of military hardware—the sounds of an army preparing to march.

As the sky began to pale, Rockwell had a clearer view of the preparations below: supply wagons being brought into line, dragoon and infantry mounts saddled, teams harnessed to gun carriages and caissons, carbines slid into saddle boots, bedrolls fastened to cantles. Remounts and spare draft animals were roped to tailgates of double-teamed wagons. Apart from the main body of troops, Rockwell could see a small group, not more than a half-dozen men, swing into their saddles and head for the camp gate. Rockwell's glass went to the head of the small column. The leaders were an officer wearing captain's boards, and the scout, Hickok. The short column, leading pack animals and spare mounts, swung to the right, away from the trail leading to Salt Lake City, heading on a southerly course.

"Wonder where they're goin'," said Luke Cartwright.

"If I were a betting man, which I am, I'd say those boys were heading for the New Mex Territory."

"New Mexico?" frowned Luke's younger brother, Will. "What for?"

"Army forts all over New Mex Territory. Maybe the general doesn't want to count too much on resupply from Platte Station. I wouldn't."

"Boots and Saddles" sounded from the camp. Dragoons and mounted infantry moved smoothly into formation as double-strength flank guards rode out to take up position. The echo of "fo-ward ho" rang out and the column began to move. There was no mistaking the man at the head of the column. General Johnston's hussar's dolman was one of a kind. The man to his right, Rockwell was certain, was Phil Cooke.

"Reckon we ought to saddle up," said Luke Cartwright.

"No hurry," answered Rockwell. "About time you put some water boiling for chocolate, isn't it, Luke?" Cartwright nodded, digging for his steel and flint as he moved away.

"How come no infantry?" asked Harve Arnold with a frown at the column below.

"Johnston must have his reasons, and I'd say they all have to do with time."

Rockwell brought the scope to this eye. The lens revealed a brace of uniformed men on each driver's bench, armed with both pistol and carbine. Rockwell was almost certain there were more soldiers hidden under the wagon canvases, ready and waiting to drive off any attack on the wagons. Johnston, he thought, was learning, or listening to Cooke: Doubled flank and rear guards made surprise attack on the column an impossibility, particularly if the attackers were defanged—forbidden the use of weapons. Rockwell centered his glass on the coach sandwiched between two companies of dragoons near the head of the column. The coach had been a curiosity since the first time he saw it back at the crossing: Who were the occupants? Whoever they were they couldn't be part of the military, not riding in a fancy, civilian coach.

Civilians, that was it; politicians would be more like it. Perhaps President Buchanan wasn't so convinced by the stories of rebellion as it first appeared; perhaps he was depending on the people in the coach to send him an unbiased report. Perhaps.

The more immediate question in Rockwell's mind would be answered when Johnston's troops reached Ham's Ford. Would they continue on to Echo Canyon, or branch southwest to the open country of Bear Valley? The fate of Utah, irrespective of the people in the coach, could well rest on Johnston's decision. If it were the Bear Valley route, his advance would be unobstructed by any natural barrier. The whole of the great basin would be at his feet, unless Brigham Young rescinded his "no blood" order and loosed the full power of the battalion. Not a very likely possibility, thought Rockwell with a grimace. Brigham was too damned stubborn to admit a mistake, if it was a mistake. Rockwell understood Young's desire to seek a peaceful solution, but would Johnston permit it to be?

There was another thing to consider: How far would the basin settlers bend? With their backs to the wall, in danger of losing all they'd worked and strived for, could they stand idly by and see it destroyed or taken away? Rockwell didn't believe they would; they'd strike back with a fury. Washington would have its rebellion, and so would Brigham Young.

The breakfast of hot chocolate and biscuit was long over by the time the last of Johnston's column disappeared in the distance.

Rockwell dispatched a young rider to General Wells, informing him that Johnston was on the march, and that he was riding ahead to beat Johnston to Ham's Ford, promising to alert Wells about which route Johnston would take from there.

It was just past midday when Rockwell's troop took to their saddles.

The second day of the march had dawned a murky, slate gray, dropping the temperature a good ten degrees from what it had been on the column's departure from Camp Scott twenty-four hours earlier. Warming rays from the pale, ill-defined sun failed to penetrate the moisture-laden blanket that covered the land from horizon to horizon, and by mid-afternoon a light drizzle began to fall, at times becoming little more than a heavy mist. The column plodded on, the midday meal of jerky and hard biscuit taken in the saddle. Corporal Terrence Riley, 2d Dragoons, nursed the two-quart, nonissue canteen that held the last of the whis-key purchased so expensively from Jubal Hathaway. Riley carefully gauged what was left in the canteen by its weight after each long sip. He was an expert: He could tell to the ounce just by the heft of the blanket cloth–covered container, and knew it would be dry long be-fore the day was out. The twenty dollars silver resting in his pouch was useless; it wouldn't buy him so much as a sniff, not the way these selfish bastards in the company held onto their own supply. Sergeant Dorn had three extra canteens tied to his McClellan, but do you think he'd have mercy for a fellow trooper with a raging thirst in his gut? "Shit," growled Riley. "What the hell ever happened to the milk of human kindness?"

"You talking to me, Riley?" asked Ezra.

"If I was, you'd know it," said the big Irishman, uncapping the can-teen for the third time in the last twenty minutes.

Ezra looked on hungrily as Riley took a long pull. "How about a little taste, Corp? Damned throat feels like I been eatin' sawdust."

"Tough!" grumbled the big man, recapping the canteen. That milk of human kindness crap was for other people, not Terrence Xavier Riley, corporal in the 2d Dragoons.

At the head of the column Colonel Cooke rode stirrup to stirrup with

General Johnston. Not a word had passed between the two since they had taken to their saddles that morning. Cooke wished he could see what was going on in the mind behind that massive brow, discover just what it was that made Johnston tick. Reluctantly, he had come to the conclusion that Johnston was right; the Utahns had no intention of armed resistance. So far, the harassing actions had diligently avoided open combat, which was something the general had good reason to be thankful for, despite his bellicose protestations.

Cooke knew what havoc a small, well-armed, highly mobile group of determined and skilled riflemen could wreak on a ponderously slow-moving military column: quick, slashing attacks, ambuscades, officers picked off by hidden sharpshooters. They'd wear down the troops in body and spirit, the way a pack of wolves would eventually bring down a bull bison, bleeding it a little at a time. Johnston would have found himself a prime target for long rifles. Cooke realized uncomfortably that his own shoulder boards would be a temptation not to be resisted by skilled marksmen.

Clearly, the Utahns determined to avoid bloodletting, were playing for time, hoping to show by their restraint that these tales of rebellion were no more than that—tales, a fiction.

Johnston seemed equally determined not to give them that time; he had his orders and intended to carry them out forthwith, come hell or high water. Of one thing Cooke was certain, they were all pawns, the people of Utah Territory and Johnston's army. The masters of the game were two thousand miles to the east, the ultimate object of the game known only to themselves, or was it? And what about Johnston himself? Was he merely a pawn, blindly following orders? Or was he a key player? Another question pulled at Cooke's agile brain: Why send an army to Utah when the problem, if there really was a problem, might easily be resolved by a delegation empowered to investigate conditions there? Then, if rebellion proved fact, there was ample time to employ force.

Like every knowledgeable career soldier, Cooke was all too aware of the disunion movement; that, to his mind, was the real threat to the nation. Buchanan's promise to hold the Union together by force if necessary would be seriously diluted with a full quarter of that force bogged down two thousand miles from where it would be desperately needed. Cooke looked searchingly at Johnston's Roman profile. The man made no secret of being a staunch states-righter, a Southerner in heart and spirit. Was it fair to suspect him of being part of some sinister plot? Cooke recalled their discussion the first day he joined the column, the fire in Johnston's eyes when he'd thought Cooke had impugned his loyalty to the uniform he wore. From what he knew of Johnston—the man's capabilities, his courage, and his reputation for honor—Cooke was forced to conclude, in spite of himself and not without some reservations, that the respected general was following orders, and was not a willing contributor to any sinister plot. Time would tell, one way or the other.

Cooke eyed the western sky, now a much deeper hue of gray, portions almost charcoal black, the normally visible peaks of the distant Bear Mountains shrouded by the thick blanket of storm clouds.

General Johnston pulled the turnip-sized pocket watch from the folds of his caped greatcoat. The gold lid snapped open under stem pressure exerted by his broad thumb. Twenty-four minutes past three. Frowning at the diffused horizon, he decided he'd call a halt at four thirty, an hour and a half earlier than he had intended, and a few miles short of Ham's Ford. Johnston was satisfied with the column's progress—thirty miles in two days, a fair rate of march considering the pace imposed by the heavily laden baggage and supply wagons, a limitation that would end when the column reached the mouth of Echo Canyon.

Johnston planned for a quick thrust through the canyon, leaving the wagons behind, protected by a full company of mounted infantry. His troops could then easily essay the canyon passage in a half day, at forced march. Captain Hauk's artillery batteries, drawn by six-ups instead of the customary four, would have no trouble keeping up with the main body. If by chance the enemy had any ideas of a canyon ambush, a few volleys of grape and canister would make short work of them. Once through the canyon, the Great Salt Lake Basin would be at his feet—open, defenseless. As for the battalion, if they did choose to fight, it would be on Johnston's terms, not their own. In his long career he had never known a time when irregular troops could stand head to head against professionals supported by heavy guns.

A half mile distant, sheltered by a copse of scrub pine, Porter Rockwell focused the telescope on Johnston's night camp preparations. The troopers went about their chores with well-practiced efficiency.

Cook fires had been lit, the wagons circled to form a corral for the saddle and draft animals, the wagons in turn encircled by a thick ring of six-man tents, they in turn encircled by a ring of picket guards—two-man teams spaced at fifty-yard intervals. Under normal conditions, Rockwell knew, a surprise attack would have little chance of success. At the first sound of alarm he and his boys would find themselves facing a hedgehog of musket barrels. They'd never get within striking distance of the supply wagons. But from all indications, tonight's conditions would be far from normal. The slow drizzle had changed to a steady downfall, the sleet-laden drops whipped by sporadic gusts of wind. Rockwell looked with satisfaction at the western sky. The dark, roiling clouds were rolling in without a break, a massive wall of black-gray that would soon be overhead, carrying the first real taste of winter. The fast-dropping temperature would change the rain into snow. It looked as though Brigham's request—or was it a demand?—for an early and severe winter was about to be granted.

Deeper in the copse Rockwell's troop busied themselves erecting lean-tos, piling thick layers of boughs on the sharply slanted roofs. All this had been done without a word from him; the boys could read weather sign as well as he. Several were already engaged in weaving snow pads from supple branches—not as good as snowshoes, but they'd serve the purpose if the need arose.

Earlier, the Cartwright brothers had questioned Rockwell about the sacks of frozen potatoes he'd ordered tied to their saddles. Why were they hauling them all over hell-and-gone; they weren't fit to eat. "Might find a use for 'em yet," said Rockwell. "Waste not, want not; isn't that the way it goes?"

The pair exchanged a puzzled look, and returned to the warmth of the smokeless chip fire at the entrance of their lean-to.

Sergeant Dorn, an old campaigner on the northern frontier, was as weather wise as Rockwell and his boys. He moved among the troopers ordering them to double-peg their tents against the gusting wind. Dorn knew things were going to get a lot worse before the night was over; a norther was coming, no question about it. The wagons would be a problem, their high, canvas tops making them vulnerable to wind pressure. Dorn ordered the drivers and their gun guards to guy the wagons down with any rope that was available. He thought of hobbling the corralled animals, but decided it would be an unnecessary precaution with the circle of wagons well anchored against the wind.

With Phil Cooke at his side, Johnston made a tour of the encampment, exchanging a word here and there with troopers and noncoms. Heavy, dime-sized flakes had begun to fall by the time they completed the circuit back to Johnston's Sibley. Walker, the general's orderly, had the evening meal prepared, simple fare of dessicated peas and tinned beef. Two place settings were on the linen-covered camp table; the brandy decanter and glasses gleamed in the light of two camphine lanterns hooked on the support pole.

"Why the glum face, Phil?" asked Johnston as Walker helped him out of his greatcoat, brushing the light layer of flakes from the cape. "Not bothered by a few snowflakes, are you?"

"We could have done without 'em," answered Cooke, shrugging out of his own coat. "Let's hope it passes over before the worst of it comes down."

A sharp gust beat on the canvas of the cone-shaped tent, causing the support pole to wobble. The lanterns swayed briefly, casting a play of shadows on the walls. Johnston poured the brandy, and extended one of the glasses of amber liquid to Cooke with a chiding smile. "Relax, Colonel. If Hannibal could do it, so can we."

"Hardly an apt comparison, Sidney," said Cooke, returning the smile.

"Nothing ever really is, when you get down to it. There's always a difference, small as it may be."

Cooke chuckled. "There's nothing small about African elephants knee deep in snow."

Johnston nodded, and indicated the camp chair opposite his own.

Walker served the stewlike mixture from a large iron pan, expressing his regrets there hadn't been time to bake fresh biscuits.

A few yards away Lamar Dawson gingerly removed an opened tin of beans from the tent stove. He slanted a lifted brow to the governor designate, barely visible under a layer of robes, the foot of his folding cot angled to receive what little warmth the camp stove could provide. "Sure you don't care for some beans, Governor?"

Alfred Cumming stifled a moan, anticipating what the night would be like when those beans worked their way through Dawson's digestive tract. "Quite sure, Lamar. If I never saw another can of beans in my life, it would be too soon."

Dawson dipped a spoon into the can to bring a heaping spoon-ful to his mouth. "Partial to 'em myself. Guess if I had to, I could live on 'em."

"I'm sure you could, Lamar," said Cumming, unable to repress a shudder. He drew the heavy robes over his head, punching out a pocket for breathing space. Damn Mormons! Damn Buchanan! Damn every-thing that got him into this; and, above all, damn Dawson!

The next three hours saw the temperature drop precipitously. A foot-thick blanket of snow covered the ground; savage wind gusts buffeted and tore at tents and wagons, piling deep drifts against everything projecting above ground level. Still the flakes fell, a wall of white, almost impenetrable to the eye, swirling, whipped in a thousand di-rections, driven with stinging force, straining the guy lines of the canvas wagon coverings to their limit. Corralled animals turned snow-coated rumps to the wind, crowding together for warmth.

The conical shape of the big Sibleys offered relatively little resis-tance to the wind, but the same could not be said for smaller tents facing into the gusts. Dozens were pulled free of their pegs to flutter off into the night, the former occupants burrowing into the nearest drift for protection. Sergeant Dorn took it upon himself to have a bugler sound recall. The pickets, fully exposed to the elements, blinded to anything more than ten to fifteen feet distant, could serve no purpose, and he sure as hell didn't want to find fifty to sixty men with frostbite come morning.

Moving around the outer ring of tents, the storm lantern held high, Dorn had the bugler repeat the call at short intervals, ignoring the muffled protests that came from the tents. Wind had a way of distorting sound, carrying it away at times, and Dorn wanted to make damned sure every man on picket post could find his way into the camp.

The sergeant saw a large figure appear out of the swirling flakes. He didn't have to be told it was the general; there was no mistaking that purposeful stride, even in foot-deep snow.

"Who ordered recall sounded, Sergeant?" said Johnston, his voice raised over the wind.

"I did, sir. Those boys out there can't do any good, and I didn't see any point in gettin' 'em froze."

Johnston was silent for a moment, then he nodded. "Carry on."

Dorn exhaled a sigh of relief as the general's form faded into the driving snow. He turned to the bugler, a corporal in the mounted infantry. "What the hell you stoppin' for? You heard the general!"

The bugler nodded, blew a warming breath on his mouthpiece, and sounded the call again.

Rockwell and his guerrillas, moving ghostlike on their snow pads, had already penetrated the picket line when the first bugle call sounded. Rockwell, like the others, carried a quarter-filled sack of the frozen potatoes that Will and Luke had been curious about. Waste not, want not. Rockwell halted the group, waiting for the brief moment of silence between the bugle calls, his ears attuned for another sound. It came, the mournful bray of an army mule, which brought instant accompaniment from equally unhappy creatures. Rockwell fixed on the direction the sound had come from, then signaled the troop into movement, leading them silently between rows of half-buried tents.

Phil Cooke was standing at the entrance to his tent as the preoccupied general passed to his Sibley. The colonel would not sleep that night. He was uneasy. They were out there, somewhere, Rockwell and his men, and had been every step of the way from Camp Scott. He could feel it. Rather than bring in the sentries, the camp should be on alert. Still, a ring of sentries might have little effect. Couldn't see your hand in front of your face. An assailant could be on you before you knew it. Either way, Cooke knew, Rockwell had the advantage.

The bugle call sounded again. Cooke had trouble pinpointing its location until a faint glimmer from Dorn's lantern was briefly visible through the swirling flakes.

"Down," hissed Rockwell, throwing himself prone in the deepening snow. The order was swiftly relayed down the line.

Two indistinct shapes crossed his line of vision. "How the hell are we going to find our tent, can't see nuthin'," said one of the shapes.

"I don't know, dammit, just gotta keep lookin'," responded the other.

The shapes disappeared in a few steps. Rockwell pulled himself to his feet; the others followed. They hadn't gone ten yards when one of the canvas-topped wagons loomed suddenly before them. A sharp gust of wind rocked the big wagon on its chassis, the wood frame groaning in protest, the anchored guy ropes alternately looscning and tightening with every change in wind direction.

Rockwell peered through the space between the wagons, parked tongue to tailgate, and got a brief glimpse of tightly packed saddle and draft animals, heads low, rumps aimed into the worst of the wind. The boys hunkered down in the lee of one of the wagons as Rockwell laid out the plan of action. Luke Cartwright would take fifteen of the lads and circle around the corral, enter it from the north side, and come in behind the animals massed against the south wall. When they were in position, Rockwell and the others would open a gap in the south wall, cutting the guy lines and manhandling two of the wagons clear of the circle. The wind, he told them, would make the task easier, the high canvas catching the wind like the sail of a ship.

"But how do we get 'em moving, Major?" asked Buck, referring to the animals. "You said we couldn't hooraw 'em with gunshots."

"Told you we'd have a use for those frozen spuds," replied Rockwell. "Once they start, grab a handful of mane and bareback out of there. Keep 'em going."

Rockwell pulled out one of his emergency ration cheroots, and cupped a sulfur match to its end. "Takes about ten minutes for this to smoke down halfway. You ought to be in position by then. Get moving."

Luke nodded. Big pockets bulging with frozen potatoes, the group moved off, to be quickly swallowed up by the wind-driven flakes.

Rockwell and the others slipped under one of the wagon beds, knives ready to cut the guy lines when he signaled the time was right. He cupped the cheroot in his big hands, protecting it from the wind. Ten minutes. . . .

Sergeant Dorn checked off the last of the two-man picket teams. Eighty men had been out, eighty brought back in, and there wasn't a one of them who wasn't damned glad of it. Picket duty, in the best of times, was a pain in the rump. Out there in the dark, not knowing what that darkness might conceal, played on a man's nerves, had him jumping at shadows, seeing things that weren't there—and sometimes were. Trouble was, a man could never be sure.

Pushing the lantern before him, Dorn crawled into his unshared tent, a privilege of his rank, and stifled an oath at what he saw—an uncapped canteen atop his blanket. Dorn snatched up the container, bringing its mouth to his nostrils, an unnecessary confirmation. He knew what the now-empty canteen had held, two quarts of gut-buster whiskey—gone, except for the residual vapor taunting his nostrils. Growling an oath, Dorn hurled the canteen at the tent wall. Some son of a bitch was going to pay for this!

The angry bray of a mule, quickly followed by others confirmed Rockwell's estimate of how long it would take Luke and his boys to come in behind the herd. The cheroot was just on the halfway point of its burn. Stubbing it out he nodded to the others. They slipped through to the inner side of the corral, silently hazing the bunched-up animals back clear of the guy lines. Then he and the boys went to work; knife blades slashed through the taut lines. Will Cartwright and several of the others laid hold of a wagon tongue, cramping it around so the wheels were angled outward. As Rockwell had said, the wagon, free of the restraining ropes, helped by the wind, moved easily. The second wagon was freed from the circle to leave a forty-foot gap in the corral wall. The first few animals took a few tentative steps through the opening, as if unsure the barrier was no longer there to prevent their passage.

Luke Cartwright slung a leg over a big dragoon mount, his left hand twisted hard into the animal's mane. The others quickly followed his actions and a barrage of frozen potatoes hammered into the rumps of horses and mules, bringing snorts and brays as they pushed forward to escape the stinging missiles. Iron-shod boots bit into hocks and fetlocks; mules and horses bucked or lashed back at their tormentors. "Mount up!" bellowed Rockwell, swinging up on the bare back of one of the lead horses. Will and the others didn't need a second invitation. With a swelling rumble of agitated hooves, mixed with the bawl of mules and the shrill neigh of horses, the entire herd began to surge blindly forward. Rockwell and his lads pelted the leaders, driving them from an aimless walk into a fast trot, then a run. "Stampede!" roared the man in buckskins, his voice rising above the sound of animals and wind. Will and the others added their voices to the alarm, and swung in to take the lead, knowing from long experience that the rest of the herd would follow.

Sleep-dazed dragoons and mounted infantrymen spilled out of their tents, their shouts adding to the confusion. Men were bowled over, some trampled before they could clear their tents as the herd thundered through, cutting a fifty-yard swath through the ring of shelters. Shots were fired in panic, the shots only spurring the animals to greater effort. Luke Cartwright's boys had fanned out behind the rear of the herd, crouching low on the bare backs of their mounts, howling at the top of their lungs. "Stampede! Get out of the way, stampede!"

A few of the more alert troopers, getting brief glimpses of the mounted figures, managed to get off a shot—ill aimed, ineffective. In less than a minute it was all over, the herd disappearing into the thickly swirling flakes. A strange silence fell over the encampment as bewildered troopers wondered what in the hell had happened.

Cooke crossed to the solitary figure standing outside the flap of the command tent. Lamar Dawson and Alfred Cumming, thick blankets around their shoulders, also approached.

Albert Sidney Johnston's face appeared as if cast in stone. He did not turn to Cooke. "Don't say it, Phil," he said in a flat, toneless voice.

"Guess there isn't any need, Sidney. Wouldn't have made any difference anyway in this blindness."

Johnston turned and entered the Sibley, his eyes never making contact with the junior officer's.

"What happened, Colonel?" said the governor designate.

"What shouldn't have, Governor, what shouldn't have."

Cumming and Dawson exchanged puzzled looks as Cooke strode away to enter his own tent. Cumming seized on the opportunity to draw in several deep breaths of untainted air as he and Dawson made their way back.

In the security of his tent, Cooke sank onto his cot, resting his elbows on his knees, hands cupped under his chin. *"Guerrilla tactica,"* he bit out. No question about it; Rockwell's orders were to stop the Utah Expedition without military confrontation—hit and run, bleed the supplies, knock Johnston off schedule.

A deep frown creased the officer's forehead. But that wouldn't be enough to keep the army from reaching Salt Lake City, he surmised, not with Albert Sidney Johnston in command. There was one other necessary factor—an uncommonly early and vicious winter with a record snowfall and debilitatingly low temperatures. Cooke shook his head. "How in the hell were they able to count on that!" he asked aloud. Then the colonel fell back on the cot and closed his eyes. He sure as hell wasn't going to try to answer that question.

It was well past midmorning when the last of the search parties re-turned, to report minimal results. The continuously falling snow, though much lighter with the coming of daylight, had effectively erased the herd's tracks. The searchers, often hampered by waist-high drifts, had recovered a number of animals that had broken away from the main herd, often singly, others in groups ranging from a half dozen to thirty or more. In all, Captain Hauk reported, four hundred and nine had been recovered, about evenly divided between horses and mules, barely enough to fill the traces of the wagons and gun carriages.

Johnston eyed the group of officers gathered in the command tent, reading the unspoken question in their carefully composed faces. The question could have only one answer, but that answer would have to come from Johnston's lips.

The previous night, Salt Lake City could have been reached within five to ten days; now, any hope of attaining that goal, or anything near it, was beyond all reason. The dismounted troopers, slogging through knee-deep snow, would run out of rations before they could cover fifty of the hundred and more miles to their destination. Echo Canyon might well be impassable, blocked by heavy drifts. The column would have to backtrack the thirty miles to Camp Scott, and wait there until it could be refurbished with fresh supplies and remounts. There could be only one answer. Johnston gave it.

Stepping out of the tent, Colonel Cooke took in the slate gray sky that deepened to near black on the northern horizon, and knew that the previous night's storm was just the beginning. The chances of the column being snowbound before it could reach Camp Scott was a very real possibility.

A half mile distant, lying prone on a windswept hummock, Porter Rockwell had much the same thought as he observed Johnston's army break camp. Pulling the sugan tighter about him, he settled down for what he hoped would not be a long wait. Would the column continue west, heading for Echo Canyon, or would it backtrack toward the east? Had Johnston's determination been blunted, or would he push on despite the clearly ominous weather conditions and loss of the bulk of his animals?

Rockwell would remain where he was until he knew for certain; he was not a man to take things for granted. He knew that generals, like lesser men, could not always be depended on to do the logical thing in a given circumstance. Too many other factors often colored judgment, the foremost being ambition, and there was no doubt in his mind that Albert Sidney Johnston was a very ambitious man, the kind to take reverses as a personal affront.

If Johnston did attempt to continue the push for Echo Canyon, he'd pay a heavy price in casualties, if not from battalion guns, then from the cold hand of winter. That was a distinction eastern politicians and newspapers wouldn't concern themselves with. In a way, they would be right. A trooper losing a hand or foot to frostbite turned gangrenous was no less a casualty than one wounded by gunfire; a dead man, whether by cold or bullet, was still a corpse, and blame would be placed where most expedient.

The hazy, ill-defined sun struggled to pierce the gray blanket covering the land. It was directly overhead when a detachment of fifty mounted dragoons began to break trail through the two-foot-deep snow, heading east. Rockwell had the answer he'd been waiting for—the army was pulling back, returning to Camp Scott. Logic had prevailed; the immediate threat to the Great Salt Basin had been averted.

Brigham Young's hopes had been realized. It *was* going to be an early and one hell of a winter. For all practical purposes Johnston's army was immobilized, and would be until spring. By then who knew what changes might take place? Nature and a handful of renegades had given the people of Utah a breathing spell. Now Brigham, and other reasoning men, would have an opportunity for their voices to be heard. Still, one important question was yet to be answered—would those voices fall on deaf ears?

Dismounted dragoons and infantrymen fell into a half-mile-long column behind the mounted troopers. The tramped-down snow would ease the burden on the animals pulling the gun carriages and wagons. Rockwell felt an unfamiliar surge of sympathy for the troopers struggling to keep some semblance of formation as they plodded through the snow, which would deepen as storm followed on the heels of storm. The column would be lucky to average two to three miles a day under such conditions, their rations exhausted long before they came within sight of Camp Scott.

"Poor, foot-slogging bastards," blurted Rockwell. Then pushing all thoughts of compassion from his mind, he snorted to himself, "To hell with 'em!"

Rockwell swung into his saddle. He'd catch up with the Cartwright brothers and the stolen herd before the light went down. They'd have their own problems to worry about. Getting that herd through Bear Valley and into the basin wasn't going to be any picnic.

On the third day of the withdrawal to Camp Scott, General Johnston ordered every able-bodied officer to surrender his mount to the troopers breaking trail. He himself was to be included in that order. The trailbreaking animals would be on the verge of exhaustion after a few hours and would have to be rotated to the rear of the column to regain their strength. Many would die in their harnesses, and each night the bitter cold would take its toll. The foot troops immediately behind the trailbreakers had the toughest going of all. By the time the last of the column had reached a given point, movement was fairly easy, the snow well tramped down by those who had gone before them.

Not a day had passed without a fresh fall, making the trailbreakers' task much more difficult. Cooke estimated they had covered slightly more than six miles in the three days, the column frequently delayed by bogged-down supply wagons and the heavier gun carriages, often taking the strength and weight of dozens of troopers to get them on the move. To make things more difficult, the grease in wheel hubs would freeze quickly once a wagon was immobilized for any length of time. There was a particular problem with the artillery pieces, the gun barrels and metal carriage fittings a constant menace to the unwary, as a substantial number of bloody bandaged hands gave evidence. Nothing metal could be touched without leaving living flesh glued to its surface.

Rations were another problem. The supplies carried for the quick push to Salt Lake City were wholly inadequate for the current situation; at the rate of two miles a day they'd be exhausted long before Camp Scott came into view. Johnston approved Cooke's suggestion to halve the daily rations for all ranks, including his own, and those of their civilian charges, Cumming and Dawson. Cooke had to give him credit; the man was no armchair general, more concerned about his own comfort than that of the men serving under him. Albert Sidney Johnston would take no more for himself than the lowest rank in the command. Cooke would have done the same, but he wasn't a general. Put a star on a man's shoulder and he instantly became something apart— the nearest thing to a law unto himself ever devised by the community of man.

Cooke's journal, still preserved to this day, recorded the rustling of the cattle ". . . by the Mormons, in consequence of which many wagons were unable to move at all. After struggling along until nightfall, the regiment camped wherever they could find shelter under the bluffs or among willows. The animals slipped to rise no more, and the mules would cluster around the abandoned night-fires to waste away from hunger and cold. In the mornings, the camp was encircled by their carcasses, coated with a film of ice."

Chapter Fifteen

The storm, or series of storms, had come down on the eastern flanks of the Bear Mountains, which acted as a buffer, keeping the worst of it out of the Great Basin. The constant winds from the northwest drove the storm south and east, crossing the Elks to blow itself out over the great Kansas plains.

The pie-shaped wedge formed by the Bear Mountains to the west and the Wind River Mountains to the east took the brunt of the week-long storm. Bridger's Fort and Camp Scott were close to the heart of that wedge.

The well-worn trail between Bridger's Fort and Camp Scott was easily discerned, even under a two-foot layer of snow, but traversing it was far from easy. By the fourth day from the Ham's Ford bivouac, Johnston's column began to lose animals to exhaustion; mules and horses dropped to their knees with mournful groans, never to rise again.

A pistol or carbine ball would put an end to their suffering, and knives would plunge into the still-warm bodies to carve fresh meat for hungry stomachs. In most instances the meat was eaten raw, the bloody residue freezing on beards and mustaches, giving their owners a savage appearance.

By the ninth day of the march, Johnston was forced to order the abandonment of the artillery pieces, which had become too great a drain on the strength of men and animals. An artilleryman without his guns was like a trooper without boots, thought Captain Hauk. So it was with reluctance that he had his gunners remove the percussion cap firing mechanisms and spike the touchholes to render the big guns inoperable. The guns would be recovered as soon as his men and animals were up to the job; the spikes would be drilled out and the firing mechanism bolted back in place.

The big grain-carrying wagons were emptied of all but what was needed to provide for the rapidly diminishing number of draft and saddle animals, now down to less than a sixth of what had marched out of Camp Scott thirteen days earlier. The space left by the discarded grain sacks was quickly filled by men suffering from exhaustion, dysentery, or frostbite—often all three. The medical officer, Major Poole, had overruled the general on a number of occasions in the last several days. A man was either incapacitated or he was not; malingerers, he informed Johnston, would be quickly culled out of the morning sick line, a line that grew longer with each passing day. Johnston bowed to the doctor's expertise.

The twelfth day of the march was particularly brutal on man and beast. The dragoons, many of whom wore nonregulation boots, designed more for appearance than utility, suffered the most. The tight-fitting, thin-grained leather offered little resistance to cold and moisture. The day had dawned with a thick mist, which hung foglike over the land. Then came the snow—huge flakes that drifted down and clung to every available surface. The wind—harsh and unrelenting—drove the flakes with stinging force into the faces of men and animals as they struggled half-blinded to make headway, barely able to see one or two steps ahead. Body heat melted the flakes on the backs of men's necks, the moisture seeping under their collars to be soaked up by the thick wool of tunics and undershirts. The snow was everywhere, a great, constantly moving shroud of impenetrable white that forced the men to squint through lashes heavy with ice. Men slipped and fell, many wanting nothing more than to just lie down in the deep snow and let the falling flakes cover them in final sleep. Their comrades pulled them up, forced them on, ignoring the bitter curses and threats that were their reward.

Colonel Cooke ordered Lieutenant Coy to mount a squad and take it to the tail of the column in search of stragglers. "Drive them with the flat of your sword, if you have to, but keep them moving!"

At midday, Johnston called a halt. The column would have to wait out this latest storm, conserving the little strength remaining in numbed,

half-frozen bodies. Foraged twigs and branches were ignited with cartridge powder, the flames giving little more than an illusion of warmth.
Some of the older hands burrowed into the sides of drifts, huddling
together in an attempt to share body heat and, more importantly, to
escape the icy fingers of piercing wind.

Corporal Terrence X. Riley cursed himself for not saving a taste of
the whiskey he'd poured from Sergeant Dorn's canteen into his own,
and double-cursed himself for sharing a portion of it, a small portion,
to be sure, but a portion nevertheless. The fact that his accomplice had
made the theft possible, by standing watch outside Dorn's tent, didn't
enter into it, not with Riley it didn't.

General Johnston plodded through the knee-deep snow, going from
group to group with a word of encouragement, at times even praise.
Johnston's pride in his men was evident as he pointed out to Cooke
that there wasn't a man who had discarded his field pack or weapons.
"When they start throwing away their equipment, then you know you're
in trouble. It isn't an army anymore, it's rabble."

"We're on the edge, Sidney," said Cooke. "I don't know how much
more of this they can take."

Johnston's dark eyes bored into Cooke's. "They'll take what they
have to, Phil. I intend to march into Camp Scott with every man present
and accounted for. They'll do it if I have to make them crawl in on
their hands and knees."

"Lead 'em or drive 'em, is that it?"

"Does it matter, as long as they get there?"

"An honest answer? No. I'd do whatever I had to, if it were my
command."

A thin smile touched Johnston's lips. "At last we agree on something."

Alfred Cumming was oblivious to the stream of unending observa-
tions spilling from Lamar Dawson's mouth. Cumming had learned to
block them from his conscious mind, the way one learned to ignore
the constant yapping of some mongrel pup. Cumming had his own reason for complaint—Albert Sidney Johnston. The man was a martinet,
determined to listen to no voice but his own; refusing to accept advice from highly competent officers such as Phil Cooke and Col. Fitz-
John Porter—advice that would have prevented this current fiasco, saved
a thousand men the discomfort and pain this retreat had inflicted upon
them. A reckless venture to say the least.

A good share of the fault, Cumming concluded, lay with Buck Buchanan and his advisers; they'd failed to look before making a more than likely unnecessary leap. A situation that might easily have been resolved by political means had been turned into a military venture, one that could have repercussions far beyond the borders of the Utah Territory. Cumming admitted to himself that he was no authority on the Mormons, but what little he did know convinced him that these people were not fools. Fools they would have to be to take up arms against the entire nation, no matter how just their cause. That was the key word—*cause*. Had anyone in Washington listened to their side of this unhappy affair? Would anyone listen? A grim tightness came to Cumming's lips; people would listen if he had anything to say about it. If that meant bucking heads with General Johnston, so be it. He was a presidential appointee, dammit, and he had no intention of buckling down to some two-for-a-penny brevet brigadier general.

A particularly sharp gust of wind rattled the coach. Lamar Dawson's litany of complaints and anecdotes droned on.

It was just past noon on the fifteenth day of the march from the Ham's Ford bivouac when Johnston rode into Camp Scott at the head of his ragtag, stumbling column of glazed-eyed troopers. Fifteen days of frozen hell lay behind them, but the men were all there, every last one of them.

Willing hands helped the incapacitated from the wagons. Company cooks doled out ladles of mule meat stew, additional fires were built, and spare clothing was donated—what there was of it. Questions were asked that received only numbed mumbles in answer.

Great changes had been made in the seventeen-day absence of the column. Fitz-John Porter took out his disappointment at being left behind by working the tails off the men sharing his temporary exile at Camp Scott. Woodcutters labored from first to last light to fill wagon after wagon with freshly cut logs. The logs were split and sawn into rough planks, and structures of sufficient size and number to house the entire complement of troops were nearing completion, all laid out as prescribed by army manual. The colonel had a feeling of satisfaction as he observed Johnston step down from his horse, legs quivering from fatigue. His highness had gotten his comeuppance. Fitz-John couldn't wait to hear all the details from Phil Cooke and the other officers. He'd make all the proper sounds of commiseration, of course, and he'd mean them—for the others, not Johnston. The arrogant ass deserved no compassion, not from Col. Fitz-John Porter.

Hank Magruder and his wagon boss, Case Carney, pushed through the ring of curious troops, all anxious to hear about what happened on the march to Salt Lake City. Most found it hard to believe that the same men who high-stepped out of Camp Scott a mere two and a half weeks before were now this ragged, physically beaten column.

Fitz-John Porter broke through the crowd. "I'll show you to your new quarters, General. I think you'll find them an improvement over the Sibley." At Johnston's nod, Fitz-John Porter led him to one of the larger structures facing the quadrangle.

Magruder and Carney stepped up to Cooke, the former grinning openly at him. "Looks like we won't see Salt Lake City this year."

A flash of anger filled Cooke's eyes as he stepped toe to toe with the big man. "The best thing you can do right now, *Mister* Magruder, is get the hell out of my presence, and take your overgrown ape with you!"

Carney bristled. "Who you calling—"

"Shut up, Carney," snapped Magruder, never losing his smug smile. "The colonel's a bit edgy, that's all. Can't say I blame him, considerin'. C'mon."

The pair stalked away, Carney's laugh trailing behind them.

"Don't let them bother you, Colonel," said Captain Frietag. "Why step in dung when you can go around it."

"If Magruder's typical of the kind of scum the government's forced Utah officials to deal with, I don't blame them for booting him out of the territory."

"And they send us out here to boot 'em right back in," said Lieutenant Coy, shaking his head.

Alfred Cumming and Judge Dawson, coach robes drawn tightly about their shoulders, approached. "What's the situation, Colonel?" Cumming asked Cooke. "How long will we be here before we start back for Salt Lake City?"

A hint of amusement touched Cooke's lips as he eyed the earnest faces of the pair. "How does April or May sound to you, Governor?"

The faces of both men blanched. "Surely you jest, Colonel. Our orders are to proceed with—"

"All possible dispatch, Governor," said Cooke, completing the sentence.

"Precisely. I'd appreciate a proper answer to my question, sir."

"The answer was as proper, as accurate, as I can give, Governor. You and Judge Dawson will have to make the best of it; we all will, I'm afraid."

Cumming and Dawson exchanged looks of disbelief. "Impossible," tweeted Dawson.

"What the colonel's saying, gentlemen, is that everything depends on the weather and our ability to resupply, neither of which seems to be in our favor, sorry to say," said Frietag.

"But . . . but this is intolerable!" stammered the governor designate.

Cooke, in spite of his weariness, couldn't resist a smile. "We all agree with you, Governor, but I can assure you, things are going to get worse before they get better."

Mike Danaher, a bull-chested man of forty, wearing the stripes of a sergeant major, took advantage of the momentary lull to step with a crash of boots and crisp salute to the senior officer in the group, Colonel Cooke. The salute, Cooke was quick to notice, was palm front, British style, rather than the down-palmed U.S. Army regulation salute. The man held the salute, waiting to be acknowledged. Ex-British army, Cooke concluded. He'd met hundreds of such men over the years, and knew that it was almost impossible to break them of a habit deeply ingrained by their earlier training.

"Yes, Sergeant Major?" said Cooke, returning the salute.

"I'm to see you officers to your quarters, sor. And the civilian gents, too, sor. I'll have some of the lads tend t' your personals. If ye'll follow me, plaze."

"Willingly, Sergeant Major, willingly," said Cooke.

The journey through South Pass had been effected with little difficulty by the three hundred heavily laden pack animals escorted by two companies of infantry under the command of Captain Buell, part of the contingent that Johnston had ordered to remain behind at Platte Station. The storm had worn itself out by the time it reached the west flank of the Wind River Mountains, but it had dropped enough snow to pose a problem for wagons. Wisely, Buell followed the advice of the Fort Laramie garrison commander, Major Hemming, transferring the supplies from wagons to pack animals. The wisdom of the decision became evident long before the column reached the midway point through South Pass. The sturdy packhorses and mules forced their way through drifts that would have been impassable to wagons. Now, well down the west slope of the pass, the going was relatively easy, the snow averaging less than a foot in depth.

The closer the pack train column got to the approaches of what had once been Bridger's Fort, the more nervous Buell became, closely scanning each and every clump of brush or stand of trees, anyplace that might offer concealment to "them Utah boys." Buell didn't doubt for a moment that they might make an attempt on the pack train. They'd sure raised enough Cain with Johnston's column, and there was a lot more of them.

The arrival of Captain Buell's pack train lifted the spirits of the troopers at Camp Scott, clear evidence that they weren't cut off from the world they knew. If one train could get through, others would be sure to follow. The camp had taken on a permanent aspect, complete with log palisade, watchtowers, and gate. Like soldiers of every time, they had settled in, prepared to make the best of what was to be had. There were grumblings; there were always grumblings, a natural part of military life.

General Johnston had worked long into the night to encipher a detailed dispatch to the secretary of war, informing him of the urgent situation and status of his command. Conditions had made occupation of Salt Lake City an impossibility, and any projection as to when the army could resume march would be pure speculation at this point in time. The primary obstacle was weather, followed by an acute shortage of supplies and the need to replace animals lost to the elements and marauders from Utah Territory. If the weather should break, and all indications were bleak in that respect, he would push on to Salt Lake City with what mounted units and infantry he could muster. The medical officer, Major Poole, had rated more than twenty percent of the command unfit for field duty due to dietary deficiencies, injuries, and frostbite. As things stood, Johnston regretted to report, even with prompt and adequate resupply, it was highly probable that the army would remain immobilized through the winter months. Resupply was absolutely essential if the Utah Expedition was to continue its mission in the spring.

Johnston handed the sealed envelope to Captain Buell, instructing him to proceed to Fort Laramie with all possible haste. A squadron of dragoons would serve as escort to ensure Buell's safe arrival. There, he was to see to it that the message was transmitted east. Then Buell was to return to the army's base of supply at Platte River Station. He was to bring what was left of the supplies to Camp Scott at all costs. "Your efforts may mean the difference between survival and disaster, Captain. I . . . we . . . are all counting on you."

"I understand, sir. I'll do my best," responded Buell icily. Then he did an about-turn and exited.

"At all costs," Buell repeated aloud to a fellow officer. "That son of a bitch. The cost will be the lives of me and my men. No way on God's earth I can make it back with all those supplies in the dead of winter. He should have brought everything with him to begin with. Hell, this weather's mild compared to what it's goin' to be, and its goin' to be bloody hell for us to get to the Platte and Fort Laramie, let alone return. The man's crazy!"

Johnston settled back in his camp chair, a brooding resignation darkening his powerful features. He had a strong aversion to anything that smacked of defeat, and for the moment, *defeat* was the only word for his current situation. He knew that some of his junior officers were criticizing his command decisions. It was not that he had ignored their suggestions out of incompetence. But his was more than a military exercise; it was a mission of the greatest importance, and its critical nature weighed heavily upon him. The risks he had taken were calculated. He had simply underestimated the stubbornness of the Mormons, their use of guerrilla warfare, and their willingness to engage the Utah Expedition far from their home base. If there was to be a battle, he had expected it to be for control of the Salt Lake Valley. And the brutal severity of this early winter—no one would have predicted it. Still, being the man he was, there was no doubt in his mind that he would ride triumphantly into Salt Lake City come spring.

Brigham Young poured over the reports coming in from all over the territory. His communication system was unmatched. He was not to know this until much later, but the estimates he received of the damage inflicted by Rockwell and his guerrillas on the army were remarkably close to those gathered by General Johnston's staff. Rockwell's guerrilla tactics, which Young termed his "first line of defense," had been successful. In the space of a few weeks, they—with help from the elements—had halted the Utah Expedition in its tracks, more than likely until at least spring.

The second line of defense—the Mormon Battalion, or Territorial Militia, or, as it was sometimes called, the Legion, under the command of General Wells—had not been idle. Ranging far and wide, before the snows came, they had burned thousands upon thousands of acres of forage that lay in the path of Johnston's army. General Kutuzov would have been proud.

Under Wells's order, several hundred battalion troopers had fortified the most direct route into the valley—Echo Canyon; within its twenty miles it contained a number of natural formations that were ideal for fortification. Large boulders and rocks were cradled on the overhanging cliffs at strategic points, ready to be tumbled down, blocking passage to unwelcome visitors. In one area a large spring had been dammed, its release capable of flooding sections of the canyon floor at a moment's notice. Trenches were dug across the canyon floor in the narrowest areas. Ten feet deep and of like width, the trenches were effective barriers to mounted troops, cannons, and wagons.

The troops had cleverly constructed makeshift bridges and platforms across these obstacles, so that friends could pass through with relative ease, but the props could be easily and quickly destroyed should an enemy seek passage.

Salt Lake City was the third line of defense. Once again the defender of Moscow came to mind. Napoleon had found the Russian capital in ashes, a hollow victory for the invaders. Johnston would be no more fortunate. The defense of Salt Lake City would lie in its destruction: fire and flame. The thought of it anguished Young, but of one thing he was certain—like the phoenix, a new city would rise from the ashes. His people would go on. Utah was their home.

Still, Young had asked himself many times: Would Johnston march through the ashes and then pursue his people? If he did, what then? Young would never order the battalion into a head-on battle with the Utah Expedition. Fine as his troops were, they'd be no match for Johnston's field guns. There'd be no Balaclava in Utah, no Light Brigade, no valiant six hundred charging into the mouths of cannons. If there was to be a battle, it would be on Young's terms; he'd choose the ground, the time, and the place. He prayed it would never come to that.

General Wells had ordered the battalion demobilized. There would be ample time to reassemble it when and if it were needed come spring. In the meantime the men had more important matters to attend to: homes and families, and another kind of warfare—the seasonal battle of the elements they all knew and feared with just cause—the battle of winter survival in a land that showed no mercy for the foolhardy.

Farmers, ranchers, and villagers in the path of Johnston's army had obeyed Brigham Young's command to leave no succor to the advancing troops; vital winter stores that could not be carried were destroyed. Homes and barns were torched or stripped of anything that might give comfort to the invaders. These people would have to be housed and fed, most of them dispersed among the communities to the west and south. There was sparse room for them in Salt Lake City, and it was a strain on food reserves to feed them. The small city–sized camp that Young had ordered constructed in Cache Valley wasn't intended for lengthy occupation. Its purpose was to provide a temporary shelter for the women and children should Johnston's troops attempt to lay waste to Salt Lake City—a very real possibility considering the political climate in the nation's capital. Now, fortunately, that danger was no longer imminent; life could go on. Perhaps, they thought, peace would come with the new spring, and they would rebuild, plant new crops, and once again be secure in their homes and beliefs.

In early October Porter Rockwell and his little band of rustlers returned to Salt Lake City. The morning had dawned bright and clear, the rays of the sun sparkling off the newest layer of virgin snow. The men were tired and cold, but their journey had been comparatively easy, considering how the Utah Expedition was suffering.

The sight of the city was curiously comforting to Rockwell. For a brief period he felt a rare sense of contentment, as though he were coming home for the holidays. There was a festive spirit in the air. Johnston's army had been stopped, until spring at least. Once again, Rockwell mused, the outcasts were nestled safely in the great valleys of the Rockies. It seemed to him that life was going on much as before. He noticed that Thanksgiving and Christmas decorations were already appearing in the center city.

Anne McCutcheon came to mind, and the thought of her made him feel warm inside. Nevertheless, since the moment he had first laid eyes on her, she had raised contradicting and confused feelings in him. He could never dissociate her from the past. Even now, in spite of himself, his mind's eye went back to Nauvoo, Illinois, Christmas Day, 1845, bleak and cold. He had stood alone, his head bowed, at the foot of a barren and forlorn elm, stripped of its foliage by the season. In one direction, it was but a short distance to the banks of the Mississippi; in another direction stood the Homestead, once the home of Joseph Smith.

Beneath the tree was a single grave, a simple stone. Buried in now-frozen earth lay the woman who had made his existence something most men only dream about, and a tiny babe carefully, tenderly nestled in her arms. A dream, he had said to himself, that's all it was—now gone.

At length he had turned and walked thirty yards or so across the snow and into a thicket. There he stopped for a minute at the foot of two barely visible mounds. In order to protect these graves from vandals, there were no markers. Here were buried Joseph Smith and his brother Hyrum. Rockwell again bowed his head in silence. Then he had gone away, never to return.

The sorrow and the guilt had taken its toll. No one had been able to say anything to Rockwell to ease the pain. He knew that the Mormon communities in Missouri and Illinois would soon be under siege, that he would be desperately needed. But nothing mattered now. Brigham Young had tried to dissuade him, and came close to being struck by him. Rockwell never wanted to see a Mormon again, or hear about a loving God. He left, and headed west. However, when, in August of 1846, Brigham Young answered the call of Pres. James K. Polk for 500 men to fight in the war with Mexico, Rockwell reluctantly "returned to the fold" for yet another season. Col. Thomas L. Kane, who directed the recruitment and induction of the Mormon troops, came upon Rockwell serving as a lawman at Fort Leavenworth, Kansas. After several days of frequently angry exchanges, Kane persuaded the gunman to accept a commission and join the battalion.

And now, here he was, deeply involved again with this people, against his will, fighting an uncontrollable feeling of obligation to them. It was as if he could not free himself from them.

Anne McCutcheon. It was bewildering to him how closely she resembled the woman he had buried beneath the elm tree in Nauvoo—her appearance, her mannerisms, the sound of her voice. At times the remarkably close resemblance almost angered Rockwell. His desire for Anne somehow caused him to feel dishonest, as if his feelings were betraying the memory of that beauty long dead. For years he had protected himself from emotional involvement with any woman. In his wildest imagination he never thought there could be another. Nor did he want there to be. To love and be loved bore a terrible responsibility, and an opening of the soul to the deepest hurt.

Now he was confused and unsure. He did not trust his feelings, did not trust himself if he were to give vent to them, as he wanted to do. "Damn!" he said aloud; what right did Anne McCutcheon have to be so appealing!

It was at this moment, before Rockwell had even dismounted, that a solemn-faced Luther James rode up to him and told him about the death of Jud Stoddard.

Self-sacrifice had its limits, and sharing his room with some stranger was out of the question as far as Porter Rockwell was concerned. One look into Rockwell's steel-hard gray eyes was sufficient for the board-inghouse owner, Mister Brandon, to withdraw the suggestion. After all, a man—especially this man—was entitled to a mite of privacy.

"You're damned right about that, mister," said Rockwell, as he slammed the door in Brandon's face. Rockwell was in a mean disposition. News of Jud's senseless death had been the last straw.

Rockwell unbuckled his guns and threw himself on the patchwork quilt. Hands laced behind his head, he stared unseeingly at the patterns in the rough-textured ceiling paint. Little Jud was gone, the lion's heart in that banty-rooster frame stilled forever, and for what? Rockwell was ready to say to hell with the whole miserable mess, Brigham Young and his all-merciful God included. Merciful! That was a damned poor word for a God who seemed to go out of His way to take the best, and let scum like Case Carney live to foul the earth with their droppings.

It was Lot's fault, no argument about that. He should have made little Jud go back when he caught up with the troop. Anybody with half an ounce of sense knew a man who was recuperating from the lung sickness took a long time to get really well. Lot could thank his lucky stars he was off somewhere in Cache Valley, out of reach of Porter Rockwell's bone-hard fists. He'd almost taken out his anger on young Luther James when the youth told him about Jud.

Half an hour later, Rockwell had stormed into Doc Ames's house, almost bowling over an astonished Anne McCutcheon when she opened the front door. He had ignored her as if she were not there. He found

Ames in the surgery, lancing an angry-looking boil on the neck of a cow-eyed farmer. Angus McCutcheon had his arms around the farmer's chest, trying to keep the man from bucking off the table as Doc Ames probed for the boil's core. For the life of him, Rockwell couldn't remember what he'd said to the two medical men who stared at him in open-mouthed bewilderment. He had vague recollections of the wide-eyed farmer leaping from the table and grabbing his shirt, almost tripping as he escaped past Anne McCutcheon standing in the surgery entrance. Only once before in his life could Rockwell remember experiencing the rage he felt at that moment—the night he got word that Joseph Smith and his brother had been murdered at Carthage jail by a lynch mob. He had been completely unreasonable.

Doc Ames's explanation fell on deaf ears; Rockwell didn't want to hear about limited duty and all that crap. Jud was dead, and as far as Rockwell was concerned, Ames bore as much responsibility as Lot Smith. But in Rockwell's mind the real guilt was Brigham Young's, him and his damned fool orders that tied the hands of good men. If you're in a fight, you fight; win, lose, or draw, you fight! And if you haven't got the stomach for that, cut and run!

Having said, or rather hollered his piece, Rockwell stormed out of the house, again failing to acknowledge Anne. When he was gone she ran up the stairs, slamming the bedroom door behind her.

Guilt gnawed in Rockwell's brain, twisting a painful knot behind his eyes. This was stupid, he chastised himself; Jud was dead, and all the anger and self-recrimination in the world wouldn't change that. But there was one regret that would haunt Porter Rockwell for the rest of his years—the day he told little Jud not to call him brother. He'd never forget the brief look of hurt that appeared in Jud's eyes.

John Atwill had three things going for him, to Rockwell's way of thinking: He wasn't a Mormon, he ran the finest livery stable in town, and he made the best corn likker this side of the Missouri. He also had a fine potbellied stove and was one helluva checker player.

The coat of Rockwell's big buckskin gleamed from three days of repeated currying as the horse munched contentedly from the oat-filled feeding trough. Rockwell's saddle gear was draped over the stall partition, the leather waxed and polished, the Merrill carbine cleaned and oiled in its scrolled leather scabbard, saddlebags packed and ready, his heavy sugan hung on a peg embedded in the stall post. All was in readiness for an instant departure—all, that is, except Rockwell. He was determined to go somewhere, but was having a time figuring out where that somewhere would be. It would come to him, in time. For now he was contented to match skills with Atwill over the worn checkerboard, dollar a game. It wasn't much of a contest; the dollars were all going one way—Atwill's.

Atwill frowned hard at the board, then made his move—a triple jump that put his black in Rockwell's king line.

"How the hell did I miss that?" grumbled Rockwell.

"Ain't got your mind on the game, Port; haven't had since we started playin', not that I mind taking your money." Atwill put a match to his odiferous, drop-stemmed pipe and puffed rapidly to start an even burn.

Rockwell fanned a hand through the billowing smoke, grimacing. "What the hell do you burn in that thing?"

"Like I tell my old woman—you don't like it, don't breathe." Atwill puffed contentedly, "Your move."

"Don't rush me."

"Hell, Port, you might just as well slide me that dollar now—you're skunked."

Rockwell knew that the old man was right; he was skunked, and his mind wasn't on the game. Twice in the past two days Brigham Young had sent a messenger asking Rockwell to ride to Cache Valley. Twice Rockwell had ignored it. Somehow he couldn't bring himself, trust himself, to a meeting with the Mormon leader. Porter Rockwell was in no mood to be reasonable.

Atwill leaned back in his chair and blew a cloud of tobacco smoke that hung like a curtain between them. Reaching for the jug nestled against the table leg, Atwill toothed out the cork and poured a generous jolt into the tin mugs sharing the table with the checkerboard. Rockwell's hand went to his mug with an action that was pure reflex, his eyes never leaving the board. The smooth corn likker went down like honeyed water. Atwill shook his head over a grin. "The way you're puttin' that away, I'll be lucky to break even on the games."

The spring bell on the street door tinkled, followed by a gust of cold, crisp air. Rockwell ignored both, slapping the red disks on the black squares on his side of the board.

Atwill eased up from the chair. "Can I help you, miss?"

Anne McCutcheon, clothed in a heavy, hooded cape, stood in the open door. It took a moment for her eyes to adjust to the dim light.

She focused on Atwill and, with a start, on the man seated with his back to her. Catching her breath, she recognized him immediately.

"Close the damned door!" said Rockwell, not turning.

Anne's face tightened. She had her pride. She slammed the door, sending the spring bell into a brief frenzy of sound. "You have the manners of a he goat, Porter Rockwell!"

Rockwell peeled unsteadily out of his chair to take in the tall figure at the door. The kiss of cold air had brought additional color to Anne's cheeks, enhancing her natural, unpretentious beauty. A lock of blond hair peeked from under her cape hood.

Atwill shuttled a puzzled look from one to the other.

"Didn't know it was you," mumbled Rockwell, cursing himself for the slur he knew was in his speech. Atwill's "corn" could sneak up on a fella.

"Whether you did or didn't is of no concern to me," she forced out, "but I'll be taking this opportunity to give you a piece of my mind, Mister Rockwell! What you did the other day was uncalled for. Doctor Ames is a fine old gentleman who deserves some respect. You had no right to come a-stormin' into his home like . . . like some Glasgow bully boy, accusing him of something that was no fault of his own! Is there no shame in you?"

The man in buckskins eyed her, saying nothing. He was miserable.

Atwill cleared his throat noisily. "Am I in the way here, or is there something I can do for you, Miss—?"

"McCutcheon. Doctor Ames asked me to stop by to ask when it would be convenient for you to put snow runners and side curtains on his buggy. You are Mister Atwill, aren't you?"

"That I am, miss. You can tell the doc anytime next week'll be fine."

"Thank you, Mister Atwill."

Anne turned for the door, her eyes sliding past the man in buckskins as if he were not there. But when her hand touched the knob, she paused and turned back, brow lifted. The tautness in her face eased. "I'm the daughter of a doctor. You're not the first man, or woman, I've seen try to ease their hurt over losing someone close by turning it into anger at the one person who did everything humanly possible to help. Doctor Ames warned your friend about overexertion—how dangerous it could be in his condition. And, for your information, there was no written permission, Mister Rockwell. I know because I was there when Doctor Ames refused to give it."

Rockwell knew that Anne was speaking the truth; still it rankled him even as he admitted to himself that writing his own letter of permission was the kind of thing little Jud would do—anything to get back into the thick of things, and to hell with the consequences. "I see," he said without emotion, feeling like a complete fool.

"Do you! Then an apology to Doctor Ames would not be out of place, would it now?"

Rockwell did not respond. Yet his eyes could not leave her.

"And with that," she concluded, "I'll be saying good-day to you." She had held her Scottish brogue in tow until the last "good-day."

The spring bell clattered and Anne McCutcheon was out the door, striding strongly to Doc Ames's buggy tied at the hitching rail. Rockwell moved to the window in time to see her drive off with a quick slap of the reins.

"Right pretty gal, that one," offered Atwill. "Pretty enough to tangle-foot a fella. . . . And let me tell ya' somethin' else. She's got it bad for ya', could see it in her eyes. What's more, she has more of an effect on you than this here corn likker. Somethin' you ain't told me?"

Rockwell glared at the older man, attempting to cut off further comment.

"If you're so sweet on that gal," continued Atwell, ignoring Rockwell's warning frown, "why don't 'cha do somethin' about it, 'stead of standing there like a drunk Injun!"

"Keep your thoughts to yourself!"

"Hell if I will! I'm your friend, though I don't know why. But that gives me the right to tell you what I think, and I've had a mind to do that for a long time!"

Rockwell returned a hint of a smile. Atwill *was* his friend. "Well, get it over with."

Atwill gulped, took a deep breath, and then spit it out. "Porter Rockwell, I don't know a helluva lot other than my business here, but I know two things—life ain't fair, and ya' can't live in the past. A man can't change the past by refusin' to live in the present. The days jest keep rollin' along anyway. Now, it's high time, and then some, for you to start livin' again; and if I just seen what I think I seen when that woman was in here, that was your future jest rode off. For God's sake, go after her!"

Rockwell shook his head. "If I was to get near that woman, her father would go for the tar bucket. And I wouldn't blame him. Turned around, that's just what I'd do. We're a decade apart, my friend. I have nothing to give her. Anyway," he said as an afterthought, "Lot Smith's thunderstruck over her. That's the way it ought to be."

Atwill started to speak again, but Rockwell jerked a thumb at the buckskin's stall. "Saddle me up. This town is beginning to cramp me."

"If you say so," sighed Atwill, heading for the stall. "Want me to put a burr under his saddle, like the one under yourn?"

Rockwell ignored the question.

"Want a jug to take along?"

"Yeah, better make it two, in case I run into somebody with a thirst."

As Rockwell mounted the buckskin, Atwill put a restraining hand on his arm. "Porter . . . you take care." The two shook hands.

Rockwell rode to the corner of Elm Street; halfway down he could see Doc Ames's buggy tied to a post ring in front of the house. Reining up the buckskin, he sat for a moment. Every instinct pulled at him to go after her, as Atwill had urged. But instead he wheeled the animal around and nudged it into a canter in the opposite direction. Twenty minutes later he was well out of the city, heading east, to the Wasatch Range and Jim Bridger. A crisp blue sky meant bitter cold weather but no additional snow—for a while.

A battered Porter Rockwell sprawled limply, almost lifeless, on the pallet of thick furs, his gaze fixed absently on the bit of velvet black sky visible through the hogan's smoke hole. The mud and wattle frame of the hogan was sheathed in several layers of scraped buffalo hide, which kept the cold out and the heat in. The tiny, almost smokeless fire under the smoke hole provided just enough warmth and light for the needs of Jim Bridger.

Finding the Paiute winter camp had been no problem. Three days out of Salt Lake City he'd crossed trails with a leather-faced old Ute laying traps at a frozen-over beaver pond. The old man had already taken and skinned a fair haul of the richly furred animals, but was determined to stay at it until he got all he could pack on his travois. "Go south to the big cut, then west to where the mountains come together. Go through the neck; on the other side you find small valley—there you find Bridger man."

Rockwell had entered the valley to find a much larger encampment than he'd expected—forty hogans, he counted, snug and secure, protected in the lee of five-hundred-foot cliffs. His appearance brought two dozen young bucks on the run, and Little Fawn. "What you come here, Rockwell man?" she bellowed, signaling the braves to lower ready weapons. Rockwell noted that the weapons were short on bows, arrows, and lances, and long on muskets and carbines. "Bridger got big mad on you, Rockwell man. Better you go 'way!"

Ignoring her protestations, Rockwell rode past her to the entrance of the hogan from whence he had seen her emerge. Dismounting from the buckskin, he retrieved one of the jugs of corn likker from a saddlebag. Maybe, he thought, a peace offering might calm somewhat Bridger's understandable anger.

As he reached to open the blanket that served as the flap to Bridger's hogan, as big a fist as any man ever possessed struck from within to catch Rockwell full in the face. His head flew back, the momentum carrying his body forcefully into the buckskin. Braced by the horse he did not go down, although his knees buckled.

Then Bridger's left fist slammed like a mule's kick into Rockwell's ribs, bending him over to the side, forcing an inhuman grunt as air exploded from his lungs. He dropped to his knees and fell back under his stoically unmoving animal. He tried to move, gasping for breath . . . then, blackness.

It was late that evening when Rockwell began to regain a momentary consciousness. He was lying flat on a pallet of furs near the center of the hogan. Sitting close to him, a jug held passionately to his breast, was Jim Bridger—pacified and sentimental, almost maudlin, thanks to the contents of the jug from Atwill's livery stable.

Rockwell slowly raised himself to a sitting position in spite of the wrenching pain in his side and the hammering ache inside his head. "Lo Jim," he said softly.

"Lo Port."

"One helluva life. . . ."

"Now that you mention it. . . ."

A full two minutes passed, then. "Ah hell," Bridger blustered across the small fire, "it weren't your fault; I know you didn't want to do what you did. We been through too much together. I tell you, Port, things just ain't simple anymore. I'm right glad I didn't kill you."

"Damned decent of you, Hos," moaned Rockwell.

Bridger nodded. "I think so, too, considerin'." With that he swung the jug to his mouth.

Rockwell's head throbbed mightily, dwarfing the hurt that wrenched where his jaws hinged. He had to breathe slowly and carefully to avoid sharp pains in his ribs. He coughed lightly with almost every breath. At length he fell back on the bed of skins. He was through talking for that night. Truly, Bridger had damned near killed him.

In a state of semiconsciousness, Rockwell's thoughts once again drifted back over the years to another time, another place. Images of people and places touched his innermost being. Through the mist of time he relived a brief moment of sublime happiness. In a town—a real, civilized town. Men in suits—without guns. Beautiful women in evening gowns. Simpson's Band—a real band, real music. *She* was there, dancing with the gracefulness of a dove, swirling, laughing, in and out of his eager arms, her flaxen hair flowing to the rhythm of her body. All eyes were watching.

Again she slipped into his arms as their bodies moved to the beat of the music. Her lips were close to his ear. "My love . . . I am with child."

"What . . . what did you say?" He had stopped abruptly in the middle of the dance floor.

"Well now, Mister Rockwell," she had said coquettishly, "why are you surprised? Did you suppose you were impotent?"

Her sparkling laughter, the depth of her blue-gray eyes, the hint of Scottish in her melodic voice, the aura of her elegance consumed him. "You're going to have a son, my love."

"A son. . . ." How could one word sound so all-encompassing of life, love, joy, pride, fulfillment. "How . . . how do you know it's a boy?"

Feigning anger, she laughingly replied loud enough for others to hear: "Now then, Mister Rockwell, did you think I didn't know I was married to the manliest fella in this or any other state? Of course it will be a boy!"

Now the scene began to fade, and Rockwell fought desperately to hold onto that brief moment when all was right with the world. Bridger had to restrain his writhing body for some minutes before he lost consciousness.

That night Little Fawn placed compresses with ice from a nearby stream on Rockwell's ribs. In the morning much of his right side was black, but the swelling had been held to a minimum. Then she changed to hot compresses by boiling them in water. For two days and two nights she cared for him, spooning him broth during his moments of semi-consciousness. Then as the third night approached, Rockwell abruptly came to his senses. His ribs on his right side still ached but he could breathe better, and the pain in his head had all but subsided. But it would still be days before he could use his jaws for chewing anything solid.

"Looks like you're alive again," offered Bridger.

Rockwell stood on his feet, vision blurring with the effort. With a feeling of uncertainty, he moved, stiff legged, to the entrance of the hogan, passing Little Fawn. He remembered vaguely that the Indian woman had cared for him. "Much obliged." Little Fawn acknowledged with a grunt.

He walked around the encampment for half an hour, until the muscles in his legs would obey him, and his lungs and head were cleared to a degree by the clean crispness of the air.

The night was cold and clear. A full moon, embellished by a never-ending array of stars, illuminated the scene. He dropped slowly to his knees by the partially icebound stream that passed through the encampment. Carefully, he grasped two stones at the edge and, bracing himself, lowered his face into the sparkling water and drank deeply.

Suddenly, a dark shadow fell across the stream, engulfing him. With effort he raised his head to confront the source of the sudden eclipse. There, legs spread and hands on hips, perfectly silhouetted in brilliant whiteness by the moon, stood the giant Simon.

Secured through a belt on his hip was a brass-studded Indian fighting ax; balancing it on the right was a .44-caliber Starr double-action revolving pistol. The combination seemed to accentuate the duality of the man's heritage.

Rockwell stiffened. His fingers seemed to dig into the supportive stones. The added pressure caused one of them to break loose from its moorings. His tenuous balance broken, he plunged headfirst into the stream, momentarily submerging his head and shoulders.

Sputtering, he thrust himself clear of the water to roll on his back, both hands clawing instinctively for the Colts that had become part of him. They were not there. A mental picture of the matched weapons, hanging on a peg by the entrance of Bridger's hogan, flashed in his brain. Something he'd never experienced before surged in his breast—a feeling of total helplessness, or was it panic?

There was nothing above him but the night sky, nonthreatening, unblemished. Had he been hallucinating, seeing things that were not there? He came to his feet in time to see Simon's massive frame disappear into the darkness.

A shudder coursed through Rockwell, and it had nothing to do with his plunge into the chill waters of the stream. He knew he'd been closer to death than at any other moment in his life. The giant had had him cold, defenseless. He loosed his pent-up breath in a long, silent sigh. He was alive for one reason alone—Simon's loyalty to Jim Bridger. Another debt owed to the famed mountain man.

Chapter Sixteen

The full force of winter had created a hiatus for Utah Territory and the Utah Expedition. Johnston's army was apparently stranded, barring a miracle, until spring, probably late spring. The general was now concerned with survival in the frozen wasteland that had him and his troops snared in its icy grasp; what he would do when he reached Salt Lake City was a decisional priority of little importance at this time. Now the great enemies were freezing temperatures, snow and sleet, dwindling food supplies, and the boredom of inactivity—waiting, waiting, waiting.

And in Salt Lake City, referred to by one eastern reporter as "Brigham Young's Great Basin Kingdom," a relative normalcy reined. To be sure, the city and its environs were more crowded with people than ever before, and there was a shortage of some goods, but in general, the community had sighed with relief with the early coming of winter. The threat of invasion had been stalled; there was no danger of famine, and life went on much as before. Only in the preparations for Thanksgiving and Christmas—the extraordinary zeal, the almost overbearing enthusiasm—could one feel the subterranean uneasiness of Salt Lake's inhabitants, as if it was feared that this might be their last holiday season in the valley.

But the hiatus did not mean that the Utah War was at a standstill. The drama went on. From several points, events were playing their part in a way that would have a significant impact, not only on the immediate present, but the future as well.

Colonel Thomas L. Kane, Maryland Militia, had arrived in a hot, relentlessly steamy, insect-ridden Panama City, well on his way to Salt Lake City with the most important document of the Utah War—the message from President James Buchanan. The trip across the isthmus had been relatively comfortable, thanks to the new, narrow-gauge railway line linking Colón to Panama City. The United States Mail Steamship Company and the Pacific Mail Steamship Company shared a U.S. government contract giving them a virtual monopoly on transit of passengers and mail between the Atlantic and Pacific.

It was the night of Kane's arrival in Panama City when the dysentery hit him, incapacitating him for nearly a week. With sleep-granulated eyes and a moan, he pulled his sweat-soaked body from the coarse sheets for what seemed to be the hundredth time in five days. The dysentery held him captive for that long in the cell-like room of the Calle Princessa Hotel. The rolling rumbles in his lower intestines heralded the imminence of another flow. He braced himself.

Where in hell did it all come from? he wondered fitfully. He hadn't eaten a solid bite since the first day, and had taken barely enough liquids to keep his mouth from drying up. He felt the loose skin on his thigh, wondering how many pounds of himself had been carried away in the repeatedly filled chamber pot.

The Colombian doctor knew a smattering of English; not that it mattered, dysentery was dysentery in any language. Its treatment shared the sameness—repeated draughts of a thick, chalky liquid that didn't seem to do a damned bit of good no matter how much you choked down. The sickness had to run its course. At the end of it you hoped to be alive.

Kane was becoming increasingly frustrated. He sensed keenly the importance of his charge. For the hundredth time his hand reached for the reassuring presence of the pouch containing Buchanan's letter, cinched about his waist even in sickness. But the next San Francisco–bound steamer, with ports of call at Acapulco, Mazatlán, and San Pedro, was not due at Panama City for another two and a half weeks.

There was, however, an alternative—the *Santa Cruz,* destined for the mouth of the Colorado where it opened into the gulf of California, or the Sea of Cortez, as the Mexicans called it. Connections could be made with the shallow-draft river steamer *Jessup* that would take Kane upriver past Fort Yuma and Fort Gaston to Beale's Crossing, saving him an overland journey of some three hundred miles. The thought had definite appeal; shipboard travel had distinct advantages over coach and horseback, particularly for someone victim to treacherous bowels. Three days' ride due north from Beale's Crossing would bring Kane to the Old Spanish Trail. From there it was coach all the way to Salt Lake City—weather permitting. Two days later, an emaciated Colonel Kane boarded the *Santa Cruz*.

The twenty-seven days it took the river steamer *Jessup* to reach Beale's Crossing from Fort Yuma was a journey that Col. Thomas L. Kane would never forget. The Colorado River was a navigational nightmare. Passengers and crew joined in lightening the sidewheeler of her entire cargo to get her through the shallows or across sandbars, which seemed to be at every bend of the winding river. The unloaded cargo was portaged past the trouble spot, then reloaded aboard. The short stretch, forty-five miles, between Fort Yuma and Fort Gaston consumed eleven of the twenty-seven days to Beale's Crossing.

Having arrived at the crossing, Kane was frustrated again to find that all carriage passage to Utah had been suspended temporarily. He had no choice; after making arrangements to purchase two horses from a local hostler, he spent the night at the company way station.

"Listen, mister," the hostler had said the next morning, while helping Kane strap his baggage and food supplies to his packhorse. "As happy as I am to sell these two horses, I gotta tell ya', yer' a damned fool. From here on north is filled with hostiles and renegades. Ridin' alone, you ain't got much of a chance of making wherever you're a-goin'. Lookie, just wait another week, head out with a group. Don't go alone!"

"Thanks," responded Kane, forcing another ten dollars into the man's hand. "I'll try to be careful." With that he began the last leg of his journey to Salt Lake City. He prayed he'd be in time.

Meanwhile, two other critical journeys had been undertaken, the success of which could well have decided the ability of Johnston's army to survive the winter without a catastrophe. In spite of the elements, a furious Captain Buell and his troop, minus five good men and a number of horses left dead along the way, stumbled half frozen into Platte River Station. His orders: Bring back to Camp Scott the remaining supplies that Johnston had left at the way station. The following morning Buell, still sick and numb from his ordeal, sent a contingent of troopers to Fort Laramie, then to drive several hundred mules into Platte River Station. There they would be loaded for the impossible journey back to Camp Scott. Buell didn't hold out much hope. It would take weeks to get all the pack animals he needed, and he dreaded the thought of herding them through that freezing hell back to Camp Scott.

*   *   *

Captain Marcy, Hickok, and five troopers had left Camp Scott for Santa Fe under darkening skies, but had soon found themselves in mild weather. It lasted all the way to Santa Fe, where they arrived on the seventeenth day, having missed the brunt of the storm that had swept down to stop Johnston in his tracks, forcing him to beat a retreat back to Camp Scott. The trip had been monotonous, uneventful, and comparatively fast. Marcy hoped against hope that conditions would be the same on the way back to Camp Scott.

Fort Union's commandant, Lt. Col. A. R. Culbertson, a native of Georgia, moved with commendable speed in response to Johnston's requisition order. But Fort Union's stock of supplies and remounts was insufficient to meet Johnston's needs. They would have to be supplemented by what could be obtained from Fort Mary, some sixty miles distant, and from civilian providers in the nearby city of Santa Fe. Drovers and rolling stock were readily available through the good offices of one Jaime Peralta—if the price was right. Peralta, it seemed, had a lock on Santa Fe's labor supply, much to the chagrin of the non-Mexican business community.

At first light the following morning, Marcy was on the trail to Fort Mary, leaving Hickok and the colonel to deal with Peralta: fifty wagons to carry the supplies provided by the Fort Union and Fort Mary garrisons, and three hundred head of prime beeves. If there were any problems dealing with Peralta, Culbertson told Hickok, they were to commandeer what was needed, and let Peralta fight it out with the War Department. But Señor Peralta was more than obliging; the wagons and beeves would be ready and waiting when the time came for them to head north for the Nebraska Territory. As an added gesture of goodwill, Peralta threw in a chuck wagon and cook, no charge. He also assured the colonel that the Mexican drivers and drovers would be top hands, no strangers to any troubles they might encounter on the journey.

James Butler Hickok, already weary and not savoring the thought of beginning the return ride to Camp Scott the following morning, leaned an elbow on the plank bar of the post sutler's store. He nursed a tankard of rum and water—grog, the sutler, James Wheeler by name, called it in his East Cambrian accent. It was a drink prized by the iron men in the wooden ships of her majesty's navy, a navy he'd been proud to serve in.

Hickok had noticed a young boy slip through the batwing doors and approach some of the customers sitting at tables. He didn't give it much thought, but when the boy moved toward Hickok, Wheeler recognized him. With a growl, Wheeler rolled around the bar and caught the youngster by the seat of his pants and the scruff of his neck. Then he rushed him across the room, yelling, "I told ye to stay outta here, ye little snipe!" and threw him through the batwings into the dirt-packed street. The boy rolled to a stop flat on his back, just in time to see a cursing Wheeler flying through the same batwings, performing an unintended somersault before coming to rest with an angry grunt beside the startled boy. Somebody had given Wheeler some of his own medicine.

Then Hickok was standing between the two. Wheeler tried to raise himself, but Hickok's boot, pressed hard against his throat, discouraged the idea. "I don't like bullies," Hickok said quietly. "If you lay a hand on this boy again, I'll cut it off!" He didn't have to tell Wheeler twice.

Hickok gave his hand to the boy, and they began walking. "Thanks, mister," the wide-eyed lad offered.

"What were you doing in there?" asked Hickok.

"I'm looking for work; gotta get outta this place. Stray dogs and kids don't count for much here. . . . You're with that outfit headin' for Nebraska Territory. Sure wish you'd let me tag along. I can earn my keep. I can rein mules and I can help cook—"

"Hold it, hold it," Hickok cut him off. How old are you, boy?"

The lad pulled himself to his full height. "Almost thirteen, but what's that got to do with anythin'?"

"Well, your folks might have something to say about you taking on a man's job, traips'n off to nowhere."

"Folks are in Kansas. Please, mister, I need t' work."

Hickok studied the boy for a moment. "What's your name?"

Cody, Bill Cody. "Tell you what, mister, if I don't pull my weight, you don't have to pay me."

"You said you knew something about cookin'?"

The boy's face brightened. "Heck, yes. I came all the way out here on the back of a chuck wagon; helped with the cookin' and cleaned up after it was done. Even got paid for it—fifty cents a day."

Hickok smiled. "Okay, Bill Cody, you're on. You'll be working with the cook, and you damned well better know how to whip up something I won't choke on. Fair enough?"

A broad smile blossomed on Cody's face. "You got yourself a deal, mister!"

Hickok thumbed a few coins into Cody's grubby palm. "The name's

Hickok. Here's an advance. We leave at sunup tomorrow; and next time I see you I want those hands to be clean. Understood?"

That day a friendship was created between James Butler Hickok and William F. Cody that was to last a lifetime. According to Cody himself, writing years later, "From that time forward Wild Bill was my protector and intimate friend, and the friendship thus begun continued until his death."

Brigham Young had been amply apprised of these two movements out of Camp Scott, and it was not difficult to surmise their destinations. Of the two groups, Young was most concerned about Marcy's attempt to get supplies from the military establishments in and about Santa Fe. They could have fair weather much of the way. If those supplies were to arrive during a warming trend—a not unlikely occurrence with an early winter—Johnston, he believed, was not above attempting another run on Salt Lake City. For reasons that Young thought he understood, the general was in a great hurry to get to the valley. As for bringing supplies in from Platte Station anytime soon, Young held the same opinion as Captain Buell—a long shot.

Young therefore made the decision to stop any movement of supplies and cattle coming up from New Mexico, while reserving judgment on any movement from Platte River or Fort Laramie. And he wanted Rockwell to lead the guerrillas! This interdiction would be one fraught with difficulties. He knew where Rockwell was, and began to think about how he could ensure the angry gunman's presence with the battalion troup.

Rockwell examined the beautifully crafted flint spearhead he'd scuffed out of the canyon floor, the edges still razor sharp, as attested to by the cut on the toe of his boot. How long had it lain there? he wondered. Surely the hands that had made and used it had turned to dust long before the first Europeans had set foot on this continent. He surveyed the protecting walls of the small canyon. How many other camps like this had they looked down on over the ages. There was no way of telling.

The days passed in fluid harmony in Bridger's sanctuary, each blending into the next like the flow of a smooth-running mountain stream. For the first time in more years than he could remember, Rockwell was slowly beginning to feel at peace with himself, gradually coming to accept what was and what had been, without guilt or self-recrimination—words that had no meaning within these ancient walls.

Still, there was a part of the outside world that clung to his thoughts, surfacing at the most unexpected moments to bring a vision of wide gray eyes, a rich, generous mouth, flaxen hair, and a voice touched with heather. At times he grew angry with himself, mooning like a lovesick whelp over a woman he had no business even thinking about; a woman, he tried to convince himself, he wished he had never seen.

Adding to his frustration, another thought pulled at his brain, one he'd made a conscious effort to quell whenever it arose. Was it Anne McCutcheon who had him in such inward turmoil, or was it another, so much like her? At times their faces, even their personalities, seemed to blend—one long dead, the other so very much alive.

Atwill was right, he told himself; life was now. Perhaps it was time to move on, leave the territory and the frustration in favor of another clime—another country, if need be, maybe the Oregon Territory, or Canada; perhaps Mexico. He told himself he needed a place to start anew. It was a big world out there, but Rockwell also feared that time and distance might change nothing. He'd carry the image of two women within him as long as life remained—each forever young, forever lovely, forever beyond his reach.

Simon presented Rockwell with the rusted remains of an ancient wheel-lock pistol. "Think you'll find this more interesting than flint arrow-heads, Rockwell. Conquistador period, about 1590, if I read the armorer's proof marks right."

Masking his surprise at the offer, Rockwell examined the still-legible markings on the weapon's side plate. "Wheel locks were pretty well out by the 1600s. Where the hell did you learn about old Spanish proof marks?"

"Same place you did, I suppose—books."

Rockwell eyed the giant half-breed with new interest. "You're full of surprises."

"Makes life interesting," was the dry response.

"Where'd you find it?" said Rockwell, turning the piece in his hand.

"I didn't. One of the women found it; was digging a fire pit."

"Pretty far north for the conquistador," mused Rockwell, again eyeing the relic.

"They were here," said Simon. "Santa Fe was a city before you damned gringos got your feet wet at Plymouth Rock."

The undercurrent of hostility was unmistakable. "Might as well get used to gringos, Simon; they're here, and from the looks of things, they're going to stay."

An enigmatic smile toyed on the half-breed's lips. "Perhaps, Rockwell, but as Saladin said to the Crusader kings, 'There is room here to bury you all.' "

"And which half of *you* shall they bury?" Rockwell asked, a touch of sarcasm in his voice.

Simon said nothing. Instead, turning on his heel, he strode off.

"Hold it!" snapped Rockwell. The giant turned, his left hand moving smoothly to the shaft of his fighting ax. "Just to put things straight, Simon, I won't take it kindly the next time you come up on me, like that night at the stream."

Simon met Rockwell's smile with one of his own. "If I do, it won't matter how you take it."

The big man moved away with long, catlike steps.

An hour later, Lot Smith led a saddle-weary twenty-man contingent into Jim Bridger's winter camp and signaled a halt some dozen yards from where the mountain man and Porter Rockwell stood in front of Bridger's hogan. Simon and several dozen well-armed young bucks moved in to form a loose circle around the newcomers, faces bland, expressionless. Rockwell recognized Harve Arnold and the Cartwright brothers, but the rest were new to him. Some of them were young; others appeared more seasoned. They weren't uniformed, but their accoutrements were battalion issue—carbines, sidearms, and sabers. Not waiting for an invite to step down, Lot swung out of his saddle, nodding for the young man beside him to do the same. "Let 'em through," Bridger called, adding as the pair approached, "You come to pay up?"

"No sir," said Lot, recalling, with a sense of guilt, the burning of Bridger's Fort. "You'll probably have to go to Salt Lake for that."

"That'll be the damned day!" snorted Bridger as Smith shot an unfriendly look at Rockwell.

"We didn't expect to find you here, Major, but since you are, I have orders for you from—"

"Ex-major."

Lot continued, ignoring Rockwell's interjection, "From General Wells. You're to report to President Young at Echo Canyon, forthwith."

"Something happen to your ears, Lot? I said *ex*-major. You can tell Brigham I've resigned."

Lot's nostrils flared in sudden anger. "I'm not your messenger boy, Rockwell. You happen to be a duly-sworn officer in the Territorial Militia; you took an oath. If you want to go back on it, at least be man enough to tell President Young to his face! When we get back, I *will* tell General Wells his order was delivered."

Rockwell's jaw knotted dangerously as he took a half step closer to the defiant younger man.

At that point, Bridger pushed between the pair. "Now hold on, both of you."

"Stay out of this, Mister Bridger," snapped Lot. "This is militia business; you have no say in it."

"Mebbe so, but this is my camp, and I'm telling you to haul tail, afore somebody gets hisself hurt."

Suddenly the anger disappeared from Rockwell's face, "Come back from what?" he asked.

"That doesn't concern you," Lot shot back, acidly.

The young man with Lot followed the exchange wide-eyed, awed by the way Lot Smith stood his ground with both the legendary mountain man and Porter Rockwell. What stories he would tell of this day.

"You said you didn't come here looking for me," said Rockwell. "What did you come here for?"

Lot frowned, hesitated a moment, then responded, "There's a supply train coming up from Fort Union. Our orders are to see that it doesn't get to General Johnston."

"You're a mite off course, aren't you?" queried Bridger. "Wrong side of the mountains; should be over on the Cherokee."

"Train won't be comin' up the Cherokee," gulped the youth with Smith, his eyes shuttling from Bridger to Rockwell and back again.

"Coley was down at Fort Union; rode out three horses getting to us with the information," explained Lot. "Accordin' to what Coley heard, the train's comin' across the San Juans, breaking new trail, west and north."

Coley nodded his head vigorously. "That's right, about forty wagons and a small beef herd, about three hundred head."

Bridger frowned thoughtfully. "Only way through the San Juans is the Chochetope Pass. If you're set on stoppin' 'em, that's the place. Once they're through, it's open country. You'll have a helluva time findin' 'em, much less stoppin' 'em with that handful of pups you've got with you."

Lot acknowleged the mounted troopers, then turned back to the mountain man with something like pride in his eyes. "Those pups have a mean bite, Mister Bridger."

A snort escaped Rockwell. "Not with the muzzle Brigham's slapped on them, or has that changed?"

"Nothing's changed," Lot said firmly. "The president's order still stands."

"Figures," growled Rockwell.

"Ease up on the lad, Port. He's doin' what he has to do; can't fault him for that." Bridger turned his attention to Coley. "You got some idea when that train was startin' out from Fort Union? Could be they're through the pass already."

"From what I heard they was havin' trouble gettin' some stuff up from Fort Mary. Figure I had at least a week jump on 'em. No way they can move that herd better'n ten, twelve miles a day."

"How large an escort?" broke in Rockwell.

"What difference does that make to you?" Lot asked in a flat tone.

Rockwell ignored Lot's interruption. "What about it, son?"

"Hardly any, Mister Rockwell. Handful of troopers and a scout, fella named Hickok. Heard they was supposed to borrow some soldiers from the fort, but the colonel couldn't spare 'em, bein' short-handed already."

Bridger turned to Lot Smith. "Chochetope's easy to miss. I'll send Simon along with you; save you some time and keep you from gettin' lost."

"No need, Mister Bridger. Coley here's been over the ground; he'll get us there."

"Let's go, Coley," said Lot, directing a final, cold look at Rockwell.

Bridger and Rockwell watched as Lot Smith and Coley swung up into their saddles. A moment later the twenty-man column was riding out of the mountain man's winter camp.

Rockwell, face devoid of any emotion, turned and entered the hogan. Bridger followed in time to see him reach for the peg holding the twin-holstered gun belt. A faint smile appeared on Bridger's lips. "Change your mind about that resignin' business, Port?"

"Temporarily," said Rockwell, buckling on the Colts. "Have one of the lads saddle my horse, will you, Jim?"

"Bridger's smile widened. "Why the sudden change? Wouldn't have anything to do with that scout that almost put a hole in your brisket, would it?"

Rockwell was silent.

"Afraid he's too much a bear for them to handle, that it?"

"Hickok's a different breed of cat, Jim," Rockwell said grimly.

Lot Smith's open hostility toward him had come as no surprise to Rockwell. Taking French leave was virtually unheard-of in the battalion. But there was more to it than that, Rockwell was sure. And that "more" was Anne McCutcheon. Lot had a real crush on the girl, and Rockwell was the competition.

Of one thing Rockwell was sure—if it came to facing James Butler Hickok, he had better be the one to do it. He had no illusions about the scout's ability; the man was good, perhaps better than Rockwell wanted to believe. Men Hickok's age had an edge by the very virtue of youth, their certainty that they were immortal. Rockwell had been the same at Hickok's age. The bullet hadn't been made that could put an end to him. But that belief, like memories, faded with time. Mortality became real. Could he take Hickok? He wasn't sure; but if he did—went against Brigham's "no blood" decree—what then? To hell with it, he snorted to himself; play it as it comes. A hundred years from now who would care?

Rockwell caught up with the column half an hour after it had departed from Bridger's camp. Riding to the head, he reined down to match pace with Lot and Coley. "Thought I'd tag along," he offered dryly.

"Suit yourself," returned Lot, looking straight ahead, "But if you do, you're under my command, *Major* Rockwell."

Rockwell gave a hint of a smile. "Wouldn't have it any other way, *Major* Smith."

Lot Smith forced back a smile. He wasn't the least bit surprised to see Rockwell riding up to join the troop. Everything had turned out just as Brigham Young had planned, including the troop's stop at Bridger's camp, where Rockwell was sure to find out where they were heading and why.

Luke Cartwright grinned at Harve Arnold. "Told you he was no deserter."

"Never said he was," protested young Arnold. "But he did go off without gettin' leave."

"Heck, everybody does that one time or t'other. Long as they come back when there's need for 'em is what counts."

"Port Rockwell likes a loose rein," said Will Cartwright. "Got to take him the way he is, or not at all."

The others agreed; he was his own man, and no rules or regulations were going to change that.

A beef herd could be driven just so far and so fast in a given number of hours—an immutable fact that Capt. Randolph Barnes Marcy found he had to live with. Marcy's suggestion that the wagons move on ahead of the herd, leaving them to catch up at day's end, was met with fierce resistance from Don Peralta's *segundo,* Hector Ramirez. Hector had never heard of "united we stand, divided we fall," but he knew only a fool moved through Indian country without all the guns he could muster in one place. He was not about to split the column on this young officer's say-so. The wagons were Don Peralta's property, and they'd be returned safely, if Hector Ramirez had anything to say about it. And Hector had a lot to say. His argument was backed up by the seventy-odd drovers and wagon handlers who looked to him for instruction. With a handful of troopers, Marcy was in no position to enforce orders. The contents of the wagons belonged to the U.S. Army, but the wagons belonged to the Mexican aristocrat in Santa Fe.

Nine days out of Fort Union, on the western downslope of the Chochetope, Captain Marcy had good cause to be thankful for the segundo's refusal to split the column. A large war party of Navajos had struck at dawn, catching troopers and Mexicans preparing to break night camp by surprise. Two of Marcy's small contingent went down in the first volley, along with a half-dozen Mexicans.

A half-mile running battle brought the column to the mouth of a box canyon, shouting drovers frantically driving the spooked cattle before them as a buffer between the Indians and themselves. The wagons made it to the relative safety of the canyon, sealing off the mouth with a wall of rolling stock. The drovers abandoned the milling herd to join their *compadres* behind the barricade.

It was a standoff; the Navajos couldn't force entry into the canyon, and the defenders couldn't get out. Before noon, the cattle had instinctively moved away from the battle site, taking the path of least resistance—the downslope of the pass.

The war party found shelter among the outcroppings and boulders on the far side of the narrow pass, and laid down a desultory fire on the men behind the barricade. Farther back among the boulders several small columns of smoke rose skyward. "Cooking fires," observed one of the surviving troopers. "The red bastards are going to wait until we have to make a break for it."

The heavy boom of Hickok's borrowed Whitworth echoed off the canyon walls, followed by a shrill scream from a brave as he tumbled from a high outcropping to crash in a bundle of broken bones at the base. "That's one who won't be around for the pickings," grimaced Hickok, ramming a fresh charge into the long gun.

The Indians' response was not long in coming. Lead balls whipped through wagon canvas and thwacked solidly into planking. A ricochet from the iron rim of a wagon wheel tore into the chest of a young drover, who fell to the ground writhing in pain. In a fury, the Mexicans loosed a fusillade toward the concealed Indians—futile, ineffective, the slugs flattening against solid rock, finding no softer target.

"Hold your fire!" shouted the frustrated Captain Marcy. "If you can't see them, you can't hit them! Hold fire!"

"Not an arrow in the bunch," said Hickok, eyeing the musket holes in canvas and wood. "Where the hell did they get all the guns?"

"*Comancheros*," answered Ramirez bitterly. "They take a share of everything the Indians get on a raid, including women."

"Ought to be hung," snapped Marcy.

"They are—when we catch them," said Hector.

Hickok turned at a touch on his elbow. Young Bill Cody, shaking slightly, held up a tin mug of coffee to the tall scout. "Still some left in the pot from this mornin', Mister Hickok. Ain't hot, but it's kind'a warm."

Hickok took the cup. "Thanks, Billy. Tell Cookie to rustle up some grub for the men. Looks like we're going to be here for a spell." Hickok shot a questioning look at Marcy, almost an afterthought. "That al'right with you, Captain?"

"Fine, Mister Hickok. I was about to suggest the same myself."

A shot whistled through the canvas wagon top, passing mere inches above Marcy's head. The group instantly crouched lower for the more sturdy protection of the wagon's wood planking. Hickok grinned at the officer. "Lucky you aren't a couple of inches taller, Captain."

"And fortunate you weren't standing where I was, Mister Hickok," said Marcy to the taller man. "More importantly, how the hell do we get out of this mess? How many do you think there are out there?"

"Big party," said Ramirez. "Fifty, maybe more."

"Enough to keep us tied down until their patience runs out," Hickok said dryly. "Looks like we've got ourselves a Mexican standoff, eh, Ramirez?"

"If you say so, señor," he said flatly. "The *Indios* are not ones to drag things out. A day, maybe two, and they will go away."

Marcy frowned; more lost time, and Lord knows how long it'll take to round up the spooked herd. The delays at Fort Union had stretched well beyond the week that Colonel Culbertson had estimated it would take to get the supplemental supplies from Fort Mary, and that damned Peralta had still come up short on the wagons—thirty-eight instead of the promised fifty. Now this. What the hell would go wrong next? To make matters worse, this prima donna Hickok seemed to find the situation humorous.

There wasn't anything funny about cold, hungry troops waiting desperately for fresh supplies—supplies that Marcy had assured Johnston would be at Camp Scott within six weeks. At this rate, they'd be lucky to reach the camp in half again that time. A day, maybe two, Ramirez had estimated. Pray to God that the Mexican was right. Marcy didn't look forward to a breakout and running fight with the Indians, but that's what it would have to be if the Indians went contrary to custom and decided to wait them out.

Another thought troubled Marcy: Ramirez and his men were civilians; would they obey an order that would take them out of the box canyon's shelter, exposing them to certain casualties? Marcy hoped fervently that he would not have to put that question to the test.

Dawn had yet to reach the depths of the box canyon as Bill Cody dutifully lugged a steaming, gallon coffeepot and a clutch of tin mugs to the two troopers and half-dozen Mexicans keeping watch at the wagon barricade. The hot drink was more than welcome to the night-chilled sentries. The camp was reluctantly coming to life, the drovers and wagon handlers rolling out of their serapes to head for the cook wagon with their tin plates and mugs. The cook, Israel, a potato-faced little tub of a man, rattled a huge spoon on an iron triangle to spur them on: "*Andele, Pendejos! Andele!*"

"Maricón!" someone shouted back, bringing a laugh from the others.

Young Cody stepped up on a wagon brace to peer across the floor of the pass, looking for some sign of the redskins. One of the troopers laid a ham-sized paw on the boy's britches to lift him bodily from the exposed position. "Mind yerself, lad."

"I didn't see anything. Betcha they've called it quits, and lighted outta here durin' the night."

"We'll find out, soon enough. In the meantime, don't go givin' those thievin' devils a target in case they ain't."

"Cody! Where the hell are you, boy?"

Cody blanched, swinging a look to the tent near the center of the camp to see Hickok standing in the open flap, face lathered, a straight razor in hand.

Cody snatched up the coffeepot and ran for the cook wagon, shouting, "Grub'll be right there, Mister Hickok."

Were the Indians gone or weren't they was the question foremost in the mind of Capt. Randolph Barnes Marcy. The sun was well up by now, the officer's tent struck and stored, the chuck wagon buttoned up and ready to travel. Anxious eyes were searching the bluffs and boulders on the far side of the pass. Not a movement could be discerned, not a sound heard. "One sure way to find out," said Hickok, slipping between two of the wagons forming the protective barricade, the long Whitworth capped and cocked in his lean hand.

"Don't be a fool, Hickok. Get back here!" commanded Marcy.

But Hickok was already on the move, running in a crouched position across the open space that separated the canyon mouth from the concealing rocks on the far side. He'd covered half the distance in his crouching run before he stopped and stood straight up, presenting himself as an open target, sure to bring a response from any brave worth his salt. There was none. Hickok turned to walk slowly back to the wagon barricade. "Time to roll, Captain, we're all on our lonesome. They've skedaddled."

Relief flooded Marcy as he turned to the segundo. "You heard the man, Ramirez. We're moving out."

Ramirez was bellowing commands in rapid-fire Spanish before Marcy had half the words out. The barricading wagons were pulled back, and teams of mules run up to take their places in the traces. Drovers swung into their saddles to assist, herding balky mules into position. Bill Cody—always there, always ready, always helpful—lead reined Hickok's and Marcy's mounts to their riders, then ran back to take his seat beside Israel on the chuck wagon bench.

From his saddle Marcy eyed the flurry of activity. Two days they'd been pinned down in this damned canyon—two days of lost travel time, and Lord only knew how much more would be lost tracking down and rounding up the beef herd, which was probably well out of the pass by now. Damn! Johnston would have his hide.

A rifle cracked; a mule screamed and went down in the traces. For a split second all activity froze. Then a shout came from one of the drovers as he pointed to the rim of the canyon. On the heels of his cry a fusillade of shots rained down on the bunched-up wagons, spilling drovers from saddles, teamsters from their benches, and dropping bellowing draft animals in their tracks. The shots were followed by burning bundles of crackling, flaming brush that showered down on men, wagons, and mules. Hector, the segundo, seemed to be everywhere at once, directing the drovers' fire at the fleeting targets on the canyon rim.

Shooting fish in a barrel came to Marcy's mind as he shouted, "Move out! Get those wagons moving!" His command was quickly relayed in high-pitched Spanish. "*Vamonos, muchachos! Rápido! Vamonos!*"

The first of the wagons was lashed into movement to rumble through the neck of the canyon. Others swung in behind, the drivers urging their teams on with shouts and blows. A hitched lead mule took a haunch shot and went down, hooves lashing in its death throes. A lean Mexican stepped around the animal's head to plunge an eight-inch blade into the mule's cervical column, bringing instant death. Others assisted to pull the beast clear of the traces and move another into its place.

The mounted drovers did their best to provide covering fire. Several flaming wagons were cut out and dragged clear of those yet untouched by fire. Two of them locked wheels, spokes splintering, the iron rims collapsing to fully disable the cumbersome vehicles. The drivers, shouting imprecations at each other, abandoned their wagons to find a place for themselves on another bench.

Israel and young Cody had their team hitched, the cooking pots dumped and stored in short order. The rotund cook clambered onto the driver's seat, slapping the reins down hard, furiously cursing the bewildered animals. Young Cody clung to the tailgate as the chuck wagon bounced and jolted toward an opening in the barricade. He caught a glimpse of Captain Marcy and his remaining two troopers, hazing the drivers to greater effort.

Dust, kicked up by grinding wheels and pawing hooves, rose from the canyon floor, mixing with the dark, billowing smoke of burning brush bundles and flaming wagons. It provided some protection from the rifles above as the last of the wagons made it through the narrow neck of the canyon. The drovers, many of them burned and bleeding, loosed a last, futile volley at the canyon rims, then followed.

By midafternoon some semblance of order returned. The train was now on the foothill downslope of the Chochetope, and before them spread a vast, open plain. A number of the beef herd had been recovered; more would be found up ahead, grazing on the stunted winter grass, or filling themselves at some water hole.

Marcy was grimly desolate. Seven wagons had been lost, wagons that had carried vitally needed stores for the troops at Camp Scott. The loss of two of his troopers and ten of Hector Ramirez's men, while deplorable, couldn't compare with the loss of supplies that might have fed and clothed a hundred of Johnston's troopers. One thing Captain Marcy had learned in a dozen years of army life was pragmatism. The fact that those dead might suffer mutilation too horrible to contemplate, and lie unburied, their bones eventually scattered by carrion eaters, was regrettable, but it was a fate that any man, soldier or civilian, might one day suffer in this untamed land. You learned to live with it. Still, he offered a silent prayer that all those left behind were dead, that no wounded would fall into the hands of the Indians.

Day's end found the wagon train, and the 263 recovered longhorns, encamped on a low rise some six miles from the western approach of the Chochetope—ideal defensive ground that provided a clear view in every direction. There would be no more surprise attacks, Marcy told himself. Still, he ordered the wagons laagered, tongue to tailgate— a protective circle of proven efficiency. The drovers had bedded down the herd at the foot of the rise, and had tended to their wounded—a dozen with flesh wounds and two with badly burned hands.

The voices of the Mexicans, singing softly to their charges, wafted to Marcy in the night breeze. It was nothing less than pastoral, a far cry from the morning's savagery. Within the laager, life went on as usual—campfires to provide warmth against the night chill, the men enjoying a hot meal. It was hot in more ways than one, thought Marcy. The Mexicans firmly believed that food had to burn its way down their gullets in order to be any good at all. Gringos weren't built for such meals, he grimaced. Still, it was better than a steady diet of hard biscuit and coffee, he admitted to himself. Several times he'd been tempted to crack open one of the boxes containing tins of cooked beef or stewed fruit he'd requisitioned from a civilian warehouse in Santa Fe. The development of tinned food had proven a godsend, both to the frontier and to home folk in the towns and cities. The day would come, Marcy assured himself, when troops on the march would not have to depend on walking commissaries—beef on the hoof—when one man could carry a week's rations in his pack, one wagon a month's supply for a company. When that day came, troops in the field would be self-sufficient, more mobile and efficient than at any time in history. But for now, every tin, every case, was meant for those who needed it most—the men at Camp Scott. Who knows, he mused with a faint grin, by the time we get there, I might develop a real taste for chili peppers, but I doubt it.

Lot Smith's troop had crept to within a quarter mile of Marcy's camp. Their horses had been left well back, guarded by two of the troopers. A neigh, or the clink of an iron-shod hoof on a rock, could quickly give away the game, reveal their presence to the alert sentries protecting the herd and encampment. The troop had made it to the western approach to Chochetope Pass, only to find that they were too late. The train had already passed through. Rockwell examined the wheel tracks left by the heavy wagons, and the freshness of horse droppings. "Can't be more than half a day ahead," he told Lot.

"Half a day, or half dozen—we're too late to catch 'em in the pass," said Lot with disappointment strong in his young face. "Now we'll have to take 'em in open country."

"Can't have everything our own way," instructed Rockwell. "Just have to make do."

Lot was irritated. "I intend to!"

Rockwell straightened up from the small mound of dung, wiping the residue on his trouser leg. "Don't you think it's about time you let up?"

Lot eyed Rockwell for a long beat, then glanced back at the column, some twenty feet distant. "Seems to me I could ask you the same question. Let's get it out in the open, Port. I don't need a wall to fall on me to know you hold me responsible for what happened to Jud. Maybe, in a way, I was, for not sending him back when I had the chance. I don't know . . . I tried."

"You didn't try hard enough," Rockwell retorted sternly.

Lot sighed resignedly. "No argument there, lookin' at it now, but talk isn't going to change what happened, and neither is desertin' your duty!"

Rockwell's demeanor now lost its hostility. "You said it right, Lot, nothing I can do will make a difference. Fact is, I'm not cut out for Brigham's kind of duty and, right or wrong, I sure as hell can't go on fighting his kind of fight. Sooner or later you're all going to get smashed again, and I don't want to be there to see it."

A heavy silence fell.

"You finished?" Lot said softly.

"For now," said Rockwell, swinging up in his saddle. "But you're right about one thing; what I've just said to you, I should be saying to *him*."

Lot nudged his mount forward. The column moved on, following the wheel tracks into open country.

Cephus James's telescope did little more than bring the outlines of the circled wagons into view. The small, objective lens didn't have the light-gathering power to do much more. Still, it was enough. Rockwell lowered the glass. "No way we're going to get close enough to get the jump on them. Have to think of some other way."

"Like what?"

Rockwell frowned hard. "I'm working on it."

"Maybe we'd just better keep tailing them until we find the right place," frowned Smith.

Rockwell shook his head. "They'd spot us, sooner or later. Our only chance is to take them by surprise."

Hector Ramirez wasn't a happy man. The segundo didn't look forward to explaining the loss of wagons and men to his *patrón*. Don Peralta took a dim view of anything that lightened the weight in his capacious pockets. Ramirez circled his mount around the outside perimeter of the laager, giving soft words of encouragement to his men, warning them to stay on the alert. You never knew what the Indios might do. Angling the mare toward the herd, he reined up at the small campfire where coffee was being brewed for the night guard, stepped down to accept the mug poured for him, then took a seat on a small rock to exchange a few words with the men around the fire. One of them had lost a brother in the fight with the Navajos. There would be compensation, he told the youth—not enough to replace a brother, but something.

Rockwell and Lot signaled the rest of the troopers to hold position while the two bellied closer to the glimmering campfire. They could hear the low exchange of conversation but had no idea of what was being said. The man seated on the rock was someone of apparent importance; that much was clear from the way the others deferred to him.

"That's it! Right in front of our noses all the time," Rockwell whispered to Lot.

"What are you talking about?" hissed Smith. "What's 'it'?"

"Mexicans."

"I'm not blind. So they're Mexicans."

"If young Coley was right, there's only a handful of troopers with the train; the rest are all Mex."

"What does that have to do with anything? We're still gonna have to—"

"Hired hands, Lot, doing a job for a dollar. The Mexicans couldn't care less about General Johnston, or Brigham Young. It's not their fight."

Lot snorted impatience. "Tell *them* that."

"Just what I intend to do."

Lot's eyes widened as Rockwell came easily to his feet. "You crazy?" Lot whispered. "They'll see you."

"I expect they will. Bring the boys up closer—be ready for whatever happens."

"Hold on, Port!" said Lot, coming to his knees.

But Rockwell was away, moving unhurriedly toward the men seated around the small campfire. "Damn you, Port Rockwell!" Lot gritted under his breath then elbowed his way back to the waiting troopers. "Whatever happens," Rockwell had said. Well, it'd better be right, whatever that was!

*   *   *

Jorge Gonzales was the first to see the tall man in buckskins emerge from the surrounding darkness. "*Jefe,*" he said softly, indicating.

Ramirez and the others came to their feet as Rockwell, fully erect, advanced with no show of urgency. The flickering light of the campfire was not strong enough to reveal his features under the broad-brimmed hat, but the butts of his high-belted pistols were unmistakable. "Señor Hickok? Is something wrong?" asked Ramirez with a puzzled frown.

Another step brought Rockwell fully into the firelight.

Alarm flooded the segundo's face. His hand moved to the gun at his waist. "You are not—"

"I wouldn't do that, señor," said Rockwell, making no move for his own weapons. His tone and almost casual stance gave Ramirez and his men pause. Rockwell continued, almost pleasantly, indicating the darkness behind him. "There are guns out there, and all of 'em are pointing in this direction."

Ramirez's hand fell away from his weapon. His men, who spoke little if any English, read the segundo's unspoken message clearly; their guns remained holstered. "Who are you, señor? What is it you want here?" he asked suspiciously.

Rockwell shrugged lightly. "Just trying to keep some people from getting killed—yours and mine."

"You have my attention, señor. What is it I can do to help in this most admirable intention?"

Rockwell angled a thumb at the coffee brewing over the campfire flames. "Mind if I have a taste of that coffee?"

Ramirez rattled off something to Jorge in rapid Spanish. A cup was poured and offered. Rockwell took a seat on a stone, facing the segundo. "Your people," queried Ramirez, lifting his own cup, "you are ones who call yourselves saints?"

A quirk of a smile touched Rockwell's lips. "There's something we have to do, amigo. All we're asking is that you and your men don't interfere. When it's done, we'll be on our way."

"This 'something,' " frowned Ramirez, "what *is* this 'something' ?"

"The wagons, they've got to be burned. We can't let them—"

Ramirez's face darkened in a scowl as he came to his feet, tossing the contents of his cup into the flames. "No, señor! The wagons will not be burned! They are the property of Don Peralta. We will protect them with our lives!"

"Simmer down, *hermano*. There's more than one way to skin a cat."

"*Qué?*" blinked Ramirez, a baffled expression on his face. "Cat? . . ." To the others: "*Dice que va a pelar un gato.*"

Lot and the rest of the troop had moved up to within fifty yards of the group around the campfire. Lying prone, they were invisible at half that distance. Luke Cartwright nudged Lot, whispering, "Having a real jaw fest, ain't they? What's the major up to? What's he tryin' t' do?"

Lot raised his shoulder. "Wish I knew, Luke. Just have to wait and see."

Rockwell and the segundo came to their feet and shook hands. As Ramirez climbed into his saddle and spurred toward the laager, Rockwell returned to Lot and the troop and threw himself down beside Smith.

Lot Smith was fit to bust a gut. "Well? What was that all about? Say something, damn you!"

"Not much to say, except that he won't let us burn the wagons; says he'll fight if we try."

Exasperation flooded the younger man's face. "Fine! Now they know we're here. They'll have every gun in there waiting for us!"

"I said he wouldn't let us burn the wagons. I didn't say he wouldn't let us burn what's *in* the wagons."

Lot stared into Rockwell's grin, the anger washing slowly out of his face to be replaced by wonderment. He shook his head. "What about the troopers? We still have to get by them."

"Only two left, and one of them is wounded. The others were killed in an Indian attack, back in the pass. The jefe'll see to those two. All that leaves is the army captain, and Hickok."

"How will we know when to move?"

At that moment an unseen hand hurled a brightly burning brand over the wagon tops. It fell to the ground, still blazing.

"That's how," said Rockwell, climbing to his feet.

"Port!" called Lot as he rose. "Can we trust him? I don't want these men walking into an ambush." His question was ignored.

With Lot and Rockwell at the center, the troopers advanced on the circled wagons in a broad skirmish line, hearts pounding with excitement, and a worm of apprehension in their bowels.

The camphine lamp threw a warm glow over the figures of the two men hunched over the checkerboard atop the small camp table. James

Butler Hickok pulled at his lip, grinned at Captain Marcy, then made a triple jump to the king line. "King me."

"How the hell did I miss that?" grumbled Marcy.

"Your mind's not on the game."

Marcy nodded absently, looking to the corner of the tent where Billy Cody buffed a high sheen on one of Marcy's knee-high cavalry boots. "That's good enough, son. No need for a parade ground polish out here."

"Just about finished, sir," said Cody, giving the boot a vigorous rub before setting it down beside its gleaming mate. Cody's eyes were drawn hungrily to the telescoped Whitworth and brace of holstered pistols on Hickok's folding cot. Some day he'd own guns that beautiful, he promised himself. He felt Hickok's eyes on him. "Want me to polish your holsters, Mister Hickok?" he said, sure that the tall scout had read his mind.

"No thanks, Billy. It's time you turned in."

"Yessir," said Billy, coming to his feet. Suddenly, his eyes widened at something past the pair at the camp table. Standing in the opening was a man—a copy of Hickok in form and dress, even to the brace of holstered pistols at his waist.

"Evening," the man said softly as a second man appeared behind him. One had a cocked carbine, which he leveled at the pair at the camp table.

At the sound of the voice, Marcy and Hickok came out of their chairs, Hickok reaching for pistols that weren't there. For a moment, the young Cody registered shock. Then, to his amazement, the tall scout smiled at the man who so closely resembled him. "You're Rockwell."

At that moment Marcy came to life. "Damn!" he growled, reaching for the pistol belt slung over the back of his camp chair. "Hold it, Captain!" barked the man with the carbine, centering the muzzle on Marcy.

The captain glared at the pair in the tent opening. His words came out as if something had a strong grip on his throat. "How . . . how did you get in here? Where are the sentries, my troopers?"

"Your troopers are okay, Captain, but this supply train has gone as far as it's going to go," Lot Smith told the officer.

"Looks like the Mexes sold out on us, Marcy," Hickok said easily. "How'd you manage it, Rockwell?"

"I told them it wasn't their fight," he responded casually.

"It was their fight when the Indians jumped us, dammit!" protested Marcy.

In their intense concern with Hickok and Marcy, the two intruders ignored the young boy. Billy Cody made his move. Quick as a young cat he snatched up the Whitworth and swung the heavy barrel toward the pair at the entrance. "I got 'em, Mister Hickok," he shouted, pulling back the hammer.

The muzzle of Lot's carbine whipped to center on the boy. It took a nerve-wrenching effort for Lot to keep his finger from squeezing the trigger. "God, no. . . ," he said silently.

"Tell him to put it down, Hickok," Rockwell said softly.

Hickok seemed to consider his options for a moment, his pale blue eyes locked on Rockwell's. Then he nodded. "You heard the man, Billy. Put it down."

"But Mister Hick—"

"Put it down!"

Reluctantly, head hanging, bottom lip puffed out, Cody placed the rifle on the bunk.

"Take the captain and the boy out of here, Lot," said Rockwell. "Mister Hickok and I have a personal matter to settle."

Lot looked from one to the other—matched pair, if ever there was one. There was no doubt in his mind what Rockwell intended, and none in his own about preventing it. "Not a chance, Port!"

"Suit yourself," Rockwell replied as he moved to sweep up Hickok's gun belt and toss it roughly at the scout's breast.

"You look naked, Hickok. Put 'em on!"

"With pleasure, Mister Rockwell."

Lot was furious. "Drop 'em, Hickok, or I'll—"

"Do nothing," snapped the scout arrogantly, slipping the gun belt around his lean waist.

"Don't be a fool, Hickok," said Marcy, alarm clear in his face, his voice trembling.

"A little late for that," he smiled. "Mister Rockwell wants to prove a point, and so do I."

Hickok cinched the belt tight, then slowly dropped his arms to his sides, his eyes boring into Rockwell's.

Ten feet separated the two men—ten feet and more than a decade—but at that moment they were as one, the same thoughts racing through their brains, the same churning in their guts. Can I take him? Will he betray himself with the flicker of an eye? It was the eyes that gave a man away, told you when he was about to make his move; the eyes that gave you that fraction-of-a-second warning. Miss it, and you were dead. A fifth of a second, maybe less, was all it took to clear leather and fire. You couldn't wait for the hand to move; by then it was already too late. The eyes. . . .

Lot Smith gritted his teeth. He felt an overwhelming helplessness as he looked from one man to the other. The heavy carbine in his hands was just so much dead weight, meaningless. "Oh, damn!" he whispered.

Billy Cody's young eyes were saucer wide, in total awe of the moment. Captain Marcy stood transfixed, feeling as though he were bound and gagged, unable to move or speak.

Then it happened. Hickok slapped leather, his palms mating themselves to the smooth grips of his Colts in less time than a blink.

The front sights had yet to clear his holsters when he found himself looking into the muzzles of Rockwell's navies, the bores looking like the gaping mouths of field guns. Hickok froze; *disbelief* was a feeble word to describe his surprise. For a fleeting moment a kaleidoscope of images flashed through his mind. This was it, then. In a split second two fireballs would tear into his chest, ripping life from his body. He'd seen it happen often enough, had caused it more than once. Why was Rockwell hesitating? Why didn't he get it over with!

"It appears you've made your point, Mister Rockwell. Shoot and be damned!"

As if in response, Rockwell slid the navies into his leather, easing the hammers down all in the same movement. "I'll settle for this," he said flatly. Turning his back to Hickok, he picked up the scoped Whitworth.

The stunned Hickok still had his hands locked around the butts of his half-drawn pistols.

"That agreeable with you?" asked Rockwell, turning back to the tall scout.

Hickok now let his weapons slide into their holsters and hooked his thumbs into the gun belt. "At this moment, I'm just about the most agreeable fella you're likely to meet, Mister Rockwell."

Rockwell returned a hint of a smile. "Try to keep it that way, Mister Hickok." Swinging around to Lot, he added, "We've got work to do."

"Port—you gonna leave them with guns?"

Rockwell looked back at Marcy, the boy, and Hickok. "I don't think that'll be a problem."

As Rockwell turned to leave, Hickok halted him. "A question, Rockwell. . . . Why?"

Rockwell eyed the scout a moment, then shrugged easily. "I had you pegged as a glorified bushwhacker, all reputation and nothing to back it up. I was wrong."

Dawn struck Hickok. "Scott's Camp! It was you up in those rocks."

"It was me," Rockwell responded matter-of-factly, then pushed his way out of the tent.

"I'll be a son of a bitch," murmured James Butler Hickok, all the pent-up emotion draining out of him.

For the first time since he was a small boy, Capt. Randolph Barnes Marcy wanted to cry. All his work and effort gone for naught, the supplies so desperately needed at Camp Scott were now nothing more than smoldering piles of ashes, the beef herd on its way somewhere to end up in Mormon bellies, and Hector Ramirez headed back to Santa Fe with empty wagons. *Disaster*—that was the only word for it. Marcy would return to Camp Scott with nothing more than a twelve-year-old boy to show for his pains—hardly a fair exchange for the two experienced troopers lost to the Indians. Marcy had ordered Billy Cody to return to Santa Fe with the wagons. The boy had flatly refused, saying he'd tag along behind Hickok on that old mule Ramirez had given him. To the devil with the boy; Marcy had more serious concerns to trouble him, and facing Brevet Brig. Gen. Albert Sidney Johnston outweighed all the rest.

"Standing there looking at it isn't going to change a thing, Marcy," said Hickok as he swung into his saddle beside the mounted troopers.

Unreasoning anger flooded Marcy's face as he turned on the scout, pushing past Cody, who stood holding the reins of the captain's mount and his mule. "You told me the Mormons would back off if it looked like they'd have to do some real fighting."

"There's always the exception, and last night we both got a clear look at one. Porter Rockwell wasn't about to back off. Believe it."

Something like a sneer tainted Marcy's words as he came back, "You could have taken him, but you didn't have the stomach to try. Admit it, Hickok, you were afraid of him!"

"That's not true, Captain," cried out Cody. "Mister Hick—"

"Shut your mouth, boy," snapped the devastated Marcy. "I'm waiting for an answer, Hickok."

Hickok's lips thinned, and he shifted in his saddle. "If you think I could have taken him, Captain, I suggest you get yourself some specs. The man had me cold. Hell, I'm not even sure he's human."

"What about when he holstered his guns and turned his back on you?"

Disgust dripped from Hickoks' lips. "You expected me to back-shoot a man who just gave me my life? What do you think I am?"

"Men are going to die because of what happened to these supplies. I'd rather see a dozen Rockwells back-shot than see one soldier die of cold, or because there isn't enough food to keep him alive. Is that so hard for you to understand? If it is, what are you doing here?"

"I've been giving that some thought, Captain. Now, if you've got it all off your chest, I think it's time we got some miles behind us."

Marcy glared at the tall scout for a moment, then, with a snort of anger, snatched the reins of his horse from young Cody and swung up into the saddle. "You haven't heard the last of this, Hickok!"

Marcy spurred his horse into an easy canter, followed by Hickok, two troopers—one with an arm in a sling—four packhorses, a mule, and a twelve-year-old boy. Billy bellied up on the mule's back and dug his heels into the flanks. The long ride back to Camp Scott would not be a pleasant one.

Years later in his memoirs, Cody recalled his friend Hickok as he remembered him during the adventure they shared in their aborted attempt to bring the supply train to the aid of Albert Sidney Johnston: "He was ten years my senior—a tall, handsome, magnificently built and powerful young fellow, who could out-run, out-jump, and out-fight any man in the territory." Cody also wrote in detail how the doomed train was surprised by Mormon raiders, who disarmed everyone, burned the supplies, and drove off the cattle, leaving only enough weapons and supplics for the frustrated train members to reach safety. Cody remembered the leader of the raiders to be "*Joe* Smith," but it was undoubtedly *Lot* Smith.

Chapter Seventeen

Lot Smith drove both men and cattle to their limits as long as the weather remained comparatively mild. As sometimes happens in the midst of an early and particularly severe winter, a temporary warming trend had developed. It could last for weeks or end in a day. As they moved north, they were happy to find that the snow had melted sufficiently for the cattle to find some nourishment under the dwindling patches of white. On Rockwell's suggestion, they had headed due west for the first twenty miles, then north, a route that would bring them to Echo Canyon in an estimated fortnight.

At last, and without serious incident, they arrived at the mouth of Echo Canyon, just as the sun was going down. There, on a small plateau, Brigham Young had ordered the construction of a temporary camp for those in need of refuge. Families in the path of Johnston's army, or in danger of Indian attack, were brought into this depot before being moved to points west or south. Young spent a good deal of time at the camp, soothing tempers and giving encouragement.

Angus and Anne McCutcheon had come following an outbreak of measles, which was now all but eradicated. Fortunately, Anne was immune, having come through the sickness as a child. Night after night she'd fall into her small cot at the rear of the camp dispensary, totally exhausted from another fourteen-hour day of ministering to the children. Some cabins held as many as five, all down with the sickness. The younger patients often had to be restrained, little wrists tied to the bed frames to keep them from scratching the red pustules. "It's for your own good" didn't make much impression on three year olds who desperately wanted to assuage the unbearable itching, and they had no intention of suffering in silence. Parental temperance was tried to its limits by the incessant wailing that seemed to blanket the camp.

The arrival of Lot's troop with the cattle relieved from Captain Marcy caused quite a stir in the camp, giving a lift to spirits sorely tried by the events of the previous few months. The tired riders were the heroes of the hour, plagued by endless questions from wide-eyed youngsters and equally curious adults.

The story of Rockwell's confrontation with James Butler Hickok spread like wildfire. Indeed, the story would gain luster over the years as Hickok became a legend in his own right.

But Rockwell walked by well-wishers, ignoring extended hands. He wanted to see Brigham Young, and he knew exactly where to go. One of the cabins had the American flag waving overhead. That would be the governor's quarters. Under the circumstances, Rockwell told himself, only a fool or Brigham Young would be flying the colors.

Without knocking, Rockwell pushed open the heavy door to the cabin, which was lighted by two large camphine lamps and a brisk, crackling fire. Brigham Young was sitting at his desk. He laid aside his pen and gave Rockwell a penetrating look. "I gather the mission was successful, Porter?" he said without emotion.

"Two hundred and sixty-seven head. They lost thirty-seven before we got to them," Rockwell reported curtly.

"The wagons?"

"On their way back to Santa Fe, empty."

Young nodded his satisfaction. "Any problems?"

"Lot was in command. He'll give you a full report. If you're asking whether we killed anyone, the answer is no."

Rockwell then reached under his sugan to bring out a folded slip of paper, which he tossed on Young's desk. The governor swept it up, unfolded it, and scanned the writing. His look shot back at Rockwell. "I suppose you've thought this through?"

"More than once, Brigham."

"Very well, your resignation is accepted."

Without another word, Rockwell turned on his heel, strode to the door, pulled it open, and passed through. The weight of the heavy panel swung it closed behind him.

Young rounded his desk, the paper crushed in his hand. Through the hazed window he watched motionless as the man stepped down from the porch to the path, and walked into the darkening night. Rockwell, he knew, would leave in the morning, never to return.

Rockwell pushed aside the flap of the tent assigned to him by a smooth-cheeked young corporal, and dropped on one of the two folding cots. He removed his boots, threw a blanket over himself, and fell into a fitful sleep.

On leaving the governor's quarters, Rockwell had walked through the small crowd that had gathered in expectation of news from the outside world. Anne McCutcheon was one of them, but Rockwell had passed her with unseeing eyes.

Lot Smith was more observant. He made his way to her side. "Hello, Anne."

"Lot! I'm sorry, my mind was elsewhere," said Anne with a forced smile.

"I'm glad you're here, Anne. I'd like to talk with you. After I report to the governor and get some of this trail dust off me, al'right if I drop by the dispensary?"

Anne hesitated a fraction of a moment. "Yes, of course."

Lot touched his fingertips to the brim of his hat. "Till later, then."

Anne felt a pang of sympathy as she watched Lot head toward the governor's quarters, a self-assured swing to his broad shoulders. She knew he had strong feelings for her. How could she keep from hurting him? What could she say that he would accept and understand?

She had taken Lot's hands into hers, looking at him gently, with feeling, as she spoke. "I've asked myself so often: How did it happen? How could I have fallen in love with a man I don't really know? The answer is always the same. There is no answer—it happened."

Lot's eyes dropped. His hands held hers tightly, but like the gentleman he was, he quickly pretended to recover, not wishing to cause her any further discomfort. With all the courage he could muster, he told her he would always be her friend, adding that if ever she needed someone to rely on, he'd be there. Anne embraced him, pressing her cheek to his, a bittersweet moment for both.

"Now," Lot said, clearing his throat, "if he doesn't know how you feel about him, you'd better tell him soon."

"What?"

"He's resigned from the militia, Anne, did it earlier this evening. He's ridin' out in the mornin'.'"

Anne was taken aback. "Why, for heaven's sake?"

"Oh, it's a long story. The man's been living in his own private hell for a long time."

"Brooding over the death of Joseph Smith?"

"Yes, that and more—much more. There'll be some who'll call him a deserter, leavin' his people in their hour of need, but they won't know all he's done, the lives he's saved at the risk of his own, how he's been forced to fight a war in ways he doesn't understand. . . . Anne, he's done more'n his share, as much as any man has the right to ask of him, including President Young."

A moment later Lot was down the steps and off into the darkness. Anne looked after him for a long moment, then passed back through the dispensary door, closing it behind her.

Fifty yards down the dirt street, in the opposite direction taken by Lot, Doc Ames and Angus McCutcheon, returning from their nightly rounds, had paused to observe what appeared to be a touching scene between Anne and Lot. A crafty twinkle came to Doc Ames's eye as he nudged his colleague. "While the cat's away, eh, Angus?"

Angus McCutcheon beamed a nod. "If I'd known about this, I'd've stayed away a lot sooner. Fine lad that Lot Smith."

"Aye," nodded Ames. "Lad'll make the girl a good husband; and I'll make it my business to tell her so."

"You'll do nothing of the kind, Milford. This is my Annie's surprise, and I won't have you cheatin' her out of it!"

"Hmmmph," snorted Ames. "A secret, is it? Fine with me, but if the firstborn is a boy, I'll expect him to have a proper name. Milford would do nicely."

"Angus Milford Smith," mused Angus. "Does have a nice ring to it. Remember now, not a word of it."

It took Rockwell less than an hour to saddle the buckskin and load a packhorse with provisions. He had awakened tired, irritable, and depressed.

The sun was nourishing the morning sky as he rode out of the corral, directing the buckskin through the narrow valley past the encampment up on the plateau.

Suddenly, Anne McCutcheon appeared directly in his path, startling both him and the buckskin.

She was somewhat disheveled from working with the sick since before dawn, yet more beautiful than ever, thought the confused Rockwell. But what was she doing at the Echo Canyon camp? One thing was certain, the woman was angry.

"And where is it you might be goin', Mr. Rockwell?" she demanded, placing her clenched fists on opposite hips, her fine-lined jaw thrust out aggressively to match the fire in her wide gray eyes. She was unaware of how pronounced her Scottish brogue became when she was angry and not consciously attempting to sublimate it.

Rockwell reined in the buckskin and looked down at her, but said nothing.

"So you're desertin' us all, are you, to say nothin' of your duty?"

Still, Rockwell said nothing. His look was one of frustration.

"That man," she jerked her head in the direction of Young's office on the plateau, her brogue hardening, "has the weight of the world on his shoulders. He needs you, and you ride off without so much as a 'by-your-leave.' "

"Brigham?" Rockwell interjected bitterly, "he doesn't need—"

"Oh, the both of you turn my stomach," Anne shot back. "Of course he needs you, tho' the good Lord himself couldn't make him say so! Don't you know you're his right arm in harm's way? And how can you think you don't need him, he who's given you reason for livin' again these past months! Oh, the both of you. You have the stupid pride of Irishmen! . . . So he's lettin' you leave, is he! Will you not remember the *other* who ordered you away! You obeyed, and will regret it always!"

These last words cut Rockwell. The *other* . . . Joseph Smith. His face began to crimson with anger.

Anne knew she had hurt him deeply, but she would have done anything to keep him from riding away. She moved to the side of the buckskin, reaching up her hand to touch his. Now her voice was subdued, her brogue diminished to a soft hint. "He needs you . . . your people need you." And then, "I need you."

A moment passed; then Rockwell reached down and, in a smooth movement, pulled her up to sit behind him on the buckskin as easily and gently as if she had been a child. Saying nothing, he reined the buckskin about, heading it back toward the corral. Her arms went about his waist.

Rockwell's mind and emotions were pulled from their moorings. He had walked out of Brigham Young's office wrenched by competing feelings of relief and guilt. Now he felt trapped. So much for my resignation, he told himself, wondering how Young, that arrogant . . . would react to his return, or more accurately, to his not having left at all. And what about this Anne McCutcheon? He didn't recall women being so downright brazen.

Up on the plateau stood Brigham Young, straight and still as a statue. Only his eyes moved as he watched Rockwell and Anne ride back toward the corral. He turned and walked slowly back to his office. Once inside, he poured himself a cup of herb tea. Then he took the resignation paper Rockwell had thrown on his desk, and let it drop into the fireplace, watching it turn to ashes.

At length he knelt down, hands clasped behind his back, and bowed his head.

The sun had escaped just below the western horizon, leaving for a brief moment the remnants of pink light embroidering the occasional explosion of towering, majestically white cumulus clouds, as if to introduce the brightening evening stars.

The warming trend had left the night extraordinarily balmy. The slight wind out of the south was curiously comfortable, certainly a far cry from the angry storms of early winter, which had been beaten into a white frenzy by polar winds streaking down out of Canada. Soon the weather would resume its belligerence, but this night was made for lovers.

Porter Rockwell and Anne McCutcheon stood silently on a rise at the brink of the small plateau, the same place where Brigham Young had witnessed their confrontation early that morning. From their vantage point they could look out through the mouth of Echo Canyon, through the valleys and flatlands, to the distant mountains beyond, which were now giving sanctuary to the setting sun. But in spite of their breathtaking view of nature, they were oblivious to all but each other.

Rockwell's hands gently cupped her face. Her arms were about his waist, holding him close. Her eyes looked deeply into his, searching. "Who is she?"

Rockwell was momentarily startled. "What . . . ?" His hands dropped from her face.

"The woman you've been comparing me with since the first day I saw you and Lot Smith riding out of the sun. Who is she?"

"Not now, Anne . . . that was long ago."

"Tell me about her, please," Anne persisted gently.

Rockwell sighed. "She is . . . you . . . so like you."

"And where would she be now?"

Rockwell's eyes looked down. "She's gone. Childbirth," he said haltingly.

Anne flushed. "Oh . . . I *am* sorry. And the child?"

"He died . . . with her."

"Dear God," she whispered.

Neither spoke for some time. Then she tightened her arms around his waist, pulling her body closer to his. She turned her face up, offering her lips to him. He took them, hesitantly, tenderly, breathing in her fragrance.

After a long moment, she slowly eased herself away. "Now, Mister Rockwell," she spoke softly but deliberately. "I am me, myself, and no one else. I'm filled with love and passion and beautiful dreams I've been saving my lifetime. I have much to give, but I'll be loved for myself alone, or not at all."

With that she threw her arms around his neck and kissed him once again—passionately—then she turned and ran gracefully down the rise to the camp, leaving Rockwell with his heart pounding and head spinning.

Brigham Young had ordered the closing of the camp at Echo Canyon, having concluded that all endangered families had been gathered in or were on their way to Salt Lake City. With moderate weather still holding, he, along with his group of volunteers, including Doc Ames, Angus and Anne McCutcheon, forty families, Lot Smith and his troopers, Porter Rockwell, and the rustled—Young preferred to use the term *requisitioned*—army cattle, began their journey. They arrived in Salt Lake City in the early morning, three days before Christmas.

It had been a miserable trip—mud in the lowlands, snow and ice at the higher elevations. Many of the streams that had previously been frozen over, providing a bridge of ice, were now flowing copiously again, the deeper and wider ones causing predictable problems. Still, as Lot assured his overworked soldiers, travel could have been a whole lot worse if the weather had turned bad.

Anne and Rockwell saw each other frequently as they performed their tasks, although only for short periods of time, given the ubiquitous problems the wagon train faced. Still, Rockwell found himself increasingly comfortable in the company of this Scotswoman.

On occasion, Rockwell and Brigham Young crossed paths but said nothing. "What a shame," Anne confided to Angus. "Two grown men, both courageous enough to cast the gauntlet in the face of the whole wide world if necessary, yet neither can find the words to speak to the other."

"Ah," Angus replied pontifically. "Pride cometh before the fall."

Significantly, Brigham Young's train was not the only one to arrive in Salt Lake City just prior to Christmas. Members of the battalion were still bringing in a few stranded immigrants, and residents from different parts of the territory. Later that afternoon, Rockwell read the following in Salt Lake City's full-grown newspaper: "Hodget's and Hunt's Companies, with those who went to their relief, have been arriving within the past few days. Bishop Stowell reports the new arrivals to be in fine spirits, notwithstanding their late hardships; and those who so liberally turned out to their relief report themselves ready to start out again were it necessary."

"Ready to start out again were it necessary." When Rockwell re-read that sentence, he thought of the courage of Lot Smith, the rough-and-tumble Cartwright brothers, and the other troopers. Most of all, he pictured the baby-faced, redheaded Zebulah Weems, gut shot and dying yet still sitting his saddle, and the small, sinewy, homely Jud Stoddard. Rockwell would have given anything to see the diminutive form of that modern David walking down Main Street, head high and singing out, "Hello there, *Brother* Rockwell."

Rockwell shook his head, asking himself where they got such men.

In this Christmas season of 1857, Salt Lake City was a unique settlement in the West. It was crowded, given the large numbers brought into the already populous community from points east.

The center city was bustling with activity. Home-fashioned and locally manufactured Christmas decorations adorned the official offices and the numerous shops and eateries that bordered Main and Temple streets. Not a shop window was without some festive display. At the Assembly Hall work was almost completed in preparation for the annual Grand Cotillion. The very air seemed to have a festive touch—crisp, vital, the essence of life. But underneath lay an urgency to make this Christmas one to remember.

Even with the unanticipated shortages of certain items, goods were being advertised with vigor. The major commerical establishments were doing a land-office business.

To the casual visitor, Salt Lake City had none of the earmarks usually associated with newborn frontier communities. In many respects it resembled more the staid environs of the better sections of Boston or Philadelphia—broad, tree-lined streets, modestly stately homes with well-tended grounds, and an air of permanence. It seemed like a city built with an eye to the future—solid, substantial, with thoughts of generations yet to come as the cornerstone.

Unlike eastern communities, Salt Lake City had no wrong side of the tracks, no division street separating the acceptable and the undesirable. There were no brothels, bang-head saloons, or gambling dens, no indigents walking the streets. This was a community built on a foundation of self-reliance, the quiet pride of accomplishment—and it showed.

Immigrants and visitors passing through would uniformly express amazement at the abundance of amenities available; well-stocked shops offered a seemingly endless variety of goods and services. There was an honest-to-goodness soda fountain at Godby's, which also featured perfumeries, a wide selection of nostrums, and copies of the ever-popular *Grafenberg Manual of Health*. Customers often chuckled over Godby's carefully worded advertisement: "A selection of choice liquors, wines, and cordials of the first quality *for medicinal purposes*."

Walking along Temple Street, one would encounter the establishments of Goddard and Hardy, which featured cakes, pies, hard bread, spruce beer, cider, lemonade, and sugar babies. In the eatery one could order anything from eggs and bacon to mutton chops and beefsteaks. Next to Goddard and Hardy's was the People's Meat and Provision Mart. A little farther on was Stewart's Groceries and Dry Goods Shop. There was Canland's Half, called Globe Rooms, complete with dining facilities, a "bakery saloon," and a barbershop. There were milliners, tailor shops, watchmakers, dry goods stores, and, of course, Kimball's Emporium, Taylor and Sons, Abram Levi's, and the Deseret Store, selling everything from soap to parasols.

The Union Hotel, and lesser hostelries such as the Utah Hotel, were filled to the bursting point, just as the shops were doing an unprecedented business. Even these wide streets were at times almost impassable with foot and wheeled traffic.

With the change in weather, a few of the more courageous freight wagon trains had begun to make it through from southern California, bringing with them the latest copies of *Harper's,* the *Knickerbocker* magazine, and eastern newspapers that had made the long journey around Cape Horn. Martin Hober and Charles Kalman, reporters for Greeley's *New York Tribune,* were safely ensconced at the Union, having traveled almost twenty thousand miles from the streets of New York to get there. Their attempts to interview Brigham Young, or anyone else in the territorial hierarchy, had, of course, been fruitless. But that did not keep them from making good use of their expense accounts, enjoying the best that Salt Lake City could provide.

On his return to Salt Lake City, Porter Rockwell, his pockets heavy with back pay he'd picked up from the militia paymaster, had found that his room at Brandon's boardinghouse was now the accommodation for the wife and daughter of a battalion captain who had brought his troop up from the south. Rockwell expected as much; he had left without notice. However, Mr. Brandon presented Rockwell with a sealed note. "This is addressed to you, sir."

The note simply directed Rockwell to the finest hotel in the territory—the Union. "Where did this come from?"

"I was asked not to say" was Brandon's pompous reply.

Rockwell's room at the Union was fit for a nabob; even had its own private bath. He was delighted, especially so when his porter told him that a party who wished to remain anonymous was footing the bill. It took just one scowl from Rockwell and the young man admitted that the anonymous party was "the governor's office."

Rockwell ordered hot water, and was soon reclining in his tub, feeling better than he had for a long time. Within an hour, he had the water changed three times.

Rockwell was no stranger to luxury. In the past, he'd enjoyed the best that metropolises such as New York, Charleston, and New Orleans could provide. But things had been different then; he was different.

Now, amid the hordes of smartly uniformed battalion officers, well turned-out ladies, and gents in broadcloth suits, he felt uncomfortable walking through the copiously chandeliered lobby of the Union. Buckskin was out of place in such surroundings.

But Rockwell knew it was more than that. Being in such surroundings took him back over time, a time of gentility, a time of love and peace, of happiness, and a hope for the future. In his mind's eye he could see *her* again. Her tall, willowy body, her strong yet delicate face that was once the be-all and end-all of him.

He wanted to capture it all again, but he knew he could not. Or could he?

There was another in his mind—Anne McCutcheon. She had stirred in him once again feelings he thought had been forever ripped away. He relived the moment on the plateau, with her arms locked tightly about his waist, the passion of her kisses. To be loved for herself alone, she had demanded. . . .

"You're a fool, Rockwell," he said aloud, as if he had suddenly made sense of his unnecessary frustration. Of course they are alike! That the sameness should have attracted him was both good and natural. For one who had loved as he had, it would take someone like Anne to rekindle the flame. Why hadn't he seen this? With her, the past became a beautiful memory, enriching rather than embittering the present; the future, a promise that ennobled rather than betrayed the past.

Earlier in the day, as he had unloaded Angus McCutcheon's medical supplies from the battalion wagon, placing them in the doctor's buckboard, Anne had asked him, "Will I see you soon?"

"Yes," he had answered, "soon." But he wasn't sure.

Now he was sure. He had never been more certain of anything in his life. Indeed, it would be soon, and not in buckskins.

Almost before he was dry from his extended bath, Rockwell, with the zeal of one who had discovered a new lease on life, entered the respected establishment of A. W. Wright and Sons, Tailors. The shop was just a short walk from the Union, and right next door to the fabled Mrs. E. Bull, Millinary, Dress, and Mantle Maker, who promised "items to be found in the first-class establishments of the Old Country."

A. W. Wright, proud that Porter Rockwell had selected his establishment, promised him a broadcloth suit by Christmas Eve, if he and his sons had to work on it through the night, a promise, Rockwell warned, he would hold them to.

Wright was a champion talker. As he took Rockwell's measurements, his mouth didn't stop for a second. "The invention of the sewing machine has made this possible, Brother Rockwell; yes, indeed. This is a great age to be living in, Brother Rockwell. Think of the inventions that have appeared in just the past half century to make life easier—the cotton gin, the harnessing of steam for power, the telegraph. Why, there are already plans being considered to lay a telegraph cable across the Atlantic. But let me tell you this, Brother Rockwell, none of these great marvels will affect the lives of the average citizen more than Mister Elias Howe's sewing machine. Because of this invention," he insisted, "the whole world will one day be affordably well clothed."

The next stop for Rockwell was the Deseret Store, for boots and shoes and shirts and a dozen other accoutrements that caught his fancy.

The twenty-fourth day of December broke brilliantly clear, the high mountains with their sparkling white blanket contrasting with the deep blue of the sky.

Early that morning, Brigham Young, governor in residence of the territory of Utah, addressed the duly elected Territorial Legislature. The bulk of his address concerned the Utah Expedition, and the actions of the federal government concerning the territory of Utah. It was directed not only at the Utah Territorial Legislature and the people of Utah, but to the United States Congress, reporters visiting Salt Lake City, and the eastern media.

The governor charged that the United States Army had been sent to Utah "with the avowed purpose, as published in almost every newspaper, of compelling American citizens, peacefully, loyally, and lawfully occupying American soil, to forego the dearest constitutional rights."

Nor was he shy about inferring that a conspiracy was afoot that reached beyond the confines of Utah. "Who is laying the ax at the root of the tree of liberty? Who are the usurpers? Who the tyrants? Who the traitors? Most assuredly those who are madly urging measures to subvert the genius of free institutions and those principles of liberty upon which our government is based, and to overthrow virtue, independence, justice, and true intelligence, the loss of which, by the people, the celebrated Judge Story has wisely affirmed would be the ruin of our Republic—the destruction of its vitality."

There is a limit, he warned, even to the highest forms of patriotism, a higher law that takes precedence. "Has Utah ever violated the least principle of the Constitution, or so much as broken the most insignificant constitutional enactment? No, nor have we the most distant occasion for so doing, but have ever striven to peacefully enjoy and extend those rights granted to all by a merciful Creator.

"No one has denied or wishes to deny the right of the government to send its troops when, where and as it pleases, so it is but done clearly within the authorities and limitations of the Constitution, and for the safety and welfare of the people; but when it sends them clearly without the pale of those authorities and limitations, unconstitutionally to oppress the people, as in the case in the so-called army sent to Utah, it commits a treason against itself which commands the resistance of all good men. Patriotism does not consist in aiding government in every base or stupid act it may perform, but rather in paralyzing its power when it violates vested rights, affronts justice, and assumes undelegated authority.

"A civilized nation is one that never infringes upon the rights of its citizens, but strives to protect and make happy all within its sphere, which our government, above all others, is obligated to accomplish. Its present course, however, is as far from that wise and just path as the earth is from the sun.

"We have long enough," concluded Young, his powerful voice ringing through the hall, "borne the insults and outrages of lawless officials, until we are compelled in self-defense to assert and maintain our God-given and constitutional rights."

There was a moment of silence after Brigham Young finished his declaration. Then the Territorial Legislature rose as one with a roar of approval that lasted some minutes. Daniel H. Wells cheered the loudest.

Apparently—but only apparently—unmoved, Young stood tall before the deafening expression of support. "God bless them," he said, "bless them all." His words were drowned out by the commotion.

In the afternoon, the tabernacle, secure within the walled temple grounds, was filled to overflowing to hear Brigham Young, now in his role as president of the church, give his annual Christmas message. It was one of hope and thanksgiving, and admonition that, in celebrating Christmas, all humble themselves before the man to whom it is dedicated, remembering His life, His love, His sacrifice. "Through the blessings of an all-wise Providence," he summarized, "we have been favored with freedom, general health, and a fair portion of the bounties of the earth. Let our gratitude and praise be given unto the Lord of Hosts for these mercies and favors; and with them may wisdom and understanding continue to flow unto us."

Then the congregation, which packed the tabernacle, flowing out onto the grounds, began to sing the traditional Christmas carols. Hundreds of voices were lifted in song. At length, those in the tabernacle moved out into the sunshine, through the gates of the walled enclosure, and a spontaneous parade began down Main Street. It was a day of rejoicing. Who among them knew when there would be another.

In the evening the streets were filled with well-wishers, merrymakers, and people just talking to one another. The extraordinary and unseasonably warm weather helped make the evening even more enjoyable.

From the great Assembly Hall, its doors opened wide, the music of Strauss, mingled with cheery voices, drifted across the grounds, over the walls, and into the streets, there to be hummed aloud by many a passerby. On one corner, a group of rosy-cheeked young people playfully and exuberantly danced to the music, the girls holding out imaginary trains with their left hands, the boys bowing properly, pretending that their scuffed shoes were in truth polished military riding boots, their largely homespun clothing, sharp uniforms with braids. After all, it was Christmas Eve.

In the crowded hall, the Grand Christmas Cotillion was at its peak. General Daniel H. Wells had led the grand march to open the evening's festivities, his impeccable white jacket adorned by the medals earned in the service of his country. At his side, her arm entwined in his, her long blond hair contrasting with her deep blue taffeta gown, marched the general's stunning wife. This was not her first cotillion. Even as she marched she recalled another such event that took place in Philadelphia, not too many years past, when she and a number of other young women were presented. Her escort that night had been a handsome, broad-shouldered, sandy-haired young lieutenant, wearing the uniform of the United States Army—the same man whose arm she held so proudly this Christmas Eve, December 24, 1857.

Directly behind General Wells marched four other officers, similarly attired. They, too, had served their country as officers of the Mormon Battalion in the war with Mexico. They had marched from Fort Leavenworth, Kansas, to San Diego, California, conquering two Mexican presidios along the way, and from there to Los Angeles in time to help counter the political ambitions of John Fremont—a march of more than two thousand miles.

Porter Rockwell was conspicuous by his absence from the grand march. He found it incongruous that these men were honoring their country, when less than two weeks' march from Salt Lake City, an army of the United States—including as one of its commanders the officer who had led the battalion on its historic trek—had been ordered by the president of the United States to force military occupation of Utah Territory.

But when the grand march was completed, and the music of Strauss filled the hall, played by the Salt Lake City Symphony Orchestra, Rockwell was there, Anne McCutcheon in his arms. Once again, the past was compressed into the present for him. Once again, he was at a ball, filled with people of gentle manner and civilized attire. The dirtiness of the frontier was washed from his body. In his eager arms, a beautiful Scotswoman looked at him with unconcealed love.

He spied Lot Smith waltzing with the daughter of General Wells—if one could call it waltzing, given his exaggerated motions—a look of utter contentment smoothing his face. Rockwell guessed that Lot's infatuation with Anne had been turned in another direction with equal fervor. "Ah," Rockwell mused aloud with a broad smile, "the resilience of youth."

"And what do you mean by that?" Anne responded pleasantly.

Rockwell swung her around so that she could see Lot and his beautiful partner. "I was thinking," he said, "that Lot's period of mourning is about over."

"And then some," Anne replied laughing.

Rockwell also wondered if his own contentment this evening was as easily recognized as Lot's. At least for the moment, all seemed right with the world again.

"I love you," he spoke quietly.

Anne responded by reaching up, touching her lips to his.

"And I thee, with all my heart."

The music swelled, filling the hall with the beauty and genius of Strauss. They moved as one to the captivating rhythm, round and round to its now haunting refrain, as if they were in a realm all their own.

There was no rejoicing in the army of the United States, marooned at Camp Scott on an island of revolving ice, snow, and mud. Dwindling rations hardly matched the food being enjoyed by their enemies in Salt Lake City.

On Christmas Eve, two soldiers joined others who had died before them of fever and the lung sickness. Since October, others had died from gangrene, resulting from frostbite, and from a variety of other illnesses. Still others had lost frostbitten toes, fingers, even ears to amputation. Each day a new group of troopers reported sick, and recovery was slow, sometimes not at all.

Uniforms were deteriorating, as were socks and boots; and wearing boots without socks invited infection from inevitable blisters. Soap was in short supply, making matters worse. The Mormon marauders had destroyed more than fourteen thousand pounds of it. Included along with this problem was the severe lack of wiping paper, or any paper at all for that matter.

A festering rash had descended on the troops like a holocaust. It was not just an ordinary rash; it was the granddaddy of all rashes, shooting bright red fingers from ankles up to calves and knee joints. The rash brought a maddening itch that could be assuaged only by frenzied scratching, which drew blood. And when the itching sometimes spread to other areas of the body, the crotch, for instance, the agony increased proportionally. Men walking stiff legged or bowlegged was not an uncommon sight.

All of the trees in the area had been felled for construction and kindling. The growing paucity of warm clothing necessitated the burning of fires both day and night. It was not unusual for temperatures to drop to fifteen or twenty degrees below zero when the sun went down. And a stiff wind could turn that into forty below. The snow layer around Camp Scott wore a mantle of black soot for a hundred yards in every direction. The perimeter where any kind of kindling could be found grew wider with each day's passage, eventually to be measured in miles rather than yards.

When suddenly a warming trend, encouraged by southerly breezes, began melting the snow, Camp Scott became a sea of grasping, sucking, infuriating mud in the daytime and half-frozen ridges and holes at night, making just walking difficult.

Johnston was facing a serious morale problem. Lost tempers and fights were commonplace. But most ominous were the men who became morbidly silent, standing or sitting off by themselves, refusing to respond to others, performing their duties slowly, silently, their expressions dulled.

Captain Marcy's report on the Fort Union train had been a bitter blow to the officers and men of Johnston's army; another nail in an icy coffin, said Major Poole. Johnston, however, appeared to take the news calmly. What was done was done. The army would have to do as all armies have done in similar situations—endure.

Still, he knew that the loss of the supplies from New Mexico had spelled the end to any remotely possible attempt to move on to Salt Lake City before spring. Johnston knew that his command would have to be completely refurbished before the Utah Expedition could resume its march. Even then, Johnston questioned whether the physical condition of his troops would, after this winter nightmare, permit an early spring movement into the rebel stronghold. At this point the Utah Expedition was stranded. It had neither the strength, facilities, and food, nor the weather to move either forward to Salt Lake, or to retreat to Fort Laramie. His recalling of Napoleon facing the Russian winter, and the similarities he shared with him, caused a chill to go up his spine.

Nevertheless, the general remained confident that his army would survive the rigors they faced. He had believed all his adult life that he was a man of destiny. He would be in command of Salt Lake City by early summer at the latest.

A foraging party from Camp Scott was to confirm his vision. No more than a week after the arrival of Captain Marcy, with his tale of disaster, troopers sifting through the ruins of Bridger's Fort found a treasure trove of stores untouched by the flames that had destroyed the fort. In a series of connecting cold cellars burrowed deep in the earth under the charred ruins, they found hanging venison, hams, sides of bacon, hundreds of jarred preserves, bins of beets and potatoes, and case upon case of dessicated vegetables.

As far as Albert Sidney Johnston was concerned, this was a sign, a godsend. Yes, now there was time for Captain Buell and his men to arrive with what remained of the stores left behind at Platte Station. He knew that Buell must be on his way, taking advantage of the warming trend. Using mules and the break in the weather, he just might make it. He had to make it!

The general had already given the order to begin the butchering of what remained of his draft animals and all but a few horses. This would serve two purposes: fresh meat for his command, if only for a short period, and the avoidance of the animals' inevitable starvation. He and his men faced a grave ordeal, he admitted to himself, but they would survive. Damned if they wouldn't survive!

James Butler Hickok was leading an especially uncomfortable life at Camp Scott. In the first place he was bored. The days passed slowly, and with predictable regularity. In the second place he was carrying a burden he'd never in his life faced before—humiliation. He knew that every man in Camp Scott had heard of his confrontation with Porter Rockwell.

During the day he spent most of his time with Billy Cody, who hung on every word the scout uttered, ready to polish his boots, bring him his meals, see to his tent, or do whatever he might ask of him. In the evening Hickok played poker with Magruder, Hathaway, Carney, and the trooper Riley. Each night he came to despise them with greater intensity.

But it was the loss of the Whitworth that bothered Hickok most. There were others who were not happy about the loss, including the rifle's owner, Lieutenant Coy. He was not pacified by Hickok's promise to replace it. Not the same, Coy had said gloomily; the Whitworth was something special, a gift from his father, a retired colonel. There was no way to replace that. All Hickok could say was he'd try to get back the original.

The year 1858 was not going to be a good one for President James Buchanan. He looked a decade older than his sixty-six years, a worn and troubled man. With a sigh he rose from his chair and turned to peer unseeingly through the frosted window overlooking Pennsylvania Avenue. A light layer of snow covered the unpaved roadway. There was little traffic on this cold Sunday morning, just a few closed carriages, the breath of their horses pluming steam clearly visible, even at this distance. Beyond lay the partially completed monument that was to be dedicated to the first president of the United States. For the thousandth time a bitter thought seared Buchanan's mind: Was he to be the last?

Word had reached the eastern press. It had streaked across the nation, even in the dead of winter—from Fort Union in the New Mexico Territory, from Platt Station through Fort Laramie in the Nebraska Territory, even from California around Cape Horn, and God knows from where else. Johnston's army, viciously harassed by the astounding guerrilla tactics of the Utah Territorial Militia, called "The Battalion," had been deprived of wagons, supplies, cattle, even infantry mounts. Its timetable demolished, the army had not reached Salt Lake City, nor would it until at least spring—if ever. The Utah Expedition, the largest mobilized army in the United States, was hopelessly trapped in the Nebraska Territory by what was undoubtedly the worst and the earliest winter in fifty years. Furthermore, it was reported that the army was dangerously low on supplies. Thus far, almost superhuman efforts to refurbish the army from Fort Union and Platt Station had proved abortive. The situation, already critical, could become desperate.

For more than a week, reporters had unsuccessfully sought an audience with Buchanan; a number of senators, led by Sam Houston, were demanding a meeting with him. Three newspapers, spread out, adorned the president's desk, sensationalizing the problems of the Utah Expedition, and asking questions. Then there was the arrival of dispatches from General Johnston himself, forwarded by Captains Marcy from Fort Union and Buell from Fort Laramie. This left no margin for doubt. What seemed an impossible occurrence to Buchanan had been confirmed, in every maddening detail.

Finally, the president addressed his niece, who had sat silently, watching him, hurting for him. "My God, Harriet," he moaned, "this is a tragedy. Who could have imagined this would happen? That is an army of the United States out there!"

Uncharacteristically, Harriet Lane said nothing. It *is* a tragedy, she thought. Talk of secession all around and the largest army of the United States stranded two thousand miles from the nation's capital. A strategic blunder if ever there was one.

"And what am I supposed to do?" the president continued. "Damned either way." He shuffled across the room, then spun around, facing her again. "The Congress will scream bloody hell if I go to them for more funds, more supplies, more troops. I'm already under fire for the cost of the first expedition. But I can't just leave them out there, can I?"

Harriet started to speak but was interrupted by a firm knock on the door.

"Yes," Buchanan answered, irritated.

It was his aide. "Excuse me, sir, Secretary Floyd is here."

"Floyd." Buchanan's voice was bitter. "Send him in."

The secretary of war inclined his head rather arrogantly. "Mister President. Miss Lane."

"Well," said Buchanan abruptly, bypassing the formalites, "what do you think of this mess?"

Floyd sucked in his breath. "A deplorable situation, Mister President, but one that is not unredeemable, not without its possibilities for future vindication."

"And just what in the hell do you mean by that?"

Floyd sucked in another breath, then raised his hands in a calming gesture. "Look, Jim, let's put this whole thing into perspective. Johnston's debacle has been a blow, an embarrassing blow, to both of us. Who could have foreseen this? The Utah Expedition is stuck, suffering—a cause célèbre for your opposition and mine, both in the press and on the floors of Congress."

Buchanan was about to interrupt, but Floyd spoke on, authoritatively. "However," he continued, a hint of a smile, "this situation won't last forever. In the spring, Johnston's army will move on. There's no question that the territory of Utah is in rebellion against the federal government. Everything that has happened, from the expulsion of federal appointees to the contents of Johnston's dispatch, points to this reality. The abuse we are now subject to will be forgotten when the Utah Expedition takes Salt Lake City. What we must do now, Mr. President, is to assure the survival of Johnston's army, with fresh troops and supplies at the earliest possible time."

"And if, in fact, the people of Utah are *not* in rebellion, Mister Secretary?" Harriet Lane's voice was more accusing than inquisitive.

The lady with the violet eyes made Floyd nervous. There was more to her than met the eye, much more. She had a brain and knew how to use it. Like most of Washington, Floyd was strongly convinced that she was the real power behind the presidential throne. Old "crook neck" didn't make a decision without consulting her.

The secretary of war tried to smile, but it was left hanging superficially on his face. He cleared his throat. "Do you have any doubts, Miss Lane?"

"Perhaps. Would you care to relieve me of them, Mister Floyd?"

Floyd cleared his throat again. "Why, yes, of course." Nervously, he reached into his inner coat pocket, fumbling for a cheroot. "May I smoke, Miss Lane?"

"No, I'm afraid not," she responded matter-of-factly.

"Oh, well, no, of course not; my apologies. . . . Will you tell me what disturbs you about my assessment of the situation?"

"Everything, Mister Floyd. First of all, I am aware of the character of Utah's former territorial appointees. Judge Drummond, for instance, is a thief and a lecher. I have met periodically with two representatives of Governor Young, Messrs. Benson and Romney. I must say, they inspire in me a great deal more confidence than those officials who took French leave of their territorial posts.

"Secondly, while I accept the fact that the Territorial Militia has harassed the Utah Expedition and has destroyed government property, the general's letter doesn't say anything about armed conflict. Don't you find that a bit unusual?"

"Merely a matter of time," responded Floyd. "Up to this point, the rebels have avoided direct confrontation with our troops, but it will come, that I assure you. Don't forget, they have already murdered one trooper, and are inciting the Indians to join them in their rebellion. General Johnston's report confirms this."

"One soldier killed? In a rebellion? Hardly a heated conflict, is it? And is it not possible that the presence of Johnston's army has caused no little concern among the Indian tribes of the area, completely aside from the influence of the territorial government? Senator Houston and the two gentlemen sent here by Governor Young tell me that if a war breaks out, it will be instigated by *our* troops.

"And another thing, Mister Secretary, don't you find it passing strange that there was no communication from the governor designate included with the dispatch from General Johnston? Surely Mister Cumming would have contributed his own views on the situation."

"I'm afraid I can't be responsible for Mister Cumming's actions, or lack of same, Miss Lane," responded Floyd, not bothering to conceal a disdainful curl to his lip. "The military is my responsibility; political appointees are not."

Blood rushed to Buchanan's face; his eyes flashed angrily. "I advise you to choose your words and tone more carefully, sir!"

Floyd effected a slight bow that took in both. "I meant no offense to Miss Lane or yourself, Mister President."

Buchanan was not appeased. "And for your information, as commander in chief, the responsibility for the military is mine alone. Against more sound advice I was foolish enough to embark on this Utah fiasco, and the ultimate responsibility rests on my shoulders. But I suspect that the motives of some members of my cabinet were not entirely what they appeared to be at the time."

Floyd bristled. "With all due respect, Mister President, I must ask you to clarify that statement!"

"Don't play me the fool. The winds of rumor don't stop at the White House gate."

Floyd's attempt to respond was silenced by Buchanan's hand. "*I have not finished!*" he roared. "You will have your relief column for General Johnston, if it means stripping the federal garrisons down to the bone to do it; and if that is not enough I'll call on Congress to authorize the raising of an army the likes of which this country has yet to see! But Utah isn't the issue here, Mister Secretary. It's bigger than that, and you know it! This country is *not* going to be torn apart—not by Mormons, disunionists, or the devil himself. "Have I made myself clear?"

The war secretary nodded stiffly, his face flushed and taut. "Quite clear, Mister President."

"Then get out!"

"You should have demanded his resignation, Cobb's and Thompson's as well," Harriet Lane offered when the door was closed firmly behind the secretary of war. "They don't wear the blue cockade on their lapels, but it's there in spirit. Avowed disunionists, all of them!"

"I know," sighed a now calmer Buchanan, "but there'll be time for that. For the moment I don't dare risk forcing them to more precipitate actions."

The president fell into his chair as if he were supporting a great weight. "When will men like Floyd realize that our strength as a people lies in unity? Twice in the memory of living men we've had to beat back European domination. The threat is still there, now perhaps more than ever. The empire builders haven't forgotten us. Why, given the opportunity, Louis Napoleon would be quick to abrogate Bonaparte's agreement on the Louisiana Purchase; and England is no less eager to restake her claims on our northwest territories. When will they learn? Disunion is but the first step to eventual dissolution. We'll be back where we were in 1775."

The relieved secretary of war made a quick exit. As soon as he was out the door, he rammed a cheroot into his mouth, coughing as he lit it.

By the time John Floyd reached his office, he was puffing smoke like an engine stack, his cheroot clamped tightly between stained teeth. He had lost the composure he was able to maintain in the presence of the president and Harriet Lane. "That fool Johnston has ruined everything," he spit at Secretary Cobb, who was lounging on a flowered couch by the fireplace. "He should have been in Salt Lake City by October! Now God knows what will happen! Imagine, a group of farmers and foreigners hog-tying an army of the United States, and forcing its commanding officer to cry for help! It doesn't make sense, dammit to hell!" He cast the stump of his well-masticated cheroot angrily into the fireplace.

At that moment Cobb came to his feet. Senator Jefferson Davis had entered the room. "I could hear your voice at the end of the hall, John. Am I to take it that your meeting with the president and his charming niece did not go well?" he asked with obvious sarcasm.

"They're on to us, Senator," Floyd bellowed, causing himself a brief coughing spell.

"The best laid plans of mice and men," Jefferson Davis mused aloud.

"Spare us your little homilies, Jefferson," growled Floyd. "He's on to us, no doubt about it!"

"Calm yourself, John, calm yourself. Whether he is or is not aware of our intentions probably makes little difference at this point."

Floyd was no less inconsolable. "What do you mean by that, Jefferson?"

"We may have more time than anticipated. I have learned from reliable sources that California will not vote on the secession question this year when the state legislature meets."

This brought grunts of surprise from both Floyd and Cobb.

"Now don't get me wrong, gentlemen. The conspicuous failure of Johnston has dealt a potentially telling blow to our hopes for a western confederacy. I say 'potentially' because I'm still not fully convinced that the Utah Expedition, succeeding *or* failing, will materially affect our efforts one way or the other.

"Nevertheless," the senator from Mississippi continued, "we must put our best foot forward, mustn't we? Now, since our time restraints can be put away for the moment, our situation quickly improves. Johnston's army is going nowhere for perhaps three months. The president can't recall it. Furthermore, he must refurbish it—he has no choice in the matter. He cannot leave the army to suffer. And for our purposes, it's nice to have a three-month breathing spell, a time to reorganize and plan.

"Come spring, if we can assure Johnston's immediate occupation of Salt Lake City and Utah Territory, we are potentially no worse off than just before the troubles began.

"Keep this in mind: Whether or not Utah Territory resists the occupation, differing, but valuable, benefits may accrue to us in any event. Remember, I said 'may.' Your task, John, is to see to it that Johnston's army occupies the territory of Utah come spring. Once that has taken place, we can evaluate our position and plan our strategy. Without this, our options diminish."

Floyd was taken aback. "How can I assure that, Jefferson, when probably at this very moment, Colonel Thomas Kane is handing Governor Cumming an executive order from Buchanan empowering him to terminate the expedition and order its return if he finds there is no actual rebellion. Remember, you were the one who insisted that the charges against the people of Utah were farcical."

The senator symbolically raised his eyebrows, giving Floyd a condescending look. "I'm sure that a bright fellow like you can find a way.

"One more thing, gentlemen. As you, John, no doubt were assured this morning by Old Buck, he'll use force to prevent disunion; and, rest assured, the northern states will rally behind him to do it. He'll get his volunteers, by the hundreds of thousands. The Yankees are itching for a fight—have been since '32.

"Time is on our side. Buchanan has made it clear that he doesn't intend to run for a second term. With the proper planning we just might see to it that the next man to occupy the White House will be much more receptive to the idea of state sovereignty."

"And who might that be?"

Davis smiled. "The Little Giant."

"Stephen Douglas," said Thompson. "He couldn't take half of the northern states."

"Perhaps not, but he will be a candidate. And if elected, he won't be another Buchanan. Furthermore, he is not antagonistic toward the South. I have come from a long and frank talk with Mister Douglas, and I must say I was pleased with his attitude. What I'm trying to say is that we have options. There is time. Now, if you'll excuse me."

"Who does he think he is?" growled Cobb, after Jefferson Davis had left.

"He *knows* who he is," responded Floyd, acknowledging his respect for the senator, "and he knows there won't be a confederacy without his help. He's right, you know; we must see to it that Johnston's army is kept in the West come spring. Salt Lake City—the crossroads of the West. Johnston *must* gain control there."

Less than a week later, Secretary of War John Floyd dispatched a ciphered message to Gen. Albert Sidney Johnston. The message would be telegraphed to Fort Kearney, and from there to Fort Laramie by army courier. The commander of Fort Laramie would arrange for the message's delivery into the hands of General Johnston at Camp Scott, Nebraska Territory—that is, when the weather would permit it.

When all the cards were finally dealt, thought John Floyd, it would be squarely up to Johnston how they would be played. So much depends on this one man. Was it an exaggeration to suggest that the future of eleven million Southerners lay in his hands—the fate of not one nation, but two?

Chapter Eighteen

I n January Porter Rockwell and Anne McCutcheon were married. Doc Ames gave away the bride. General Wells, whose daughter was accompanied by Lot Smith, stood with Rockwell. John Atwill presented the couple with a gift of two large beaver-pelt Indian blankets.

Brigham Young and Angus McCutcheon did not attend, each for his own reason.

Angus was devastated. All these years his daughter had refused to marry, causing him no little embarrassment. And now, in a land filled with men who were suitable in every way, she brazenly chose a backslider, a gunman, a saddle tramp. He had tried to reason with Anne, but to no avail. There was no question about it, he told himself, Rockwell had cast an evil spell over her. This libertine, this man of the world had beguiled her sweet innocence, taken advantage of her unworldliness, her trust.

"Marry him?" he had bellowed. "Are ye daft, girl? Hae' ye lost what little sense the good Lord gave ye? The man's a backslidin' scallywag with nothin' more than the clothes on his back and the saddle he sits in. What kind of life can he offer ye? Answer me that! How can ye even think of such a scoundrel when the likes of Lot Smith is yours for the noddin'. Think, girl, think!"

I have, Da," she had wept, "more than you'll ever know, but all the thinking in the world won't change what's in my heart. Tell me how

I can stop loving him and I'll do as you say. Tell me how to cure the longing I have for him, and for the babies I want to make with him, and I'll look the other way. I'm sorry, Da, but that's the way of it. Don't force me to choose between the two of you; please don't do that to me."

"It's yerself that's done the choosin', girl. Go off with him, if that pleases you, but ye'll have no blessing of mine in the doing!"

Angus had stormed out of the room. He hadn't gotten ten feet when doubt assailed him. Right or wrong, she was flesh of his flesh, his lassie. Could he turn away from her? For a long moment he wrestled with an urge to recall the words spoken in anger and frustration. The moment passed; there would be no turning back. Angus McCutcheon was a Scot.

Earlier on the morning of the wedding, General Wells had come to Rockwell's room at the Union to hand deliver a message from Brigham Young: "Major Porter Rockwell, Territorial Militia. Urgent. I have instructed General Wells to order your immediate departure for southern Utah. You will command a troop of Territorial Militia. I have reports of tribal unrest in the St. George area. Your first assignment is to secure the peace there, and enlist additional recruits from among our people. May I suggest that you and your wife occupy my winter home in St. George."

There was a postscript to the message. A hint of poetic warmth—not really unlike Young, Rockwell knew. "May God's blessing and shield go before you as you begin a new life. When the daffodil and the swallow appear, return to Salt Lake."

Rockwell shook his head and smiled at Wells in spite of himself. "Well, Brigham does know nature's way; and he knows his Shakespeare—Shakespeare's daffodil 'that comes before the swallow dares, and he takes the winds with beauty.' "

Then Rockwell grimaced. "Now, what do I tell Anne? Hell of a way to start a marriage."

"If you don't mind my saying so," offered Wells, "any way to start a marriage with that woman is a rare gift, Major. At any rate, she already knows."

"What?"

"Yes, a personal note to her from Brigham Young early this morning. He was concerned how she might feel about it."

"Really. And her response?"

"Exactly what you would expect it to be."

"The man knows how to honey both sides of the bread," Rockwell mumbled.

It was a simple, warm ceremony, a small chapel, a few close friends, the weather outside threatening.

As Rockwell repeated his vows, a sensation of peace suddenly enveloped him. A gentle hand reached out of the past to touch him, reassuring him that all was well.

Rockwell brought the wagon he'd rented from Atwill to a stop, ordering his mounted troop to camp at Point of the Mountain, where the foothills of the mighty Wasatch and the Oquirrh touched like two giant fingers. On a clear day, one could see the entirety of the Great Salt Lake Valley, including the great lake to the north, and Utah Valley, with its grand freshwater lake, to the south.

This night there was little to be seen, however. The sky was overcast, threatening snow, and a cold wind whistled through the pass with angry intent.

Rockwell was damned if he was going to spend his wedding night in a wagon. Grasping the tightly rolled beaver-pelt blankets, he led Anne up a low rise, snow mist churning about them, to a grove of majestic fir trees. After a few minutes' search, he found a magnificent ancient blue spruce with a richly endowed base, its great extremities touching the ground. The endless layers of branches, with their innumerable outcroppings of needles and cones, formed a fifteen-foot umbrella around the trunk so impenetrable as to have not yet admitted a flake of snow or a drop of water.

Lifting some of the heavy, snow-crusted branches, Rockwell bid his bride enter their pristine chamber.

The wind and snow swirled futilely about their sanctuary as if to protest the security of their nest, while inside, the fur blankets warmly caressed their naked bodies. Then, as the storm raged, they gently, tenderly, became one.

Anne was taken with Brigham Young's winter home in St. George. Comfortable was the best word for it. It was modestly furnished, with two oversized fireplaces on both floors. The master bedroom on the upper floor opened out onto a sturdy balcony that overlooked the small city.

Most of all, Anne enjoyed becoming acquainted with Brigham Young through the books in his study. On one shelf she found Thomas Paine's *Common Sense,* the works of Thomas Jefferson, *The Federalist Papers,* the essays of Addison and Steele, Milton's *Paradise Lost,* Locke's *Essays on Government,* Smith's *The Wealth of Nations,* Grotius's *On the Law of War and Peace,* and Trenchard and Gordon's *Cato's Letters.*

On another shelf she found the Bible, the *Book of Mormon,* Rutherford's *Lex Rex, or the Law and the Prince,* and Hutcheson's *A System of Moral Philosophy.* On still another, the works of Shakespeare, the works of Plato, Washington Irving's *The Knickerbocker Gallery,* Franklin's *Poor Richard's Almanac,* Jonathan Edwards's *Sinners in the Hands of an Angry God,* and Emerson's *The Divinity School Address* and *Essay on Nature.*

Anne immediately fell in love with St. George—the people, the soft, red earth, the mountains, the river that passed through the settlement. But most of all, she came to love the Indians, whose many villages in the area intrigued her. She could see that the chieftains of these villages respected her husband. They listened to him, and apparently assumed that what he told them was the truth. Slowly, Anne came to see these people in a different light—their customs and traditions, their dress, their festivities, indeed, their nobility. No longer did she see them as heathen savages, little more than animals.

It was not long before she turned her nursing skills in their direction, and even Rockwell was surprised at the willingness of the Indians to allow her to minister to them. Against Rockwell's firm advice—that with Indians it was best to let nature take its course—she brought a small Indian child, suffering with severe fever, into Brigham Young's home, where she cared for it day and night for a week. The recovery of the child was a cause for celebration in the village, and the Indians brought gifts galore for Anne, now called "Sister Ah-han."

Each time she visited a village, she carried candy and cookies for the young people, even taught them some old Scottish games. Whenever she visited, they surrounded her. Several times she went riding with them.

As the weeks went by, Anne saw more and more of the depth of Porter Rockwell—the way he dealt with the Indian leaders, the respect his troopers had for him, his evenhanded justice when things went wrong. How she wished her father could see him in this setting. "Saddle tramp," indeed!

It took some time for Rockwell to feel at ease with the Indians, however. They were naturally concerned with the coming of Johnston's army, about which they knew nothing. The relationship between the Indians in southern Utah and the Mormon settlers had been fairly good, but the situation had always been tenuous. The slightest thing could kick it off track.

Therefore, when Rockwell was informed that a group of renegades had begun attacking travelers coming to St. George from Vegear, he was properly concerned. The attacks appeared to be concentrated about sixty miles south.

It took Porter Rockwell, battalion scout Woodrow Taylor, and three Indian trackers less than four days to find the renegades, just as the blistering desert sun was going down. They were heading toward St. George without any attempt to conceal themselves. From the edge of a cliff, Rockwell watched the Indians slowly wind their way through a dry riverbed deep in a reddish walled canyon.

Finally, he put down his scope and turned to the others. "Fifteen of them. They've got a white man with them. His hands are roped behind his back. The head man is wearing an officer's jacket. Must belong to the prisoner. Should be stopping to make night camp anytime now." He motioned to Taylor and one of the trackers. "Woodie, you two follow along on this side of the gorge till they stop. Then get down as close as you can to their campsite." And to the other trackers: "You two cross over to the other side and do the same thing, so we have them in a crossfire. I'll ride up ahead of them, and come back down the riverbed. Give me fifteen minutes to get into position, then open fire. I'll try to get to the prisoner before they have a chance to kill him."

Rockwell raced the buckskin along the ridge of the gorge for a half mile. Then he left the animal in a clump of Joshua trees, and descended to the bottom of the canyon.

The renegades had decided to stop for the night in a sandy patch, almost in the center of the riverbed. The captive sat on a small boulder on the edge, his hands still roped behind him. Rockwell had it figured: By edging close to the canyon wall, he could get within fifteen to twenty yards of the white man without being detected. From there he could belly-crawl. By that time, Taylor and the others would be ready to open fire.

Everything was going smoothly. Rockwell had another five yards to crawl to reach the prisoner when he heard the spine-tingling sound that has struck fear into the hearts of men since time immemorial—the buzz of a disturbed rattler.

He froze, every muscle taut. His mouth suddenly went dry. Without moving his head, his eyes scanned the area in front of him. There it was: three feet in front of him and slightly to the right—a thick five-footer, its large diamond-wedged head above its coils in striking position, tongue whipping frantically in and out of its deadly mouth.

Too early for the snake to be out of hibernation, Rockwell told himself; but there it was. What had been a perfect plan collapsed in the face of Eden's monstrosity. Woodrow Taylor and the trackers, now just a few yards from the encampment, opened fire with murderous accuracy. Shrill cries of alarm joined with the sharp sound of gunfire echoing up and down the canyon walls. The renegades and their spooked ponies fell right and left. It was a chaos of terrified horses and panicking Indians, neither knowing which way to turn. Some of the renegades managed to return fire, but it was ineffective.

In the confusion, some were able to reach their ponies and attempt to escape up the riverbed. Most never made it. Two of the braves ran toward the prisoner, one raising his rifle, the other a war ax.

Rockwell sprang to his feet, his left hand pulling his Colt with the same speed that the rattler's fangs struck deep into his right forearm. Two shots dropped the Indians; the third blew the head off the snake. Then he quickly pushed the prisoner to the side as the thundering hooves of Indian ponies barely missed them.

"BEHIND YOU!" the bearded man cried out, and Rockwell turned just in time to ward off the plunging blade of the buck wearing the officer's jacket. He went over backward, the attacker on top of him. They rolled to the middle of the riverbed, Rockwell holding the knife hand, while the Indian struggled desperately to keep Rockwell's Colt from turning into his body. For a moment they held each other at bay.

Finally, Rockwell was on top, a vicelike grip on the Indian's wrist, pounding the hand holding the knife against a rock until the blade was dislodged. Then Rockwell jammed his thumb an inch into the Indian's left eye. A gurgling scream of agony exploded from the brave's mouth as his hand instinctively went to his bloody socket. In a split second, Rockwell forced the muzzle of the navy under the Indian's chin and fired. The top of the brave's head was blown off.

Dropping the pistol, Rockwell pulled out his boot knife and quickly cut deep crosses into the rattler's puncture marks, then began to suck the wounds.

Before the last echoes sounded from the canyon walls, Woodrow

Taylor was at his side, cutting the sleeve from his shirt and tying a tourniquet on Rockwell's arm just above the elbow, twisting it tight with one of his Colt barrels.

"Any get away?" Rockwell asked Taylor.

"Yeah, two, but one of 'em's wounded."

"Get after them, Woodie. If you take 'em alive, tie them backward on their ponies. On your way back, pass through some of the Indian villages. I want the young bucks to see what happens to renegades. When you get to St. George, hang 'em. Malvado," Rockwell nodded at one of the trackers, a big man with sculptured, bronzed muscles, "will get me back."

"See you soon, Port," yelled Taylor with a wave, as he and the other two trackers ran for their mounts.

The prisoner, sitting in the dust, hands behind him, had said nothing. His eyes were fixed on Rockwell. "Seems we meet in strange places, Porter," he said at last.

Rockwell turned swiftly to confront the voice. He peered suspiciously into the man's bloodshot eyes, studying him—the dark beard, the red blistered nose and cheekbones, the scaled, cracked lips. It took a moment for Rockwell to see behind the mask. "My God . . . Kane! Is that really you?"

"I'm afraid so. Lucky for me you happened by. For you, I'm not so sure."

In a second Rockwell was at his side, cutting his bonds. "Malvado, bring this man some water!"

Rockwell turned again to Kane. "What the hell are you doing here, Tom?"

"On my way with messages for Governor Cumming and Brigham Young."

Rockwell shook his head, as if he was having difficulty fathoming it all. "How did you get into this mess?"

"Being stupid. By going through a canyon I should have gone around. They had me before I knew what hit me."

"Lucky you're alive. Renegades seldom take male captives."

Kane jerked his head toward the corpse wearing the officer's tunic. "When toadface there found my uniform and the pouch with the messages, he got the idea he could trade me for guns and ammunition in St. George. They've been pulling me around for I don't know how many weeks, arguing among themselves how they were going to do it. I expected any day they'd get frustrated and kill me. But ol' toad-face took pride in having a long-knife officer as his prisoner."

Kane slowly, stiffly walked over to the dead renegade wearing his jacket. He jerked away the pouch tied around the man's waist. "Thought I'd never get to deliver these. Hope I'm not too late."

Rockwell knew the symptoms of rattlesnake poisoning. It wasn't the first time he'd been bitten, and repetition didn't make it any easier. Swelling began in less than an hour, accompanied by throbbing pain. That night the telltale metallic taste appeared in his mouth, introducing a retching nausea, followed by intermittent chills and sweating. By morning, he was dizzy, and his whole forearm had become painfully swollen and black-and-blue. Rockwell knew that the king of rattlers had given him a good jolt of venom.

The next day he found it difficult to sit his horse. Kane rode close to him but was weak himself. The Indian tracker was philosophical: If Rockwell weathered the next twenty-four hours, he'd probably survive, unless gangrene set in—a very real possibility.

Three miserable days later they arrived in St. George. With Anne's patient and professional ministering to her charges, Kane and Rockwell quickly regained their strength.

Two weeks later, Col. Thomas L. Kane bid a fond farewell to his friends as his coach, with military escort, headed for Salt Lake City, with orders from Major Rockwell not to spare the horses.

General Wells was beginning to sound a lot like Porter Rockwell, Brigham Young told John Kimball, "and one Rockwell is enough for any army."

"I am sorry, sir," Wells had said, having requested an audience with the governor, "but I don't understand your reasoning in sending supplies to Johnston. You don't fatten up an enemy so he can hit you that much harder. What is the purpose in sending out troops, at the risk of their lives, to stop the supply train from Fort Union?"

Brigham Young was annoyed. "I'm getting a little weary of having to explain my actions to everyone."

"Sir, I'd walk through hell with you, but this—"

"Really, Dan," Young interrupted, a glint of humor in his eyes, "I had supposed our journey would take us in another direction."

Wells, as he had learned to do with Young, ignored the quip. "I want to know why. I believe I have that right."

Brigham Young nodded. "Yes, Daniel, I suppose you do. I was

concerned that the supply train from New Mexico might give Johnston just the edge he would need to make an attempt to reach the valley, should there be an easing of the weather. I couldn't take that chance. I had to have it stopped.

"At this point in time, Johnston's position is hopeless. Reports from the scouts watching Camp Scott tell us that the Utah Expedition has serious difficulties—not enough food, clothing, or medicine. Many are sick. Some have died, and they still have a long winter ahead of them.

"They are our countrymen. We may be shooting each other in the spring, God forbid, but as for now, I believe we ought to try to ease their suffering."

Brigham Young sighed. "I confess I've had doubts that what I'm doing is wise. I'm not even sure Johnston will accept what we offer, but offer it we will."

General Wells said nothing for a minute. Then he rose, extending his hand to Young. "Your order will be carried out, Governor."

"Thank you, Daniel."

Preparations for the relief column were well underway when the escorted passenger coach from St. George bearing Col. Thomas L. Kane arrived in Salt Lake City.

Young took Colonel Kane in a rib-cracking embrace, his face filled with genuine, comradely affection. "Good to see you again, Thomas. You bring a moment of light into these dark hours. Welcome!"

"Thank you, Governor," said Kane, when he was able to draw a breath. "A lot of years have gone by since those days at Council Bluffs, years I might not have had if it weren't for you, sir. And now, again, dear friends in St. George save me from certain death. My debt can never be repaid."

"Nonsense," smiled Young. "Your friendship for this people will always be remembered. You humble us by your courage and sacrifice in our behalf. Would there were more like you, Thomas."

"There are, Governor. There are still those in Washington who haven't forgotten the stench of what happened in Missouri and Illinois. Sam Houston is one of them, and more are turning to his way of thinking every day. The senator asked me to give you this."

Young carefully broke the seal and unfolded the single page. The message was short, almost terse, but it said all that mattered: "Governor Young. You have my oath that every effort will be bent to bring this unfortunate affair to a just and honorable conclusion. I have every assurance that Governor Designate Cumming and Judge Dawson are gentlemen worthy of the term, men who value truth above all." The note was signed with a scrawling flourish that John Hancock might have envied.

Young carefully folded the note. "Would that Sam Houston were sitting in the White House instead of the Senate. How is the old war-horse?"

Kane laughed easily. "He can still take on a grizzly with a birch switch, Governor. If anyone can put another crick in old Buck Buchanan's neck, it's Sam. He backed up every word your Romney and Benson said to the president. Buchanan called him a damned Texican fool for standing up for men he scarcely knew. If they'd been a few years younger they'd probably have gone at it like a pair of river toughs.

"Buchanan's niece, Miss Lane, finally cooled things down and persuaded the president to dictate a letter for me to deliver to the governor designate. In short, it instructs Cumming to make a thorough investigation of the charges against the people of Utah Territory. If those charges are proved to be true, Cumming is to take whatever steps necessary to restore order."

"I find no fault in that," Young nodded with satisfaction. "All we've ever desired is a fair and impartial hearing."

"That isn't all, Governor," interjected Kane. "If, in the opinion of Cumming, these charges are *unfounded,* then he is commissioned by the president to order an immediate withdrawal of the Utah Expedition."

Brigham Young's smile was a big one. "Johnston's encamped near Bridger's Fort. We'll get you safely there, Thomas. Deliver the president's letter to the new governor, and one from me, assuring him safe conduct and our full cooperation."

The twenty provision wagons had left Salt Lake City at first light on a cold February morning. Each of the wagons trailed a saddle horse—transportation for the wagon driver's return to the city once their charitable cargo was delivered to Camp Scott. One of those wagons carried eight hundred pounds of sacked salt. Two others were laden with sacks of good white flour and salt, an offering as old as time, symbols of friendship. Another wagon carried stacks of beef jerky. The loaders had taken special pride in the fact that the jerky had been provided by a number of the cattle that Lot Smith and Porter Rockwell had rustled from the army at Chochetope Pass.

There was a twenty-first vehicle, Brigham Young's personal carriage, occupied by Thomas Kane, now attired in his Maryland Militia uniform. The governor designate and Judge Dawson would be carried to Brigham Young in comfort and style, thought Kane, covering his knees with a coach blanket. Brigham's letter offering Cumming and Dawson safe conduct was nestled inside his tunic along with Buchanan's message to the governor designate.

The first sixty miles had been covered with relative ease, and in good time. Reaching the snow-covered higher elevations, the wheels had been locked in position, and snow runners affixed.

The four-up teams of stout, sixteen-hand mules easily managed an average of three miles an hour, thanks to the runners that helped the heavy wagons glide over the surface of the snow. It was just past noon on the fifth day when the palisaded walls of Camp Scott came into view, the flag of the United States flying bravely in the bitter wind.

Captain Lot Smith, in battalion uniform as were the twenty-one men on the driving benches, rode to the head of the column to signal a halt three hundred yards from the camp gate.

The crisp urgency of a bugle sounding call to arms carried from the camp, and in moments the palisade walls were manned with riflemen. The gates swung closed.

Smith took a folded five-by-three flag from his saddlebag and affixed it to a ten-foot pole brought along for that purpose. With a crisp cracking sound, the wind snapped the cloth. It was white, whiter than the surrounding snow—a flag of truce.

General Albert Sidney Johnston mounted the gun rail steps flanking the gate, buttoning his greatcoat. "Truce flag, sir," said Philip St. George Cooke, offering his field glasses to Johnston. The general peered through the lenses, then lowered them, his brow furrowed with suspicion.

"Maybe they've come to surrender, sir," offered Captain Frietag.

"Hardly," snorted Fitz-John Porter. "Some kind of trick, if you ask me."

Johnston returned the glasses to Cooke. "Get out there, Phil. Find out what they want. I'll be in my quarters."

Johnston started down the steps as Henry Magruder, followed by Case Carney, started up. "What's going on, General?" asked Magruder.

"Nothing that concerns you, Magruder," Johnston answered coldly, forcing the pair to flatten themselves against the palisade walls as he passed on the narrow steps.

"I don't like that sonovabitch," growled Carney when he was sure that Johnston was out of earshot.

"Don't worry about it. He'll get his comeuppance when the time comes. I'll see to that," said Magruder, thin lipped.

Kane had exited the coach to stand high in the driver's well, his eyes trained on the encampment. "They're coming out," he called down to Lot Smith from his vantage point.

Smith stood in his stirrups to see the camp gates swing wide and five mounted men pass through. He was relieved to see that one of the riders carried a white cloth fixed to his upheld sabre. As the riders drew closer he could distinguish a familiar figure, Col. Philip St. George Cooke. Thank God for Phil, he told himself. Cooke is a man you can talk to, reason with. The general is an unknown entity. "We'll meet them halfway," he said to Kane, signaling one of the drivers to bring up a saddle mount for the colonel.

Lot passed the white flag to Cephus James, now wearing sergeant's stripes, and the three rode to meet the riders approaching from Camp Scott.

The balance of the battalion members abandoned their driver's seats to mount saddle horses and form up in column. The wagons were now the responsibility of the men at Camp Scott. The man on the coach bench remained seated; his job was only half over.

At midpoint both parties reined up. Lot Smith snapped a salute to Cooke. The colonel returned it with a trace of a smile. "See you've gotten yourself a promotion, Lot. My congratulations."

Then his eyes swung to the man in blue with a flicker of recognition. "Kane?"

"That's right, Colonel. Been a long time since you were back in Washington."

Cooke's smile turned a bit wry as he nodded. "Not long enough. I've had my fill of parlor-room campaigns, Colonel. What brings you here?"

"Orders from the president, Colonel. I'm to deliver a communication to Governor Cumming."

"It appears you've come to the right place," smiled Cooke, then added with a gesture to the distant wagons and formed-up legion troop. "Must be quite a message to require all those wagons for delivery."

"The wagons are from President Young, Colonel," said Lot. "Supplies . . . A gift from the people of Utah Territory."

Cooke chuckled. "If I didn't know you better, I'd be a bit wary of Mormons bearing gifts these days, Lot." The humor left Cooke's face. "You and the sergeant had better wait here. You're not very popular with our troops at the moment." Turning to Kane he added, "If you will accompany me, Colonel, the general is waiting."

Kane rode through a sea of curious faces, some suspicious, a few appearing hostile. "Who is he? What's he doin' with them?" was heard from the ranks of troopers.

Johnston didn't bother to return Colonel Kane's salute. Militia colonels, even those dispatched from Washington on presidential orders, ranked poorly in this general's esteem.

Kane flushed at the unspoken rebuff. "I have a communication from the president to Governor Cumming, General," he said, removing two envelopes from his tunic.

"So Colonel Cooke informed me," said Johnston, extending his palm for the envelopes. "I'll see that he gets it."

"Sorry, sir. My instructions were to deliver them personally."

"Them? Two messages, Colonel?"

Kane could have kicked himself for his slip of the tongue, and the mistake of showing both envelopes. His effort to dissemble was a failure from the start, and he knew it. "The second message is not from the president, sir. It's something personal."

"From whom, Colonel?" said Johnston, his hooded eyes boring into Kane's.

Kane's lips thinned stubbornly. "I'm not at liberty to say, General. I—"

"You damned well better say, Colonel!" thundered Johnston. "I'm not asking to learn the contents of those letters, but I do demand to know their source. I'm giving you a direct order—hand me those envelopes, now!"

"Under protest, General," Kane said tightly as he handed over the documents.

Johnston ignored the statement. The first envelope bore the presidential seal. The second had an impression of a beehive in the sealing wax; there was nothing else to indicate who the sender might be. "If you must know, General," said Kane without bothering to conceal his anger, "the second letter is from Governor Young. A guarantee of safe conduct, nothing more."

Johnston's face grew stonelike, his look boring into Kane. "Safe conduct! You expect me to permit that damned politician to leave here with the rabble you've brought? Is that what you're telling me?"

"That decision is Governor Cumming's, sir, not yours, or mine."

"He's right about that, Sidney," said Cooke. "Cumming and Dawson aren't doing much here to sort things out. Might do better in Salt Lake. Besides, if they want to go, we have no authority to prevent it."

Johnston glowered at Cooke. "Thank you, Phil. I can always depend on you, can't I?"

"Up to a point, General; I'm not much for crossing Rubicons." Johnston held his glower for a long beat, then snapped a command to his orderly. "Tell Governor Cumming and Judge Dawson their presence is requested."

Johnston returned the envelopes to Kane. "You may carry out your instructions, Colonel."

Governor Designate Cumming quickly scanned the contents of the envelopes and passed them to the curious Dawson. "How soon can we leave, Colonel?" he asked Kane.

"At your convenience, sir."

"An hour, time to get our kits together. That al'right with you, Judge?"

"Sooner the better," nodded Dawson.

Johnston turned to Kane. "You've accomplished your mission, Colonel. You can tell your rebel friends they can take their wagons back with them. They are not wanted here."

"Oh, for God's sake, Sidney!" blurted Cooke. "We need everything we can get, no matter where in hell it comes from."

"I'll have no arguments, Cooke; the wagons go back. Have I made myself clear, Colonel?"

"You're talking to the wrong man, General. Major Smith and his troopers are in charge of the wagons, not I."

"Then you can tell your Major Smith that if he leaves those wagons, they, and everything in them, will be destroyed."

Kane looked at Johnston with disbelief, then shrugged. "Whatever you say, General. But it seems an unnecessary waste."

An hour later the coach containing Kane, Cumming, and Dawson was gone, and with it, Lot Smith and the battalion escort troop.

Word of Johnston's threat to destroy the wagons raced through Camp Scott like wildfire. Not a man, with the exception of Cooke, believed that Johnston would carry out his threat. Men lined the parapets, their eyes fixed on the distant wagons, wind buffeted and alone.

At dusk, Captain Hauk and a squad of his artillerymen planted fused charges in the abandoned wagons. The resultant explosions brought an angry moan of frustration from the troops lining the parapets, clearly heard over the rolling echoes of the detonations. Some of the bolder troopers cursed Johnston openly within the earshot of officers who halfheartedly attempted to silence the outbursts of an emotion they, too, shared.

Magruder shook his head. "Damn fool trick. Now if Buell don't get here soon there won't be any army."

"Ain't much of one now," smirked Carney, "way I see it."

"That's the damned truth," echoed Corporal Riley. "Bunch of scarecrows, draggin' their butts around like they was half dead already."

Phil Cooke made a determined effort to keep his temper under control. It wasn't entirely successful. "Man to man?"

Johnston leaned back in his camp chair with an audible sigh, closing his journal and pushing it to one side of the camp table. "Why not. Speak your piece, if it'll make you feel any better."

"It won't, but I've got to say it anyway. What you did is unconscionable, a slap in the face of every man here with his belly wrapped around his backbone. Why, for God's sake? What conceivable harm could it have done to take those supplies?"

"I have my reasons. Why don't we leave it at that?"

"Not this time, Sidney."

Johnston rose from his chair as if to signify an end to the discussion. "*My* command, Phil!"

But Cooke did not move. His icy stare remained riveted on the commanding officer. Johnston's dark eyes flinted. "Look beyond your nose. You're an officer. Granted, the men are angry. At the moment that anger is directed at me, but when they take time to think about it, they'll realize where it should be directed—at the people who've plagued this command every step of the way between here and the Platt. It was they who destroyed our supplies, they who sabotaged our wagons, they who laid waste to the surrounding country, ran off our beef, and burned forage. That's where the blame lies, Phil, and I'm not about to let them buy their way out of it with a few wagon loads of supplies."

Johnston seated himself in the camp chair. Now his voice became less argumentative. "There's something else, Phil. Take a look outside. If you haven't already, you will witness an army in the throes of physical and mental defeat. Now, am I to go to them with scraps from the hands of those who have brought them to this humiliating condition? Shall I say to them, 'Here, eat, your victors have taken pity on you'? No, I won't do that to them. In the spring we ride into Utah with the pride of fighting men. And I can guarantee you, anything that stands in our way will pay the price."

The twenty-mile night journey through Echo Canyon had been carefully planned to make the right impression on the governor designate and his companion, Judge Dawson. The escort, bearing torches, was stopped and challenged repeatedly by well-armed sentries. And above, what appeared to be countless campfires on the ridge of the cliffs burned brightly. Cumming expressed amazement at the number of troops guarding Zion's portals.

Colonel Kane was far too experienced an officer to be taken in, however. He was sure that many of the same troopers who had stopped and challenged had moved quickly ahead to challenge again, and again, giving the impression of a far greater number of troops than actually existed. And each of the supposed campfires was more than likely stoked by just one man. Old tricks, but ones that worked more often than not. Kane saw no reason to reveal the ploy to his coach companions. They would assuredly paint a formidable picture of Utah's military strength when they returned to Camp Scott.

Remounts and a fresh team for the coach were waiting at a heavily guarded relay station just west of the canyon mouth when the party arrived a bit past dawn. The smell of frying bacon, mingled with the savory aroma of freshly brewed coffee, was all the invitation Governor Designate Cumming and Judge Dawson needed to climb the steps to the station waiting room. The pair dug in with no attempt to conceal their voracious appetites, each putting away several rashers of thick bacon and a half-dozen eggs. Then they sipped steaming, rich, fragrant coffee before settling back with loosened waist belts. "It's been a long time," Cumming apologized to Kane.

As they returned to the coach, a company of battalion troopers, en route to relieve the canyon guard posts, arrived at the station. Cumming and Dawson were objects of curiosity to them. Word of their coming was common knowledge throughout the basin. What that coming would mean was open to speculation. A young fifer, with a mischievous glint in his eye, piped the opening notes of "Camptown Races." As if on cue, fifty voices rang out with grinning faces:

> Old Buck has sent, I understand,
>> Du dah, du dah,
> A Missouri ass to rule our land,
>> Oh, du dah day!

Cumming, one foot on the coach step, swung around with a wave and a smile. "A Georgia ass, boys. Georgia!"

The good-humored response brought a spontaneous cheer from the troopers.

"Was that necessary, Governor?" frowned Dawson just before the coach got underway.

"Damned right it was, Judge. These people are not the enemy—not until they prove differently."

Suddenly, Colonel Kane felt reassured; Alfred Cumming appeared to be more than he'd hoped for.

As a matter of fact, it was the good judge who caused Kane some discomfort. Dawson's stomach now full and tight, he was unable to control his flatulence. The colonel spent the remainder of the trip sitting outside on the coach bench with the driver, a blanket wrapped tightly around his body, chilled to the bone, but still thinking he had the advantage over Cumming in the fetid air of the carriage.

Actually, Cumming hadn't given the problem too much notice. Then, suddenly, it dawned upon him: "My God!" he cried out in utter frustration, "I'm getting used to it!"

On their arrival in Salt Lake City, Kane, Cumming, and Dawson were taken to the Union Hotel, where they were given rooms, a hot bath, and a hearty meal.

Later that afternoon church official John Kimball walked with them to the governor's offices, cornered on Temple and Main streets in the center city. Cumming and Dawson were literally dumbfounded with what they saw along the way—the hustle and bustle, the bright-looking faces, the dress of the people, the quality of the stores and eateries, the cleanliness—scarcely the "cesspool of sedition and anarchy" described by the secretary of war.

Brigham Young could not have been a more gracious host. Clerks
and bureaucrats had piled territorial records and court proceedings—
to say nothing of stacks of budgetary and accounting records—on three
tables in the governor's office.

Young had immediately offered to turn over the reins of government to Cumming, but the latter refused. "I don't think this is the time,
Governor. I don't want to add to the tension that must be hanging heavily
over you. Let the people get used to me. Then, in the spring, when,
as I hope, all of this conflict will have ceased, we can make an orderly transition. In the meantime, sir, I would like to learn what I can
from you. Being governor of Utah Territory has got to be a different
kind of experience."

For the next three mornings, Cumming went over the territorial records,
assisted by clerks and secretaries and other territorial officials. Every
stitch was in order; every decision made had been a legal one; every
penny accounted for; every gubernatorial and legislative action carried out within the confines of the separation of powers system of the
territory and its constitutional mandates. Every report required of the
territory by the federal government had been forwarded. The functioning
of the territory had not missed a beat by the absence of its federal
appointees.

Dawson brought back to the governor's office a similar report from
the court building—which he found, incidentally, had not been burned
to the ground with all its records, as reported. Everything was as it
should be—almost. Dawson did find copious evidence of corruption
during the judgeship of one William Drummond, corruption that ceased
when he took French leave of the territory. Dawson promised himself
that his first act as territorial judge would be to use his influence to
see that charges were brought against Drummond in Washington.

Cumming and Dawson spent each afternoon walking through the
center city, talking with people, passing in and out of stores, sampling
the ambiance. They visited the militia headquarters and the temple grounds,
where the foundation was already underway for the great edifice, all
the while feeling safe and unfettered.

They asked for and received another meeting with Brigham Young.
Cumming raised himself to his full stature, his right hand grasping the
lapel of his coat, and drew a deep breath. His countenance gave every indication that he was going to pontificate. "Governor Young, I

have seen enough. You and your people have been unconscionably and falsely maligned. What I have to say about the duplicity and intrigue of the territorial appointees who attempted to plunder you will be made in an official report to the president.

"I must say that the decision to dispatch federal troops to a peaceful and legally constituted territory of the United States has perpetrated a gross injustice to its people, and an affront to all fair-minded men.

"I wish that I could dispel the worry and tension this regrettable affair has caused you and your people these past months, but I cannot. However, I can put an end to it, and I intend to do so with all possible dispatch.

"Your good friend, Colonel Kane, has brought me authorization from the president of the United States to investigate the charges of treason against you and the people of Utah, and to then proceed accordingly. By the president's commission, I am at this time the superior officer of both the territory of Utah, and the army of the United States encamped on its borders. I now declare that hostilities are at an end. Furthermore, by the authority vested in me by the president, I extend his right of pardon and amnesty for treason in your behalf. This, too, I solemnly declare."

"The devil you do!" bellowed Brigham Young, teeth clenched.

The startled Cumming jumped as if he had been touched by an electric current. His mouth fell open and his chest collapsed. "I beg your pardon, sir!"

"And well you should!" was the thunderous response.

"Really, sir, I do not understand."

"Then let me explain myself," Young responded. "Your statement upon entering this room gives reason why we will not accept pardon, amnesty, or anything of the sort. You're right, *we have been* 'unconscionably and falsely maligned.' A 'gross injustice' *has been* perpetrated on this people. From the day Utah was declared a territory, we have been preyed upon by Washington appointees with the moral character of swine, men whose only thought was to glut at the trough of political advantage, to pillage both white man and Indian.

"Yet, when these scoundrels took French leave of the territory, informing the president of the United States that the people of Utah were in rebellion, Buchanan took the words from their lying mouths as truth without so much as making an attempt to investigate the charges. Once again, we are judged by allegations coming from the nation's most debauched denizens, without an opportunity to answer their false charges. Are you now suggesting, Governor Cumming, that it is *we* who should seek the *government*'s pardon?"

Cumming opened his mouth to reply, but Brigham Young was not finished. "Are you suggesting *we* accept amnesty from the president of the United States because *he* has, and without the slightest cause, threatened *us* with military occupation? Are we to beg *his* indulgence because *our* constitutional rights have been illegally placed in deadly jeopardy, and our very existence as citizens of the United States opened to question? Not likely! Mister Cumming, not likely!"

Governor Cumming was thoroughly frustrated. He had hardly expected this response. Looking a gift horse in the mouth, that's what it was. "Sir, —"

But Brigham Young still wasn't finished. "Perhaps, Mister Cumming, if I live long enough, *I* may one day be persuaded to pardon the *United States*."

"See here, Governor," interjected Dawson, "this is a mere formality. With your acceptance, the Utah Expedition will be on its way east in a matter of weeks. Further hostilities will be averted."

Cumming tried again. "Sir, I beg you to be reasonable."

"I'm sorry," said Young, his voice now less contentious. He had accepted the sincerity, if not the wisdom, of these well-meaning officials. "You must understand that our acceptance of amnesty for rebellion and treason would simultaneously infer a confession of guilt. You are asking that these loyal citizens, who have had the courage to stand for their constitutional liberties, be condemned in perpetuity as a treasonous people, who required the forgiveness of a generous government in order to continue living in the land. You speak of injustice. Is this not the greatest injustice of all?"

The room became silent. Cumming hung his head. Dawson fidgeted with his fingernails, his brow heavily furrowed. Neither wished to look Brigham Young in the eye. Cumming confessed to himself that under the circumstances, his response would have been exactly the same as Young's.

Finally, Kane broke the silence. "Gentlemen," he nodded at Cumming and Dawson. "May I have a word with you in the next room?" Both agreed.

Kane turned to Young. "If you'll excuse us."

Kane and the two officials remained in the outer room of the governor's office for some time. Their muted, unintelligible voices sometimes rose in apparent anger, other times descending to a relative silence.

Finally, the three conferees returned to the governor's office. Cumming had regained his composure and assumed his authoritative stature. "Governor Young," he began, after a harrumph. "May I present to you a few questions, sir?"

Young nodded. "If you must."

"Sir, during this period of conflict with the federal government, have you, as territorial governor, served also as commander in chief of the Territorial Militia, commonly known as 'The Battalion'?"

"Yes, of course."

"Did the battalion, under your orders, attack the army of the United States under the command of General Albert Sidney Johnston, and outside the territory of your jurisdiction?"

"In a manner of speaking, yes."

"Have you issued a proclamation forbidding passage through your territory of a duly constituted army of the United States?"

"Yes, I have."

"Under your direction, did the battalion burn and destroy tons of supplies and military equipment belonging to the United States, worth undetermined millions of dollars?"

"Yes."

"Under your direction, did members of the battalion rustle many hundreds of cattle, including cavalry mounts, and drive them into Utah Territory?"

"Yes."

"Under your direction, did the battalion burn hundreds of square miles of grasslands and dam streams and rivers, at the same time destroying scores of wagons and disrupting, by diverse means, the passage of a United States Army?"

"Yes, yes?"

Cumming's rapid-fire questions ceased. He seemed to be searching his mind for something else to say.

Brigham Young was becoming annoyed again. "Are you *quite* finished?" he asked.

"Almost," was Cumming's frustrated response. Beads of perspiration had broken out on his forehead. "Now, I have but one more question to ask. And for God's sake, for the sake of your people, and for the sake of the United States, will you answer it in the affirmative?"

"The question?"

"Will you allow the president of the United States to grant you pardon, and the people of Utah Territory amnesty for destroying government property, and impeding the movement of federal troops?"

Anxious eyes were fixed on Brigham Young. He knew that this new offer—avoiding the charge of treason against the United States—had been Kane's suggestion. He had convinced Cumming that the people of Utah would never submit to the searing brand of traitor. A compromise had to be made that would be acceptable to them, would allow the president to save face, and give reason for General Johnston to turn his command east, from whence they had come.

As much as it galled him, Young knew he had to compromise, and although he despised the very word, this was one he could live with. He waited for what seemed an eternity to Cumming. Then, at last, dryly, "Yes, that will be acceptable."

Faces brightened with smiles. The anxious expression on Cumming's face turned to one of blessed relief. Kane clasped his hands together. "Good show!" he remarked, mimicking a common expression from an English-born fellow officer.

Major Poole, senior medical officer, pushed open the plank door, accompanied by a strong gust of icy wind that caused the flames of the camphine lamps to flicker wildly. They settled down to a steady glow as Poole used his weight to close the portal. The warming spell enjoyed by Rockwell and the battalion troops, who were bringing the army cattle into Echo Canyon, had long since been replaced by periodic cold winds propelling down from the north. Temperatures dropped to below zero, followed by a cloud bank of depressing, icy fog, which had lain over Camp Scott for nearly three weeks, refusing to let even a whimper of sunlight through the murky grayness. There was one blessing, however; there had been no snow for weeks. If, as Johnston insisted, Buell was on his way, his army of mules would have some natural forage, plunging their snouts under the now thin layer of white.

"Country's not fit for man or beast," Poole growled to Colonels Fitz-John Porter and Cooke, seated comfortably close to the cast-iron camp stove, which was heating an enameled coffeepot.

Porter acknowledged the medic with a grunt.

"Coffee?" questioned Cooke, reaching for the pot.

"Anything if it's hot," replied Poole, peeling off his double-mufflered greatcoat and advancing to spread his hands to the stove's warmth. He accepted the mug, sipping it with a groan of appreciation. Fitz-John Porter toe-hooked a camp stool over for Poole, who sank into it with a grateful sigh, hunching it closer to the stove. "We're in deep trouble, gentlemen," he said through the steam rising from his cup, "deep trouble."

"Tell us something we don't know, Poole," Cooke said dryly.

Poole lowered the mug, looking solemnly from one to the other. "Scurvy, gentlemen. It's with us."

"Oh, dear God," Porter exclaimed.

"Are you sure, Henry?" frowned Cooke.

Poole nodded glumly, "Had nineteen cases this morning. All the symptoms: inanition, asthenia, swelling and bleeding of the gums. . . . I'm sure."

As an old campaigner, Phil Cooke was well aware of the havoc that scurvy could wreak on a body of troops. In the recent Crimean War, the French lost twenty-three thousand men to the disease, fifteen percent of the entire command. Dietary deficiency can prove as lethal as grapeshot. It just takes longer to kill.

"Have you reported this to Johnston?" asked Cooke.

"Of course, for all the damned good it did. He's counting on Buell to get here with fresh supplies."

"The bloody fool!" shouted Porter, losing his temper. "Every time I think of him turning down supplies from the Mormons I could kill him! Nineteen dead and more to follow. He's responsible for this, and all he can say is that Buell will be here soon."

Two weeks after the first outbreak of scurvy at Camp Scott, a sentry spotted Buell's pack train on the horizon. A pandemonium of cheers and excited shouts and gestures broke out that carried for miles across the snow. Johnston let them celebrate. He knew he'd been right. This would help them gain back their pride, their spirit. How Buell ever made it. . . . Providence was the only answer.

Two hours later a thoroughly exhausted Captain Buell, with seven hundred tired, starving mules and eighty emaciated troopers, arrived at their destination. It had cost—twelve troopers dead, others in serious condition, and a hundred mules gone, all to the elements.

Nevertheless, Johnston was elated over the courage of the relief unit. "If it's the last thing I do on this earth," he told Captain Buell, "I'll see you wearing the Medal of Honor for this."

Indeed, the arrival of the pack train brought with it new life, literally and figuratively. Each of the seven hundred mules was laden with 350 pounds of food. The 245,000 pounds of vitally needed stores would provide a subsistence-level ration of 2.35 pounds of food per man for forty days: pemmican (1.25), desiccated vegetables (0.10), flour (0.33), sugar (0.14), grease (0.25), tea (0.03), and biscuit (0.25).

Under the direction of Major Poole, scurvy patients' rations were supplemented with daily doses of citric acid mixed with sugar and water, and a double ration of desiccated vegetables, a proven antiscorbutic.

But 2.3 pounds of food would be a minimum for healthy garrison troops in a more moderate clime. At Camp Scott it was barely enough to allow the men to function. The bitter cold seemed to drain the food's energy from their bodies. Still, they now had a large herd of mules for meat. It was stringy and totally devoid of fat, and had little nourishment value. But it did help fill gnawing bellies.

Because the limited space in the wagon was filled with the top priority—food—there was no room left for soap, blankets, uniforms, and boots, and little space even for medicine. The soldiers of the Utah Expedition had been saved from possible starvation and decimation by scurvy, but the days ahead were going to tax their strength and determination.

No pessimist, Albert Sidney Johnston. He knew beyond a shadow of a doubt that Buell's arrival was a godsend. They would make do until supplies, which he was certain were well on their way from the East, arrived in proper time.

And then, he would lead his men to victory, and revenge.

Chapter Nineteen

S ecretary of War John Floyd had never worked as hard as he was now, assembling the *second* Utah Expedition. It did him good to see Buchanan's back nailed to the wall. The debacle of Johnston's army had seemed to diminish the confidence of this man, who had promised the American people he would hold the Union together at any cost.

Buchanan had no choice: Johnston's army had to be refurbished—from uniforms to mounts, wagons, food, and ammunition. When he estimated the cost, both in economic and political terms, it made him sick to his stomach. Gradually, he pulled away from the details of procurement, leaving those up to Floyd; he took note only of the aggregates, with grunts of dissatisfaction. In effect, the secretary of war had been given virtual carte blanche.

Floyd found it interesting that after the initial flurry over the humiliation of Johnston's army in the press and in the Houston-led debates in the Senate, other timely events began to intrude on its sensationalism. Foremost among these was the trauma over Kansas and Nebraska.

In 1854, the Great Plains area had been divided into the two territories of Kansas and Nebraska. As territories, both would be open to slavery, but before gaining statehood the people of those territories would decide for themselves whether they would come into the Union as slave or free states—a process called popular sovereignty. Kansas, adjacent to Missouri and subject to immigrants from that state, was expected to vote proslavery. The South would gain desperately needed new territory and additional representation in Washington.

What few saw, however, was the virulent reaction from Northern abolitionists, which, in time, gave birth to the new Republican Party. The Dred Scott decision in 1857 was a clarion call to both free-staters and proslavers to seek mastery over the Kansas Territory. "Bloody Kansas" would be brought into the Union—by ballot or, as John Brown declaimed, "Bible and Bullet."

In contemplating all of this, along with the Utah War, Sam Houston sighed wearily. Country was going to hell in a hand basket, and no one knew what to do about it, except him, of course. But no one would listen.

When the actual process of raising a relief expedition under the command of a hero of the Seminole Wars—Col. Uriah P. "Old Iron Ass" Wilson—was revealed, however, attention quickly focused on the Utah War again.

In the unpredictable character of American democracy, public opinion in the East was undergoing a radical change, shifting favorably to the people of Utah Territory. Stories of their valor with restraint, embellished in print, captured the imagination of a growing number of citizens. The image of a courageous people battling against insufferable odds touched more than just a few hearts. Americans had a way of pulling for the underdog. Sometimes, right or wrong didn't matter. It was the feeling that counted.

Brigham Young, once portrayed as a tyrant and a fanatic, was now depicted by the press as a hero—indeed, as another Prince of Orange. Among other newspapers, the *New York Tribune,* which had once described the people of Utah as "ecstatico religious, tyrannico politic, and poly-uxorial loafers," now used superlatives in praising Young, the Utahns, and their stand. The *New York Times,* which once charged that the Mormons "should be utterly exterminated," now referred to Johnston's army as an "unwise posse comitatus." Even the London *Times* took swipes at the Utah Expedition. States-righters and popular-sovereignty advocates lauded Young's insistence on the importance of local government and decision-making.

Some of the more sophisticated began to fear sinister plots behind the Utah Expedition that involved the threat of secession more than a territorial rebellion. Others, including many in Congress, feared that once started, a war between the territory of Utah and federal troops could lead, and had led, to the most dangerous and disastrous circumstances. To continue the Utah War was looked upon by many as sheer madness.

Overnight, Buchanan and Floyd found themselves the subject of press tirades and congressional investigations. Horace Greeley, who had changed his mind about the necessity of the Utah Expedition, was the first to use his newspaper chain to call for an investigation into Floyd's awarding of government contracts for that endeavor. And according to the *New York Times,* "No dispassionate person, whatever his political partialities, can fail to see that the various enterprises undertaken by Mr. Buchanan do not seem to prosper in his hands. The latest news from Utah places the Administration in a position marked by a singular mixture of farce and tragedy, and the whole story of the war is crowded by as much ignorance, stupidity, and dishonesty as any government ever managed to get in the annals of a single year."

Now, Senator Sam Houston gained an audience of his fellow congressmen. "The more men you send to the Utah War, the more you increase the difficulty," he warned the United States Senate. "They have to be fed. For some sixteen hundred miles you have to transport provisions. The regiments sent there have found Fort Bridger and other places, as they have approached them, a heap of ashes. They will find Salt Lake City, if they ever reach it, a heap of ashes. They will find that they have to fight against Russia and the Russians. As for troops to conquer Utah Territory, fifty thousand would be as insufficient as two or three thousand. Whoever goes there will meet the fate of Napoleon's army when he went to Moscow." Houston excoriated General Johnston for having refused Brigham Young's traditional "act of civility"—the gift of salt and flour.

The claim made by Senator Albert G. Brown, of Mississippi, that continuation of the Utah War would bring on "civil war beyond all question," caused a flurry of comments and whispers in the Senate. He insisted that "General Johnston be deposed from the command. I say the man who goes there thirsting for blood will bring war, disgrace, and dishonor to your country."

When the senator pointed out that supplies to Johnston's army would probably eventually reach a cost of forty million in a time aggravated by the financial panic of 1857, boos echoed throughout the Senate chamber.

And, indeed, eyebrows were raised when he charged that Floyd had awarded government contracts for the Utah Expedition, without competitive bids, to secessionists and slavocrats. "Gigantic contracts involving an amount of several million dollars were distributed with a view to influencing votes to bring Kansas into the Union as a slave state."

With the arrival of spring, the Utah War had come to be known universally as "Buchanan's Blunder." Even the remarkable Harriet Lane was unable to help the president. On January 27, 1858, the House of Representatives had requested information from Buchanan concerning the Utah War, and why a new governor had been selected for Utah Territory. That body was never satisfied with Buchanan's answers. He was accused by members of both political parties of accepting false "rumors and reports" as true without adequate investigation.

John Floyd's activities came under the scrutiny of investigation and later indictment. The secretary of war was charged with chicanery but never convicted. From a variety of sources he was accused of promoting the Utah War to give the South an advantage in the West in case of secession; of promoting violence in the territories as a forerunner to destroying the union; of using the Utah Expedition as a means to bankrupt the federal treasury; of seeking to scatter the nation's military forces, leaving the North powerless to preserve the Union; of transferring arms from Northern to Southern arsenals to weaken the North; and of being the source of a "boondoggling scheme" in awarding government contracts, leading some media sources to refer to the Utah War as the "contractors' war."

The resilient secretary of war was not without some satisfaction, however. Relief columns and wagon trains were already well on their way, stretching across the plains to Camp Scott and Gen. Albert Sidney Johnston. On a cold, wintry morn, the first contingent had marched out of Fort Leavenworth, sped on its way by the post band's brassy rendition of the "Garry Owen," a Gaelic tune that would one day become the favorite of George Armstrong Custer's 7th Cavalry.

Given the tragic situation of the Utah Expedition, an angry, reluctant Congress—just as had the president—could find no other alternative but to begrudgingly come to Johnston's assistance with fresh supplies and the troops to assure their safe arrival, overcompensating their numbers, given what had happened to the earlier supply trains.

One senator later wrote that when Congress passed the appropriations for the relief of Johnston's army, "the atmosphere in both Houses was like that of a funeral parlor."

Floyd's order requisitioning troops from the federal forts along the Southern seaboard brought a storm of protest from the garrison commanders. They received short shrift from the war secretary. By the time Sam Houston saw that Floyd was leaving these forts outgunned and outnumbered by the state militias, it was too late. Floyd and friends had planned and executed well. Substantially more than a third of the federal forces were now west of the Mississippi, weakening Buchanan's vow to use the army to keep the Union intact. Vows could be taken, promises sworn, but without power to back them up, they meant nothing. John Floyd had effectively stripped Buchanan of a good portion of that power.

Once again, in spite of his personal problems, Floyd resurrected his dream of a western confederacy. Utah! Perhaps the rebellion would start right there, draining the Union of its manhood and resources. And then? Well, Fremont had conquered California with a hundred and fifty men.

Alfred Cumming had thought all along that the charges of rebellion and treason against the Utahns were greatly exaggerated. Now he had found by his own investigation and observation that they were false in their entirety. He was greatly relieved. He had not been blind. From the very beginning he had believed them to be scapegoats. As he saw it, a blundering James Buchanan, who lacked both the deceit and the finesse to carry out a clandestine operation, had ordered the Utah Expedition primarily as a warning example to the South that he would not tolerate secession or rebellion. On the other hand, Cumming strongly suspected that Floyd and the other secessionists in the president's cabinet sprang on this opportunity to create a conflict—perhaps the entering wedge to disunion—and to remove a substantial portion of the federal army from the East. Nor did Cumming rule out the possibility of Johnston's army being used to ensure the secession of California and the West.

It was, then, with great satisfaction that he penned the following report to Brigham Young, James Buchanan, Sam Houston, and Albert Sidney Johnston, with other copies reserved for the eastern newpapermen

in Salt Lake City. His orders had been to report his findings only to
Buchanan and Johnston, but he no longer trusted either the wisdom
or the stability of the lame-duck president. As for Johnston . . .

> Since my arrival I have been everywhere recognized as the Gover-
> nor of Utah; and so far from having encountered insults and indigni-
> ties, I am gratified in being able to state to you that in passing through
> the settlements, I have been universally greeted with such respectful
> attentions as are due to the representative of the executive authority of
> the United States in the territory.
>
> Judge Dawson and I have been employed in examining the records
> of the supreme and district courts, which we are now prepared to re-
> port upon as being perfect and unimpaired. This will doubtless be ac-
> ceptable to those who have entertained the impression to the contrary.
> I have also examined the legislative records and other books belong-
> ing to the secretary of state, which are in perfect preservation.

As time went by, however, Cumming became increasingly uneasy.
Weeks had come and gone since he had sent his report to General Johnston
at Camp Scott via a battalion courier. Was the courier sure that Johnston
had gotten the message? "Yes, sir," had been the reply.

Then more than a month slipped by, and Cumming began to feel a
sense of foreboding. He asked for a meeting with Brigham Young,
explaining to him his concern, one he found was shared by the governor. It was decided that Cumming, along with Colonel Kane, would
return to Camp Scott under escort and confront General Johnston.

Two weeks later they stood before the general in his quarters. Johnston
was curt; he evinced no surprise at seeing the duo. "You must enjoy
the ride between here and Salt Lake City, Mister Cumming."

"I decidedly do not, General, and my inconvenient and uncomfortable return here could have been avoided had you answered my communication!"

"I saw no compelling reason to reply to your superficial observa-
tions, let alone risk the life of a rider going from here to Salt Lake in
the dead of winter," was the cold reply.

Cumming tried to hold his temper. "You know very well that any
courier leaving this encampment would be picked up in less than a
mile by the battalion, relieved of his message, and returned to camp;
and that the message would have been in my hands in a few days.
Furthermore, as I informed you, by the authority of the president of

the United States vested in me, I declare hostilities between the Utah Expedition and Utah Territory at an end!" Cumming hesitated long enough to let his declaration sink in. "You will, therefore, prepare your command to return to Fort Leavenworth as soon as weather and supplies permit! Do you understand me?"

General Johnston sprang from his camp chair growling, furious. "You popinjay! Did you really think you could waltz into this camp and dictate terms to me! Do you believe for a minute I would bring these brave soldiers through this frozen hell only to tell them they must turn tail without ever seeing their objective? You listen to me, you insignificant buffoon." Johnston's face was red and puffed. "I will ride with my command into Salt Lake City, there to invest the territory and declare martial law. Anyone who attempts to impede me will be met with force. From the territorial offices *I* will dictate terms. And hear this well: *I*, not you, not Buchanan, will decide whether or not Utah is in rebellion!"

Kane stepped forward, anger in his eyes. "You're acting like a martinet, General. There is no rebellion in Utah Territory, but there will be if you attempt to occupy Salt Lake City. You must know this! If you force them to fight, I tell you, the bones of your troops will whiten those mountain valleys!"

Johnston was becoming furious. "That's enough, Kane. You're dismissed!"

"Dismiss your own officers, General," Kane answered with contempt. "You're in an untenable position, militarily and politically—a no-win situation. Will you throw away an army to satisfy your arrogance?"

"Kane," growled Johnston, his teeth clenched, "I told you to—"

"Or is it something more than arrogance," Kane interrupted, nearly shouting, "something none of us knows about!"

With that Johnston strode to the door and whipped it open. "Sentry!"

The young sentry popped into view, coming rigidly to attention. "Sir?"

"These gentlemen are to be escorted from this post, forthwith!"

The sentry shot a puzzled look at Kane and Cumming. "Yes, sir."

As Kane moved through the open door, he addressed Johnston once more. "Under other circumstances, I would call you to account. We'll meet again, General."

"I shall be at your service!"

"And I, sir," added Cumming before exiting, a firm eye on the ledgebrowed commanding officer, "intend to see that you are brought up on charges!"

Brigham Young had been looking out his window facing the temple grounds when General Wells was admitted to his office. "Come in, Daniel. It's always good to see you."

"Thank you, sir. I came as soon as I got your summons."

As always, Brigham Young came directly to the point. "Daniel. What I have to say is not very pleasant. Governor Cumming and Colonel Kane have just returned from Camp Scott. Johnston has refused to acknowledge President Buchanan's authorization to Cumming. He intends to occupy Salt Lake City, and establish military control over the territory."

Wells was startled. "Disobeying orders from the president? He'll be court-martialled."

"Perhaps, but that's some time down the road. Right now, he apparently doesn't look at that consequence with much fear. The question is, what are we going to do about it?"

"A decision you have already made, no doubt, and have called me here this morning to give me direction." Wells's frustration was clearly evident in his voice.

"It's not an easy task, Daniel. You're not going to like it."

"Whatever it is, it'll be done, sir."

"I know, Daniel. The plan is that we are going to evacuate Salt Lake City and the surrounding communities."

Wells's sigh was heavy, almost a groan. "I was praying this wouldn't happen."

"And I."

"There is no alternative?"

"Yes. We can sit here and let them occupy the city. And you know what will come with that. Martial law will be directed against our people, not the invaders. It will be stringent, Daniel. Our people won't bend to it easily. Sooner or later there'd be violence, and it would be Missouri and Illinois all over again. We can wait to be pillaged, raped, and murdered, without legal recourse, or we can move out."

"So, we seek a new place. We're running out of territory, sir."

"No, Daniel, we're here to stay. This is our home. We may have to rebuild it. But we'll be here when they've gone."

Wells raised his eyes. "I don't understand."

"And you are about to tell me I owe you an explanation."

"I'd appreciate hearing it," responded Wells.

"Let's look at the situation. In the East, opinion is moving in our direction. The major newspapers have taken up our cause. Sam Houston and others have turned much of Congress in our favor. The new governor is with us as our guest, not with the army. When Johnston invades Utah over the protests of the new and respected governor, a great outcry will be directed against him. The Utah Expedition has already lost its legitimacy. Its days are numbered.

"Now, Johnston must face a deserted city, ready to be put to the torch. He will end up conquering ashes, and the destruction of the city will be on his head. Then, there are his fellow officers, men like Phil Cooke. I'm sure he is feeling pressure from them as well.

"I'm playing a dangerous game with Johnston. I'm betting that my hand will force him to throw in his. I'll allow him to ride unopposed through Salt Lake City. But the city will be deserted. I want every home and store evacuated, with all their goods, and hay, straw, or anything else combustible, placed inside. I want explosives in the larger buildings. As the army marches through the city, I want volunteers with torches stationed at intervals along the streets. The moment Johnston attempts to stop and occupy the city, it is to be burned to the ground."

Wells looked devastated. "Burned . . . , everything we have built up with our hands and our hearts?"

"We may have to burn it to save it. We can build again, but the territory must be ours. We must have roots, a center place. One day Utah will be a state; then our constitutional liberties will be guaranteed."

Now a darkness seemed to cover Brigham Young's face. Wells knew he was about to hear the kicker. "Daniel, we have one imponderable—General Johnston himself. I'm not quite sure what makes him run. He gives every indication of a man possessed. Is he consumed with thoughts of revenge because of the humiliation he's suffered at our hand? Does he believe that he owes it to his men and to himself to achieve some victory? Does he intend to gain his objective, throw a scare into us, and then ride away, having made his point?"

"Or," interrupted General Wells, "is he operating under secret orders to instigate war in Utah Territory, and then move on to California, to ensure a western alignment with the Southern states?"

"Indeed! That's a real possibility. There are those who believe it to be true—Tom Kane and Sam Houston are but two. The question is, how do we adjust for these possibilities?"

"I'm sorry, sir, that's your cross."

Brigham Young dropped into his desk chair, appearing emotionally drained. "Now, Daniel, hear me carefully. We have a month to six weeks to prepare. I want this city and its environs vacated, with the exception of enough troopers to ignite and scuttle it. *You* are in charge. Take this people into southern Utah. For the time being, they'll be safe there. Rockwell has ensured peace with the Indians and has built up a solid military establishment at St. George.

"If Johnston succeeds in forcing a military occupation of Salt Lake City, he will declare martial law over the territory, and send out troops to 'pacify' every village and settlement. You know what that means."

"Oh, Lord," Wells said quietly. "Perhaps Rockwell was right all along—punish the invaders, make them bleed until the cost is no longer worth the prize."

Young leaned forward in his chair, his face taut. "And that, Daniel, is exactly the strategy you will follow, should these dark predictions become a reality!"

Wells took a step backward, his mouth open, as Young continued. "We'll make them pay dearly for every foot of this territory they seek to conquer!"

Young got up from his chair and walked to the west window. Without looking back at Wells, he spoke softly. "Know this beyond a shadow of a doubt—we'll be victorious. We'll never again give up our land and our homes. What is destroyed here we shall destroy. If Johnston follows the path of tyranny, there will rise such a clamor in the East as will eventually bring his downfall and our return to our rights. In a short while, just as certain as you live, you'll see the North divided against the South in civil war. If nothing else, that tragedy will empty Utah of troops, and we'll return home, there to stay.

"One final note, Daniel. If the worst happens, draw Porter Rockwell close to you. He was meant to be a champion of this people. And remember this, the finest general within two thousand miles is not Albert Sidney Johnston; it is you. If you meet in battle, you'll be the victor."

Daniel Wells walked slowly down the stairs of the governor's office and out into the warmth of brilliant sunlight. For the first time in twenty-five years, tears filled the eyes of this tough career officer.

*   *   *

Spring had arrived late in northern Utah Territory, and with a foul temper. The awakening of the earth was slow and tortured. The obstinate winds of March brought extended periods of snow and freezing temperatures. April began with a tantrum, only gradually and begrudgingly giving way to the warm Santa Ana winds blowing up from the deserts to the south and west.

Word to Rockwell from General Wells in Salt Lake City confirmed that Johnston's army remained helplessly snowbound. So, thought Rockwell, Johnston had yet to win one. Not only had Young gotten his early winter, his cup runneth over—a blustering spring.

But the final battle is the only one that matters in the long run. However late its start, the Utah Expedition would sooner or later break out of its prison of ice and head for Salt Lake City, no doubt burning with sentiments of revenge. The final chapter to the Utah War was yet to be written, Rockwell knew—and it could well be written in blood.

For the time being, the late departure of winter in the north suited Porter Rockwell just fine, for he had fulfilled the greatest quest of man— the victory without which every other achievement pales to insignificance—to love and be loved.

In the community of St. George, spring came typically a month or so earlier than in the northern part of the territory. As the last vestiges of winter were rooted out of the valleys by the warmth of the sun, wildflowers of every description and every color made their grand entrance, led by the daffodil and the sego lily.

The willow trees along the banks of the Virgin River were the first to pop their bright yellow—soon to be brilliant green—leaves. Then, overnight it seemed, orchards of apricot, cherry, and apple trees burst into clouds of delicate whiteness, followed by the pink bouquets of the peach.

The skies were filled with countless birds. They came singly or in waves, weaving their way melodically through the skies. Others came in precision formation, a great V, as they formed two lines, gradually narrowing on the tail of their point leader.

In the pastures, each morning heralded a variety of new arrivals. Calves, lambs, and colts greeted their adventure on unsteady legs, hungry and bawling—their wary mothers close by to ensure their survival.

Anne McCutcheon Rockwell was overwhelmed by nature's yearly miracle. The beauty of spring; the smell of it; the sense of newness and rejuvenation. If winter were necessary to prepare the earth for this beautiful resurrection, Anne reasoned, then every bitter-cold day one had to endure was worth it.

For Anne, this was the spring of springs. She was now gloriously certain, she was going to have a baby. Thoughts of war and killing were far from her mind.

But for Rockwell, the change of season brought with it increased tension. As he worked diligently to bring strength back to his right arm, he knew that soon one of the weekly communiques from General Wells would inform him that supplies had reached General Johnston, and that he was mobilizing for his move on Salt Lake City.

It came by a rider, his pony lathered, one calm evening just as the sun was setting. "Johnston being resupplied," it read. "Much activity at Camp Scott. Return immediately." It was signed by Gen. Daniel Wells with a postscript: "Sorry, old friend."

Anne turned pale when she read the order. Her arm dropped to her side, her hand releasing the paper, which drifted to the ground. A feeling of near despair came over her.

Rockwell took her hands in his. "I must leave in the morning."

"*We* must leave in the mornin'."

"Anne, you can't, the baby—"

"Come in the house, Mister Rockwell," she interrupted, "so I can sit while you give me all the reasons I can't go. But I trust you won't belabor it. You see, I've a lot of packing to do." And with a warm smile, "The child I carry in my body will be fine; it's of hearty blood."

Most of the trip was hot, dusty, and uneventful. Six young Utes on bright speckled ponies escorted Anne's carriage for two days, just to be near their beloved "Sister Ah-han."

Soon the green valleys, the great red buttes, and the sun-baked, spiraled canyons of southern Utah were left behind, and Rockwell's troop passed through what seemed to be countless miles of sagebrush, scrub oak, and juniper, broken periodically at the higher elevations with cool, sparkling streams surrounded by fir and pine.

As they at last descended into Utah Valley, they emerged from a forest of quaking aspen to be greeted with grand meadows of wildflowers in bloom, and herds of deer and elk. They stopped for some time on the northern shores of Utah Lake to swim and bathe. Then they moved on toward the Point of the Mountain.

It was shortly after this that Rockwell, at the head of his troop, saw it: movement on the crest of Point of the Mountain, coming down into Utah Valley. From that distance it looked like ants swarming around an anthill.

A half hour later, Rockwell could see that it was an extensive movement of people and wagons. He took the scope from his saddlebag, pulled it to its farthest extension, and focused it on the commotion ahead.

The sight left him stunned. Wagons, Conestogas, carriages, coaches, handcarts—anything that had wheels and could move—headed south, sometimes four, five abreast, drawn by mules, donkeys, horses, oxen, and human muscle down the gentle incline of the pass into Utah Valley. Battalion troopers were scattered among the wagons, giving assistance where necessary. Rockwell surmised that bringing up the rear of this great caravan would be men and boys on horseback, with their tireless dogs, directing herds of cattle and sheep. At the front rode General Wells.

Rockwell could not help but wonder if this was how the children of Israel must have looked, carrying all their belongings, driving and marching through the Red Sea, towering walls of water on either side. In this case, the slopes of the Wasatch rose on the east and the Oquirrh on the west; the modern Moses—Gen. Daniel H. Wells, Utah Territorial Militia; the modern pharoah—Gen. Albert Sidney Johnston, United States Army—in hot pursuit.

When Wells saw Rockwell's company, pulled to the side and waiting for him, a look of relief crossed his face. "Glad to see you, Major. And, indeed, you too, Missus Rockwell."

"What in hell is happening here!" demanded Rockwell.

"An exodus, Porter. Johnston is bent on invading the territory and taking over Salt Lake. President Young has ordered the evacuation of the northern part of the territory. And I mean evacuation—right down to pins and pots. We're the first train heading south. There'll be more in the next two weeks—many more. I'm leaving troopers at points all along the way to guide them in. Lot Smith has remained behind with three hundred troopers. They've nearly finished preparing the city for burning and demolition."

"Running again!" Rockwell bit out.

"Not exactly, Porter; it takes a lot of explaining."

"And you approve of this?"

"I . . . I don't really know."

"Why wasn't I informed?"

"It wasn't my idea, Porter. Brigham Young said to let you be until we needed you. Said you needed a moment of peace." Rockwell did not reply.

The general turned to Anne, who was trying to fathom the enormity of what was happening. "Your father and Doc Ames are still in Salt Lake City. President Young has asked them to stay through the occupation, just in case their services might be needed for those who must remain. You two might consider staying in Doc Ames's home. They're expecting you. Major Smith will contact you there. He has further orders for you, Porter. Now, I'd better be on my way."

"Is Brigham going to remain behind when Johnston invades the city?" asked Rockwell.

"What do *you* think!" the general yelled back as he spurred his horse into a gallop.

"Da."

"Who is it?" came a voice from upstairs.

"Tis your daughter, come to pay her respects."

Silence.

"Da?"

Finally, "I have no daughter."

"Well, now," she called back in pure Scottish, "that's a fine way to treat yer kin, come home as pregnant as a heifer in spring."

There was a rustling at the top of the stairs. Angus McCutcheon appeared slowly, unsure, then began to descend. "Pregnant, is it? I might have known—that animal Rockwell."

"Da," Anne laughed, "he's my husband. I love him."

Finally Angus reached the bottom of the stairs. In a moment they were in each other's arms, tears flowing.

"Are ye well?" he choked out, trying to regain his composure, and looking at her carefully.

"Da, I'm as fit as a fiddle."

"That," replied Angus, authoritatively, "will be for me and Doc Ames to decide. Now then, where is that predator who ran off with my virgin daughter?"

"He's out in the carriage, waiting for you to invite him in."

Angus raised his eyebrows, puffed out his chest, and walked to the door. "Oh he is, is he?" Standing in the doorway, his arms folded belligerently, he glared at Rockwell. "If ye have any gentleman in ye a'toll, then bring that big hulk of yerself in here and pay yer respects to yer father-in-law . . . who'll be the namesake of yer bairn!"

That same evening Lot Smith came to the Ames home to deliver Rockwell's instructions from Brigham Young. It didn't take much for him to see that his friend was in a foul mood. After a few amenities, he handed the dispatch to Rockwell, smiled at Anne, and left.

It was several hours later when Rockwell, now alone in the downstairs parlor, opened the envelope and read its contents by the light of a flickering lamp.

> Porter. I suppose one would say that the "moment of truth" has arrived. Johnston's army will soon be on the move. I plan to allow the Utah Expedition safe passage through Salt Lake City and its environs. But should Johnston carry out his threat to occupy the city and declare martial law throughout the territory, he'll be met with fire and ashes.
>
> You and Lot Smith direct your men to the Point of the Mountain. If the worst happens, there is little doubt that Johnston will dispatch troops in pursuit of our people fleeing south. He won't be satisfied ruling over rubble.
>
> If this happens, you will trail Johnston's troops from the Point of the Mountain, south. If they in any way attempt to impede or molest our people, you may then consider the "shed no blood" edict rescinded. Link up with General Wells in St. George, and join hands. Obey him. God bless you.
>
> P.S. You must be out of the city before Johnston arrives. As you know there is a price on your head. At best we will be faced with a tenuous situation. Nothing must upset it.

When Rockwell was finished reading the orders, he dropped his hand heavily on his lap, the paper crushed in his fingers. He leaned his head back on the soft rim of his chair and gazed at the patterns of light and darkness the lamp had created on the ceiling. The first rays of morning had begun to appear before he finally went upstairs.

Two smaller wagon trains with provisions of flour and tinned goods had broken through to Camp Scott from New Mexico during the latter part of March, although one of them had been harassed much of the way by Indians.

Then, in May, the big trains, from Platte Station and Fort Leavenworth, through Fort Laramie, began to arrive almost in tandem. The troops, skinners, and teamsters seemed to be just as relieved as the occupants of Camp Scott. The way west had been a trip through hell. Each section had its horror stories, its burials along the way. Dead animals, broken wagons, and a fortune in cast-aside goods lined the unhappy trail. All the arrogance had been driven out of the once-proud Col. Uriah P. Wilson. He arrived seriously ill, spending the next weeks in bed. When Johnston's army began its march to Salt Lake City, he was unable to take to his saddle.

In less time than it took to unload the wagons, Albert Sidney Johnston had pulled his command into action. From dawn till dusk the bark of sergeants and corporals filled the crisp air, as troopers went through the drill, for the most part, wearing new uniforms and new boots. Whinnies and neighs, together with the thundering sound of hoofbeats, rose from a dozen makeshift corrals, as fresh horses were being broken, and as the mounted dragoons went through their paces. Officers planned and reviewed the activities, shouting praises one minute and condemnations the next. Anxious soldiers, waiting in mess lines, were no longer met with half, or one-third, or one-fourth rations with a paucity of nourishment. Best of all, they had succulent, greasy stew made with steer meat rather than mule. The heavy silence and the atmosphere of resignation disappeared from Camp Scott. Johnston had his army back. And it was an army well fed and well armed.

A makeshift map of Salt Lake's center city was spread out, overlapping the camp table in Johnston's quarters. Surrounding the table were the general, his top-ranking officers, and Hank Magruder.

The general was speaking. "Gentlemen, in three days' time we begin our move on Salt Lake City. We will mobilize at the ruins of Bridger's Fort, preparatory to marching through Echo Canyon."

Echo Canyon! Cooke had to fight to control his temper. The damned fool! Had he learned nothing? After all that had happened, would he still lead his command into a potential death trap?

Colonel Porter and Captain Marcy turned their eyes to Cooke. His shock was mirrored in their faces.

"From there," Johnston continued, pretending he did not notice the look of consternation that had come over his officers, "we pass over the Mormon Trail, through Emigration Canyon, and into Salt Lake City."

Emigration Canyon! Cooke's face flushed. Had Johnston gone mad?

Emigration Canyon! One would have to search long and hard for better and more extensive natural locations for ambush. An uninvited thought suddenly sprang into Cooke's mind: It was almost as if Johnston was engineering a confrontation with the battalion, one that the Utah Expedition might very well lose.

Captain Marcy brought the heel of his hand up to his forehead, body language expressing his frustration.

"A headache, Captain?" Johnston asked with obvious sarcasm.

Marcy dropped his hand. "A rather severe one, I'm afraid."

"Not so severe as to inhibit you from attending to your duties, I trust." Johnston's voice was bordering on the vitriolic. He continued his instructions.

"I expect to be in Salt Lake City within ten days of our departure. We will bivouc at the mouth of Emigration Canyon overlooking Salt Lake Valley, and occupy the city the following morning. Leaving the canyon, we follow the trail northwest along the foothills until it connects with Temple Street on the outskirts of the city."

Johnston's attention turned to the crude map overlapping the tabletop. "Our good friend and wagon master Mister Magruder is hardly a draftsman, as you can see. However, having been a frequent visitor to the Salt Lake Valley—*before they threw him and his wagons out*—he assures me that this map of the inner city, which he has drawn from memory, is an accurate one. Is that not true, Mister Magruder?" the general asked in a taunting voice.

Magruder, furious, looked away and said nothing.

After an embarrassing moment, Johnston continued his briefing, jamming his forefinger in the center of the map. "The core of the center city is where Temple Street—which, as you know, runs east and west—intersects with Main Street, running, of course, north and south. There," he indicated, "on the northeast corner are the territorial offices, including the governor's office, with the governor's mansion just to the east.

"On the northwest corner, and surrounding a full block, is a wall, probably ten feet in height. They call this the temple grounds. It contains some buildings and a large foundation where they would build their pagan shrine. That wall is a potential danger to us. It could become a fortress."

Indeed, thought Cooke, if we ever get that far. A hell of a time to start worrying about security!

"On the southeast corner is a mercantile building, bordered by commercial establishments. On the southwest corner, a bank, also bordered by commercial establishments.

"This is the heart of Utah Territory, gentlemen—our destination!

"Now," the general's brow darkened, his manner becoming increasingly intense, "hear this well: At this point I do not know what kind of reception Brigham Young and his brigands have planned for us, but I tell you, it will be nothing with which we cannot cope. I caution you—any failure to carry out your orders will be severely dealt with.

"We all have much to do," he concluded. "Our final briefing will take place the morning we occupy Salt Lake City. That will be all."

Colonel Cooke was the last to leave. He stopped at the door and turned back to face Johnston, who had returned his attention to Magruder's map. Johnston looked up, a questioning lift to his brow. "Questions, Colonel?"

Cooke stood in the doorway for a few moments. "No, sir, I guess you've said it all." Cooke spun about and walked away, closing the door firmly behind him. He strode briskly to Marcy's quarters, bursting in on Marcy and Fitz-John Porter. "My quarters, gentlemen, *now!*"

The surprised pair glanced at each other, then obediently followed the colonel. The three officers talked the night away. It was near dawn before Cooke's guests returned to their rooms.

General Albert Sidney Johnston, resplendent in his dark blue, gold-frogged dolman, gleaming leather, and highly polished brass, sat easily in the saddle of the impatient big gray he'd appropriated from the ailing Col. Uriah Wilson.

The harsh morning light accentuated the rugged cast to Johnston's formidable jaw, but didn't reach the dark, brooding eyes sheltered by the peak of his soft-topped campaign hat. Not that it mattered; Johnston's eyes rarely betrayed his inner thoughts. He knew he was something of an enigma to his subordinates, and not a few of his superiors. That's the way he wanted it.

The column, four abreast, stretched back for a good two miles—dragoons, mounted riflemen, Hauk's retrieved artillery, and the infantry companies—ready for the order to march. Bringing up the rear, and this time heavily guarded, were the quartermaster and sanitation units, followed by what was left of Magruder's wagon companies.

Immediately behind Johnston were Colonels Philip St. George Cooke and Fitz-John Porter. They, in turn, were followed by Captains Marcy and Frietag.

Eight drummers, accompanied by a mounted bugler, waited on the heels of the senior officers, beating a rhythmic, almost lulling cadence. The junior officers—Coy, Hauk, Buell, and others—were mounted at the heads of their respective commands.

A sense of anticipation wafted through the ranks. Johnston stretched himself high in the saddle. He nodded to Cooke.

"FORWARD, HO!" echoed down the line, each of twenty commanding voices picking up the order in turn. The colors caught the morning breeze.

When the formidable entrance to Echo Canyon came into view, an uncomfortable feeling descended on General Johnston. He noticed, too—or was it just his imagination?—that an uneasy stillness had come over the troops.

Echo Canyon was a paradox. In some places a winding, twisting path was hemmed in by high, sheer cliffs. There were dank, dark, sunless stretches where cutbacks and massive overhangs of rock conspired to make the canyon everything Phil Cooke said it was—a natural death trap for an unwelcome invader. But periodically these unpleasant conditions would give way to bright, wide passages, with slowly rising hills of willows and quaking aspen on either side.

The column was brought to a stop just before entering the canyon to wait for the return of Johnston's advance party, led by Hickok. The news was both good and bad. Hickok reported fortified strongpoints high on the canyon's walls—impressive strongpoints, where a deadly fusillade could be poured down on those below. But they were apparently unmanned, deserted. Johnston breathed an unintended sigh, then looked about, hoping no one had heard him.

However, the great rock cradles that the battalion had perched on the lip of the canyon walls had all been triggered, apparently just hours before. Tons of rock had plummeted into several of the narrower spots on the canyon floor, closing off passage. It could be cleared, but it would take time and energy. To add to that, streams had been turned onto the roadway, in some places creating deep, muddy pools.

All along the way there were wide trenches dug into the trail that would have to be filled or bridged.

Cooke reined up to Johnston's side. "Look, Sidney, there is nothing to be proved here. There are other routes into the city."

The general shook his head. "You still don't understand, do you?"

"I understand we're damned fools if we attempt to plow through here."

"It's the men, Phil, the men! Can't you see it? They're frightened, hesitant. And after what they've been through I can't blame them. They haven't as yet quite returned to being soldiers. They still see Echo Canyon as a barrier. This is the best thing that can happen under the circumstances—attack this canyon, clear its obstacles. I tell you they'll be better men, have more confidence, once we're on the other side."

Cooke raised his eyebrows indicating partial agreement. "Well put; perhaps you're right."

"We'll see," was Johnston's response. "Get me Hickok and Hauk. I want a hundred men, including demolition squads, to precede us."

The Utah Expedition strained painfully through the canyon. Periodic explosions of gunpowder, clearing walls of boulders off the roadway, rang along the gray cliffs, shaking the valley floor like so many earthquakes. Sometimes hours were spent hauling away rocks and boulders, damming streams, or filling in the trenches. Most infuriating of all were the muddy bogs. It took Herculean efforts to get some of the heavier wagons through them. Once again, Johnston's schedule had been disrupted. The twenty-mile passage through Echo Canyon held the Utah Expedition to an average of two miles a day.

Johnston was right, Cooke admitted to himself. When the first troops broke into the bright sunlight of Echo Canyon's west entrance, a thunderous cheer broke out all down the line. Its tone was not one of relief, but of pride. The colonel turned to his commanding officer. "My compliments."

Chapter Twenty

I t had been another full day for Brigham Young. Salt Lake City was all but deserted, its inhabitants well on their way south. The erstwhile governor was now making final arrangements for the approach of Johnston's army, which, by the latest report, was three days' march away.

His last guests, late in the evening, were the somber Kane, Cumming, and Dawson. The distraught Cumming was the first to speak. "Governor," he began—Kane thought it ironic that each called the other "Governor"—"what can I say to you? For all my good intentions, I have failed. I have been unable to carry out the directions of the president, or to assist you and your people in this miserable affair. To express to you my deepest apologies is hopelessly insufficient."

Young put his hand on Cumming's shoulder. "On the contrary, Governor," he said with feeling, "your presence here is more important than you know. And your report, which will soon be, if it is not already, in the hands of the president and the national press, will make *all* the difference to us. Believe me, you'll be governor to the people of this territory long after the Utah Expedition is a bad memory."

Young placed his other hand on Kane's shoulder. "You, Thomas, and you, Judge Dawson, we can never thank you enough as well for your efforts in our behalf.

"As you know, Johnston's army will be here in a few days. When it arrives, I'll be standing in front of the governor's office. The colors will be raised, and Professor Holt's brass band will welcome it.

However, if Johnston attempts a military occupation of the city, he'll see it reduced to ashes."

"God!" blurted Kane, "this beautiful city . . . it would be a tragedy."

"True," answered Young solemnly, "but a tragedy that would hasten the end of Johnston and his army. Now, we can't rule out the possibility of violence. For your protection, I've ordered Major Lot Smith to conduct you to an area where you will be out of danger."

"You dishonor me, sir!" blurted Alfred Cumming.

"I intended no—"

"We are in this together, Governor Young. Surely you can't believe I would desert you at this crucial time! When the story of the Utah War is written, it will read that Governor Alfred Cumming stood at your side."

"Along with the chief justice of the Utah Territorial Court," added Dawson, with a firm lift to his chin.

"Let me make it unanimous, Governor," said Kane. "I have no intention of leaving."

Brigham Young was touched. "Is there nothing I can say that will change your minds?"

"Certainly not!" Cumming spoke for all three.

"Well," Young said finally, "it appears my little corner on Temple Street will be rather crowded when Johnston rides by."

On this last day before the Utah Expedition would emerge out of Emigration Canyon onto the panorama of the Salt Lake Valley, Johnston called an early halt. "I want to be through here first thing in the morning," he told Cooke. "I want the entire day tomorrow to view the city from the foothills and to make my final plans. I don't want to arrive there tonight in the dark."

James Butler Hickok had slept for a few hours in the early evening, but awoke as the night pressed on. He tossed and turned for a half hour before he dressed, then silently moved out of his tent. Off in the distance he could hear muffled voices. He wasn't the only one who couldn't sleep.

There was an invigorating cool breeze meandering through the canyon, bringing with it the satisfying smell of pine needles. He filled his lungs a number of times, letting the air slip out slowly in a soft whistle. Above the mountains on either side and across the open canyon, stars sparkled with unusual brightness. Even though Hickok was in a small valley, hemmed in by richly forested mountains, his pathway was illuminated. He stopped for a moment to check the noose around his horse's neck, patting the animal lightly on the snout. Then he walked the path he knew would lead him to the river without disturbing a sentry.

The sounds of water dashing exuberantly over smooth granite rocks were comforting to him. He came to a stop at a large boulder, about ten yards from the river. Leaning against it, and looking up again at the diamond-studded sky, he began to roll a cigarette.·

It was then that he heard voices, directly below him, on the riverbank. One he recognized immediately—Magruder. Ordinarily, Hickok wasn't interested in others' conversations. But something made him curious about this clandestine meeting. What were they up to? Nothing good, of that he was sure.

Silently, he moved closer. Soon he was able to make out Carney, Hathaway, Magruder, and Riley—his poker partners. No problem with recognizing them in the half-light. There were three others, men he had seen before but did not know their names. Some of Magruder's gunmen, he surmised.

"So that's the way it is." Magruder was talking. "Cumming and Dawson will try to negotiate. If Young allows the city to be occupied, we'll be cut out of everything. And we'll be no better off if Johnston backs down."

"That'll be the day," interjected Riley, "when that sonovabitch backs down to anybody."

"Shut up, Riley," responded an angry Carney.

"We have a lot at stake," continued Magruder. "If there's a fight, everything'll be up for grabs. Land, mines, farms, homes—ours for the takin'. When all the others come in to pick up the pieces, we'll already have the cream."

Now Carney and Riley began to argue.

"Al'right, al'right," interrupted Magruder. "Point is, we got to find a way to lay out both Cumming and Young. The army'll come down Temple Street past the governor's office. It's a safe bet Cumming and Young will be there. If we can get them both while the army's in the city, all hell's gonna break loose. If not, we'll have to find some other way. Chances are, fightin'll break out without our help anyway. But if it don't . . ."

Carney shook his head. "That's an awful lot of 'ifs,' Magruder."

"I know, I know. No one said we wasn't takin' a chance. Goin' to have to play it as it comes. But you remember this, Case. We got nothin'.

You mark my words: Once we get to Salt Lake, Johnston'll have what damned few wagons we got left seized, and all our back pay forfeited. Cooke as much as told me so. And don't you forget Brigham Young. We got something to settle there. He ran me out of this territory and took everything I had. I tell you, I'm going to get it back in spades."

Hickok remained where he was for some time after the others had left, his face expressionless. At length he walked slowly back to his tent.

The following morning, General Johnston led his army out of Emigration Canyon, and through the wooded area of oak, poplar, and aspen that formed the plateau where Brigham Young was first informed about a federal army on its way to Utah, just a few days less than a year before. To Johnston's left, the playful waters of City Creek, beginning their descent into the valley, added to the pleasantness of the glen. For a few minutes the general felt curiously at peace.

Gradually the glen gave way to an expansive alluvial fan, extending from the foothills of the rugged mountains out toward the valley below. It was nearly treeless, supporting numerous grasses and the ubiquitous clumps of oak brush. It dropped slowly, in a series of muted steps, until it met the lush greenness of the valley. From that point on, the outskirts of Salt Lake City began to appear, culminating in the central city. Beyond that was a glassy sea, sparkling brilliantly in the sunlight, causing Johnston to squint—the Great Salt Lake. To the south were obviously fertile farms and orchards, marked off in various shades of green and yellow plots. Johnston could even see brief sections of the Jordan River along the valley floor winding its way from the Point of the Mountain; it joined the freshwater of Utah Lake with the Great Salt Lake, just as its namesake joined the Sea of Galilee and the Dead Sea.

Johnston rose in his stirrups, scanning the valley below. The top step of the gently sloping hill, he reasoned, would be the perfect place to bivouac—the city in full view, and no way for an enemy to mount a sneak attack.

Johnston scanned the valley from right to left, attempting to capture its unique panorama. The mountains, stretching up, up in the sky, diminishing all else, crested in gray rock, the steep slopes dressed in endless outcroppings of summer green patterned on tan. Beyond were the bright green valley, the precision of the city, the great lake, and still more mountains beyond that. He had never seen a more beautiful setting. Through his scope he surveyed the city, the tree-lined streets, the well-designed buildings, its obviously planned symmetry. He saw no evidence of military activity.

Was it really possible that this magnificent place was inhabited by a pagan people, the refuse of two continents—moral outcasts, devoid of culture and gentility? Could these pastoral farmlands be the product of degenerate minds, the work of mindless zealots, unworthy of citizenship in a Protestant America? Was it a weak and cowardly people who had the gristle to challenge the United States?

Then, as quickly as he had brought these questions to mind, Johnston dismissed them. Under the circumstances, what difference did it make? There were more important and far-reaching factors at stake. So much depended on the next few hours.

Making camp was much like raising a small city, and just the task of feeding the troops was overwhelming. The process of corraling wagon stock and cavalry mounts often turned into a comedy of errors. Even the most disciplined armies were plagued with this orderly chaos. So it was not unusual that no one noticed the man in buckskins lead his horse into the reeds that bordered the banks of City Creek, following its course to an extended protective gully, where he was hidden from sight as he moved toward the valley.

A uniformed rider galloped up the street to rein up at Doc Ames's home, where Rockwell, Anne, and Lot were preparing to leave for Point of the Mountain.

The rider dropped from his horse, bounded up the steps, and hammered on the door. Rockwell opened it.

"Major Rockwell?"

"Yes, Corporal?"

"Corporal Hanig here, sir. Beg the Major's pardon. Lieutenant Jamison sent me to tell you somebody's looking for you. Gives his name as Hickok. Been ridin' through the central city. Now he's askin' for you. Should be comin' along any minute now. He's armed—the lieutenant thought you ought to know."

Rockwell frowned.

"May I be of assistance, Major?"

"Ah, no," Rockwell responded absently. "Thank you, and thank the lieutenant for me."

The young trooper snapped a salute. "I will, sir." Turning on his heel, he strode to his horse, sprang into the saddle, and was away.

"Hickok?" queried Lot, a worried cast to his face. "What could he want?"

"We'll find out when he gets here," Rockwell answered softly.

"What's wrong?" Anne asked, concern knitting her brow.

Rockwell walked into the parlor and took his Colts from the wood clothing peg. "Nothing to worry about," he responded dryly.

"He's coming now," Lot said from his vantage point at the bay window.

Anne gasped, tenting her fingers over her mouth.

Rockwell crossed to join Lot at the window in time to see Hickok rein up at Ames's hitching rail. The tall man swung easily from his saddle, scanning the house and the empty street before stepping down. With studied casualness he unbuckled his gun belt and swung it over the saddle horn. Then, with the same almost lackadaisical air, he walked around to the front of the hitching rail, leaned back against it on his buttocks, and crossed his feet.

Soon he reached into a hidden pocket, retrieving a small pouch and an even smaller packet of paper. He expertly poured some of the contents of the pouch into one of the papers, and rolled a cigarette, sealing its length with tongue and nimble fingers. Finally, he cinched the pouch, using his teeth and left hand, and returned it with the unused paper inside his buckskin tunic.

Rockwell had seen enough. "Won't need these," he said, handing his brace of Colts to Lot. He looked at Anne, cupping her chin. "I'll be back in a minute," he assured her.

"What if it's a trick?" interjected Lot.

"Not this time."

The sound of Rockwell's boots on the small porch brought Hickok's eyes up in the midst of touching a match to his smoke.

In the meantime, at the window, Lot pulled one of Rockwell's Colts from the holster, thumb on the hammer. "Just bein' careful," he said to Anne, with what he thought was a comforting smile. She nodded, her eyes locked on the pair outside.

Rockwell stepped from the porch and walked down the short path. "Mister Hickok."

"Mister Rockwell."

"This a social call, Mister Hickok?"

"In a manner of speaking," nodded the scout, a hint of a smile touching his face, "knowing how you feel about back-shooters."

"Mind spelling that out? I seem a little slow this morning."

Now a frown darkened Hickok's countenance. He was visibly perplexed. "Magruder, Carney, maybe four, five others—going to break off from the main body in the morning, I believe. Going to bushwhack Young and Cumming, and make sure the occupation turns into a war. War, Mister Rockwell! Magruder's a jackal. When the bloodletting's over, he and others like him will tear this territory apart, gobble up everything worth having."

Rockwell's face clouded. "How're they coming in?"

"Don't know yet, but I think it will be while the troops are in the city. Troops'll be coming west, down Temple Street."

"Figures," stated Rockwell, dejectedly.

"As soon as they break off in the morning, or whatever, I'll let you know," continued Hickok. "Where will I find you?"

Rockwell thought for a moment. "The two doctors who live here," he motioned back at the house, "will be inside the south gates of the temple grounds, in case they're needed. I'll be with them."

"Good," responded Hickok. "Just rode by there a half hour ago."

Untying the rein, he swung up into his saddle, careful to keep his hand away from the holsters hooked on the saddle horn, and prepared to ride off.

Rockwell took a step closer. "One question, Mister Hickok."

"Mister Rockwell?"

"Why? Why are you doing this?"

Hickok could not hide a self-satisfied smile. "I had you pegged as a glorified bushwacker—all reputation and nothing to back it up. I was wrong"—the same words Rockwell had said to him at Chochetope Pass.

Hickok reined his mount into the street, spurs nudging the animal into a smooth canter.

"What was that all about?" Lot demanded as soon as Rockwell had reentered the house.

"Hickok," Anne repeated. "Who is he? He looks enough like you to be your brother."

"Right now he's a friend," responded Rockwell. Then to Lot, "Magruder and some others are going to try to assassinate Brigham." He placed a hand on each of Lot's shoulders. "You have to understand this: Orders or no orders, neither of us can leave now. This changes everything. I'm not going to have any trouble with you, am I?"

Lot shook his head slowly.

"Ride in, warn Brigham. Tell him he's got to keep out of sight, off the streets."

The moment Lot was out the door, Anne was in Rockwell's arms, her body shaking with emotion. Rockwell had read somewhere that pregnant women tended to be overly sensitive. He raised her face gently to look into her misty eyes. "Come now," he said, trying unsuccessfully to mimic a Scottish accent, "where's my brazen hussy?"

She tried to smile, also unsuccessfully. "When will we be free of this?" she sighed.

Rockwell carefully stroked her flaxen hair. "Anne, I have no choice."

Anne was in no mood to be reasonable. "But President Young ordered you to leave. You don't have to stay. You've done enough."

"Anne," he spoke softly. "You said it that night at Echo Canyon. Once I rode away, and I've regretted it from that day on. Now I must stay."

For a long time they held each other in silence.

"I told him!" Lot blurted out, bursting into the house, slamming the front door behind him, his voice edged with frustration. "Damned if he didn't tell me he figured they'd try something like that, just as though it was nothin'. And then he said you and I had our orders and we were to obey them—that nothin' had changed."

Rockwell shook his head. "So you accepted that, and walked out of his office with your tail between your legs."

Rockwell could see it coming, but not quite soon enough. He stepped back as Lot's fist grazed his chin. His backward motion combined with the muted blow sent him to the floor on his backside.

Anne quickly sprang in between the two. "Stop it!" she cried out in the fullness of her Scottish brogue. "What's the matter with ye! Insultin' and hittin' one another like tavern brawlers! I will nae' stand for it a moment more!"

"Sorry, Anne," Lot said sheepishly. But he wasn't finished. He turned to Rockwell, who was now sitting with his legs crossed, a hand on each knee, Indian fashion, surprise still written on his face. "Just so you'll know, Port," he shouted, "I told President Young we were staying, and if that was violating his orders, then so be it!"

"*Aha!*" responded Rockwell with gusto, coming to his feet with a grin, contemplating Lot. "You did it! You really did it! *You stood up to him!* What I wouldn't give to have seen his face." Then looking whimsically at Anne, he raised one hand in a Shakespearean gesture. "Behold, our Lot Smith, come of age at last."

The sun was setting over the Oquirrhs, generating a bright pink hue in the waters of the Great Salt Lake, when it was pointed out to Cooke that four civilians were riding up the trail from the city. Cooke pulled out his scope. After focusing on the group, he slammed the scope shut and walked briskly to Johnston's Sibley. "General, there's a group approaching the camp under a flag of truce."

"Can you make them out?"

"Young, Kane, Cumming, Dawson."

"They dare to come here!"

"Sidney, they've all come under a flag of truce, for God's sake!"

Johnston shot a look at Cooke. "Then we must give them a fitting welcome, mustn't we? Colonel, have the bugler sound Battle Formation."

Cooke was startled. "Now wait a minute!"

"Calm yourself, Phil; a show of force, nothing more. I want them to see what they're up against."

Cooke wheeled and exited the Sibley. A flick of the wrist brought a bugler on the run. "Sound Battle Formation!" Cooke growled.

The bugler rattled out the call, the clear, commanding notes picked up and relayed throughout the camp. Officers and noncoms bellowed orders as the troops swung into battle line. Captain Hauk's artillery raced forward to take the center, the guns lining up wheel hub to wheel hub, gunners cocking the already primed firing mechanisms while the gun layers checked for elevation. Hauk moved quickly along the line of his field guns, checking to make sure that they were set for direct fire. The loads were canister, filled with plumb-sized shot—a gift to the art of war from Napoleon Bonaparte.

The drummers beat a rapid tattoo, spurring the men on. Rapidly mobilizing infantry units surged forward to flank the fieldpieces, leaving gaps in their formations to give the dragoons freedom of movement for the time they would be called upon to charge. Mounted riflemen, now without their mules, took up skirmish formation to support the infantry. Bayonets were affixed, muskets brought to full cock, primers thumbed down hard on the cones. Sabers slithered out of scabbards in a glittering array of bright steel, at the ready. The infantry lines were in depth, the first rank kneeling, the one behind standing erect to fire over their heads. Behind these two lines waited another two, ready to step in when their companions fired and drew back to reload. Sanitation and quartermaster units formed a perimeter defense at the rear, along with Magruder's decimated wagon companies.

Johnston's army was ready for battle in a few short minutes, an exercise that could not help but please its commanding officers. It was no wonder, then, that when the troops saw a small group sporting a white flag, coming up over a grassy rise, a loud and long groan of disappointment exploded from the line and echoed down the slope. This army wanted revenge.

Johnston and Cooke alone rode down to meet the approaching delegation.

"An impressive sight," Brigham Young addressed Gen. Albert Sidney Johnston, his hand pointing to the array of firepower fifty yards beyond and slightly above them. "For our benefit?"

"Yes, indeed, Governor Young," responded Johnston, insincerity in his voice. "But I must ask why a man of your stature and perception would bring *these* persons with you to talk terms." The general's dark eyes swung scathingly over Young's companions.

"I've found *these* to be persons of integrity, of honor, General. I trust I may place you in that same category."

Johnston smiled sardonically. "What you trust is of no concern to me, Governor. Tomorrow morning I ride at the head of my troops to occupy Salt Lake City. I will invest the territorial offices and declare martial law in this territory. Any attempt to impede my troops will be met with force. Is that plain enough for you, Governor?"

"A fine attempt, General," responded Young, unintimidated, "but seriously lacking prescience. With your permission, I will tell *you* what will happen. Your command will be allowed to pass through Salt Lake City. I think we owe that to you after all you and your troops have suffered. I'll be at the territorial offices, to bid you Godspeed. But if you attempt to carry out any of your egotistical threats, Salt Lake City will be burned to the ground. If you wish to rule over ashes, that is your choice. Those are *my* terms, General."

With that, Brigham Young reined his stallion about and began to ride down the incline, followed by his friends.

Johnston was furious. *"Just a minute! I'm not finished with you!"*

Young reined in, and looked back at the incensed officer. *"You had damned well better be finished with me, General, for your own sake and that of your troops!"*

It was dusk when Hickok took young Cody for an evening's fishing on the banks of City Creek. "Fishin's good for a man," he told him, "gives a feller time to relax and think."

"Where'd you go this mornin', Mister Hickok? I was lookin' all over for you."

"Just for a ride, son. May have to do the same tomorrow."

"Lemee go with you, Mister Hickok, please?"

"Can't do that. But I won't be far. You stay put till I get back. You got that?"

"Yeah, I guess so" was the dejected reply.

Just then, the boy snagged a trout, an angry one. Hickok took two steps out into the stream to net it. At that moment his eye caught something moving downstream, into the gully—a dark figure leading a horse. "Appears someone else has business in town," he said, a look of concern on his face.

On this summer's eve, two thousand miles to the east, Lord Edmund Lyons, in his Washington apartment, completed a communique to Whitehall. As he wrote the last line, he wondered if this was not the most unusual report that had ever appeared under his signature. Actually, Prime Minister Palmerstone, upon reading it several weeks later, commented that the ambassador must have "gone 'round the bend!"

> With this message I write finis to the secessionist dream of a confederacy that would include California and the great American West. The dream died in the snowbound wilds of Nebraska Territory.
>
> A secessionist South will not survive without the moral legitimacy, the space, and the wealth of the West; and the schemes, ploys, and conspiracies of the Floyd cabal directed to that end are becoming unraveled, from Kansas to California. They were given an extraordinary boon by the bumptuous Buchanan, who was going to make the rebellious people of Utah Territory an example of his strength and determination. But, I must say, they have not played it out well. If they had, secession might even now be in process.
>
> The Utah Expedition presented to them a host of potential opportunities. Allow me to list one or two: Had war erupted between Johnston's

army and the territory of Utah, violence may have spread, becoming the catalyst for rebellion in other parts. At the very least, it could have become a caldron, devouring increasing numbers of federal troops, thereby diminishing the power of the federal government to restrain secession by force.

If Johnston had gained quick and decisive control over Utah, he may have been able to use that strategic location to bring substantial influence on the West, including California. What if he had invested Utah and quickly moved on to California? With the advent of secession—and it will occur—the federal government will probably seek to reunite the country under force of arms. I have been led to believe that, in the event of war, an integral part of Southern military strategy will be the invasion of New Mexico and California by Texas regulars and volunteers. What if that army were able to occupy Los Angeles, and Johnston's army, Sacramento? Surely, Johnston would have enough influence over his troops to convince many of them to follow him. California is a heady prize, is it not?

What has happened? Time, the weather, and a nation of outcasts have conspired to deny them these options. It was absolutely essential that General Johnston and the Utah Expedition make a quick thrust into Salt Lake City, before the truth were known. The victory would have been hailed in the nation's press, saluted by Congress, cheered by public opinion, and acclaimed by the nation's religious leaders. And if the Mormons had shed blood in the defense of their homes, institutions, and rights, the above groups would have clamored relentlessly for their annihilation.

Instead, these unwanted citizens cleverly avoided military confrontation, while nipping at the heels of the beast. In ghostlike forays, they swept down upon the Utah Expedition, burning its wagons, running off its stock, crippling its progress, and intercepting, with tactical superiority, efforts to relieve the army. They burned the prairie in front of their would-be conquerors, blew up dammed rivers, crushing their advance with walls of water, until this great land armada was reduced to a crawl, and finally buried under great waves of snow and ice.

In the meantime, the newspapers of the land, now decidedly more informed, began to see both Johnston's army and the people of Utah in a new light. To say that some newspapers have become champions of the Utahns is not an exaggeration. Now, public opinion shifts to their camp.

Congress begins to stir from its slumber, gradually to realize the depth of this farce it helped perpetuate. Generally, Southerners, states-righters, and the devotees of popular sovereignty see the Utahns as another group of Americans whose independence is being crushed by the arrogance of the federal government, while Northerners look upon them as pawns in the deadly game of state. They ask with loud voices what a significant portion of the military forces of the United States is doing "tilting at windmills" two thousand miles from the real dangers that face the country.

Admittedly the Utah Expedition has been relieved and resupplied by the government. This had to be done to salvage it as an institution. Johnston may yet reach Salt Lake City, but he will go no farther. This time 'round, if there is violence, if, as has been predicted, Salt Lake City burns, Johnston, not Brigham Young, will be blamed. Punishment will be exacted against the general, not the governor. The forces of American democracy have overpowered Gen. Albert Sidney Johnston. We have only to see how long it takes him to realize this.

How ironic that these stubborn citizens of Utah Territory should have successfully challenged the government of the United States, humiliated its military forces, destroyed the reputation of the war secretary, severely and irrevocably damaged the presidency of James Buchanan, and contributed significantly to the demise of any hopes for a confederacy in the West, and the postponement of secession for at least two years, by my calculations. Perhaps, they have altered the course of history.

Lyons

At dawn, the senior officers of the Utah Expedition were assembled in Johnston's tent, Magruder's crude map once again laid out before them. "Questions?" asked Johnston. None were forthcoming. These men were peculiarly quiet, he thought, even somewhat morose.

"One final word, then. Nothing is going to happen that I do not order. I want no mistakes, no accidents, no heroics. I, not events in Salt Lake City, will decide our course. My orders will be passed to you, and from there down the line. I want all noncommissioned officers out of the ranks and on the wings, staggered down both sides of the line. I want them to see all that is happening, to hear all that is ordered, and to pass those directions on to the troops instantaneously. Is that clear?" There were murmurs of affirmation. "Fine. Begin assembly in half an hour. Dismissed."

The one-horse carriage moved slowly along Main Street toward the city center. The two doctors sat on either side of Anne. To the right rode Rockwell and Lot. The city was silent and deserted, except for the sounds of an occasional battalion volunteer, unlighted torch in hand, shuffling into position.

A chill made Anne shudder. She tried to suppress a feeling of foreboding, but could not. All the people gone; the stores closed; straw and hay stacked up in front of windows and doors; no children; no crowds of shoppers wending their way down the street, talking, laughing, the sound of their voices giving evidence of life and happiness. She recalled Christmas Eve: the music, the dancing, the singing, the spirit of it, the joy of it all. Now all gone; only the cold material props remained to give silent witness of what once was, and might never be again. She took a handkerchief from the sleeve of her blouse and pressed it against her tear-filled eyes. Her grim-faced father gently took her hand in his. "There, there, lass."

At length they came to the intersection with Temple Street. There seemed to be some movement in the governor's office, on the northeast corner, but as yet no one had come out to the street. The carriage and riders turned west on Temple and, a half block later, entered through the opened iron gates into the temple grounds. It was then that they heard the distant, mournful sound of military trumpets, echoing off the mountains.

A confused murmur swept along the ranks as Johnston's army began its turn east on Temple Street and into the city. Deserted it was, except for silent figures, every so often along the way, holding unlighted torches. Each one of these silent sentries calmly ignited his torch as the general passed. Out of the corners of his eyes Johnston could see the flames ominously spring into life on either side of the street, held steady by determined hands. He felt the eyes of the stoic torchbearers following his every move, their owners ready to spring into action at the slightest provocation. His mouth tightened.

So, Brigham Young was no braggard, no spewer of false bravado. He intended to do exactly as he had threatened. And Johnston, being the man he was, could not help but silently extend to the governor of Utah Territory his respect.

A half hour later, to the sound of horses' hooves, the shrill cry of an occasional cannon wheel, and the clank of military accoutrements, alone breaking the eerie stillness, the army moved inexorably toward the center of the city, the pace indicated from a distance by the periodic lighting of torches on either side of the street.

It was then that General Johnston noticed that Cooke had reined up even with him on the right, and Colonel Porter on the left.

"What is this, Cooke?"

"A word with you, General."

Johnston's face suffused with anger. "In line, Colonel!" he ground out, "and I'll be having a word with *you* when this is over!"

"A word with you *now,* General" was Cooke's steady response.

"By God, Colonel! You're under arrest! Marcy, get up here!"

But Marcy remained in his position.

"Colonel Porter!"

Fitz-John Porter looked straight ahead, unmoving.

"You fools, you're asking for the firing squad—every damned one of you!"

"You're right," said Cooke, carefully. "Every damned one of us is willing to take that risk."

Johnston's face portrayed shock. "A conspiracy! All of you!" His hands were trembling, not out of fear, but anger. "Traitor! You expect me to turn over my command!"

"No, General! I expect to keep you from making a mistake that will reek with dishonor every time honest men discuss it. You can't play God. No purpose, however monumental the goal, is worth the stain that will follow all of us."

Johnston had no choice. He could attempt to draw his pistol against his fellow officers, but that would accomplish nothing. His tense body relaxed. He looked straight ahead and did not respond to Cooke.

"Sidney, listen to me. For God's sake *listen* to me! Whatever worth the Utah Expedition had a year ago has passed. We're marching into a city ready to be put to the torch, and its citizens scattered God knows where. No enemy awaits us here, no soldiers to do battle!

"In a minute we'll be passing the territorial offices. Brigham Young and Governor Cumming will be there. So will reporters from the eastern press. The world will know what happens here today, and it will be judged. Sidney, *we* will be judged."

Cooke now spoke softly, reassuringly. "You command an army of the United States, General. It has reached its destination. Now, in the sacred memory of all those we buried along the way, lead it through and out. It deserves no disgrace. The decision is yours!"

Cooke nodded to Marcy on Johnston's left. Both riders reined back to assume their original positions.

James Butler Hickok was getting nervous. None of the conspirators were close to each other. Unable to see Magruder, he decided to watch Case Carney. Whatever happened, that animal would be in the thick of it. He took a position by one of Magruder's wagons, some thirty yards behind the mounted gunman.

Still no movement on their part. Hickok was about to conclude that they had thought the better of their assassination plot, when they began to peel off onto side steets heading north.

So, they were going to go around the northern part of the city and come at their prey from the back. As soon as Carney slipped up one of the streets, Hickok spurred his horse in the opposite direction. His objective was to drop south a block, race through the city until he was parallel with the temple grounds, then cut north to Temple Street and through the gates, where Rockwell was waiting.

With only an occasional torchbearer to watch him, he executed the route perfectly. When he reached the intersection and was about to turn the corner, he noticed the approaching army column coming down the street, Johnston in the lead. To his surprise, he saw Brigham Young standing on the northeast corner in front of the territorial offices, dry torch in hand and flanked by four other men. Most peculiar of all was the sight of numerous flags, and a uniformed brass band, directly behind the group, extending out to the middle of Main Street. And on the northwest corner four civilians leaned against the wall, paper and pencils in hand, by their expressions apparently wondering what business the buckskinned intruder had poking his nose into this historic event.

Rockwell was relieved to see Hickok ride through the temple grounds gates. "Thought you might not get here."

"I had to be sure. They're coming down the back. They've gone around north. I reckon they'll swing down Main Street and try to take Cumming and Young from the back."

"Let's get moving," said Rockwell, beckoning to Lot Smith.

"Plenty of time," responded Hickok.

Rockwell regarded Hickok for a long moment. "This is not your fight."

"Wouldn't miss it, Mr. Rockwell" was the calm response.

The trio rode across the grounds to the east gates. Before leaving, Rockwell kissed Anne gently. "Stay here. I'll be back."

"God be with you," she said simply.

James Wilson and his eight year old, James Jr., stood on the porch of the now empty Utah Hotel, which adjoined the governor's office on Main Street. Each held an as-yet-unlit torch in his hand. Behind them, the double doors to the hotel were open, exposing the foyer. It was filled with hay and newspapers.

Missus Wilson and the three girls had already left the city. As James Jr. put it, what had to be done here was a man's job. And James Sr. insisted that if his hotel had to be burned, he'd be the one to do it.

Main Street, above Temple Street, was deserted save for Wilson and his son. The two were taken back when they saw Rockwell, Smith, and Hickok ride through the open gates of the east entrance of the temple grounds. They watched them dismount, check the charges in their handguns, then begin to walk, three abreast, north on Main. Smith and Rockwell took the wings, with Hickok in the middle.

James Wilson's instincts roared at him to take his son and bolt for it. But a thrilling curiosity got the better of him. There was going to be a shoot-out, no doubt about that, and Wilson and son didn't intend to miss it.

The command of the Utah Expedition—Gen. Albert Sidney Johnston at the fore—reached the crossing of Temple and Main streets. It was approaching eleven o'clock, and the sun was bright in the sky.

Tension filled the air. Noncommissioned officers strained their ears, many leaning forward on their mounts, waiting for orders to be shouted in their direction. The officers behind Johnston sat high in their saddles, every muscle strained. The reporters by the temple grounds wall put down their pads, bracing themselves. Across the street from them to the east, Kane's hands tightened into fists, opening, closing. Cumming and Dawson literally held their breath.

Johnston, the muscles in his face taut, rode past Brigham Young and the governor designate without so much as throwing a glance in their direction. For a moment, the tension gripping Brigham Young subsided. Johnston was not going to stop at the territorial offices! He was not going to order the military occupation of the city! The Utah Expedition was going to march through the city and out!

Then, Colonel Cooke reined out of the column and directed his mount to the group standing on the corner. Once there, he presented a crisp salute to the uniformed Colonel Kane. It was returned with equal crispness.

Finally, the former commander of the battalion turned to meet the gaze of Brigham Young. Slowly, Cooke raised his right hand and removed his field cap, placing it over his heart. He held this position of ultimate respect for some seconds, eyes never leaving the Mormon leader, before abruptly spurring his horse back to the head of the column. Only then did he replace the cap. Among the many accounts written of these brief seconds, not just a few consider this to have been one of the great moments of the Utah War, a moment that by itself spoke volumes.

It was when Cooke resumed his position, now a half block past the Main Street intersection, that six riders in near-perfect military order turned south from Adams Road onto Main, a long block above Temple Street.

No sooner had they done so, however, than they stopped abruptly, in unison, as if someone had shouted a command. There, no more than thirty yards distant, strode Rockwell, Hickok, and Lot Smith.

Case Carney's heart skipped a beat. A chill shot through his body as if he had suddenly fallen into a mountain stream. "Rockwell," he bit out between clenched teeth. Instinctively he loosed his dustcoat, letting it fall over the back of his horse. The other riders followed suit.

Riley caught his breath. What were Rockwell and Hickok doing together? In cahoots from the beginning, he surmised; no other way to explain it. He had a score to settle with that arrogant bastard Rockwell. Before this day was out, he swore, he'd be riding the gunman's buckskin, or his name wasn't Terrence Xavier Riley.

Jubal Hathaway, his emasculated nose cradled in its leather pouch, gasped as the adrenaline automatically poured into his system. Confused thoughts of terror and revenge surged through his mind. Without thinking, he repeatedly wiped the palms of his hands on his thighs.

The brief hiatus—the contenders facing one another, thoughts, questions, and strategies rampaging through their minds, hearts drumming, stomachs tight—ended abruptly.

With something like the cry of a bull ape, a maddened Case Carney suddenly dug his spurs into the flanks of his horse, simultaneously drawing his Remington. In an instant the other mounts sprang forward, the battle cries of their riders echoing down Main Street.

The scream was not fully out of Carney's throat before the guns of Porter Rockwell, Lot Smith, and James Butler Hickok were spitting fire.

The fusillade echoed through the streets like the combined explosion of a dozen thunderstorms. Startled troops reached for their rifles;

nervous, inexperienced horses broke ranks, their riders cursing and jerking reins in an attempt to control them. Mormons moved to cast their burning torches into buildings. Brigham Young quickly nodded to Professor Wilfred Holt, and the brass band struck up with deafening urgency.

"AS YOU WERE!" shouted Colonel Cooke angrily, looking back down the line. "EYES FRONT!"

The command was quickly taken up by Marcy, Porter, Buell, Hauk, and the other officers. In an instant, but only just in time, it was rolling out of the mouths of the sergeants, all down the line.

As garish as it was, the music of Holt's band played its role in restoring a strained equilibrium. The sound of it had a calming effect, giving the impression that all was as it should be. Almost as quickly as the firing had begun, it ceased.

Slowly, order began to be restored. Rifles were returned to scabbards. Torches were steadied, and a few small fires were stomped out. The Utah Expedition continued its momentarily interrupted trek down Temple Street. All the while, Johnston's eyes bore straight ahead, as if he were a world apart from all that was taking place.

The tension among those standing with Brigham Young was searing. This was the worst day of Judge Dawson's life. He swore that if he could get through this one without being shot or having a nervous breakdown, he would never complain again. He had nearly fainted when the shots rang out.

Kane reacted by attempting to wheel about, his hand reaching through his coat for his handgun, but Brigham Young's arm stayed him. "As you were, Colonel!" he shouted over the din of Holt's band, and then to the others, "Stand fast, gentlemen, as if nothing has happened!" After a moment he pulled the sleeve of John Kimball. "Carefully, now, slip up there and find out what's going on."

At the sound of the shots, Anne, Angus, and Doc Ames burst frantically through the temple grounds, running toward the east gate, Anne racing ahead of the old men. All thoughts of Rockwell's stern order to remain where she was had vanished with the shots.

From the porch of the Utah Hotel, James Wilson and son held their position, the latter riveted to his spot, eyes wide as a raccoon's with the awe and amazement only a child can convey. James Sr. had begun to hyperventilate. Wrapping his arms around a porch post, he nevertheless remained standing, gasping for air. Time and again over the years he would play back a detailed scenario to spellbound listeners, with only an exaggeration here and there.

John Kimball reached the front of the Utah Hotel just as Anne, followed by the two doctors, came through the east gate, across the street from him. He only momentarily noticed the father and son on the hotel porch.

Lot's first shot had grazed Riley's scalp as the Irishman crouched in the saddle, leaning far to his right, firing as he rode. A bullet rammed into Lot's hip, throwing him back on his haunches. From that position he managed two rapid shots at the oncoming riders. The first hit Benjamin Smilie full in the chest, killing him instantly. The second shot tore through Riley's throat at an angle, blowing him backward off his mount.

In an instant the two riderless horses were bearing down on Lot. With a painful grimace, he rolled his body to the side as iron-shod hooves thundered past him, one of them slicing a deep cut in his shoulder.

Still, his instincts ruled his actions and moved his body. The instant the avalanche of hooves had passed, he rolled in the opposite direction, rising up on an elbow, his Colt pointing uncertainly in the direction of Riley.

The Irishman lay on his side, head slightly raised, eyes bulging, mouth open. His hands were clutching his throat in a futile effort to stem the spurts of blood that squeezed through his fingers with every heartbeat. His legs stiffened with powerful jerks as shock waves passed through his body. His mouth opened wider, twisting, as if he were crying for help. But no sound issued from his throat. Terrence Xavier Riley was never going to sit astride Rockwell's buckskin.

Lot spun his attention to the others. Jubal Hathaway and Erskine Crabb had charged Hickok straight on, their stomachs planted on the saddle horns, crouching and firing behind the heads of their mounts. Bullets exploded around Hickok's feet and beyond. He weaved from side to side, firing at his partially concealed targets. One of his shots found Crabb's shoulder, spinning him backward, twisting his body and lodging his boot in the stirrup. Face first he hit the ground, violently wrenching his captive lower leg out of the knee socket, his mount dragging him onward. As he was pulled screaming past Hickok, the gunman finished him with a single shot.

Hickok got off two rapid shots at Jubal Hathaway, one ripping through his upper arm, the other smacking the forehead of his horse. The animal collapsed as if it had hit a wall, dropping to its knees. Jubal was thrown forward, heels over head, hitting the street with a thud and rolling to Hickok's feet.

Dazed and bleeding, Jubal painfully raised himself to his hands and knees. He slowly lifted his head, just in time for the full impact of a ferocious kick from Hickok's boot directly in his face. His whole body seemed to raise up, then he fell again into the dust, spread-eagled and unconscious.

Hickok was furious. He cursed himself for his poor marksmanship; his shot had been aimed at *Jubal*'s forehead, not at that of a *perfectly good horse.*

Fear and hate had maddened Case Carney. Bellowing insanely, he had initiated the charge standing tall in his stirrups, legs straight, leaning forward, squeezing off shots at Rockwell.

The nearest to Carney—Clarence Carson—went down with Rockwell's first shot, straight through the sternum. His horse had jolted ahead but a few feet before Carson's life was snuffed out. He hadn't gotten off a shot.

In an instant Rockwell had leveled two shots into the recklessly exposed Case Carney; but Carney kept on coming, bellowing like a gored bull, thumbing shots at Rockwell!

A slug passed between Rockwell's upper arm and his side, nipping flesh as it passed through.

Then Rockwell sped another shot that slammed into Carney's shoulder, causing him to yank the reins as he was thrown back by the impact. The animal came to a halt, front legs stiff, hooves sliding, coming to rest barely a yard in front of him.

Carney sank slowly back into the saddle. His arms hung loosely at his sides, his right hand still clinging to his smoking Remington.

With Hickok's resounding kick into Jubal's already pulverized face, the noises of violence had ceased. Now only the boisterous strains from Professor Holt's band flowed up Main Street.

Finally, Carney's Remington dropped from his hand. Still he sat his horse. The contortion in his face, the puffed veins in his neck, and the strain in his eyes spoke of his suffering—*gut shot!* With a groan of agony he looked into his adversary's steely eyes. "For God's sake, Rockwell, finish me!"

For a moment Rockwell stared back at the man who had murdered Joseph Smith and had gut-shot Zebulah Weems. Finally, he casually walked around the back of Carney's horse and slapped it on the rump. It moved forward, slowly at first, then increasing its pace to the beat of Holt's band. At the intersection, it turned the corner, oblivious to the rider on its back, and proudly, instinctively, joined the cadence of the other cavalry mounts as they moved down Temple Street and out of the city.

Anne shuddered when Carney's horse passed her with its grisly baggage, but when she saw Rockwell still standing she sighed, "Thank you, dear Lord."

She ran into Rockwell's arms, her hair caressing his cheek. "You're hurt," she cried out when she saw his blood-stained shirt.

"No," he assured her, "just a cut." Then, turning to Doc Ames, "See to Lot."

"Is there nae' anyone else alive out there?" shouted Angus McCutcheon.

Hickok gave a disinterested nod in the direction of Jubal Hathaway. "He is, but he wishes he wasn't."

John Kimball, the last to arrive on the scene, joined the others in a feeling of blessed relief. He said nothing, but quickly took a mental picture of all that had happened. Brigham Young, he knew, would want an exact account. He congratulated himself. He had stridden full-bore up the street; tense, yes, but without fear for his personal safety. Young's order was all that was needed.

Suddenly Hickok stiffened. "MAGRUDER!"

Rockwell pushed Anne away. "What?"

"Magruder's missing! There were seven of them!" The realization raced through Hickok's mind: Last night, at the creek. The man heading down the valley had to have been Magruder!

Anne felt the tension return. "What is it?" she cried.

Rockwell felt helpless. "Has to be at that end," he jerked toward Temple Street.

Rockwell and Hickok ran down Main Street. "Where?" growled the distraught Rockwell as he ran. "Where is the son of a bitch!"

Then, just as he reached the east gates of the temple grounds, he saw it! From the roof of Zion's Bank—a bright flash, like the rays of the sun reflecting off the polished barrel of a rifle.

Hank Magruder's heart was pounding. The shots he heard and the confusion below could only mean that Carney and the others were already stirring things up. There was indeed shooting going on up the street, but he couldn't make out the characters. They hadn't reached Brigham Young, which gave him a stitch of concern; but no matter. He'd take care of that—two quick shots, one for Young and one for Cumming. Those idiots—the cacophony coming from the brass band would muffle his shots. No one would hear him or see him. For a minute a short string of passing wagons disturbed his target, but Magruder was patient.

By the time Rockwell and Hickok had reached the east gate, Magruder was presented with a clear shot. His sights narrowed on Brigham Young.

Furiously, Rockwell ripped the Whitworth from the buckskin's saddle scabbard as the sniper squeezed off his first shot. At that precise moment Colonel Kane threw a jarring bump into Young's shoulder with his own, forcing him to the right.

Kane had turned to see Rockwell and Hickok running toward the east gate, and guessed that the shooting was not over. Following Rockwell's gaze, his eyes focused on the roof of the bank. He saw Magruder's head raise up behind the small abutment, the barrel of his carbine pointed menacingly in his direction. Kane knew instantly that the sights would be on Brigham Young.

Only a faint crack was heard above the horses, the accoutrements of the troopers, and Holt's brass band. Magruder's bullet sped between the heads of Kane and Young to slam the horn of the startled Chauncy Clark's tuba, a yard behind the target.

"Sorry," Kane hollered out to Young, as he now stepped in front of him, shielding him from a second shot. "Lost my balance."

"DAMN KANE!" screeched Magruder at the top of his voice, as he again took aim.

The Whitworth was now braced across the buckskin's saddle. The instant Magruder raised up a second time, Rockwell fired. A small explosion of blood and bone directly above Magruder's left eye was visible to Rockwell through the scope.

The impact of the Whitworth's bullet, combined with the recoil of the carbine, spun Magruder about, causing him to jerk the rifle's trigger. Its bullet blew out a windowpane in the governor's office, three feet above the heads of Young and Kane, showering those below with glass splinters. Then Magruder fell backward over the abutment and into the street below.

Several bewildered troopers caught a glimpse of him hitting the street, but none of them reacted more than casting occasional confused glances at the body. Sergeants on the wings repeatedly shouted, "Eyes front!" For the next two hours, soldiers of the Utah Expedition passed within a few feet of Magruder's twisted remains, giving them scant attention.

On the northeast side of Temple Street, Young, Kane, and Cumming saw Magruder fall, accompanied by his carbine. Now Young understood Kane's peculiar behavior. "My deepest gratitude, Tom," he said in all humility.

"An honor, sir" was the response.

Both Cumming and Dawson had stood their ground. But Dawson was numb. His face was ashen white. Had everyone gone mad? Firing all around, mustn't turn around, windows exploding, bodies falling from rooftops, that infernal band playing as if their lives depended upon it, noncoms shouting "Eyes front!" and troopers riding right on through with an attitude of almost nonchalance. It seemed like a nightmare!

Rockwell, his face bathed in perspiration, slowly dropped the Whitworth to the ground. He turned and leaned back against the buckskin, wiping his brow with his forearm. Anne came into his arms again, steadying him.

At length, Hickok mounted his horse, then contemplated Rockwell. "I'd best get my butt outta here, Mr. Rockwell." Yet he hesitated. There was something else on his mind. "I can't go without the Whitworth. I have to take it," he said finally.

Rockwell hesitated a moment before reaching down and picking up the scoped rifle, his eyes fixed on Hickok. He slid it carefully into its scabbard, untied the straps, turned slowly, and handed it to him. "With my compliments, Mister Hickok."

Hickok smiled and nodded. He looked at Anne. With his right hand he touched the brim of his hat. "Missus Rockwell." Then he rode away.

While Angus McCutcheon was trying to tie Jubal's unrecognizable face together, Rockwell and Anne watched Doc Ames work on Lot Smith's hip. "Slug's still in there, but I don't think anything's broken. He'll be fine."

Rockwell dropped on one knee, putting his hand on the shoulder of the young man. "I've fought by the side of worse soldiers, Lot Smith."

Lot's exuberant smile split his face from ear to ear. "And I've rode with worse partners, Porter Rockwell."

*   *   *

Brigham Young had finally asked the perspiring and bedraggled Wilfred Holt to give his band a rest, even though troopers were still moving down Temple Street.

When John Kimball reached Brigham Young's side, he was out of breath. "A shoot-out, President."

"I gathered that, Brother Kimball" was the irritated response.

Ignoring the rebuff, Kimball went on: "They were going to kill you."

"I figured that, too, Brother Kimball, and from more directions than one; isn't that so, Colonel Kane? Now, tell me what happened."

"Seven of them, President, against Lot Smith, Port Rockwell, and a man I didn't recognize."

"And?" Young closed his eyes for a moment.

"They got all of them, President, all of them."

"And Lot, Porter?"

"Bloodied up a bit, but they're alright. You know Port Rockwell; no one's going to kill him."

"Ah, my dear friend, no one *CAN* kill Porter Rockwell."

John Kimball's eyes widened. "What did you say, sir?"

"Oh, I thought you knew," responded Brigham Young mischievously. "It isn't permitted, Brother Kimball, it isn't permitted."

Epilogue

"THE BATTALION"

With the coming of the War Between the States, President Lincoln reactivated "The Battalion," ironically, under orders to guard and control the overland route against attack, and maintain communication between the West—including California—and the East.

The battalion answered its country's call when the Spanish-American War broke out, and again during the Mexican border troubles of 1916.

The fragments of these military units formed the nucleus of the Utah military section of the 145th Field Artillery during World War I. Twenty-three members of this modern battalion were direct descendants of the members of the original Mormon Battalion in the war with Mexico, commanded by Col. Philip St. George Cooke.

With the commencement of World War II, the battalion was reactivated for the last time, now in the uniform of the United States Marines.

ALBERT SIDNEY JOHNSTON

No sooner had Gen. Albert Sidney Johnston been dismissed as commander of the Utah Expedition than the beleaguered secretary of war, John B. Floyd, was able to secure the general's appointment as commander of the Department of the Pacific, stationed in California. It was later charged that the general was a force behind the secessionist organizations in that state. So it was that Johnston finally made it to the Golden State, but a little late, and without his army. Early in 1861, Winfield Scott, general in chief of the army, forced Johnston's resignation as commander of the Department of the Pacific, replacing him with Unionist Gen. E. V. Sumner. One of General Sumner's first official acts was to arrest and imprison California Senator William Gwinn.

As a general of the Confederacy, Johnston was killed in the midst of the South's nearest approach to victory. At the Battle of Shiloh, he was wounded while directing the attack of his troops. Undaunted, he propped himself against a tree and continued to oversee the battle, refusing medical aid, insisting that his wounded soldiers be treated first. And thus he died.

JOHN B. FLOYD

According to Bryant-Gay Brooks, in his *History of the United States,* Secretary of War John B. Floyd was a leader in the conspiracy that was "especially influential in hurrying the steps that led to the attempt to dissolve the Union."

The Utah War was only part of Floyd's strategy for the West and Southwest. He had seen to it that the South and the western territories had been well stocked with the implements of war, while at the same time the arsenals of the North were dangerously deficient.

Having failed in Utah, Floyd turned elsewhere. One Confederate sympathizer communicated to Jefferson Davis that "the stores, supplies and munitions of war in New Mexico and Arizona are immense." When the outbreak of hostilities between North and South began, it was apparently Floyd's intention that an army from Texas would invade the territory of New Mexico, to combine with secessionist sympathizers there, gain easy control of the well-stocked forts, and move on to California.

During the latter part of 1860, Floyd faced a congressional investigation and was brought to trial for fraud and for having transferred arms from Northern to Southern arsenals.

Floyd was later commissioned a brigadier general in the Confederate army, and while defending Fort Donelson, Tennessee, against the forces commanded by Gen. Ulysses S. Grant, surrendered his command and fled with his personal guard. Ironically, Floyd was then relieved of his duties by Confederate President Jefferson Davis. In 1863, he died a broken man.

THOMAS L. KANE

Thomas L. Kane remained a fast friend of Brigham Young and the Mormon people throughout his lifetime. It was Brigham Young's wish that he be forever remembered.

Today, in the rotunda of the Utah State Capitol Building stands a bigger-than-life statue of Colonel Kane, at the foot of which is inscribed the gratitude of the people of Utah.

During the War Between the States, he was commissioned a lieutenant colonel in the Union army. He was wounded at Drainesville, Virginia, but recovered. He commanded the 2d Brigade, 2d Division, XII Army Corps, at Chancellorsville, Virginia. In 1863 he was brevetted major general for "gallant and meritorious services at Gettysburg."

Kane was the author of three books: *The Mormons, Alaska,* and *Coahuila.*

PHILIP ST. GEORGE COOKE

When the War Between the States began, Philip St. George Cooke, a graduate of West Point, rose to high distinction as a *Union* officer. He was commissioned a brigadier general on November 12, 1861.

However, his son, John R. Cooke, and his soon to be famous son-in-law, J. E. B. Stuart, became general officers in the *Confederate* army.

After the war, General Cooke was sent as an observer of the war in Italy. He later commanded successfully the Departments of the Platte, the Cumberland, and the Lakes.

He retired from duty in 1873.

JAMES BUTLER HICKOK

James Butler "Wild Bill" Hickok went on to serve the Union army as a scout and spy during the War Between the States. Twice captured and condemned to be shot, he managed to escape.

After the war he was appointed United States marshal at Fort Riley, Kansas, his territory covering an area of 400 by 500 miles. During this period he also acted as scout for Generals Hancock, Sheridan, and George Armstrong Custer.

In 1871 he was appointed marshal of Abilene, Kansas, which had the distinction of being known as the most lawless town on the frontier.

On August 2, 1876, he was shot dead by one Jack McCall while playing poker in a Deadwood, Dakota Territory, saloon. The shot entered the back of his head. At the moment of his death he held two pair, aces and eights, forever after to be known as the "dead man's hand."

BRIGHAM YOUNG

Brigham Young remained highly influential in the territory of Utah until his death. However, problems plagued his relationship with the federal government. He had not seen the last of corrupt territorial officials, or even belligerent generals. Nor was Utah to be immune from carpetbaggers. With the growth the mining industry, and the junction of the Transcontinental Railroads at Promontory Point in May 1869, attempt after attempt was made to divest territorial citizens of their property. Not only did clones of Hank Magruder appear, but so did numbers of more sophisticated landgrabbers, wearing the robes of judges and the smart suits of lawyers.

Under the determined and persistent leadership of Young, however, the people of Utah held on. But it was not until Utah was granted its statehood that its citizens began to feel truly secure in their rights.

Young continued his role as colonizer and religious leader, directing groups to build communities throughout Utah, and into Idaho and Arizona. He sent great numbers of missionaries throughout the United States, Canada, and Mexico, and to Western Europe.

No doubt after a lengthy debate with his Creator, Brigham Young agreed to die of natural causes on August 29, 1877.

PORTER ROCKWELL

The saga of Porter Rockwell did not end with the Utah War. To meet the growth of a vicious criminal element in Utah Territory, he was appointed United States marshal.

Ignored by modern writers on the Old West, Rockwell's reputation as an unexcelled gunfighter was well known. The mention of his name usually struck fear in the hearts of other gunmen. His mystique grew with the popular belief that he was the "Samson of the West," and could not be killed. Ballads were sung about him by young and old. In spite of his many deadly encounters, he lived a long and fruitful life, fathering his twelfth child at the age of sixty-five. He died with his boots off.

LOT SMITH

A young veteran of "The Battalion" in the war with Mexico, and a hero to the people of Utah in the Utah War, Lot Smith maintained his rank of major in the Utah Territorial Militia. He participated in several Indian engagements, and. in 1862 under the call of Abraham Lincoln, headed a company of battalion cavalry dispatched to guard and control the overland route and maintain communication between West and East.

In 1875, Brigham Young selected Smith to lead a large group into northern Arizona to colonize the Little Colorado River area. There Smith prospered as a stockman, building up thriving herds. He developed a superior strain of horses, by importing blooded stallions from Kentucky and crossing them with range mares. His brand was a Circle S. According to historian Charles S. Peterson, "There were no better horses ever in Arizona than those Circle S."

Lot Smith was killed on June 21, 1892, in an altercation with Navajos. He was shot in the back, the bullet passing through his lungs. Yet, he sat his horse until he reached home, where he died an hour later.

Authors

Leo Gordon

Leo Gordon is well known to Western fans as a screen "heavy," the bad guy in a black hat. In his alter ego as a screenwriter he has garnered an impressive list of feature film and television credits, among which are multiple episodes of "Maverick," "Cheyenne," and "Bonanza." A long-time military history buff, Gordon has scripted such major war films as "Tobruk," starring Rock Hudson and George Peppard, and "You Can't Win 'em All," with Charles Bronson and Tony Curtis. His experience as a screenwriter is evident in the fast-moving pace of *Powderkeg*.

His collaboration with Richard Vetterli is his first effort as a novelist. Gordon and Vetterli are currently at work on their second book, a sequel to *Powderkeg*.

Richard Vetterli

A long-time friend of Gordon's, Richard Vetterli is a prolific writer. Most of his work has been in the form of textbooks. A Professor of Political Science at Brigham Young University, he received his MA at UCLA and his PhD at UC Riverside.

Among his publications are *In Search of the Republic* (Roman and Littlefield), a study of the American founding, and a charming book about the first years in office of U.S. Senator Orrin Hatch, *Challenging the Washington Establishment* (Regnery).

Powderkeg is Vetterli's first novel, and there is nothing "textbookish" about it. His cosmopolitan nature is revealed in this new dimension. He writes with passion and a flair that is both vital and refreshing.

[IDAHO]

[UTAH]

Great Salt Lake

Echo Canyon

Emigration
Canyon

SALT
LAKE
CITY

To
St.
George